SUNLIGHT AND SHADOW

THE ORIGINS OF CYLLA

BOOK THREE

HARLEIGH KNIGHT

TRIGGER WARNINGS

This book may discuss topics that are not suitable for everyone and may be difficult for some readers. This book includes mentions of parental neglect, emotional abuse, torture, grief, self-worth trouble, gore, violence, memory loss, violation, coercive dynamics, infant death, dismemberment, physical abuse, panic attacks, forced infertility, child death, sex slavery, sex trafficking, and attempted sexual assault. This is a story about deities with loose inspiration from mythology. If topics of violence and death are too much for you, put the book aside and take care of your mental health first.

*To those with a love of mythology
and complicated relationships*

CHAPTER ONE

HIDING IN PLAIN SIGHT

OREST: THE ONLY EDUCATION CENTER IN THE REALM.

A stone castle built on the top of the largest mountain and guarded by giant stone golems. The education center can hold thousands of students every year and train them for any job in the realm. Orest was built by the false God of Rebirth. It has been directed by and thrived under the Goddess of Space in disguise. Mortals and deities alike teach classes together. Orest trades with multiple other kingdoms closely, not in exchange for coins, but instead, they give extra students classes every year to the lands that supply the food, uniforms, and other essentials for a functional learning environment.

RURI

The sound of steel rang out around us, echoing against the stone walls like a metallic symphony. It was the last day that I had class with General Nightjade. The last day that he could spend beating me and calling it weapons training. Exhaustion wasn't the word for it. My muscles ached with a deep fatigue that seeped into my bones. His regular assault had to count as bullying. He proclaimed it was useless to pair me with someone that I could easily beat. That I would not grow if I were never met with a challenge. He must have been too humble. He wasn't a challenge; he was an impossible feat. He assured me he would find me a new challenge as soon as I could find his weakness.

After the last year, I rested firmly on the idea that he did not have one. Koa was unbeatable.

If the discussion came up, he would talk to me as if he only helped me, and I was to be grateful. The bitter taste of resentment lingered on my tongue whenever I thought about it.

It wasn't that I didn't know how to use either of my sai's. It wasn't that his size was too much. It was simply his ability to guess everything that I was going to do before I did it. Sometimes, he knew my moves before even I did. If I had ever considered myself mysterious, he taught me it was a lie.

Lines were drawn on the floor in the shape of a circle. The circle kept the ones outside of the fight safe and gave a way to tap out if you were in the fight. They were allowed to remove themselves from the lines at any point and call the match.

I twirled my left blade, then the right, feeling the familiar weight of the metal in my palms, and like he knew that I wasn't ready, he lunged. I lifted a blade to block just in time to catch him. The impact vibrated up my arm, nearly making me lose my grip. He was better with a bow, but he wasn't that bad with a sword. I pushed him off, but he flung himself back at me just as fast. While I was distracted by his sword, he took the chance to kick me in the knee and shove. I hit the floor with an echo, the cold stone sending a shock through my body, and he was on top of me. He was relentless.

Although he was my professor, I considered us friends. That was until we stepped inside of the circle. I could stay on defense and hope that he would tire eventually; I knew he would not. I could lose again and leave Orest, knowing that I never beat him. I could try to take the lower option and cheat. I could say that a win was a win no matter how it was achieved.

Did it matter? If I were to stick with his teachings, he would be very clear on the concept that if I needed the skills he taught me, nothing would be fair.

I lifted my knee and made contact between his legs. I threw him sideways and onto his back, trying my best not to show how hard it was to move his weight. The strain in my muscles burned like fire. I thought I had won when I locked an arm behind him, but he lifted his leg under to raise his back and sent me flying. He recovered faster than I did and had an arm around my neck. He pulled me back into him. He showed little mercy with how tight he held it.

I lifted my arm as far as I could manage and shoved my elbow into his ribs with everything I had. His grip only tightened, and my heart beat harder. The scent of sweat and leather filled my nostrils as I struggled for breath. I lifted my arm a second time, higher than the first time. Air became harder to get, and each breath brought terror. I brought my elbow down into the same spot on his rib cage as the first, and he finally let go.

I gasped for air and filled with adrenaline and panic; my thoughts hardly made sense. Before I thought anything through, my fist landed in the middle of his throat. I watched him drop to his knees and start coughing, but I was not a fool.

I knew he would keep coming until one of us had to give up. I slid on the floor and rushed to my blades. I gripped the handle in what I knew to be too tight.

He was on his feet, to my dismay, and found his sword as if I had done nothing. Another clash of blades, and my arms shook under his weight. The metal screeched in protest. The pressure he applied was far too heavy for me to hold up. My feet screamed at me just as loud as my arms. They tried their best to hold me in place and prevent me from skidding back-ward, but they wouldn't last, either. The three-tipped blades I used were the only things that kept us in place.

What I was about to do was stupid, but the things I seemed to think would work never did, so it was worth a try. I lifted my leg, bending closer to the ground under his weight, and kicked. I kicked as hard as I could manage, as fast as I could, into his shin. It took him a moment to process what I had done; I saw it in his eyes in the seconds between my movements and his pain radiating through him.

Instead of the sound of his blade against mine, it was the sound of his blade that dropped to the ground. Then silence. The entire room was filled with a quiet that could have eaten me alive. I heard my heartbeat faster than it had been yet. Louder than it had been when I watched the sharp edge reflect light next to my cheek. I watched him fall to a knee. I saw him register the pain and drop in a slowed motion. When he finally hit the ground and howled something at me that I did not take in, time started to move at its normal pace, and so did sound.

Cheers filled my ears so loud I thought they would have shattered. The noise washed over me like a wave of vindication.

I would beat him fairly one day. One day, I would come out on top with only combat skills. It wouldn't be today, but it would be one day. I would have to try harder than my best, but today wasn't the last day the world turned, or breath entered my lungs, so there was time. I just needed to try harder, and I would.

For now, I allowed myself to enjoy a little bit of a win.

The head of Orest was in the doorway. He watched me as if he were dissatisfied. He always seemed disappointed. Time must have passed faster than I paid attention to because I hadn't realized it was time for me to meet him. Professor Thann, someone we knew was a God, was never late for anything. I always seemed to be late, however. Part of my agreement was to see him weekly until graduation.

Word circulated that I had nightmares. They made me violent. I hurt more than one person, but could not recall it. One of the common dreams I had was a man who led me to the fires of a blacksmith. He guided me to an egg that sat in the flames. It was plucked from its flower. He made me fill it with magic that I didn't understand. Magic that I hadn't ever seen before. After it was filled, it cracked, and a woman with eight legs lunged at me.

Professor Thann moved to the side and made me walk ahead. He didn't make me nervous until the sessions began. My entire life's goal was to be a member of the Dragon Guard. My ability to successfully accomplish that goal sat in what words we spoke during our sessions.

I fidgeted with the seam of my leather uniform while we walked through the grey stone halls. The fabric was smooth in some places, rough in others from years of wear. Normally, I enjoyed seeing all of the pictures while I walked. Every group to graduate in the history of Orest hung throughout the entire castle. Faces of past students stared down at me, some with expressions of pride, others with determination etched into their features.

I turned and entered the Professor's office. The chair that always awaited me sat in front of his darkwood desk. The sound of both of our chairs being pulled across the floor and back echoed through the room. The scent of old parchment and ink filled the air, overlaid with the faint aroma of the herbal tea he always kept nearby.

"I know you don't want to be here all day, so I won't stop you from speaking," Professor Thann remarked.

There was always something about him that made me feel like he was someone else. He looked the part of an old man filled with knowledge. He felt like a God in his presence. Still, it somehow felt wrong. As if he were someone else in a shell.

"I didn't have a nightmare for a few nights now." I paused to consider my words and how far I wanted to go. "Last night was different. I started to have a nightmare, but this time, I was able to wake myself up. I convinced myself it was just a dream, and that was that." I spoke with my hands.

He looked at me as if he didn't believe me. His piercing gaze seemed to search for the truth beneath my words. He was right. I was a liar. Every single night, I had one. If it wasn't an egg, then it was a man with dark emerald lightning streaks on his sun-kissed skin that visited me in my sleep. What he did was never the same. Sometimes, he hurt me. Sometimes, he killed me. Sometimes, he made me watch while he destroyed the temple I had worked so hard to get into.

He scared me, but it was the tree that always came after that terrified me.

She was always screaming for me to wake up.

"It really is amazing the kind of progress you've made with only our discussions. It's almost like you aren't telling me the truth," he observed.

The two of us locked eyes, and we silently battled each other before he leaned both elbows on his desk. The wood creaked slightly under his weight.

"I know you wouldn't do that, though. So, it looks like I can sign off on you leaving in peace." He smiled.

I was too cautious to be outwardly excited. He picked up his quill and dipped it in ink before putting it on a piece of paper that I did not recognize. The scratching of the nib against parchment was oddly comforting.

"Here," he declared. He picked it up and sat it back down in front of me. "This is your official paperwork stating I deemed you sane and safe after our sessions."

Was it wrong of me to take the paper when I knew that I wasn't safe or sane? I looked between him and the paper more than once. The guilt weighed heavily in my chest, a stone that wouldn't dissolve. This would be something that I would have to work out at another time. I grabbed the paper and got to my feet. I pushed the chair and moved to leave the office.

"Thank you!" I called behind me.

"Watch where you're running, Ruri!" He called back to me.

I did not stop to say another word. I ran through the too-long hallways and their candle-lit glow. The dancing flames cast shifting shadows on the walls as I passed. I moved my feet down the winding black iron stairwell to the huge wooden doors that lead to the courtyard. I still hadn't gotten to my favorite part of the day yet. Classes were fun, and the friends I made were always there for me.

Still, there was one thing I looked forward to more than anything else.

I saw him before the doors finished opening. The warm breeze carried his scent to me—something wild and earthy, like pine after rain. The love of my life waited to hear how my day was. He did not attend Orest, but he still made the journey to see me. His smile was already on me; it allowed his pointed canines to show. I jumped into his arms, and he caught me by my thighs. I kissed his cheek and then his chin before I looked into his eyes.

One red and one black eye stared back at me before I cradled his cheeks and kissed his lips.

"She signed me off today. No more appointments." I kissed him on the lips again. "This is it. It's done now. I have one more day of official things to do, and then I've done it."

"It'll leave more time to focus on your magic," he murmured. I could feel his smile through my own lips.

"Or more time that I can spend on you." I kissed him again.

"Right here? What if a classmate were to walk by?" He squeezed my legs before he put me back on my feet.

"Deimos, when has that thought ever bothered you before?" I was unable to hide the disappointment in my tone.

He grabbed my hand and pulled me into his chest. "I have a lot going on right now. I have a lot of things I've put into motion for us. I can't stay long, and I don't want you to make any mistakes on your last day. The two of us unleashing some of your magic helps you in everything you do the next day," Deimos whispered. "I couldn't skip making sure that you're okay."

The feel of his thumb over my cheek sent a wave of relaxation through me. His touch was like a gentle current, washing away my worries. "All right, fine."

I pulled away from him and instead took his hand in mine. The two of us snuck down a stone path that pointed us to the back of the castle. Not just us, but many lovers in the shadow snuck through the path enough that it was carved out by feet.

I checked inside of the grotto first to ensure it was empty. The cool, damp air inside was a stark contrast to the warmth outside. Once I confirmed, I tugged Deimos hard enough that he stumbled inside behind me. I knew what he said was true. I couldn't afford a slip in my magic. It was magic that I shouldn't have to begin with. I had to keep it a secret. Our world relied on magic from crystals that the Goddess of Magic left us before her death. There was no other natural elemental magic in mortals.

The first time I lost control of it, I heard a voice. It called to me from the grotto. I followed it, and Deimos waited for me as if we were bound by fate. He helped me calm the surges and explained to me that we were soul-bonded. That we had lived a life together already. I felt like we had known each other before. It was hard to explain, but his eyes told me that I knew him. The way he could help me learn how to control the surges of magic only confirmed to me that he had to be telling the truth.

It was easy to fall in love with him. It was not easy to listen to him and keep my hands to myself. Even knowing every-thing that was on the line for tomorrow, I only wanted to run my hands across every inch of him. To feel the heat of his skin under my fingertips, to trace the contours of his body that I'd already memorized.

"Ruri, I know what that look means. Focus," Deimos cautioned.

I clicked my tongue at him in disapproval; surely, we could have spared an hour or two. I held my hand over the warm, clear water that sat around us and tossed it at him. I shifted the droplets into ice shards, and he used a mist that I still didn't understand to deflect them and throw them back into the water. I pulled from somewhere deep inside of me and formed a fireball in my palm. The heat licked at my skin without burning. I tossed the flame at him before I repeatedly lifted the water droplets and tossed the shards of ice at him.

He turned into mist and dodged both. Small blue flowers behind him set on fire, and I covered them in water, which I picked up without using my physical hands. I moved to them and bent down. There was something else that I could do. Something else that I did not understand, either. I cupped my hands around the burnt flower petals, and small green shimmers came from me to the petals. I healed them as if they had never been touched.

Deimos leaned over. I knelt and ran his hands through my hair. The sensation sent pleasant tingles down my spine. "You really do learn fast."

I stood and left the flower behind. I wrapped my arms around his neck. "It's all thanks to you."

The smile on his face usually brought a bigger one to my own, but there was a glint of something else behind his lips. Something I hadn't noticed before. I couldn't put my finger on what it was, but it sent a rush of panic through me. A brief thought that he was not being fully open with me. The lingering doubt settled in my stomach like a cold stone.

"Have you thought about what I asked last time?" He inquired.

"I'm still not sure," I admitted.

"If you love me, there is no reason not to do it." He pressured me with his tone and words. The gentle warmth in his voice had hardened into something more demanding.

He wanted us to take our commitment to the next stage by participating in a bonding ritual. He asked me to go to the temple of rebirth so that we could take part in a blood ritual that I hardly understood. I managed to avoid the topic because I had taken so many classes. It left no time to leave Orest.

The temple of rebirth and all of the rumors that surrounded it made me uneasy. Stories of failed rituals and mysterious disappearances haunted my thoughts whenever he brought it up.

"All right. If you still don't want to discuss it, we won't. We do need to finish with your magic before someone finds us," he conceded.

I nodded. I placed my hands on Deimos' chest. I glanced up at him, and the way his eyes looked down at me set my body on fire. He always looked at me with a hunger. I pushed my magic from my palms into his chest, and he glowed golden like the sun. I shoved every spark I had to give into him. When I had nothing left, I collapsed into his chest. The scent of him, like thunderstorms and pine, enveloped me.

"Good job," he whispered.

It brought a smile to my face. I would give him anything he asked for, even if it left me weak after.

"Ru! Are you in here?" A voice called, its echo bouncing off the stone walls.

Deimos kissed me one last time before he turned to mist and was gone. I was relieved and sad to watch him go. He left so fast that I nearly collapsed into the pool of water.

"I'm in here," I answered.

"Was that a man with you? Are you seeing someone in

secret!" Hesperia practically ran inside, her footsteps splashing through the shallow water at the entrance.

"No!" I yelled.

"Keep your secrets then; I guess it'll stay between you and the keeper of the underworld for now." She winked at me.

Her wink let me know that I should have understood what she was saying, but I had no idea what the underworld had to do with anything. Hesperia was strange, and if I questioned everything she did or said, I'd have no time for much else.

"Why are you here?" I asked.

She placed both of her hands on her hips and lowered her brows enough that I wondered if it hurt.

"It's not that I don't want to see you! It's just—" I stuttered my words.

"You wanted more time with your mystery man. No, I get it. I can't provide you with the same appendages as he can, but that doesn't mean you can toss me to the side! I came to congratulate you on no more meetings with the professor," she explained, her voice rising and falling dramatically with each word.

"I don't know if I should say thanks or tell you to stop talking," I said.

"How about we go have dinner instead!" Hesperia's normal cheery voice was back.

It was exactly what we should have been doing. Eating and resting. The next part of my journey would be long, but the best part. Hesperia and I would have less time together, but it couldn't be helped. I would miss the way, even with a smile on her face, she would become the most terrifying thing I had ever seen.

CHAPTER TWO
MEMORIES OF THE PAST

OURANOS: A FLOATING ISLAND MADE OF GOLD AND CLEAR CRYSTAL.

The island was erected with the help of the God of Death and the Goddess of Space. It was built as a safe haven for the angels after the false Goddess of Time took charge of Semper and created blood guards. The angels that weren't slaughtered entered into an agreement with the God of Death and his Nola. The Nola would provide protection for their island in exchange for the angel's help in any conflicts that may come. The inhabitants of Ouranos generally stay to themselves, sending only the necessary number of citizens to Orest to learn about healing and the current combat style.

RURI

For the first night in such a long time, I slept without anything to disturb me. If I had a dream, I did not remember it. I was still not in my bed because I was woken by a voice. It was the voice of a woman that called to me. She begged me to come to her. I felt the urgency in my own chest. It pounded so hard

I thought it might escape. The sound of my heartbeat filled my ears like thunder as I rose from my bed.

The voice guided me to the library.

The Nola spirit that guarded the entrance did not look in my direction, nor did he show any sign that he paid any attention to me. His translucent form hovered silently, the edges of his being shimmering with an otherworldly light. I did not stop to ask his permission for access, and he did not acknowledge me to deny it. The voice stopped on a book. I placed my hand on it, and it shocked me like lightning. I pulled my hand back and shook it until the pain wore off, the tingling sensation running up my arm.

The second time that I touched the book, it did not shock me. I lifted it off of the shelf and opened the book. The pages were cut out, and inside was a necklace. A thin silver chain held the clearest piece of citrine I had ever seen. I held it up to the light, and the rainbows inside the stone were endless, dancing like captured fragments of sunlight.

The Nola shifted through the air faster than I blinked to be by my side. It didn't scare me, but it was unsettling to see it move without feet on the ground. The chill of his presence raised goosebumps along my arms. He stood in front of me as if I should know him.

He pointed to his chest, "Jeb. I help." He took the chain from me and held it around my neck to close the clasp. His touch was like the brush of cold mist against my skin.

I pointed to myself, "Ruri. Thank you."

Jeb nodded. "Ruri, friend."

"Yes!" I smiled and pointed to myself. "Ruri, friend."

"Jeb, miss you," he murmured.

Missed me? I shook my head. "What do you mean?"

He looked at the necklace one more time before he disappeared completely from my sight, leaving behind only a faint scent like morning frost.

I didn't know that I should be wearing the necklace. It was

a strange item found in a place that was clearly hidden on purpose. The necklace came with every indication that I needed to leave it alone. Jeb gave it to me, which had to make it somehow all right. The weight of it against my collarbone felt oddly familiar, like something long forgotten.

Maybe he confused me with someone else. He said he missed me, but he couldn't have known me.

I lost the line of thinking that I was walking down when my head pounded. I felt as if my skull was being ripped open, and I let out a scream while I gripped it. The pain blazed white-hot behind my eyes. I felt the door of my mind open; someone was there—a presence I did not recognize was lurking in my head.

"I've been waiting too long for that book to get picked up," the man's voice intoned.

"Who are you?" I asked. I still had a hold on my head.

"Names are meaningless. It would mean nothing to you today," he replied, his voice like distant thunder.

"Are you a dragon?" I asked next.

His voice was amused. "Why would you say that?"

"I'm just trying to understand how you're speaking to me like this," I said.

"How did you find my necklace?" he questioned.

"A voice led me to it," I answered.

"Do you recognize the voice?" he pressed.

I shook my head as if he could see me.

"Then we have nothing to discuss further," he declared. "It means my name would mean nothing to you, yet."

I felt alone in my mind again. I didn't know how or why I knew he wasn't there anymore, but I knew it. There was only one place or person that I knew who may have had an answer to what happened. That was our head professor. The same professor who had only just signed off on me being sane and safe.

I grabbed the Nola's hand and shook it. He looked at me with a titled head but did not speak.

"Thanks!" I yelled back before I ran out of the room.

I didn't have time for much else. Today was already a big day. I could not let anything push me off of my path when it was so close to being complete. The cool stone floor beneath my bare feet reminded me of my purpose.

I needed to speak to the professor before the dragons showed up because I still had to make the trip for my weapon to be made. I crashed into two separate people through the hallways and said my apologies. When I pushed the doors to the professor's office open, and he sat quietly with a book, I suddenly felt foolish.

"Shouldn't you be in the courtyard?" he inquired, not looking up from the yellowed pages.

"I just needed to speak with you first," I stumbled out my words.

"I approve your request," he stated.

"What?" I asked in confusion.

"Your request to stay another year. I approve it." He closed his book and sat it down, the sound echoing in the quiet room.

"What? No! Of course not!" I spat out.

His brow rose in my direction, his eyes reflecting the soft light from the window.

"It's not you. It's just that I couldn't learn anything else here."

"Fine, I suppose I'll watch you graduate then," he conceded.

"I wanted to ask you about this, actually." I lifted the stone on my chest. It caught the light, sending prisms dancing across the walls.

He stood quickly as if he had forgotten the chair behind him and moved to me. His sudden interest made my pulse quicken.

"Where did you get this?" he demanded.

"The library," I said.

He looked at me in the eyes for what felt like an eternity. It was as if he searched for something and had not found it. There was a sparkle of disappointment in his eyes.

"There are artifacts from the gods all over the realm. You should keep it close. If you have it, it looks like a God wants you to keep it. Maybe it's your gift for becoming a temple guardian," he offered.

He touched the stone only once and then shoved me until I was out of his office. His hand was cold against my shoulder, and his dismissal stung like a slap.

"I wasn't done talking!" I yelled. I slammed my fist against the door, but he did not answer. The wood vibrated beneath my knuckles.

He was supposed to be helpful. He was supposed to be the ultimate guide and the answer to all questions. That wasn't helpful. It wasn't anything that I couldn't have gotten from asking around.

A voice came out of the Fiia that flew around. "Dragons inbound!" Staff often used them to send messages around the school quicker than a person could. Their little glittery wings carried them quickly, leaving trails of sparkling dust that hung in the air momentarily before fading.

The Fiia was said to be a gift between the Goddess of Magic and the Goddess of Nature when the realm was created. We had many stories of how they used the Fiia to send messages in secret or to play games. The Fiia were given to mortals as a gift when the sisters died. Some mortals tell their children that if they speak their dreams to the Fiia, they will carry the message to the underworld, and the God of Death will fulfill the wish in the name of his beloved.

I left the door of the professor's office and hurried down the hall to the bottom of a long, brown, winding staircase that opened up to a large room filled with doorways and halls. The pathway was covered in fur rugs, and the brick wall was filled with candlelight and greenery. It was a beautiful sight to see. I still hadn't grown tired of it. The scent of beeswax and herbs filled the air, mingling with the earthy smell of the rugs beneath my feet. The ceilings were topped with glass in every spot they could be. When it rained, it created a stunning picture of the sky. I pushed the door, two times my size, open to reveal the courtyard.

The school opened up to an oversized area made for dragon landings. The edges were decorated with more plant life and benches. Orest was the only place in the mountains where plants grew. The rough edges of the mountain were very different than the school.

It was common for students to sit and watch dragons come and go. Some days were much more involved than others. Some days, we only checked on the dragons and helped with any basic care they may need. The dragons didn't need us to care for them, but as riders, we all took pride in not just being riders but bonded friends.

An uptick in wind came first; then, the mountainside shuddered in the presence of their landing. The ground trembled beneath my feet. Dragons came in different sizes, colors, and elements. Some walked on four legs and had wings; some stood on two legs. Others, like from Daxon, land of water, had no wings, but they were beyond skilled swimmers. It was easy to tell where dragons were from by their magic; they were elemental, like the lands. Some smaller dragons could have shown up unnoticed; some dragons shook everything around when they landed.

Belladonna was mine, and she did not go unnoticed.

Belladonna's scales were hidden underneath pounds of burgundy fur, and there was only one horn on her head. The only time I truly wished for assistance was when she needed to be brushed out. I appreciated the easier grip when I needed to climb her for flight. Fur was easier to grip than scales, but that was the only blessing.

I have no knowledge of the bond between anyone else and their dragon. It was private, but she and I were like one mind. Even if she didn't need anything from me, she would still come for the visit. She lowered her head to me, and I laid mine on hers. Her familiar scent, like cedar smoke and mountain air, filled my lungs.

"It's the final flight, Belladonna," I said.

"Yes. I'll accept a cow as payment for all my hard work," Belladonna remarked.

"A whole cow? Do you know how much that costs? I don't make money here!" I scoffed.

"My problems are many, little one. That problem is yours alone," she retorted, her voice rumbling through my chest.

"You're greedy," I mumbled.

I climbed up the side of her, but I didn't sit on a saddle like many other riders did. She and I had flown together for a long time. She used to take me into the sky on nights when I couldn't sleep when I was young. I think there had to be an indent in her fur by now from the length of time we were together. The familiar warmth of her body enveloped me as I settled into my spot.

Belladonna took flight. She dived off the side of the Orest courtyard. The wind rushed past, stealing my breath as gravity pulled at me. She swerved in and out of the stone golems that stood guard of the school. They lived around the mountains; some of them were the size of mountains, but they were mostly quiet as long as no one tried to sneak in or out. They were a topic of debate often. They didn't know boundaries, and sometimes students would sneak out to visit Edur, the land of ice, for their taverns. Those students would end up a bug on the side of a mountain instead.

Belladonna twirled, and I spun upside down several times before we were upright again. My stomach lurched, but I laughed with exhilaration. We sat high enough above the clouds to see nothing but sky in every direction. The only glint of life was the outline of Ouranos, the floating island in the distance behind us, its gold and crystal surface catching the sunlight.

"I think we passed today's final flight lesson," I laughed.

"Yes, little one. I think I did fine. You could loosen up on my fur," Belladonna noted.

Belladonna and I flew high enough that we lost track of the ground entirely. We needed to get to Erebus today. I planned this trip to sit perfectly between the end of final flights and entering our weekend before being sent to our assignments. I saved every coin that I could make doing odd jobs around the school so I could gift myself a new weapon for graduation. The small pouch at my side jingled with each movement.

I was hoping for a little discount so that I didn't have to spend all of it. I was going to see the most sought-after blacksmith in all of Cylla. His work was beyond anything anyone else could do. People said he had the arm of a God, and that was why his weapons held up so well. Others said he was so good because he was a God; he never confirmed or denied it himself. Gods were hard to deal with because we had to toss a coin on if they wanted to blend in or be worshipped.

God or not, I was excited, and I'd pay for the chance to have blades from him, but I'd like to visit a few other places, too, with the extra coin.

"Belladonna," I said.

"Hm?"

"Do you think he makes dragon armor?" I asked.

"Are you preparing for battle, little one?" she questioned.

"Well, no, but you would look lovely showing up to the temple of magic wearing shiny new armor," I said.

"He may, but you would not save any coin," she pointed out.

It was a good point. She was right. There's no war, and eating would be better.

I didn't need to ask; Belladonna dove herself down and back under the clouds so we could see Ashbell while we flew over it. We weren't far from Erebus once we entered Ashbell, but I would take every glance I got of home. Even up high, the heat from the volcano could be felt, a warm embrace against my skin.

Belladonna completed her dive by landing all four claws on the ground of Erebus. The impact reverberated through my bones. From the ground, it was nothing impressive. The only things in sight were a few trees and some patches of half-burnt blades of grass.

The entrance to the main cave stood tall and decorated in the middle of the mountains. The cave entrance was surrounded by hand-carved stone statues. A dragon was carved over the top in a pouncing stance as the guardian to anyone who may enter unattended. The stone had been polished until it gleamed, catching the light and showing intricate details in the carved scales.

I stood and waited alongside Belladonna. She didn't speak, but I could feel her searching the space around us. I watched Belladonna lift her head and sniff the air before turning her snout behind us, where a dragon resembling the carving tried his best to shake the ground. He pounced in front of her and stopped playfully.

Usha, Erebus's stone dragon, looked for her, too.

He had a bite behind him, but he looked like just a baby beside her. I took my chance to hug Usha before I left them to play. His scales were cool and rough against my cheek. She would find me, and I was not there to keep her from having her own friendships.

I went inside until the bioluminescent blue glow of mushrooms lit up every bit of mossy foliage around me. The air was moist, and the water was crystal clear. Droplets of condensation ran down the cave walls like tears. I had only been one other time, and it wasn't for long enough.

Bearded men and women gave me a few lookovers; some even stopped and stared at me, but no one said a word. They had long lives and had to be used by tourists. It didn't make sense for them to see me as out of place.

I didn't dwell; I had only been there once, and there was a list of things I wanted to do that I did not get to do then. The caves of Erebus were home to the Vinna. They flew with oversized wings of leather connected to their arms, and fangs sat inside their mouths. Affected by the mushrooms, they came in all colors and spots. Some poisonous, some not. They all glowed, though.

I crouched down by a gathering of mushrooms and searched around and under to find one. Instead, one dropped from above. It let out angered hisses. It sniffed me for what felt like an eternity before it wrapped around me, and I felt the air from it sniffing and chittering. Its tiny claws pricked at my skin through my clothes.

"I think I'll take you with me," I smiled.

I pulled off a little piece of mushroom to pick apart and feed it. Our next location was a shop known to carry every fabric imaginable. I heard they carried furs and silks from Brisa, and even if I didn't buy them, I had to see them. I kept a map in the back pocket of my pants. I pulled it out to ensure we didn't get lost.

When I turned a corner to follow the stone walkway, I realized I probably didn't need the map as much as I thought I did. It was clear a lot of people came for the same reason I was here. Signs were posted on every corner and in front of every store, and if that had not been enough to guide me, the shimmering dresses in the window would have been. The fabrics caught the light of the mushrooms, creating a rainbow of soft colors.

I fed the last of the mushroom to the Vinna and sat it down before I went inside the shop. I pushed the door of glass open and was surrounded by more clothes than I could wear in a lifetime. The rich scents of dye and fabric filled my nostrils, earthy indigos, spicy reds, and the subtle perfume of silk.

I ran my hands through cotton, silk, and velvet. Leather in all colors even hung in its own corner. I spent all my time in pants for training, but if I had the chance, I would have worn a gown or two. I was stopped when I saw a simple crimson silk dress with pearls from Daxon down the side. It was long enough that I wasn't sure if I could have even walked in it, but light enough, it would have been perfect for the heat in Ashbell. I thought about trying it on, but I knew it would make it harder to part from it. The fabric whispered beneath my fingers, cool and smooth like water.

"You would look good in it," the voice in my head spoke.

"You can see me?" I searched the room, my heart skipping a beat.

He gave no answer, and I convinced myself to leave before I was watched any longer. When I left, I put my map away and followed the signs posted around to the blacksmith.

The looks I received while I cut in front of people already waiting for this blacksmith could have killed me if magic were still around. I did my best to keep my eyes on the ground even though I searched for any sign of the man behind the voice that followed me. The weight of their stares burned into my back.

I made arrangements for my meeting in advance. I could have said it out loud, but I wasn't confident I could handle the backlash if I didn't just keep walking.

I showed the man guarding the shop the card I received when I made my appointment, and he motioned for me to follow. The room he led me into was filled with what I was sure was the only giant half-breed left in the world, not a man. When he held his hand out to me, waiting for me to shake it, I thought for sure I'd never graduate. He was sure to break every one of my fingers. The heat from the forge made sweat bead on my forehead. I questioned if being polite was even worth the risk, but if he considered me rude, I'd not survive the hit. Death or a broken hand seemed to be my only choice.

I held out my hand and scrunched my eyes shut, waiting to hear the crunching before I felt it, but instead, I just heard laughter roar out. I opened one eye and saw his hand in mine, so I opened the second eye and looked from his golden eyes to my hand. I had to look like a fool. I was embarrassing myself in front of someone who was famous. The scent of hot metal and coal filled the air around us.

I should never have come. I should have kept my head in the books.

I did my best to force a laugh and shake his hand. "Nice to meet you; here is my sketch. Do it, please. Thank you. Enjoy your breakfast, goodnight." I tossed him my bag of coins and turned to run.

I mindlessly walked, then jogged my way out of the building, which was almost as hot as my face felt. I moved past the crowd and was back on the street. I was a fool. A fool. I-collided with a person. It was a girl with the brightest teal eyes. Her mouth was covered, and her black hair, which was nearly all tucked under her cloak, matched her skin. She looked to be sneaking around, but I wasn't sure that I wanted to be involved.

"Sorry," I mumbled and backed up.

She pointed her dark finger at me. "One free, you pay for the rest."

She shoved me to the side and kept going like I was an insect. The brief contact left a chill running down my spine. I didn't want to dwell on it. I was lucky to escape my earlier near-death with a giant man. I didn't want a second problem. I flung the door open to the tavern and took the furthest table I could find to throw myself into. The smells of roasted meat and fresh bread filled the air, making my stomach growl despite my mood.

"Great!" I yelled and threw my hands up.

I left all my coins with him. I threw my head on the table and groaned. The wood was cool against my forehead. I wouldn't be trying any sweet, fluffy cakes with strawberries and cream this time, either.

A dwarf tapped me on the shoulder, and when I sat up, there were several plates in front of me. The dessert I had been looking forward to. Too many meals for me to eat, and two boxes. When I lifted the corner of one, it was the red dress I had looked at earlier. The other held a small pair of citrine stud earrings. I asked the woman where they came from, but she had no answer for me. When I looked around, I only caught the back of a crimson-cloaked figure leaving the tavern.

A man in a black cloak came in after I tucked the boxes under my chair, but I knew who he was. He was my lover.

He sat across from me, but he only lowered his cloak enough for me to see bits of his face. The scent of thunderstorms clung to him, as always.

"I can not be here with you today. There are things going on that require my presence. I will meet you when I can, but until then, we will have to make do," Deimos explained, his voice low and urgent.

"It's all right," I lied. "Thank you for the gifts and food."

He looked at them and back at me, but only gave a nod before he and his cloak were in the wind. The chair he vacated still held his warmth.

Throbbing filled my mind. "If you thank him for my generosity again, I won't be so nice."

"You did this?" I asked the voice in my mind.

There was no response, and I was alone again. The tavern's chatter continued around me, but I felt isolated in my confusion, the plates of food in front of me suddenly less appetizing.

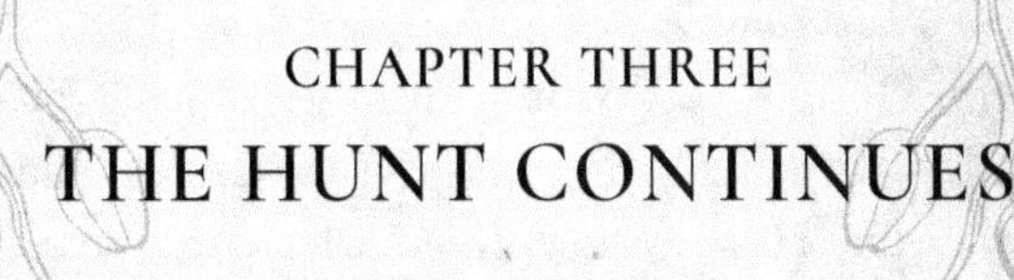

CHAPTER THREE
THE HUNT CONTINUES

BRONTIDE, THE LAND OF THUNDER.

The rocky land was started by the Goddess of Envy. After some time of trying, she learned that she could not use her abilities correctly, and the land never flourished. The Goddess of Magic and the God of Death created a child kept in secret and staged as Envy's daughter. The Goddess of Storms took charge of the land, and it flourished. The citizens live in homes built inside of giant rock pillars. They are the only closed land in all of Cylla. Protected by a barrier the Goddess of Magic put up, only close friends and select people not born inside the borders have ever entered.

HESPERIA

Astra's office was never what I thought it would be. She was so committed to being Thann that sometimes, even I believed her. Everything went down to the smell that filled the air—mildew, and it felt like Thann. The musty scent clung to the furniture, a constant reminder of the persona she maintained. The sound of my boot tapping against the ground could have made a beat, each tap echoing through the silent room. She was supposed to have been there before I was. Coy and my nameless informant were supposed to have been there, too. I was not hopeful that any good news would come. There was nearly never good news.

Sina, the Goddess of Winter in dragon form, sat unbothered, with her head held high despite the antlers that had to have been heavy. Her powder blue scales were beautiful; she was beautiful, but she was also different. The cold emanating from her body created a visible mist around her talons. She didn't seem to be the friend I left behind so long ago. I reasoned with myself that none of us were truly the same as we had been.

How could we be?

We all lost so much and went through even more. I didn't experience death like so many of them had. I tried to consider that's why she was different, but I never could get a straight answer from her on anything. Once, we shared everything we thought we had. We hardly shared anything in the Age of Starlight. The weight of this realization sat heavy on my shoulders, a constant reminder of all we'd lost.

I learned that there was a large difference between those of us who died and were reborn through the stars and Yumi versus the ones who didn't die in the separation or were brought back into dragons. The ones reborn through Yumi and the stars had no memory, no idea who they were. They had to live and try their best to get things back. So far, some things have still not come back. Those of us who did not die or were put into dragons seemed to have everything. Every detail of our past, but we could not use our tongues to discuss most of it.

There was a celestial silencing that only worked on our mouths. I looked for any way around it, but Sina was satisfied to only give the basics of what was needed and never speak of it again. It wasn't like her, or at least her that I remembered to hold things in. The frustration of this inability to speak freely felt like a constant pressure at the back of my throat.

Bodies entered the room, and Astra shifted from Thann's disguise back to her own appearance. The chandelier filled with candles the size of my fist that hung from the roof lit her up well. The warm glow danced across her features, highlighting the contours of her face. She had something that I had not seen before in anyone: pink eyes. They were more stunning against her silver hair than any jewel or crystal I had ever seen.

"Sorry, we're late," she apologized.

"We learned Caym started talking to Ruri through her mind. That meeting took a little longer than we thought it would have," Coy explained.

The God of Famine, my guardian. The sweetest baby blue eyes looked at me with longing while he spoke. We tried so hard, but he still did not recall who I was or any of our memories. Although I could recall every kiss we exchanged, every time I ran my hands through his white locks, and every conversation we shared in the late hours of the night, he held nothing but our time together in the shattered realm. The ache of this one-sided remembrance felt like a hollow carved inside my chest, a space that couldn't be filled.

"We tried to reason with Caym that him speaking to her like that could set us back again, but he was hearing none of it, of course," Astra continued as she took her own seat at her desk. The wooden chair creaked under her weight.

Coy stood beside me, and my informant sat in the green velvet seat beside me.

"I don't know why you tried to have the conversation at all," I admitted.

He would sooner let us all meet our end and create a small slice of the underworld for him and Ruri to endlessly live rebirths than hear a word of how he can't interact with her. I never blamed him, and I damn sure never tried. It was because I knew for sure that I would be a hypocrite if I did.

I would take Coy and make the same choices if I had to. I would spend every day trying to help Coy remember or build a new life together endlessly, rather than live as long as I did in that locket without him. The memory of that isolation sent a chill down my spine.

"Someone has to," Astra disagreed, her voice firm.

"I just think if you're going to worry about anyone, it should be Sage and not Ruri. Ruri has been and will remain well protected. Sage is the one that can't seem to catch a break," I countered.

My informant loudly cleared his throat. Even after all of the time we spent together, he was still uncomfortable to know he was in a room of deities. The nervous tremor in his hands betrayed his unease. It was why I trusted him so much. He never lost the fear of knowing we could shatter him. It was a conversation that he heard us have often. Some of us needed to follow a set of rules that I wasn't sure who wrote. They needed an ordered list. Some of us only wanted to rip the realms apart.

I wanted to rip the realm apart.

"Please, start speaking," I urged the informant.

"I've received word that Nikola has been to the temple of vampires. They say he was there looking for Creation blood, but no one wanted to take the job of trying to get it from the one under the God of Death's protection," the informant reported, his voice dropping to barely above a whisper.

I nodded but received no chance to speak.

"We found traces of Nikola's creatures in Sephtis," Coy revealed.

"Koa's land?" Sina interjected, her scales glinting in the candlelight. "I didn't expect to hear he was caught up with Nikola. Is this a sign that he may be the traitor?"

Coy and I locked eyes at her suggestion. Neither of us

believed such an idea. It was as foolish as thinking Coy himself was the traitor. He was the only one we could trust, without a doubt. He wasn't in the realm during Yumi's rule. He couldn't have helped her. Sina had such a hunger for the subject of a traitor. Sometimes, it gave me a twirling in my stomach. A hint of tenseness. I felt as if she held some secret information that she hadn't even tried to share.

"I don't want to jump to conclusions," I cautioned.

"I think not suspecting him is jumping to the conclusion. Being sure without proof is how you get killed," Sina asserted. Her head was still held high, antlers casting elongated shadows on the wall behind her.

"I think we've spent enough time already pointing fingers. Haven't we?" Astra shifted her gaze between us, the pink of her eyes flashing with impatience. "If there are no other real talking points, then we have a dear friend who has a graduation today."

"Actually, I'd like something clarified," Sina pressed. "You never fully explained how you avoided dying."

Her tone took me by surprise. The chill from her body seemed to intensify, frosting the edges of her antlers.

"Nikola locked me inside a different realm. He separated my soul from my body. I was all but dead. I was only a spirit roaming until I reconnected with my body."

"I would like to speak to Hesperia alone," Coy interjected.

I thought it was probably only in my head, but it felt as though he did it to help me out of an uncomfortable situation. The gratitude I felt warmed me from within.

Astra shivered with her lips turned down. "Out, everyone out. The last thing I want to see is what this request is for."

The informant and Sina followed her out. Coy clicked the lock on the door behind them. It was I who held a scrunched brow after the sound.

"Is something wrong?" I asked, the tension in the room palpable.

He shook his head. "I'm going to be gone a while. I intend to relaunch my investigation of the Guardians."

I wanted to oppose and deny him. It was as if he were making a plea or a request to me directly. I saw in his face that he wasn't asking. He felt as though he had to stay with me because of his title. No amount of time around me made him remember. He doubted himself, and so he committed himself fully to weeding out the false guardian. He thought that because he could not remember who he was or us, and we could not find a clear reason, he could not allow himself to get close to me until he could clear his own name. The realization hit me like a physical blow, making my chest ache.

I tried to reason with him, to assure him that I knew he did not have that kind of blood on his hands, but my words gave him no comfort.

"I've found what I think is the way to do it. In the temple of magic, they use a crystal to see someone's true nature. To find out if they are lying. I plan to use it with them," he disclosed, his voice barely above a whisper.

"Why not on yourself? If it works that well, then why not clear your name and stay?" I questioned, unable to keep the desperation from my voice.

"You know I can not. This needs to be done, or none of us live in peace," he answered, his blue eyes filled with resolve.

It wasn't the answer I wanted, but it was one that I could be proud of. His goal was to be the guardian, so I made it mine to focus on Nikola. If I could not have Coy, then I could have my vengeance at least. I found traces of him in more than one land, but any time I was too close, I lost him as quickly as I found him.

He looked at me and searched for a response, but I had nothing. Coy leaned himself down and kissed my forehead before he left. The warmth of his lips lingered on my skin. He left without words, but every time he left me that way, with silence, he broke off another piece of me and took it with him. He kissed me in formality. It was a gesture he felt as though he had to give.

I wanted to tell him that he didn't need to act in a way that he didn't feel, but I was afraid if he didn't feel a sense of forced duty to me that, he might not even glance at me again. I wanted to stay positive. I kept telling myself that we just had to climb one last hill to find our bright side. The hope felt fragile, like a tiny flame I cupped in my hands against a harsh wind.

I used the side of my finger to flick away the moisture forming in the corners of my eyes. There was no use dwelling or crying over things that I could not change. It wouldn't solve anything or help anyone. The salt of my tears stung as I wiped them away.

I left Astra's office and shut the doors behind me. The halls were silent and empty. It was a rare sight. The only other time Orest was as silent was during balls. A tradition I enjoyed, too. My footsteps echoed on the stone floor, the only sound in the vast corridor.

In the courtyard, dragons and riders moved into place to receive their medals. It was something they would wear anytime they were doing their new duties. A symbol of commitment and training. They were worn with honor. The afternoon sun glinted off the polished metal of the medals, creating dazzling patterns of light.

An emerald cloak was placed in the back corner of the gathering. If he wanted to be hidden, he should have picked a different color. The vivid green stood out among the more subdued colors of the crowd. I moved myself to his side of the crowd and crossed my arms.

"She looks good in those leathers," I remarked.

His cloaked head turned to me but didn't speak. The shadow cast by his hood made it impossible to see his face clearly.

"I suppose you already knew that. Why didn't you tell me the two of you were sneaking around?" I inquired.

"What?" Caym's growl told me I was mistaken, the sound rumbling like distant thunder.

"Seems they're going to start. I've got to go," I laughed out.

He didn't try to stop me, which I was thankful for. I did not want to be put in the position to find and kill some poor student that Ru thought she was in love with for a day. This was an unfortunate side effect of the situation, and I did not want between Caym and the rage he would have.

Astra, disguised as Thann with the use of illusion crystals, stood in front of the students. She called names with a voice that was not hers, but they happily accepted without question. I looked forward to the day when she could have her own name, besides all of the hard work she had done in Orest. The illusion crystals embedded in her ceremonial staff shimmered as she spoke, reinforcing the magic that maintained her disguise.

Ruri and Belladonna received their medals, and I clapped and screamed until my throat ached. I saw her cheeks flush with embarrassment with every scream of her name I let out. The pride that swelled in my chest felt almost painful in its intensity.

Astra finally finished the list of riders, and everyone broke into groups. They wanted to congratulate and go over what plans they had for the rest of the night. I wanted to enjoy the events as they were, but I could not. I could hardly find joy in much for too long before my thoughts drifted to all of the things that we should or could be doing. All of the progress we still needed to make.

Ru found me in the crowd and sought me out. I spent as much time with her as I could. Sina felt off to me, but Ruri felt like my sister. Her confidence in her abilities was lower than it had been, but that didn't make her feel any less powerful. It made sense. She had every reason to have doubt in herself. I hated to see it, but I understood.

"Hesperia!" She called to me.

Her dark emerald hair matched her eyes. Her hair was as long as her eyes deep. It was a concept I could never get used to. The idea that she could be reborn one hundred times and look like the girl we knew every single time. Her voice, her eyes. It was always the same, but her memory of it all was never there.

The idea of it happening to me terrified me. It haunted me to think that I could live an entire life and forget it. Leave it behind as if it never existed. The idea that I could cause such an ache in someone's heart and be clueless about the way that aches shaped their footsteps made me lose sleep at night. The very thought sent a cold dread seeping through my veins.

She embraced me, and I returned the affection. The familiar scent of her cinnamon and smoke filled my senses. When we pulled apart, she looked at me with guilt, and I knew she wanted to say she had plans. The look on her face allowed me to let out a sigh of relief. Neither of us wanted to waste time on a celebration filled with students. We wanted to keep moving forward. To march on to the next thing, and it was that need that made the two of us so close in our past life together as well.

"I feel awful saying this, but I can't stay to celebrate. I have a few things I need to do before I meet you at the temple," I had to shout now to lift my voice over all of the ones around us. The cacophony of cheers and conversations created a wall of sound.

Ruri nodded. "I do, too! I have to go see someone."

I wanted to ask who, but it was better that I didn't know. Caym's reaction made it clear that it was not him she was seeing.

"You will be safe, right?" I called out.

"Of course!" She yelled in return.

She gave me a second hug, one much quicker and more out of a need to hurry our goodbye so that she could leave. I didn't stop her, but the need to know what she was doing to keep her safe almost outweighed the little voice that told me she was allowed to live and make choices that I didn't agree with. She deserved her freedom, even if it was hard for me not to look after her.

I lost her in the crowd before I turned to leave, too. The sea of bodies swallowed her emerald hair from view.

I needed to travel to a different temple and ask some vampires what they knew about a God who should have died several times over already. I pushed past student after happy student, but I stopped when I saw him in the crowd. My heart seized in my chest.

Nikola stood out among all of the other smiling faces. His smile was hard, glaring. His teeth flashed white against his dark features. He disappeared in front of my eyes, and his breath is what reappeared first. His mouth hovered just above my skin. The heat of it sent goosebumps rising along my neck.

"Have you missed me?" He whispered, his voice like silk against my ear.

I turned, but he was gone again. He haunted me, but I couldn't tell anyone. He was in my dreams, my waking life. He was inside of my head. I felt more bonded to Nikola than Coy since entering Cylla. One blink was all it took for him to pull me into the world he created for us. He altered my reality and put me in a false space. The first few times, I thought I had been put back inside of the locket.

Instead, I walked on shimmering stars in a black abyss. The only thing that I was able to touch and see was him. He stood behind me and brushed his hands in my hair. The sensation was both intimate and violating.

"I know that I missed you," his breath was in my hair again, warm and invasive.

"Nikola, do we have to do this? You know how it's going to go," I remarked, unable to keep the weariness from my voice.

"I'll get to put my hands on you, you'll shove your pretty little dagger through my fake heart, and I'll fall further in love with you," he murmured with a smirk.

I rolled my eyes. "You don't know what love is. I've seen your heart enough times to know it's empty."

"My sweet girl, I love as much as I can. If you and your sisters weren't forced into the connection you have with your 'lovers,' you'd understand that love is fleeting, like a mortal's life span. Fleeting like the way the shape of our world changes. You would enjoy eternity more if you loved more," he proposed, moving to stand in front of me. His eyes, black as the void around us, reflected pinpricks of starlight.

"What do you want," I spoke with space between each word. I wanted each one to sound rougher than the last. Each syllable was edged with contempt.

"You. I simply want to check on you," his thumb ran across my bottom lip and down my chin, his touch cold despite its apparent warmth.

I moved the white silk fabric draped over my torso and moved my fingers across my dagger. The metal was cool beneath my fingertips, a comfort in this disorienting space. "You don't need to keep checking on me. I'm coming for you."

"Aren't you afraid I'll kill you this time?" Nikola probed.

I gave him no smile. "We both know that you can not kill me. I am the dead. If I am not here on this form, it'll be another. So long as there are things to die, you won't be rid of me."

I pulled the dagger out and plunged it into where his heart would have been if he were more than a projection placed inside of my head. The blade met resistance before sinking in, as though piercing something solid. His laugh boomed out and filled the empty abyss with echo after echo. The sound reverberated through me, vibrating in my bones.

"I look forward to it. I'd much rather have my hands on you in person," he taunted before disappearing without a single hint that he was ever there at all.

No mist. No shell. Just a black abyss and my thoughts. He set me free without punishment for the first time in ages. Our routine had become such a ritual that I could count down to the second how every movement occurred. I was let free of the cage he kept me in without the scenes of my mother dying. Without having to replay the way, my father was murdered. I would continue my day without watching my sisters die.

If there was anything Nikola hated more than being told no, it was seeing the bond my family had with each other. He wanted nothing more than to see me in pain. This sudden mercy felt more unsettling than his usual torment, leaving me with a sense of foreboding that clung to me like a second skin.

CHAPTER FOUR

IT'S TIME TO DO WHAT I DO BEST

SEPHTIS, THE LAND OF SHIFTERS.

The land of sand, was created by the Goddess of Pride. One of the first to be brought back by the stars, she also failed to terraform the land beyond the sand. She was murdered by the Goddess of Chaos, and the land was left to Pride's children. The land plunged further into despair when the God of Dreams stole the one thought to be in charge. Dreams kept the landlocked tightly. The God of War has done his best to recover what he can. He has done his best to open trade routes, build homes, and repair the mistakes that were made. Sephtis now holds shifters in all shapes and sizes, and the land is covered in rich architecture with a pyramid in the center. It is used for the temple of the Goddess of Healing.

HESPERIA

Sina was not a big dragon by any stretch of the imagination. She had to be one of the smaller dragons that I had seen. Luckily for me, she was sizable enough for me to ride. The smooth scales beneath me were cold to the touch, like polished ice against my skin. The flight made things easier. I could move through the veil and get where I wanted quicker, but it came with the downside of being stopped by anyone on the other side who needed me. I felt guilty when I avoided the dead, even if I never said it out loud, but if I didn't prioritize, the living would have no chance while the dead had unending days.

The dead would have to wait to be sent to Caym until the living were settled.

"Do you enjoy being a dragon?" I asked Sina, the wind whipping my words away almost before they left my mouth.

"Not at all. Do you know what It feels like to be looked at like an animal? I hit walls, and I could not sit in a tavern to enjoy a meal. I am alive, but I can not live unless I want to live as a beast," she growled, her voice rumbling beneath me.

I did know what it felt like to live as an animal. Nikola made sure of it. The memory sent a tremor through my body that had nothing to do with the rushing wind.

"I don't see you as a beast, Sina," I offered, knowing my words would make no difference.

"It means nothing how you see me. You may see me as a flower, but if the rest of the world sees me as a weed, then I am nothing more than a weed," she shot her words at me, each one sharp as an icicle.

"I'm sure we can find a way to fix it—" I ventured.

"We will. When things are settled and sorted. When you ascend, and all is right, I will have my body back. Not until then," Sina declared, bitterness frosting each syllable.

I had not considered how hard the changes had to have been on her. The realization settled in my chest like a stone. I dreamt of wings, and she dreamt of solid land. The gulf between our experiences seemed to widen with each passing day.

She spiraled out of the clouds and dived, nose first for the ground. I gripped her scales harder so that I could lean further back and enjoy the rush of the breeze. My stomach lurched as we plummeted, the world blurring around us. Her talons gripped the dirt on landing, and the grass beneath her was sure to be ruined, leaving deep grooves in the earth.

The camp Shivani insisted on living in was set up for so long that it started to look more like a city and less like temporary housing. Tents of every size and color sprawled across the landscape, some adorned with symbols I couldn't decipher. More and more vampires showed up and asked for a safe haven every day since Shivani laid the first stake down. The head vampires in the Temple of Rebirth had not yet agreed on what to make of Shivani.

Some temple leaders thought she had to be their true leader, that all of the things they had been through couldn't be their future as well. Others thought she was a test of their loyalty. It hadn't been the first test they would have been given. Helia was cruel to them. The stories of her slaughtering every child under fifteen were still discussed around the realm, whispered in hushed tones around campfires.

Shivani had been through every diplomatic avenue she could think of. She was open and heard Koa's ideas for a more forceful approach. She was content to move slowly and earn their trust. I admired her for that. My patience was not as deep as hers, however. I also wanted her to push them harder, even if only a little. The waiting felt like an itch under my skin that I couldn't scratch.

Sina waited outside of the camp, and her words rippled through my mind. I hadn't realized these things made her so upset. Although Shivani was patient, she was not lenient. She did not allow anyone to enter outside of a very small circle. I did not ask for an explanation because I assumed she was better off safe than sorry, and we could all understand her point of view. It did not occur to me that maybe Sina didn't see it the way that I saw it.

It didn't consider that she may be upset with me for not

standing up for her. The thought made my chest tighten with guilt.

Maybe that was the answer to why she felt so different to me now.

"Hesperia!" Shivani called. Her arms were already open for me, her crimson eyes bright against her pale skin.

I embraced her, breathing in her familiar scent of cloves and night air. I did not miss a chance to touch anything after being a ghost for so long. It never felt quite the same as it once did. Sometimes, I had a small wish to be born under Yumi and the Age of Starlight so that I could not remember the way life was. I knew everyone was struggling, so I kept my inside thoughts separate, but being put in a cage to think of our life and then see it far from what it was was something hard to grasp.

"How are things here?" I inquired, pulling back to study her face.

"Good. I think we are making real progress now!" Her voice was filled with enthusiasm, unlike my face. I could feel my skepticism etched in the furrow of my brow.

I tried my best not to let my skepticism for any progress show, but the twitch at the corner of my mouth betrayed me.

"Not like last time. Real progress," she countered my expression, pressing a finger to the crease between my eyebrows.

I hadn't said anything, and yet my face spoke it all for me.

"I mean it! The elders in the temple have agreed to meet with me for the first time," she insisted, waving a finger at me that was in sync with her words.

"All right, that does sound promising," I agreed, allowing a small smile.

"Why are you here?" She questioned, eyes narrowed in suspicion. The sudden shift in her tone made the hairs on my arms stand up.

"I can't check in on my baby sister?" I cooed, placing a hand on her shoulder.

"We are the exact same age," she reminded me with a roll of her eyes.

"But mature in different ways," I nodded, keeping my tone light.

"Why are you really here?" she demanded, stepping back from my touch.

"I can't come and see you because I miss you?"

"No," she stated flatly.

She was right. I had not and did not ever come just to check on her. I wanted to make it a habit after I found Nikola. That hadn't gone as well, as quickly for me, either. I always told myself a little while longer. A little while turned into a bit longer. That turned into maybe next year. I hated the idea of adding the title of liar next to my name and shoving that wedge between us, but if I told her why I was really in front of her, she would turn me away in an instant.

If I said I needed to break into the temple, interrogate a vampire for answers, and possibly kill them, she would shun me. Her deep red eyes beat down on me with a pressing weight. The tension between us was a tangible thing, thick as smoke.

I had to follow my leads, even if they led me to places I really didn't want to break into. We had to find Nikola, even if the cost was spending an eternity trying for a repaired relationship.

"Sister, I simply wanted to see if you needed me before I went to Ashbell. Ruri is done at Orest, and we are moving on to the next phase of her journey. It gave me time between events. I wanted to make sure that you didn't need me," I explained, doing my best to hold myself together. I could feel a bead of sweat forming at my temple, despite the cool air.

She looked me in the eyes for several long moments and then nodded. "Fine. Whatever it is you're here for, don't cause any trouble. I mean it!" Her finger was practically in my nose, her nail sharp as a talon.

"I swear I will not cause immediate trouble," I promised with a small bow and wasted no time to leave her presence, the weight of my lie settling like lead in my stomach.

I dodged every face I saw and kept myself behind tents and shrubbery. The scent of cooking fires and murmured conversations filled the air around me. Their camp was only a few beats from the temple. If I was lucky for the day, Helia would be inside, too. I could find where Nikola was hiding, and at the same time, I could beat Helia until she was weak enough to be drug to Shivani's feet to finish the job. The thought sent a thrill of anticipation through me that I tried to ignore.

I entered the back door of the stone temple. It had been neglected enough that even the stone on the outside was tinged red. The smell hit me first, copper and decay, like old blood and forgotten bodies. I was sure no one cleaned. It looked as if no one lit a candle either, with how dark the inside was. I felt half-blind as I attempted to navigate, my hands trailing along the cold, damp walls to guide me. It was to my benefit and potential detriment. If I could not see, how was I to abduct a vampire that looked worth anything?

I walked and hugged against the walls until I heard voices. They were loud and angry, echoing off the stone.

"We can't keep stealing people and turning them to make up for the losses that girl outside keeps causing. We will start a war, or worse, we will be unprepared, and they'll sneak in to slaughter us!"

"No one would dare. They're too afraid of what may lurk inside our walls."

"Thank the Goddess, then, for the filth we live in. It'll be the only thing protecting us in the end."

"It's not our only protection. Helia promised us that the

God of Insanity would shield us from any fallout as long as we offered him the correct blood."

"Yes, we just need to find an original. No, excuse me, the originals and bleed them without losing our heads."

"If you don't want to be part of this anymore, then leave. Go with the other deserters."

"Must that be our only option? Do you not ever think we are on the wrong side?"

Silence filled the air, and the only voice of reason in the room left first. The sound of footsteps receded down another corridor. He did not see me, and I waited with hope that the other man would leave as well. It would be easiest for me if I could take him out while he was leaving the room, but he did not.

I turned the corner and entered the still dimly lit room. Red was the only color against the stone, dark stains on the floor that I didn't want to think about. The temple was hardly built for architecture. It was placed for a quick roof, with uneven walls and a ceiling that dripped in places.

"Where is he?" I asked, my voice startlingly loud in the quiet room.

The man turned, jumped out of his skin, and looked me up and down. His eyes widened, reflecting what little light there was. "Who?"

"The God of Insanity. Where is he? Is he to meet you here?" I interrogated, taking slow steps closer. My boots made no sound on the stone floor.

"If he was, you wouldn't want to be here," he warned, his voice dropping to a growl.

"Trust me, I would. I don't need to hear your thoughts on my capability. What I need is your information. I'm tired of asking nicely," I asserted. I flicked a button on my hip to release my dagger and sat it on the small table beside us. The metallic sound as it touched the wood seemed to echo through the room.

The man laughed. "Do you think that would scare me? Is that what you came with?" His laughter grew thicker, filling the small space.

I curled my fingers inward against themselves until the full sight of my palm was visible, and I shoved the flat base of my hand into his nose until I saw the blood drip down his chin. The crunch of cartilage was sickeningly satisfying.

"I'm already getting very tired of how many mortals think they can't be crushed," I snarled, grabbing him by the arm and pulling him to the only chair in sight before I lowered myself to a crouched position. The scent of his blood, richer and older than human blood, filled my nostrils. "Once there was respect. A pecking order, if you will. Mortals understood that they had better be sure of themselves before they tried anything, and sure, some of them did. They could at least say they didn't piss themselves from the first hit." I gestured to his crotch. "I'll ask you again, where is he."

The man started to bite down on his tongue. He attempted to get rid of the one thing that allowed him to spill secrets. I allowed him to do it. I watched in patient silence until he chewed through his own tongue and spat it out between my legs. The wet sound it made as it hit the floor turned my stomach, but I kept my face impassive.

"I don't know how to explain to you that you made the wrong choice. I'll show you instead."

I turned my hand to the same ghostly form I would use to walk through the veil and reached it through his chest to where his life root sat. The sensation was strange, not quite solid, not quite air, like pushing through thick fog. I touched it and commanded it to die, and so it did. His body went limp, eyes glazing over.

When I touched it a second time, he was revived with his tongue intact. The horror in his eyes at the sight of me made me feel alive, and I was ashamed to admit it, even to myself.

The power that surged through me was intoxicating and terrifying all at once.

I worried that the time I spent with Nikola had a larger effect on me than I wanted to admit. I was afraid that his ideas and his tactics had worn off on me. As I watched myself from a different point of view, I was closer to that fear being true than I had been. The realization sent a chill down my spine.

"I can kill you as many times as you need to answer me," I threatened, my voice soft but deadly.

"Who are you?" he whimpered, his body trembling.

"No one liked my speech the first time. Something tells me you won't either," I sighed, running a hand through my hair. "I am Hesperia. Keeper of the in-between, daughter of the moon, Goddess of Fate. Your eternity is mine to decide. I can send you to the keeper of the dead. I can send you to an eternity of suffering. The choice is purely mine. Pick your next answer well."

He looked at me, and I saw his body shake, a fine tremor running from his head to his feet.

"Would you like further proof?" I inquired, raising an eyebrow.

He shook his head frantically.

This slow chatter was grinding my nerves. I put my hand back through his chest until he took his last breath again and brought him back. His gasping inhale was like music to my ears.

"Do you think I want to waste hours here with you? Things are going to get worse than your imagination could lead you to conclude," I warned, picking my dagger back up and pointing it at him. The blade gleamed dully in the dim light.

"Daxon. Daxon," he stuttered, his voice breaking. "The last thing I was told was that he was going to the land of water. He isn't supposed to be back for several weeks. He should still be there."

"See how easy that was?"

I stood and put my dagger back on my hip where it belonged and clipped it back in place. The familiar weight of it against my side was comforting.

"You won't get far with him. He's been taking blood from someone to heal himself. He's strong, stronger than he should be," the man cautioned, unable to stop his stutter. Fear had made him loose-tongued at last.

I gripped the claymore on my back and pulled it over my head until it was fully visible in the dim light and swung into the delicate skin on his neck. The blade sliced through flesh and bone with little resistance. His head rolled across the floor with a wet thud, and I whipped my blade on his pants before putting it back where it belonged. The coppery scent of blood filled the air, mixing with the pre-existing smell of decay.

Shivani would be upset to know what happened here. She would be hurt if I went behind her back. One day, I'd take the time to apologize appropriately. I would make it up to her. Whatever it took, but for today, there was enough compassion going around. It hadn't gotten us anywhere yet. The word mercy did not allow us to move forward.

For now, I'd keep this secret. Getting to Daxon was more important. The weight of my actions settled into my bones as I slipped back into the shadows, leaving no trace behind but a headless corpse.

CHAPTER FIVE
THE MASKED KING

DAXON: THE LAND OF WATER.

The Goddess of water carved the land into two separate continents. She dug the area between the continents so deep that only she had ever been to the depths. When there was nothing touching the island in the center of the continents, she filled the area she dug out with water. She moved on to build the city, but it took days to consider what she would do with it. She considered her mother, the Goddess of Chaos, in the plans for her city. The Goddess of Water feared that her mother would one day wreck her lands, so she built half of her city on the island and the other half on the underside of the land; that half of the city was to be kept underwater. Her kingdom thrived until her mother showed up. The goddess of Chaos chained Izaria, the Goddess of Water, to the bottom of the ocean, leaving only the secret child she gave birth to with a mortal siren behind.

SAGE

Everyone at the table around me advised me to let my breath out slowly and quietly. Breathing techniques can help you relax, they'd say. They waved their hands by my face and pushed air onto me. The scent of their perfumed wrists only made my irritation grow, sweet floral notes mixing with my bitter mood.

"What do you mean he said he won't do it?" I gritted, my jaw clenched so tight I could feel a headache forming at my temples.

"He said he won't take any requests unless they come directly from you," the girl explained, her voice barely above a whisper.

I threw the bone from my chicken leg back on the plate in front of me with force. The ceramic plate rattled against the wooden table, drawing glances from nearby patrons. I watched the girl in front of me startle and squirm at its suddenness, and that made me struggle even more to keep my laugh inside. A bubble of amusement rose in my chest despite my frustration.

She was a new recruit, one that hardly had any experience, but my right hand thought she would be the perfect fit for taking my requests on this trip. It was customary for the new recruits to the Daughters of Steel to be shown how terrifying I could be. The poor thing's fingers trembled against the edge of the table.

"Pay for the meal," I growled, letting my voice drop to its lowest register.

I narrowed my eyes at her as hard as I could until she stood straight and looked ahead. It was my right hand's idea. She found it amusing to hear who took it seriously and who left thinking I was a fool. For her, I'd do it. I wouldn't tell Vespera that I was doing it for her. If she took it the wrong way, that was a rejection I couldn't handle. My heart fluttered at the mere thought of disappointing her.

I tossed the hood of my navy cloak up and left through the back of the tavern, preferring not to be seen. The worn fabric brushed against my cheek, still carrying the scent of woodsmoke from last night's campfire. We joked with the recruits about how cruel I was, but after they were in a while, they called me a bleeding heart.

I preferred to avoid confrontation. The moment every eye was on me when I entered or left a room made me uncomfortable. My skin prickled at the thought of being the center of attention.

Stone lined the path in the alley behind Erebus, the land of Shadows, and its busy town center. The uneven stones forced me to watch my step, still slick from an earlier rain. Taverns and custom dress shops sat around inns and the blacksmith. The man I was looking for.

The man who made deals to supply my mercenaries with weapons and gear for his own cut in the money I made from running the guild. The man who was the center of my frustration in Erebus. The man that I knew was in love with me. The knowledge of his feelings sat heavy in my stomach, an uncomfortable weight I couldn't seem to shake.

There were always many visitors; the entire land was underground. It was carved from the hands of the Goddess of Night and filled with crystals by her daughter, the Goddess of Magic.

The clearest ponds of water surrounded the brightest sparkling gems and mushrooms, bigger than one could imagine without laying eyes on them, lit the place up with a glow. The blue-green luminescence cast strange shadows on the faces of passersby, turning familiar features alien.

The land above looked empty and sad—hardly any grass but many, many caves. Once inside, no one ever wanted to leave. The dwarves of Erebus made a killing by giving tours.

I'd be confident in saying there were more inns than anything else. That was why I made a deal with the blacksmith. So I did not have to work around tourists or armies.

If it wasn't for the reputation this man had, I might have already found a new blacksmith. If there was anything he was better at than grinding my gears, it was pounding out metals. The rhythmic clanging of his hammer could be heard before I even reached his shop.

"You can't go in, ma'am. The owner is in a private meeting with a general. He demanded I keep everyone out," a burly guard declared, his hand resting on the pommel of his sword. His armor gleamed in the strange light of the underground world.

"I'll only ask you once to move out of my way," I warned, my voice dropping to a dangerous whisper.

My hope was that my serious voice would scare him enough to get out of my way. It didn't look like it was going to work. I always had a backup plan, always. I lifted the bottom corner of my grey shirt and pulled out a small bag of coins. The leather pouch felt heavy in my palm, each coin representing a job completed, a risk taken. I tossed it into his hand and motioned with my head for him to get lost.

"I repeat-"

This guard was stronger than the last. The last took half of the coin and ran with it. I unclipped a second pouch and sat that in his hand next. He looked at them both and back to me before he took his hand off his blade and jogged out of the entrance. The sound of his retreating footsteps echoed off the stone walls. If the blacksmith kept guards that stingy, I'd go broke faster than I could complete jobs.

The voices on the other side of the door were audible once the guard was out of the way. The rich baritone I recognized as Onyx's carried through the thick wood.

"I'm positive."

"You had a bright idea last time, too. It almost caused a war between us all!"

"This isn't about last time. This is about now. If we can get them to touch, it'll set off a reaction."

They were silent for a moment, and when I heard a squeak from the door opening, I pulled my weapon from my boot and lifted the blade in preparation to meet the throat of my blacksmith. The metal felt cold against my palm, a familiar comfort. Knife's seemed to be our love language. The thought made my cheeks warm unexpectedly.

"It's not very professional of you to spy like this," Onyx whispered, his breath warm against my ear.

"It's not very professional of you to deny every one of my messengers," I answered, pressing the blade closer to his throat.

I watched every swallow he gave force his adam's apple into the tip of my blade, and I had to try my best to fight the smirk I felt growing. He was cocky for someone so close to death. The pulse in his neck quickened visibly beneath my knife.

Maybe it was because he knew that I was unlikely to do it that he flirted with the idea.

Maybe this was also why I didn't actually find a new blacksmith. Part of me liked playing his game, too. The realization sent a flutter through my stomach that I quickly suppressed.

I sighed and removed the knife, sliding it back into its sheath with practiced ease.

"That's the third guard this year. You can't keep paying off everyone who tells you not to do something," Onyx chided, rubbing his neck where my blade had been.

"I can, and I will. If you hired from me, they wouldn't sell you out so easily. Though, maybe you could stop requesting I be the one to show up every time I need you to repair a few blades," I gritted my teeth, the words coming out sharper than intended.

"If I don't force your hand, you'd never come see me," he remarked, a hint of genuine hurt beneath his teasing tone.

"So, you do understand basic signals, then?" I shook my head, trying to ignore the twinge of guilt his words provoked.

This man was lucky he had the looks that he did. Red hair hung around orange eyes. They glowed against his tan skin, and he was built for his job. Muscles rippled beneath his shirt as he moved, testament to years spent at the forge. If ever there was a man who looked like his hands could crush a skull with ease and turn around to—

"Are you just going to stare at me forever?" Onyx smirked, his eyes twinkling with amusement.

"Don't flatter yourself," I moved past him to enter the room, brushing against his shoulder as I passed. The brief contact sent an unwanted spark through me. "Is your friend going to stay for our business talks?"

"Caym, this is Sage," Onyx introduced, gesturing between us. The forge's heat filled the room, making sweat bead at my hairline.

"You're the one stealing crystals?" Caym questioned, his voice deep and resonant.

"Maybe. Maybe not. I don't ask questions; I take payment and complete the jobs. It may be crystals, or it may be heads," I answered, lifting my chin defiantly.

I tried my best to make myself look larger than I was. I thought maybe if I had an intimidating presence too, the second man, who looked as big as Onyx, might want to leave. I squared my shoulders and planted my feet firmly on the ground.

Caym lowered his cloak off his head, revealing long black hair. His eyes let me know he wasn't from any of the lands I'd ever been to. They were completely black, like looking into an endless void. It was unnerving. I felt my shoulders slump, and I had to scream at my feet not to move. My heart hammered against my ribcage, and I forced myself to breathe evenly.

Did I run the assassins guild? Sure. Did I do half of the missions that involved death or fighting? No. I took jobs that involved the theft of empty buildings. This simple meeting was starting to get out of hand quickly. The air in the room felt suddenly too thick to breathe.

"Who is requesting you gather them?" Caym demanded.

"What part of I don't ask questions do you not understand," I yelled.

A poor choice that I regretted immediately. My voice echoed off the stone walls, making me wince.

"Now, now, Caym. Let's play nice," Onyx intervened, stepping between us. The scent of metal and coal clung to him, familiar and oddly comforting.

Yes, please. What that little pounder said. Listen to him!

"Why don't we bargain? I'll answer a question for you after you answer mine," Caym offered, his black eyes unblinking.

I let my eyes shift back to Onyx, who hadn't taken his gaze off of me yet. I did like to bargain. If I said I wasn't curious about their conversation before, I'd be lying to myself. Maybe I could even get paid to help them find the people they mentioned. The possibility of profit made my fingers twitch in anticipation.

It would be another job well done and filled with coin, without bloodied hands.

"Fine. But it's one answer: anything from there takes payment," I stipulated, crossing my arms over my chest.

"Deal. Who is gathering crystals," Caym inquired.

"The Vampires. What's important about the two people that you need to touch each other," I replied.

That didn't sound as serious as I hoped it would. I felt heat rise to my cheeks at my clumsy wording.

"So, you were eavesdropping," Onyx observed, raising an eyebrow.

"No, you just have a loudmouth," I retorted, flashing him a quick glare.

"They may have the power to bring back the Goddess of Magic and the Goddess of Nature," Caym interjected, his voice dropping to barely above a whisper.

"How much would you pay for their capture?" I asked, unable to hide the eager edge in my voice.

Onyx did his best to hide a smile, but I saw it. The corners of his mouth twitched upward, and I found myself momentarily distracted by the sight.

"I can't hire you," Caym stated flatly.

"Why? You won't find better," I protested, my lips turning down in disappointment.

"I need their safety as the first priority. I don't need to see much more to know you have no spine," Caym declared, pulling his cloak back on and making his way out. The insult stung more than I cared to admit.

My jaw hung open, and I moved my feet to give him a stern talking, but Onyx grabbed my arm and stopped me before I could. His fingers were warm against my skin, calloused from years of work.

"Trust me when I tell you, it's a fight you don't want," Onyx whispered, his breath tickling my ear.

In fact, I would trust him. I would take the warning and listen to it well, but I would pretend otherwise. The stubborn part of me refused to look like I was backing down.

"I wouldn't be here at all if it wasn't for your attitude. Why can't you just do your job and take my requests!" I snapped, jerking my arm away from his grasp.

"If I didn't force you here, you'd never come see me," Onyx repeated, his voice softer now, tinged with something that sounded too much like longing.

"Maybe there's a reason for that. You clearly don't need me to do your job, and I have other business to attend to," I said, avoiding his gaze.

"I'll have your gear for you; send one of your girls in three nights for it," Onyx conceded. There was a wave of sadness that washed over him. The light in his orange eyes dimmed noticeably. He moved past me to leave but stopped short. "I would accept visits from you without having to force you."

"That's not what I meant," I backpedaled. I grabbed his arm to stop him from leaving, feeling the warmth of his skin beneath my fingers.

"It's fine. I wanted to see you and check in on you because I care about you. I even made you something special, but I can see you don't care about seeing me like I care about seeing you," Onyx confessed, his back still to me. His shoulders slumped slightly, betraying his hurt.

My heart sank, and I dropped his arm. Guilt washed over me like a cold wave. "I'm sorry. Show me what you made."

"No. You're busy. I get it. I'll see you some other time when you can spare a few minutes for me. In the meantime, I'll make sure to do your half-cost labor," he remarked, the bitterness in his voice unmistakable.

I didn't say anything. I watched him leave in silence. The door closed behind him with a soft click that seemed to echo in the sudden quiet. He was the reason that I didn't commit to anyone. He made me feel conflicted. As if I didn't know my own emotions. I liked Onyx, and I felt as if I had a sense of duty to him.

It was a feeling I hadn't been able to sort out since I met him. I felt as if I owed him something. Time, love, I wasn't sure what. I was sure that any time I was close to thinking I didn't care about him, he would fill me with guilt until I did care again.

I would spend my days with Vespera and be so sure that I was beyond head over heels in love with her. I would be willing to die on the thought that she was my soul bonded. Her laugh, her smile, the way her eyes lit up when she discovered something new in her books, all of it filled me with a warmth I couldn't describe. Then I would be around him, and all of that would come into question. The certainty would waver, like a flame in a draft.

Could we have more than one bond? Sometimes, I hoped we did so that what I felt made sense. The only thing I could sort out was that the guilt had to tie back to some kind of double bond. The possibility both excited and terrified me.

I pulled my cloak over my head and tucked the black hairs that still stuck out away. I made my steps light and left as quickly as I could. It wasn't being at the blacksmiths that was a problem. Regardless of what I thought of him, he was known far and wide for his work. It wouldn't be a surprise to see that I was there.

It's where I needed to go next that I wanted to keep under cover. I took every precaution I could, and I stayed as out of sight as the mice in the allies. No names and no faces. That was the first rule of my guild. It kept my girls safe.

I received word that I was invited to the coronation of the new king. I didn't understand why, of all the people who needed me, the future king was on the list. He had enough hands at his disposal to do what he wanted, and I couldn't imagine why he would need another pair. Suspicion crawled up my spine like a spider.

Children ran through the streets in their best dresses. The glow of the mushrooms made the decorations shimmer in a way they wouldn't have been a sight available above ground. Gold and silver banners caught the light, creating dazzling patterns on the walls of the cave. The bioluminescence of the mushrooms gave the caves a feeling of being inside of another world. The air was filled with the scents of celebration, roasting meats, sweet pastries, and the earthy smell of the underground.

I showed the letter I received as my invitation to the guards who stood at the entrance to the coronation. The parchment felt heavy in my hand, the royal seal gleaming in the strange light. I would have assumed the coronation would be held at the castle, but the new king was holding it in Erebus. He had an entire block shut down with guards. When I asked around as to why he would do such a thing, people were beyond happy to tell me.

They thought he was a gem. They gushed about how he worked so hard to get to where he was. That he started at the bottom and, through hard work, became king. He was a loyal servant of the people, and it was only right that the ceremony that crowned him also helped the economy and brought joy to citizens. Their voices rose with excitement as they spoke of him, eyes shining with admiration.

His coronation was just another notch of approval from the people. Further proof that he cared where most other men didn't take a second glance. He was their savior.

I thought it was all a load of shit. He had never even shown his face. He was called the masked leader or the faceless king. It sounded to me like he had a secret motive. I had never met a man who fought endlessly for power; that was a man of the people. My instincts screamed caution.

A guard grabbed my arm and lifted me off my feet and onto his shoulder. The sudden movement forced the air from my lungs. I could have struggled, but would I ever sleep well again if I knew that I caused so many innocent citizens' festivities to be ruined? It was better for me not to resist until we were somewhere much more private, somewhere where I could unleash my beyond-amazing skills without the risk of large-scale shock and panic from my combat abilities. I let my body go slack, biding my time.

The guard carried me behind several sets of stone archways and into a golden tent set up clearly for the king to be and sat me in a chair. The plush velvet cushion sank beneath my weight. I felt as though I should have been blindfolded. Something a little more kidnapped feeling. It seemed the guard must have been new to his duties. I didn't feel very threatened yet. The tent smelled of expensive incense, sandal-wood, and something spicier I couldn't name.

He moved behind me, and the clink of his armor told me he hardly moved far enough for me to try to leave. It was a good thing that my plans were to stay put and wait patiently. After all, was there truly a reason to become violent? Yet.

The next set of footsteps entered, but I still did not turn around. The soft swish of fabric against the carpet announced the arrival of someone important. The masked king, in golden robes, sat in the chair across from me. He practically glided in the room, his movements fluid and graceful.

I wished I had fought a bit harder against the guard, not much, but at least enough that if I were murdered, I could have some sort of tale of resistance to repeat in the afterlife. My hand instinctively reached for the knife at my hip, though I didn't draw it.

Looking at him gave me a feeling of Déjà vu. He sat in front of me in a simple chair and elegant clothes. Everything from his chin to the accessories around the tent was fit for a king. I saw him differently somewhere in the pages of my memory. He sat, with the same pointed chin, on a crumbled throne. He was lit only by the dim glow of torches that hardly held on to the flame. The air around him was thick with an oppressive energy.

Where were those memories from? It must have been a dream. The sense of familiarity made my skin crawl.

"I'm glad you decided to accept my invitation. I am sorry to keep you from all of the fun outside, but I felt it important we spoke before I was officially crowned. I fear there may be too much excitement to meet after," the masked man purred, his voice smooth as silk.

"Mhm," I grunted, keeping my expression carefully neutral.

I needed to keep my cool about myself. I needed to close

the door to my mind and be present. The strange sense of recognition was too distracting.

"I heard whispers that you are the leaders of the Daughters of Steel. I've been told there's no better group of mercenaries.." He paused to look me over, his gaze almost tangible as it trailed from my face to my boots and back.

I ensured my lips were pressed together in a way that spoke of my unamused attitude. At least the one I was trying my best to wear. The attention made my skin prickle uncomfortably.

"I'd like to offer you a job," he proposed.

"I don't come cheap," I demanded. I knew his pockets were deep. The gems adorning his fingers alone could probably feed my entire guild for months.

"Of course. I wouldn't want to underpay someone I plan to work so closely with," he agreed with a nod. The gems in his mask caught the light, sending rainbow fragments dancing across the tent walls.

I hardly heard anything he said outside of 'pay.' The word had a way of drawing my full attention, like a moth to flame.

"Go on," I urged, leaning forward slightly.

"I heard that you successfully stole crystals. A feat not many have done without casualties," he noted. His voice held a note of admiration that didn't quite reach whatever eyes lay behind that mask.

It was easy when I planned it to avoid every single person who could have been around. A small surge of pride rose in my chest despite my wariness.

I cleared my throat. "I did."

"I'd like you to do it again. I'd like you to go to Daxon, to the temple of water, and steal those crystals," he instructed, clasping his hands together on his lap. His fingers were long and elegant, adorned with more rings than seemed practical.

I could only stare at him and blink. The request was so direct, so brazen, that it momentarily left me speechless.

"I will pay you well," he continued. "3,000 coins." He lifted his hand to remove his mask and set it in his lap. "If that isn't enough, as a show of trust. You can be one of only a small circle of people who can see my face."

I did not expect the perfectly pointed jaw he was showing to be his worst feature. The white hair and the dark eyes were visible through his mask, but I expected to see some scars or misshapen details. Some reason for the mask. The revelation left me oddly disappointed.

There was none. He was shaped and molded to perfection. Too perfect, like a sculpture rather than a man. Not a single flaw marred his pale skin.

"You may call me Nikola, but only in private. That name must never leave you and I," he commanded. His eyes looked into me so deeply that I was not going to tempt fate and find out what would happen if I didn't listen to him. A chill ran down my spine that had nothing to do with the temperature in the tent.

"Why do you want the crystals, Nikola?" I questioned, fighting to keep my voice steady.

"I want to unite the realm in a new way, a better way. I want to bring us all together under one ruler. I don't think the lands should be broken up as they are. To do what I intend, it will take a war unlike any we have ever seen before," he explained, rising from his chair and moving closer to me. His scent enveloped me something cold and clean, like mountain air in winter.

He was on one knee in my space before I could refute the closeness. The proximity made my heart race, but not in the pleasant way it did around Vespera or even Onyx. This was pure fight-or-flight.

"Maybe, if this goes well, we can discuss strengthening our partnership further. I will need a queen. Someone to be my hand and strike down enemies. My word will give you the ability to do things out in the open that you haven't even dreamt of yet. Things you don't even know you want yet," he murmured, his breath warm on my chin.

I felt my lip quiver in disgust. It was hard to find a way, with how close he was and his current offer, to say that I had only considered one male in my entire life, and I was confused about why I entertained even that singular one. How would I tell him that he does not have the right equipment for me without dying? I had enough trouble with romances; I did not need more. My stomach churned at the thought.

"One deal at a time," I managed to say, my voice strained. I shoved my chair backward to offer us some space, the legs scraping against the floor. "I don't want part of any war, but I will get your crystals. I want double the coin. 6,000 and half upfront."

"Deal," he accepted without hesitation, which only increased my suspicion. No one agreed to double payment without negotiation unless the job was more dangerous than they were letting on.

"I've got to go, then. I'll need time to make preparations," I announced, standing and twisting my body to avoid touching him. Even the thought of contact made my skin crawl.

I tossed my hood back up and jogged away from the tent. I ducked and contorted my way through the crowd. If I was going to complete the job he was asking, I'd need to double what I told Onyx to do. At least. I ran once I was free from the crowd, my boots pounding against the stone floor. My heart hammered in my chest, partly from exertion and partly from the unease that clung to me like a second skin.

I was foolish. I shouldn't have accepted. I received dumb luck from the Gods my first time around, and now I push my boundaries with a second attempt. Why did he have to offer me so many beautiful coins? Enough that I could buy a buffet every day. Trips to buy Vespera more books. Foolish, I was foolish! The self-recrimination looped in my mind like a mantra.

There was no guard to stop me when I entered the blacksmith shop the second time. I stopped myself. The door was not closed all the way, and I watched Onyx turn around, holding not one but two dragon eggs. The sight was so unexpected that for a moment I thought I was seeing things.

Why did he have them? They should have been at Ashbell. The smooth, iridescent shells gleamed in the firelight, one a deep crimson, the other a midnight blue.

I shoved the door open, and it startled him. I jumped at my own quick and rash movements. I wasn't sure what came over me. The bang of the door against the wall startled us both.

"We do a lot of things, but this? Stealing dragon eggs?" I pointed at him and opened my mouth again to start yelling, indignation rising hot in my chest.

"I didn't steal them! I was given them to protect in secret," Onyx insisted. He tucked them back into two spots beside the fire he had roaring. The heat from the forge washed over me in waves, making sweat bead on my forehead.

"What?" I didn't believe him. My eyes narrowed in suspicion.

"I was given them to protect in secret. I wouldn't steal them; I don't have a death wish. They have to do with the meeting you overheard earlier. We are trying to do something important, so I suggest if you want to live to see the rest of your coin spent, you hush," he demanded, his voice dropping to a harsh whisper.

"Onyx, did you just threaten me?" There it was again. That feeling that said I was into him. The flutter in my stomach was becoming harder to ignore.

"Did you like it? If you did, then yes," he smirked, his orange eyes gleaming with mischief.

"Of course, I did not. I only came because I'm going to need to double my order and have it ready in half the time," I stated, crossing my arms over my chest.

"Now you better say you loved it and that you're going with me to dinner," he bargained, leaning against his workbench with casual confidence.

"I hated it, and I'll let you watch me eat dinner. That's my final offer," I countered, widening my eyes in an attempt to look feral. The effect was probably less intimidating than I hoped.

"You let me come with on whatever it is you're doing, and I'll supply you with the weapons for free," he offered at the counter, his expression suddenly serious.

No coin spent? None at all, and all I had to do was avoid him on a trip. I was a professional at avoiding people. It's what I was paid for and what I lived for. The offer was too good to pass up, despite the complications it would surely bring.

"Deal!" I exclaimed as I held out my hand.

"Deal," he agreed as he shook it.

He lingered too long for it to stay considered a binding shake, and now I feared it crossed into hand-holding. His palm was warm against mine, calloused but surprisingly gentle. It could have been all right, just once. How would I know what it was I felt for him if I didn't at least try a time or two? I shook my head. No, I needed to save this effort to court Vespera. The internal battle made me dizzy.

"Are you all right?" Onyx asked, concern evident in his voice.

"I'm fine. Send word when you and the weapons are ready!" I called over my shoulder as I fled the shop, desperate to escape the confusion his presence always seemed to bring.

CHAPTER SIX

AS PREPARED AS WE COULD HAVE BEEN

ELOWEN: THE LAND OF THE DRAGONS.

After the goddess of Magic died and elemental magic was lost from the realm, dragons became one of the only sources left for magic. Crystals remained closely guarded and handed out if cause was shown. The realm was on the brink of war over ownership of the dragons; many called for them to be in chains. The Goddess's lover and friends carved out a piece of land separate from the rest for the dragons to live. The dragons formed their own social standards and lived in complete peace. They appointed an elder to go back and forth for any discussions that may be needed with other dragons or kingdoms, but they have vowed in large numbers not to leave until their Goddess has returned.

SAGE

I checked endlessly for the first sign of land, my eyes straining against the endless expanse of blue. The salt-laden air clung to my skin, making it feel tight and gritty. I decided not to

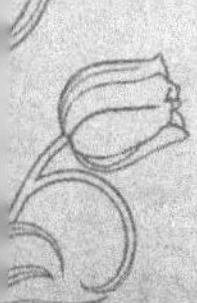

become a pirate because the nausea I felt at sea was unbearable, a constant rolling in my gut that refused to subside.

I gripped the rail again and spilled bile over the side of the ship for the third time. The acidic taste burned my throat, and the spray of seawater against my face only made it worse.

I should have asked for more coins.

The sea and I didn't mix. It was more than just sickness. I hardly bathed in the springs or bathhouses because water and I didn't belong together. The sight of water sent my mind into a frenzy. It felt suffocating. My fear of drowning kept me from enjoying anything beyond a quick and well-controlled washing. Even the gentle lapping of waves against the hull sent shivers down my spine.

A priestess once told me that my fear came from a past life. I was drowned by surprise, and I still carry the marks with me. I thought she was a fool willing to say anything for my coin. Now, hanging over the rail, I wasn't so sure she'd been wrong.

Vespera's hand was on my shoulder, but I did not want to look at her, with the thought that I smelled like vomit. Her touch was gentle, a stark contrast to the violent churning in my stomach.

"Do you need anything?" she asked, her voice soft with concern.

"Land," I remarked, wiping my mouth with the back of my hand.

"It won't be that much longer. I think you should know that we can still go home instead." Vespera nudged my shoulder with her own. She leaned herself over the rail with me, her jasmine scent cutting through the smell of salt and sick. "It's not too late to change your mind."

"We do the jobs we're paid to do, and then we go home," I said as I held back more nausea, swallowing hard against the rising bile.

"But we shouldn't be stealing things like this." She

persisted. "The crystals aren't meant to be used in spiraling the realm to chaos."

"One of our rules is to not ask questions about the aftermath," I mumbled, gripping the rail tighter as the ship rose and fell with the waves. "The coin will help everyone."

"Isn't there a time to break the rules? If you know what you're doing is wrong and is going to cost lives, don't you have a responsibility to stop it? An invisible rule can't truly be what you stick to?" Vespera offered me no mercy with her eyes, their blue depths reflecting her disappointment. "If you sacrifice the realm for coin, what will be left to spend it on? What will be left for the girls waiting on us? What good will payment do for any of us when we are held responsible for not stopping a tyrant?"

Of course, I didn't want to hand over crystals to the king. I didn't want to be called to meet with him at all, but what did she expect me to do? If I told the new king no, did she think that I would just walk out with a hearty handshake and carry on? Did she think he would do nothing? Had she forgotten all the books she had read about what had happened to little nothings that said no to kings? Did she take me for a rebel? The weight of her expectations felt heavier than any treasure chest I'd ever stolen.

Absolutely not. What could I have done as an ant against a boot?

"I won't fault you for staying behind while we get the crystals," I said, straightening despite my churning stomach.

I left the bow of the ship to find Onyx instead. He sat on a pile of crates and watched me walk, his fiery hair whipping in the sea breeze. I took a seat in the open space beside him, the wooden crates creaking under our combined weight.

"Feeling any better?" He inquired, eyeing me with concern.

"Not at all," I admitted, wrapping my arms around my middle.

He placed his palm on my back and rubbed it. The heat from his hand was calming, spreading warmth through my chilled body. I hated myself for the way I felt between the two of them. I was in love with Vespera, but I loved being with Onyx, too. Under his hand, I felt connected to him. I'd never admit it out loud; I don't think that I could. With Vespera, I bite my tongue every time I see her so that I don't spill the words out. With Onyx, I'm positive he knows what I have to say without my mouth saying any words. The realization made me feel like a traitor to my own heart.

"Do you need to talk?" He prompted, his voice a low rumble that seemed to vibrate through me.

His gaze was gentle, even if his appearance was not. The orange of his eyes caught the sunlight, turning them almost gold.

"Do you think we should go home?" I asked, my voice barely audible over the crashing waves.

His brows scrunched only for a moment. "Why would we do that? You need the coin to keep the guild running. To keep bringing more girls off the streets and keep everyone fed. Unless you want to ask me for a loan?" He smirked, and my stomach fluttered despite the nausea. "I would give it to you, but why when you could earn it free and clear today?"

"I don't want to know what the price of that would be. I'm being serious. Do you think it was wrong to take the job knowing the king plans to use the crystals to hurt people?" I studied his face to try and find the words he wasn't going to say, searching for some hint of doubt in his confident expression.

"What about everyone depending on your coin? Someone always takes the sacrifice somewhere down the line. You can ensure your girls thrive, or you can try and save the world." He stated, his voice hardening. "You can't do both. No one can. You're one small person on a bigger plan. You could stand up for this poor notion that the king is wrong and needs to be stopped, but what happens when you fail? No single person ever defeated anything so powerful. Your guild will fall away and perish; your name will be forgotten to time." He shrugged, the motion dismissive. "Or you can take care of what matters most to you, your guild, and be remembered by them."

I was taken aback by how blunt he was. It took me by surprise the way he phrased his words, each one striking like a small blow. "Maybe you're right," I conceded.

I wasn't sure I believed it, but I also didn't think that I wanted to hear anything else so blunt while I hardly held down whatever was left in my stomach. I didn't want to hear that I was useless from his lips one more time. The words stung more than I cared to admit.

The way he spoke reminded me of the dragon eggs he was hiding. Did he think the same way about them? That lying to everyone to keep such a big secret was worth doing to protect whatever group he was trying to protect? I wanted to ask him more about it, to press him harder. I wanted to believe his story, but I didn't. If I were to listen to his words, then what he was doing would really be none of my business. The thought left a bitter taste in my mouth

I needed to focus on what I was doing. If I wanted to continue on and finish it, or if I wanted to turn around and go home. I knew I already had the answer. I accepted the job, to begin with. The amount of coin the king was to pay would have taken months to get otherwise. I was going to do it, but was it going to make me a bad person? Would everyone consider me as such when they found out I handed the tools the king needed to kill their families? The weight of this choice pressed down on me, making it hard to breathe.

It was hard to sort my own thoughts out when I was surrounded by two people who took very different approaches with me. Vespera always talked to me as if I were a child. She treated me as if I would break; sometimes, it bordered on feeling as if she saw me as incompetent. Onyx would follow me into the fire if I walked into it. He supported and found logic in any choice I made. He was hard to trust because of it.

"Land ahead!" The captain called, his voice carrying over the sound of the waves.

A wave of relief washed over me, and I scrambled to my feet. I positioned myself in the middle of the crew, gathering around to watch the scenery. The shoreline appeared on the horizon, a thin strip of green against the endless blue. I was able to get a ship so fast, for such a low price, by dealing in treasure. They'd get entrance to the temple, too, and take what they looked for. I never turned down the chance to do a double job.

I hopped off the edge of the ship into the smaller boat waiting below. The wood creaked beneath my weight, rocking precariously. It took no time for the two crew members to start rowing with excitement. Watching them row felt as if it took longer than the entire journey. I wanted my feet on solid ground again. I needed to kiss the grass underneath me.

When the boat pushed against the shore, I didn't wait. I pushed over the other bodies and got out first. I tossed myself onto the ground and rubbed my face against the grass. It was beautiful. Soft, solid. I could have cried. The earthy scent filled my nostrils, replacing the salt that had been there for days.

"All right, let's go," Onyx urged, shaking his head at me.

It was the crew of pirates that grumbled about being pushed to move too quickly before I could do it. My crew didn't make a sound. Even though I only brought a handful of my own, I knew it would be fine because they were good at what they did. We would be in, and we would be out without any notice. The confidence helped settle my still-uneasy stomach.

The captain got us in the most ideal position. The distance between where our boat sat, half on soil and half in water, to the back of the temple was short enough that it would take no time to get inside. The group was large, but we marched silently, our footsteps muffled by the soft ground.

I had to stop for a moment to take in the sight. Daxon was stunning. I didn't understand how they built their architecture. The stairs were made of water, and I could see straight through their clear blue notches. Schools of tiny fish swam inside of the stairways, flashes of silver and gold darting through the liquid steps. Bundles of coral decorated and grew from the ground, in vibrant pinks and oranges that seemed to glow in the sunlight, and everything smelled of salt. The beauty almost made me forget my fear of water. Almost.

I stopped at the entrance and motioned to my mercenaries- two in front and one with me. Their weapons gleamed in the sun, ready to be drawn at a moment's notice. I knew I could trust Vespera to not need me by her side. She insisted that she caused the distraction and that I get the crates of crystals and leave. I agreed, with a small amount of guilt, because I did not want to fight, and I knew this job, unlike the first, would require it. The knowledge sat heavy in my chest.

The door in front was large and bound to be loud. I had to hope that whatever Vespera had planned would be louder than it. The temple of water had rumors surrounding it. I pushed the back door open as slowly as I could and moved myself inside. The hinges creaked slightly, making me wince. It was whispered through the realm that the temple was haunted. That the souls of the sirens killed in the past remain to keep watch. When I saw no one inside, I motioned back for my partner to follow. The empty hallway stretched before us, eerily silent.

When I heard Vespera yell from the other side, I knew it was time to put extra haste behind my steps. I unsheathed my sword, the metal sliding against the scabbard with a soft hiss, whispered to the long-gone Goddess of Water that I didn't need to use it, and entered the first room I saw. There was nothing and no one. I left it and went to the next. Only pastel walls and more coral. Windows were on every wall, letting in natural light, but I couldn't see past the fact that they were also made of liquid. The water somehow held its shape, defying everything I knew about how the world worked.

It became clear that I didn't frequent many temples because I was already lost. The corridors seemed to shift and change, disorienting me further. I had to be in the center. In front of me stood a tall statue made of the bluest color. She cradled an infant that was guarded by her flowing hair. The detail was exquisite, every strand of hair perfectly carved, her expression both fierce and tender. An altar placed in front of her was covered in fruits and silks. I noticed a shine at the back of her feet. It looked to be a cellar of some sort. Maybe somewhere you'd hide crystals. My heart quickened at the prospect.

I was careful to stay vigilant about my surroundings, my eyes scanning for any movement, my ears strained for the slightest sound. I squatted down to lift the handle, but when I did, a gust of wind kicked up. It came from nowhere but was strong enough to throw me down. The force of it knocked the breath from my lungs. Before I had time to react and get back up, a figure appeared in the wind. She was like a ghost. Large, too large. She towered over me with lavender hair and brown eyes. Even as an apparition, her skin looked as if it were melted off or covered in a rash in most places. The sight made my blood run cold.

I could only look her up and down. My hands shook, and my mouth hung open. Fear paralyzed me, freezing me in place.

"Who gave you the right to come here? To snoop in my daughter's temple?"

Her voice sent me into a dread. A panic that made my mind throb, and I stumbled to my knee. The sound seemed to penetrate my very bones, vibrating through me painfully.

Images of a woman with the same lavender-colored hair standing at the caves of Erebus flashed through my mind. She released spiders from her womb, and they entered the caves without the need to be directed. She was haunting. Deep and dark. Swallowing. I gripped my sword as if it would do anything, the hilt slick with sweat in my palm.

I felt as nauseous as I had on the ship, bile rising in my throat.

I breathed the biggest sigh of relief I had ever experienced when I saw Onyx, an axe in one hand and a crystal in the other. The crystal glowed with a fierce inner light, pulsing like a heartbeat. He flung magic into the woman, and she was gone so quickly that it was as if she had never been there at all. The air where she had stood shimmered briefly before settling.

"Who was that?" I almost screamed, my voice shrill with fear.

"The long-dead Goddess of Chaos," he replied, his voice unnervingly calm.

"So, this place is haunted?" I frowned, trying to compose myself despite my racing heart.

"I saved you, didn't I?" He countered, a hint of smugness in his tone.

He moved closer to me, close enough that I thought for sure his hands were going to be on me. I could feel the heat radiating from him, a stark contrast to the chill that had settled over me.

"Only because you are always watching me," my words came out jumbled, my tongue feeling too large for my mouth.

"I would rather you call me a protector than imply I'm a stalker," Onyx said. He held his hand out for me to take, his palm upturned, inviting.

I glanced at his hand, "what?"

"We don't have time to waste. Let me help you," his voice was still soft, a gentleness beneath the urgency.

The stance we were in, the words he said. They felt familiar to me in a way I didn't know how to handle. I felt like the two of us had been in the same situation before. That the same woman had put us in the same dynamic before. The part of my mind that told me I liked Onyx told me to take his hand. The part of my heart that told me I needed Vespera told me to kill him. I understood that feeling even less than the others. The conflict tore at me from the inside.

I took a breath and, with it, his hand. His skin was warm against mine, calloused but somehow comforting.

He grabbed me and ripped me onto my feet. He was followed in by more creatures unlike any I had seen before. They carried a stench with them, like rotting meat left too long in the sun. Their skin and wings were shredded, and bits of their faces were missing as they flew in with rage. The sound of their screeching filled the chamber, bouncing off the walls until it was almost deafening.

Onyx looked at me as if he already knew what I was going to ask. "They belong to the God of Dreams."

I opened my lips to ask why they were there. Why would they care about the water temple crystals or any of us? It didn't make sense to me. Of all the places to be or things to do, why that temple? The questions piled up in my mind, demanding answers.

How did Onyx know so much? Why did they show up when we did? The coincidence seemed too perfect to be chance.

I tried my best to gather myself. I needed to grab my sword and help fight our way out. I turned to grab it, but he used the last of his crystal to throw fire through the room, sending them screaming to the ground. The flames licked at the walls, casting wild shadows that danced like demons.

He gripped my arm, and I thought he'd take it from its socket and run out with it, leaving the rest of me behind. He didn't know his strength well enough. My feet screamed as we went through the open pathways, stumbling over uneven ground. The light environment we had passed through was an entirely different scene. The walls were streaked with crimson, and the bodies of the temple attendants lay throughout the entire place. The metallic scent of blood mixed with the salt air, turning my stomach.

So did my girls. My mercenaries. So did the pirates. I heard no sound from inside, but there was more than enough blood to tell me why. Their vacant eyes stared up at nothing, accusations in their lifeless gazes. Guilt crashed over me like a wave.

A group of the creatures came through a strange portal that opened beside us. The tear in reality rippled like disturbed water, edges glowing with an unnatural light. They dived for me as if they were placed at the temple specifically for me. Onyx used my arm to guide me where he wanted me. He tugged me down, and I was lowered out of the way, the creatures' claws missing me by inches.

Onyx lifted me back to my feet and pulled me into his chest until I was nearly cut off from all airflow. The solid wall of him behind me was oddly reassuring. He still used his blade as if it was weightless, effortless. Blood sprayed with each swing, spattering warm drops across my face.

Was he trying to convince me that he was a hero? A protector just for me? The thought made me dizzy with confusion.

A dragon stood in front of us when we moved through the doorway. Its scales gleamed like polished armor in the sunlight, shifting between deep blue and purple. I saw Vespira already sitting atop him. She was leaning against a crate bigger than she was, her expression grim. I opened my mouth to protest, but Onyx tossed me up and followed close enough behind. The dragon's back was warm beneath me, its scales smooth against my palms. In the distance, the ship we had arrived on was already leaving, white sails billowing as it retreated.

Silence surrounded me. I knew part of my feelings came from being in the sky and not on land. The wind whipped my hair around my face as we soared higher, the ground falling away beneath us. The other part was me trying to wrap myself around the idea that a goddess just stood in front of me. I felt as if my world had just shifted under my feet. Nothing would ever be the same again.

My mind was trying to wrap itself around the images that I had seen, the new feeling I felt wave over me for Onyx, and the fact that every girl I brought with me, besides Vespera, was dead. Vespera looked more angry than I had ever seen her, her usually gentle features hardened into something dangerous.

I didn't understand how things had escalated so quickly. Without me hearing a word. Without me knowing anything. Onyx tried to cover my view of the ground below, but I could see the king guard by their golden color. They marched in formation into the temple and came out with temple staff in toe. I watched the king's guard start heading the highest of the members, their swords flashing in the sun.

I turned my head away and felt my stomach turn. Was I a distraction for the king? Did he even need the crystals? The realization that I might have been used, that we all might have been used, sat like poison in my veins, burning me from the inside out.

CHAPTER SEVEN
SOMETHING RED THIS WAY FLOWS

ELD: THE FAE HIGH COURT.

The high king resides in Eld alongside his many Fae advisors. Eld is a land made by the mortals, for the mortals. When deities started dying, and the others largely pulled away from how much time they spent in the mortal realm, the mortals needed a place to meet and discuss the changes and how to move forward. Enough mortals decided they needed one leader to oversee all lands, and so Eld evolved further. It is now the place where all political encounters occur, and the high king calls home.

SHIVANI

I was tired of living in a tent. I was tired of walking outside and seeing that we still had no permanent residence set up. I was tired of the slow trickle of trust that flowed down to me. The canvas walls that had been my home for years now seemed to close in tighter each day, the musty smell of damp fabric a constant reminder of our impermanence.

I wouldn't say it out loud.

Koa would say that all progress is good progress. He would try his best to reassure me that we had endless time to sort out anything we needed to. I didn't find it comforting. When we were dropped in Cylla, I was so optimistic when the fear wore off. I spent days wandering around the forests. Countless more days taking in the scent and shapes of flowers. The sweet perfume of wildflowers and the earthy richness of the soil had filled me with hope then. When I learned of the vampires and that they were a creation from me, I dropped all of that. The weight of responsibility had crushed those simple joys.

I've worked to help the vampires be free of Helia since I learned of them. I thought we would build a city around their temple by now. That we could discuss demolishing it and creating something entirely new for them. That maybe we could enter talks with other lands and they could branch out and live anywhere in Cylla that they wanted to. Instead, I had only made the smallest amount of progress. The reality of our situation felt like a stone in my chest.

I was sitting in the same tent that we had conducted business in for years, waiting for another small group of vampires to meet with me and discuss leaving the temple and finding a home with me and the smaller population that had already left the temple. The wooden chair beneath me creaked with each subtle shift of my weight.

"They should be here soon," Koa said. He twirled his thumb on the side of my hand, which his fingers were already entwined in. The gentle warmth of his skin against mine was a small comfort.

I nodded in response. The one thing that went exactly how I hoped it would was him. He never made me doubt him or myself. If I wanted to stay in the community of tents for one hundred more years, he'd offer to build me something a bit more stable. Koa would have built an entire city for me without hesitation if I asked him to. He'd tear it down with his bare hands and move it when I was ready. The certainty of his devotion both reassured and terrified me.

Sometimes I thought that I didn't deserve him. That I hadn't done anything to earn his love. Sometimes, I wanted to ask him why he wanted to be by my side so badly. I didn't because I was too afraid of the answer. I wanted to believe in love at first sight, but that required more trust in fate than I had to lend. My mind enjoyed playing games with me. I'd get lost in his hazel eyes while I dreamt of a future for us, and halfway through, I would shatter my own hope by whispering of how he would grow tired of me, the passion would extinguish, and I'd be alone. The fear of abandonment crept like frost across my heart.

My own whispering voice kept me from giving him everything that I could.

The tent cloth was pulled back, and six vampires entered. The fabric rustled against their shoulders as they ducked inside. They looked beyond malnourished. As if they hadn't seen blood in weeks. Their skin stretched taut over sharp cheekbones, their movements slow and deliberate. The vampire race was naturally dark as the night sky, but the group in front of me had lost so much color. They all took seats, one by one, at our wooden table. The meeting table was the first thing that Koa built for me by hand. The same sun setting behind a full moon was etched on the top of every leg. My fingers traced the familiar pattern absently.

All of the vampires looked down at their own feet and refused to make eye contact with Koa or I but one. He looked at me as if he were ready to fight, not ask for a new home. His crimson eyes burned with barely contained rage. Vero, my dragon. The Goddess of Fall. Stood tightly beside me as if she could feel it, too. Her scales shifted between gold and amber, catching the flickering lantern light.

I parted my lips to speak, but so did the vampire. I felt

Koa's fingers tense around mine underneath the table. I felt much less offended by the look of anger on the vampire's face than Koa did. The protective energy radiating from him was almost tangible.

"We want to join the rest of our people here," he stated, his voice raspy from thirst.

I nodded. "There are rules."

His lips turned further down as if I had just offended his favorite person. "We are trying to leave a dictator, not join a new one."

"You must find something to do to help out. Things work because everyone lends a hand. Fighting is not allowed, and you must erect your own tents," I explained, keeping my voice level despite the tension crackling in the air.

He narrowed his eyes at me, and he closed his mouth for the first time since he entered the tent. A muscle in his jaw twitched with suppressed words.

"We have agreements with other lands for food and salves. We also have agreements with mortals for blood. It's also yours once you agree to carry your weight and put away your weapons," I continued. I could still feel the tense energy from Koa and Vero on each side of me, like heat radiating from twin furnaces.

"Before I agree, I want an answer," he demanded. His voice was sharp, cutting through the heavy air of the tent.

"Can you first tell me your name?" I asked. I kept my voice as soft as I could.

"Dimitri," he answered. He leaned himself further onto my table and rested his elbows on the edge. The wood creaked beneath his weight.

"Let me ask you a question first," I interjected. I wanted to be kind but stern. "What changed to make you come to see me?"

"Helia showed herself. She has an iron attitude and a fist to match. She tried to keep her normal appearance today, but she failed. It was easy for many of us to see that she was weaker than usual, just like you said. Her exhaustion could be heard in her voice. Her pain was seen in her eyes. It must mean that you were telling the truth," Dimitri revealed, a hint of vindication in his tone.

"Yes, It has to mean that you can kill her!" A girl on his side exclaimed, her thin fingers clutching the edge of the table.

"It's my turn. Why do you stay here and claim to care about our freedom, but give us no proof? You say you want to help, but you aren't. You could simply show everyone at the temple that you wield blood magic and solve all of our problems. They would believe in you. Most of us can not believe while blind, and you can't expect us to." His words struck like small daggers, each one finding a vulnerable spot in my resolve.

I hadn't used magic since I learned of them. Not from crystals or my own hands. I did my best to bind and tuck my wings every morning as well. Knowing that it was my blood magic that created them and that it was the reason they all suffered made me unable to look at it the same way. The weight of guilt pressed down on me like a physical burden.

"I swore off using magic," I answered, the words tasting bitter on my tongue.

It was the simplest truth I could offer him. Koa and Vero often tried to convince me of the same thing he tried his best to do.

"They deserve proof after everything that they've been through and continue to go through. They are used as blood bags for gods, and you won't end it simply because it makes you feel a little bad?" Dimitri leaned back in his chair with a scoff, the sound harsh in the confined space.

"It's not that simple," I insisted, feeling my resolve beginning to crumble.

"Isn't it? Vampires were created when your counter-god,

Helia, used your blood magic and your time-shifting abilities that didn't belong to her and triggered a curse on us. She cursed us to need blood and live never-ending lifespans. You show up and claim to be our savior, but can't you do something as simple as a party trick? Seems maybe the two of you aren't so different after all," Dimitri crossed his arms, his words hanging in the air like poison.

I knew he was upset. Maybe I would have been, too, if I were in his position. The truth in his accusations made my chest ache.

"I don't think it's the right move. I can truly understand what you're trying to say. I'll take it into consideration. In the meantime, we can have you fed and put you into tents before nightfall if you would like to stay," I offered, dropping Koa's fingers and standing from my chair. The wooden legs scraped against the dirt floor.

The group of vampires followed my movement and stood. Dimitri gave me one last, long look before they left with two wolf shifters that Koa assigned to be guards at the camp. The tent flap fell closed behind them with a soft thud.

"I think that went well," I said and turned to look at the two beside me, forcing a smile I didn't feel.

"I think he was right," Vero stated bluntly, her tail swishing irritably against the ground.

Her orange and red scales shimmered when she moved. They were the perfect copy of color-changing leaves on trees. I paid attention to them anytime she decided she wanted to discuss my magic use again. Today, they seemed particularly vibrant, as if emphasizing her agitation.

"They do deserve to know that you are the true Goddess of Time," she continued to speak. "Pieces of history are still missing, shattered, or in the dark. This realm was created on the idea that a specific group of deities were their creators. They need to be shown that the version of you and your sisters that Yumi and Nikola created isn't you. That you're different, kinder."

I needed to check with the other guards and see if we still had plenty of space to expand tents or if I was going to need to meet with the Queen of Brisa and ask for more land. She and I had made a relationship quickly. She told me what her people needed, and I made sure there were trade deals put in place for it. Koa was training her army alongside his own shifters. The mental diversion was safer than facing Vero's truth.

"You can't really expect to never use blood magic again, can you? Never?" Vero pressed on, smoke curling from her nostrils. "Ignoring my words won't change them!"

I'd need to inform our volunteers to add a few more blood bags to their list, too.

"Koa," I turned to face him. "Can you let the volunteers know we will need more blood? I need to check with the guardsmen and write a letter to the Queen of Brisa."

"Did you listen to anything I said? To anything Dimitri said?" Vero growled. She wanted to be far more intimidating than she was. The ground beneath us trembled slightly with her frustration.

"Of course I did. I'll take it into consideration," I assured, forcing another smile.

"You know, we all have your best interests in mind. You don't need to treat me like I'm not worth listening to. I don't want to be rude, but if you keep ignoring us, it'll be everyone else who pays the higher price," Vero warned, stomping her oversized paws on the ground. A loud protest that sent dust swirling into the air.

I cared for her, not her constant refusal to accept my stance. I turned to Koa. I was prepared to hear from him, too. I expected the lecture to keep itself going. They didn't under-stand my position. He surprised me when he leaned himself into me, and instead of speaking, he kissed my forehead. The gentle press of his lips against my skin was unexpectedly tender.

"I'll let them know about the blood," he murmured before he left the tent, too. The flap rustled as he ducked through it.

The shock of him leaving without a word flipped a switch inside my mind. I felt in my chest that the beating quickened. The unusual silence from him was more unsettling than any argument.

Did he disapprove so intensely that he had nothing to say to me? Was I letting my imagination get the best of me again? The doubts swirled like autumn leaves in a storm.

I sat back down at the table and grabbed a blank page of paper and ink. I did need to write the letter and get it sent. I lifted the quill to write but lowered it just as quickly. The day that I could write to her about a small city being built near the temple would be the day I hoped we would celebrate soon. The feather bent slightly beneath my nervous fingers.

"Ma'am! Miss Shivani, there's an emergency!" A guard called, his voice breaking through my thoughts.

He was flustered; panic filled his voice. It sent the same panic through me, a cold rush that started at the base of my spine and spread outward. I was on my feet and out of the tent before he could enter it. The sky darkened above the temple of rebirth. Rifts like Vesim used to make in our realm were ripped into the sky, and creatures flew out the same way as our own. They were attacking the temple. The air itself seemed to tear apart, revealing a darkness beyond that stung my eyes.

"The vampires are under attack by night harvesters. They're a creation of the god of Dreams. He uses them to pull fears from souls, and they help him create nightmares," Koa explained, suddenly beside me. His arms were crossed as if he had seen it a hundred times, and there was nothing to do about it. His posture was rigid, but I could see the concern in his eyes.

"Why is everyone standing around?" I yelled, my voice rising with panic.

"What are we to do?" Vero questioned, her tail lashing back and forth.

"Not this!" I waved my hands around, frustration making my gestures sharp and frantic.

Vero stood taller. She lifted her golden head until her candy apple red spikes pointed to the sky. "If only there were a deity around that possessed a power far greater than any we had access to. A deity that could end the night harvesters and save countless vampire lives. If such a deity won't lift a finger, neither shall I," she declared before stomping her paws harder than necessary on her walk away from me. Each step left small craters in the soft earth.

I didn't know what to say to her. How could she act as if she wasn't a dragon wielding the last natural source of magic outside of my sisters and I. The hypocrisy stung, but a small voice whispered that perhaps she wasn't wrong.

"The crystals are gone!" A man huffed out. He shifted from a lion to a man in front of us, his transformation fluid despite his evident exhaustion. "A man with two colored eyes left with every single crystal in the temple."

Koa looked as if he had finally heard something he cared about, his posture straightening with sudden alertness, but I didn't understand its significance. I had hardly been welcomed into the world since my arrival into the realm. Most of the deities left in power wanted mine. The confusion must have shown on my face.

"Deimos," Koa ground his words through clenched teeth. "I didn't think he would be so bold."

He turned to storm off, but I grabbed his arm to stop him. The muscle beneath my fingers was tense as steel. "Where are you going?"

I tried my best to keep my voice from shaking while I asked. I knew. I knew he was going to say that he was on his way to find this Deimos, but I had hoped he wouldn't say it. Hope was becoming a scarce commodity.

Shifter soldiers ran past us, organized and swift, their armor glinting in the strange half-light cast by the rifts above.

"I'm going to find out what he's doing and put a stop to it," Koa declared, lifting his hand and pointing to the sky where the rifts were closing. "Do you want this to happen again? Do you want me to worry about your safety when I have to go?"

I wanted to tell him that he wouldn't need to worry about my safety if he stayed, but I didn't. I kept my lips sealed shut and let go of him. The words died in my throat, trapped behind my pride. He and the lion shifted and were off before I could change his mind. The wind of their departure rustled my hair.

"Ma'am, we've received word that several temples have been attacked at the same time," a second guard rushed in to announce, his face pale with shock.

My sisters, even if half of us couldn't remember who we were, could handle themselves if they were part of the other temple attacks. I rushed outside to take in what was going on, my heart pounding against my ribs.

My camp was filled with the screams and cries of more than just a vampire or two. The edge of the camp had been invaded in the same way as the temple. The only thing that spared us the same fate as what was being reported from the temple was my partner. Koa kept a high volume of his guard with me, just in case. I didn't enjoy having such a large presence of soldiers until now. The sight of them engaged in battle against the nightmare creatures filled me with a complicated mixture of relief and guilt.

The edge of the camp closest to the temple was a disaster, and the ones that made it out weren't in good shape, but I was glad the night harvesters were stopped so quickly. Bodies lay scattered, some moving, others terrifyingly still.

I moved the tent opening back and entered. Three of the vampires that had just joined us today were lying on cots. None of them were making a sound. One was missing an arm; another had so much blood on them that I couldn't be sure where they were the most injured. The metallic scent of blood mixed with the sharp smell of medicinal herbs filled the air, making my stomach turn.

"We've given them a sedative. We couldn't stop their pain faster than we could put them to sleep," a cleric from Ashbell explained, her hands stained crimson as she worked.

I nodded. Although the vampirism curse gave them long lives, it didn't make them invincible. They would still die without aid. The realization pressed against my chest like a weight.

I wanted my place to be in a tent helping, not stepping foot in the temple, and facing that I had only been doing half of my part while I pointed fingers. The guilt of my inaction was becoming too heavy to bear.

My mind sent me into a freeze every time the weight of acting like a real goddess sat in front of me. The responsibility I had avoided for so long was now demanding my attention.

Dimitri stormed in with a rage swirling through him that I expected. "This is your fault!" He accused, pointing a shaking finger. "You think being a pacifist makes you some kind of greater being, but you're wrong. It makes you weak. You have the ability to change things, yet you don't. You have the ability to show everyone why they should believe you and follow you, but you don't use it. You're fine with waiting another fifty years camped out in tents outside of our temple? That's fifty years worth of lives that you willingly let suffer and die at the hands of someone else you could have stopped by now!" He moved closer to me until I could feel his breath on my face, the scent of copper and desperation. "Tell me, what makes you any better than Helia?"

I searched his eyes with my own, but I held my lips shut. There had to be a way to fix these problems without my magic. But even as I thought it, doubt crept in like a shadow.

A second cleric came running in with the body of a small child. A girl that couldn't have been any older than five. She choked on her blood the entire distance the cleric ran, the gurgling sounds haunting in their desperation. He was screaming words at the other, but it was only static to me. A third and fourth cleric ran inside. A fifth and sixth shoved me out of the way while they worked together to carry someone else. They left a blood trail behind them, bright crimson against the dirt floor.

Dimitri still looked at me, unmoving. He blamed me, but I only wanted to help. I only wanted to find a way to help them without using the thing that cursed them to be with. If I had used it, then I would have been no better than Helia. Dimitri was wrong. He was wrong. Using my blood magic wouldn't have changed anything that happened. The mantra felt hollow even as I repeated it to myself.

I stumbled outside of the tent, still only able to hear ringing in my ears. So much more chaos had erupted while I was inside. Koa's soldiers ran in all directions, their shouts mixing with the cries of the wounded.

"Get inside, ma'am. Another wave of them arrived!" A soldier warned, his voice cutting through the ringing in my ears.

The green grass was streaked with red in every direction now. The contrast was sickening - life and death painted across the landscape.

I needed to get to the temple. I needed to assess the damage done to the rest of my children. I needed to see if Hesperia was inside. She had to be inside. She was always there when something went wrong. The thought of my sister gave me a sudden resolve.

I dug my boots into the dirt and took off in a run up the hillside that the temple sat on. It was silent the closer I got. My camp was so loud, not just with sound but with movement. The closer I became to the temple, the more I felt as if I were entering an entirely different world. The quiet was eerie, unnatural.

The door was already open, and the inside was dimly lit. There was so much blood I couldn't believe anything had made it out alive. The walls were painted with it, pooling on the floor in dark puddles that reflected the flickering torches.

"Stop! Don't come any closer! Let us die in peace!" A voice cried out from the shadows.

I lifted my hands in the air as a sign of surrender. "Do you need help?"

"Not from you!" The voice spat back, raw with pain and anger.

"It doesn't have to be from me; I can send someone," I called back, taking a tentative step forward.

"No!"

I wanted to listen to their request. I was going to leave and not push myself on them, but maybe Dimitri was right. Maybe a bit of pushback was what they needed. I moved further inside, just enough that the torches lined the wall made them a bit easier to see. A group of vampires sat over a man. It was clear that he was on his last breaths, his chest rising and falling in shallow, irregular movements.

"Who is he?" I asked, my voice soft with reverence for their grief.

"He's our high priest," one answered, voice thick with emotion.

Maybe I should have pushed harder from the start. They hardly knew me. They didn't trust me, but the man they were huddled over, the one they were mourning, they did know him. They trusted him to lead them, and as much as I hoped to be in that same position, I wasn't. The realization was humbling.

"May I?" I asked, kneeling down beside the group.

A woman pulled him closer into her chest and cradled him despite the clear struggle in his breath. The sight pulled at my chest. Was she his lover? His mother? Was this another woman who was losing everything she cared about because a deity refused to use their abilities for the betterment of their life? Her tears fell onto his face, mingling with the blood there.

I knelt down in front of her, but I didn't reach for him. The stone floor was cold against my knees.

"I'm going to put this hand on his chest," I said as I lifted my right hand, trying to keep my voice steady.

I watched her nails dig into his arm in protest, but I proceeded anyway. I put my palm to his chest until I could see his life root. The vampires were easy to tell apart when they were open in that way. Their roots were glazed with a purple fuzz. A velvet sign of their curse. I felt my eyes shake, and the clock wheels turn back. His breath rasped once more before it became clear. He gasped for air, grabbing at his with his lungs as if it were his first breath. Color returned to his ashen face in a rush.

The woman broke out in hysterical sobs, and the sight made me bite my lip and hold my breath to shove down my own sorrow. The sound tore at something deep inside me.

She was crying because she was grateful to have a second chance with whoever the man was to her. I wanted to match her tears because I failed everything I tried to help. We could not bring Mori back from Nikola killing him. Fennic couldn't take being around me anymore. Vesim did not leave Juniper's Garden. She was the only one of us to be invited to stay in the realm of the gods, and now this. The weight of all my failures threatened to crush me.

My entire time was invested in trying to help the vampires

move away from Helia and into a better life, just for them to be slaughtered. The futility of it all pressed down on me.

"This doesn't prove anything about her. We've seen healers do incredible things!" A man yelled, his voice cutting through the moment.

A wave of anger washed over me for the first time in such a long time that I almost forgot how to push it back down. It rose like a tide, hot and powerful.

"Who else has come here and done something like what I just did?" I challenged, my voice taking on an edge I barely recognized.

"Healers," he answered dismissively.

His voice mocked me, and something inside me snapped like a taut string.

I held up both of my hands and released strings of blood from my fingertips. I commanded them forward, and the strings danced until they reached his skull. They glowed with an inner light, pulsing with my heartbeat. I forced them inside and took control of his mind. We were connected by blood magic until I released him. I wiggled my fingers, and his body danced in response to my commands. The power flowed through me, familiar and intoxicating.

It wasn't the magic that made me as bad as Helia; it was doing things like that. I released him, and he dropped to his knees. He looked up at me in horror, his eyes wide with a fear I had never wanted to inspire.

"I told you!" Another man from the group yelled. "I told you she was the true goddess!"

The man I healed managed to get the girl to hold onto him with everything she had to allow him to sit up. "Will you save us? Or will you keep standing on the sidelines, allowing anyone to walk inside and hurt us?" His voice was stronger now, but still held an edge of warning.

He paused and allowed me the space to answer, but I didn't know how. The words wouldn't come.

"If you only want to say that you helped, you can say that now."

"No," I shook my head. "I don't want to say it; I want to do it. I just wanted to do it without my magic."

"Why? You're blessed with a gift, and you want to pretend otherwise? You don't look like a foolish girl, but you do sound like one." His words cut deeper than any blade could have.

His eyes resembled a cat's, just like all of the vampires did. It added to the feeling that he was looking inside of me, seeing all my fears and doubts laid bare.

"My magic is what caused all of you to be where you are," I confessed, the admission painful.

"No, bad people took advantage of something good, and we are a living trail of proof. You are a good being with the ability to alter our course, but instead, you are playing with the petals of a flower. You are making wishes for a world and an idea that does not exist here. If you want to liberate us, then do it. Do it because you see injustice and want to fix it, not because you pity us, but only until it requires you to be uncomfortable." Each word landed like a physical blow.

A knot formed in my throat that I had a hard time shoving down. His words bit at me. Had I really wasted years? Was I one choice away this whole time? The possibility made me dizzy with regret.

He got to his feet with the help of the girl and rested half of his weight on her. His fangs caught the light with all of his words. "If you want to help, you may follow me to a room where I may sit and rest properly. Otherwise, I trust you know how to leave."

I watched them all leave. They walked in a perfectly organized line without exchanging any words. I didn't follow immediately. The man they called their high priest made me feel small and riddled with mistakes. I was a Goddess, and a vampire was making me feel beyond flawed. The irony wasn't lost on me.

I allowed a small chuckle of disbelief to leave my lips. What would my mother think of me? What did Hesperia think of me? Did she think so low of me because of my choices that she couldn't be around me? The questions swirled in my mind like autumn leaves in a storm.

Was it why she picked to stay with Ruri? The thought hurt more than I cared to admit, a sharp pain that settled beneath my breastbone and refused to leave.

<h1 align="center">CHAPTER EIGHT</h1>

<h1 align="center">TIME TO MAKE A CHOICE</h1>

BRISA: THE LAND OF AIR.

Brisa is one of the newer established lands in Cylla. The God of Justice helped a lost soul that was taken out of the stars on accident find its way into a dragon egg. When she hatched, she was a small dragon and spoke of a white-haired girl with white markings. She told the God of Justice that the girl was her creator. That she taught her and all of her people how to live by the rules of magic and its uses. The god of Justice kept her secret and took her to Cylla. He helped create the land of air in his name to keep prying eyes away. Nila the dragon, once the first witch under Hesperia, moved humans to the land of air, where she taught them her knowledge. They established the temple of Hesperia, and all inhabitants of the realm often visit them for blessings, spells, fertility assistance, and more.

SHIVANI

The temple was nothing like what I had imagined temples for deities would look like. I heard of the other temples and how they were the peak of the architecture in their lands, but the temple of rebirth was a far cry from what Brisa had to offer. The cool stone walls seemed to absorb the light rather than reflect it. I visited the main city in Brisa, and it was breathtaking. This temple smelled of rot and was decorated with bones. The scent of decay and mildew filled my nostrils with each breath. The torches were the only light, casting long, dancing shadows that seemed to reach for me, and I wondered if I wasn't in a cave. The flickering flames did little to dispel the darkness that pressed in from all sides.

I followed the group of vampires into what looked like it could have been a meeting room or, a dining hall, or maybe even both. There was nothing but a slab of splinted wood on four legs and chairs that had nails still poking out of the sides. The wood was dark with age and stained with substances I didn't want to identify. The priest whispered to a vampire, and he rushed out of the room in a jog, his footsteps echoing down the corridor.

I pulled out one of the chairs and sat slowly, the wood creaking ominously beneath me. The group acted as if they had no doubt about the seat's stability. The seating made me as nervous as the vampire leaving did. My fingertips traced the rough grain of the wood, catching on splinters.

"My name is Dominic. I am the high priest. The entire temple and the vampires inside of it are my duty." He sat across from me as if he was not afraid of me. As if I were a friend to him. His eyes, crimson like all vampires, held a weariness that spoke of centuries of burden.

"My name is Shivani," I replied, trying to match his calm demeanor.

"What is it you want, Shivani?" He inquired. "You've spent a lot of time sitting outside of our temple. You've invested a lot of energy into trying to convince us we should follow you, but very little time has shown us that you're worth following." The directness of his question caught me off guard.

He was right. The truth of it settled in my chest like a stone.

"I want to kill Helia. I want to carve out a home for you all. A real home where you can not just live but thrive. Where you can be safe," I answered, the words flowing with a conviction that surprised me.

There was no need to lie now. The weight of truth felt strangely liberating.

Dominic looked between my eyes with what I thought was a sign of approval. A slight softening around his mouth, a subtle nod.

"Good. That's what I was hoping you'd say. Let me tell you what's been going on here. Helia and Deimos visits us weekly. It's always the same time and the same day. Deimos takes three to four of us with him every visit. None of them have ever come back. We've never even heard a whisper from some of them. We are told that they get to ascend to godhood and live in paradise with them. I am not a fool. I know it's false. It seems things can't be going as well as they lead us to believe if Deimos is releasing his demons onto us. Do what you need to with this information. I look forward to hearing from you again so that we may plan further on how you will kill her. For now, if you could heal the vampires in your camp, I would be forever grateful." His words said he did not want me to respond. The finality in his tone brooked no argument.

I pushed the hardly together chair out from under me and stood, the legs scraping against the stone floor. I considered the proper way to say goodbye but decided to do nothing. I wanted us to work together and form a relationship, but I needed to remember that I was a goddess. I should start acting like one, shouldn't I? The question echoed in my mind.

I stood still for what had to be an uncomfortable amount of time for them. The silence stretched between us like a tangible thing.

"Actually, I have something else to ask," I said, breaking

the heavy quiet. "I want to form a council. I know that none of you have true reason not to trust me, and asking you to call me anything other than the cause of your curse is a lot to ask. I'm going to ask it anyway. I think that you and Dimitri would be a good start to a council. I'll need to learn a lot, and I'll need to learn it quickly. I only know what I've learned from the vampires in my camp, and out of respect for you, they haven't given much. I think if vampires they trust are standing by my side as equals, they would feel more at ease." My heart pounded in my chest as I made the proposal.

Dominic nodded, a thoughtful expression crossing his face. "You heal the injured vampires and prove that you're not like Helia, and I think we can work together for the good of us all."

I jogged out of the temple, not wanting to let any more time pass than I had to, my footsteps echoing in the cavernous space. The fresh air outside was a welcome relief after the stifling atmosphere within. Vero stood waiting. She was pacing back and forth, her claws leaving small furrows in the earth, but I wrapped my arms around her giant neck. I had to dodge spike to do it, but I didn't regret the comfort it brought. The feel of her scales against my cheek was cool and smooth. She felt tense under me. I didn't blame her, In all of our time together, I hadn't hugged her. She stayed by my side, but I never allowed her inside.

She had memories of our time together before all of this. Memories that I still did not have. I couldn't stop myself from considering how much I had been hurting her, too. How many people I had hurt because I was too afraid, no too selfish to move forward. The realization sent a pang through my chest.

"Are you okay?" Vero asked, her voice rumbling beneath my arms.

I ignored her because the simple truth was no. I wasn't okay. I had one hundred thoughts flying around in my head of how wrong I was and how many people I hurt because of it, but I was hardly holding on to the thinnest of threads. I wasn't the only one, though. Many others were hardly holding on to their lives, and I knew the clerics had to be exhausted. The knowledge spurred me to action.

"How are things going at camp?" I asked as I ran ahead of her and down the hill, the wind whipping my hair around my face.

"Just as you would expect, the dead are piling up," she yelled as she ran behind me, her heavy footfalls shaking the ground.

"We need to get back and help then," I shouted behind me, determination rising like a tide.

I shot the blood magic from my fingertips. The crimson strands glowed with an inner light as they extended from my body. I was ready to use it to save lives, but I was still uneasy using it. The feel of it flowing through me was both familiar and frightening. It couldn't save the people of my realm. Even if it was a shattered realm, it was still the only home that I knew. I still hadn't regained the memories of our original life. All I had was the stories that Hesperia had the time to share with me. She did so very sparingly. She told me that I wasn't unbreakable. That, as easy as it was for Ruri and Sage to be reset, was the same for me. I was left out of meetings and planning and kept from the other seasonal deities.

I was kept in my corner, left alone. I had nothing to do but replay how much I had failed at the cost of lives. I was naïve and thought that I could outsmart everyone without learning anything myself. It was everything else that carried the weight of that for me. The bitterness of that realization tasted like ash in my mouth.

I used the strings of blood from my fingers to rip open the first tent I saw that held a trail of blood going inside. The canvas tore with a sound like distant thunder. I knelt beside a girl, younger than any other vampire I had seen yet. The coppery scent of blood filled the air, almost overwhelming. I held my hand on her chest, and her root was broken in half. I closed my eyes; I didn't want them to scare her. I had learned that when I used my abilities to turn back time, not only did they shake, but small clock hands spun in my pupils. The energy flowed through me, a curious mixture of power and vulnerability.

For a moment, an image of Helia formed in my mind. It would have been easy. To take control of them, of anyone I wanted, and rampage. To do what Helia almost did. The temptation whispered darkly in the corners of my mind.

The idea of a family, a real family, pulled me back. The thought anchored me like a lifeline.

I opened my eyes again, and her roots were back together. It was her eyes that were closed. She was resting. Her pain had lessened enough to sleep. The steady rise and fall of her chest was the most beautiful sight I'd seen in ages.

I spun on my knee to the cot behind me and shifted time for his body, too. He was young but nowhere near as young as the girl had been. He was missing the skin on his jaw, and I watched it grow back as if it were string being threaded into a design. The sensation of flesh regrowing beneath my touch was strange but deeply satisfying.

"Get them some blood," I demanded to the shifter who stood over me, my voice hoarse from exertion.

I rushed out of the tent and moved to the next. Things became too much of a blur for me. I had entered and left one, two, six. Twelve filled tents. Cot after cot of injury and faded breaths. It was my breath that felt as if it were fading away. My mind was nothing but static. Every healing drained more of my strength, but I couldn't stop, wouldn't stop.

I hardly had any idea how I had returned to my own tent. I couldn't remember how I got into my chair. The world around me seemed distant and muffled. I could still hear the sound of screaming and tears through the ringing in my ears. I didn't know if I still had blood on my hands through my blurred vision, but I still felt the warmth of it all over me. The sticky sensation clung to me like a second skin.

I reached for my cup. It should have been in the same spot that it always was. I had to have my desk in a specific way; everything had its own place. Its own perfectly thought out spot, but my hands shook too much to know if it were in the spot it should have been. My fingers brushed against empty air.

"Shivani!" Vero yelled. She stomped her paws inside of the tent, shaking the ground beneath me. "You go from refusing to acknowledge you have abilities to using them so intensely you're on death's door? Do you expect me to explain this to Koa myself? To your sisters? What do you think their punishment will be?"

Her shouts moved closer, but it was the molten hands of the Seere cleric that gripped my jaw. The heat from them burned pleasantly against my cold skin. They opened my mouth and put a leaf under my tongue before they put a mist in my nose that caused me to pull the deepest breath in and start coughing. The bitter taste of the leaf mingled with the sharp scent of the mist.

I used my hands to try and shove them away, but my shaking fingers hardly did anything. I didn't struggle as much as I should have. The heat of their hands sent a wave of calm over me. The Seere used their hands to open my mouth a second time. This time, they put a glob of something inside and held my mouth closed until I swallowed it. The substance tasted of honey and ash, sliding thickly down my throat.

My vision came back quicker than the ringing in my ears stopped. The world coming into focus in increments. The Seere bowed to Vero and left the tent, their footsteps fading into the background noise.

"Don't move yet. Give it a few more minutes," Vero

advised. She took a seat on the ground in front of my desk, her massive form making the space seem even smaller. "I'm not going to tell anyone about what today cost you, and neither are you. Koa is still adjusting to his new wolf things that, quite frankly, I don't even understand. I don't want to deal with him, and neither do you. He will yap and yap." The concern beneath her gruff words touched me.

I nodded. The ringing finally stopped. My hands were still covered in blood. The dried crimson cracked with every movement of my fingers.

"You remind me of your father," she sighed, her eyes taking on a distant look. "He fought the same kind of battle once. He challenged his body to push harder than he thought it could, and I remember seeing your mother lecture him for months about what could have happened if she hadn't arrived on time. He was the sunlight clearing out the shadows Nikola caused in every corner his fingers could reach." Vero's eyes glazed over for a moment before she shook her head, scales shimmering with the movement. "There are a group of vampires outside that want to see you. I assume you would want to clean up and rest first, so I did not invite them in."

"No, let them in!" I tried to stand, but my legs failed me, buckling beneath my weight.

There was no use in asking her anything further about my father. Even if she wanted to go into detail, she couldn't. The silence around our past felt almost physical sometimes.

Vero ran her eyes down me and back up, taking in my disheveled appearance. "I'm only saying okay because I think you deserve to have someone on your side that doesn't treat you as a breakable child."

She whistled, and the tent opened. The canvas flap was pulled back, letting in a stream of evening light. In came Dominic and Dimitri. They took seats without questioning their places. They held the confidence that I wanted to hold. Their composure was something I envied in my current state.

"I've spoken to Dimitri, and he agreed that he would like to be by your side and offer advice as well. We watched you in silence today, and we both agree that you can't be the same as Helia. She would have sooner watched us die and found a way to make more than use up her own body and risk permanent damage to help any of us," Dominic explained, his voice tinged with reluctant respect.

Dimitri nodded, his earlier hostility noticeably absent. "I don't know what our future looks like to you, but after what I watched today, I know it has to be brighter than it has been yet."

I wasn't sure if they were inviting me to tell them what their future looked like or not, but I took the time to answer them all the same. I gathered my thoughts, trying to organize the vision I had for them.

"I've already been working on a relationship with the Queen of Brisa. I want us to come together and build a home here for everyone. The queen has what there is of the witches. Two people trying to piece themselves back together will have to understand each other's side. We can help them by helping you," I proposed, my voice stronger than I felt.

The two of them looked at each other, silently exchanging words. Their glances carried conversations I couldn't hear. I wished they would say them out loud. The moment stretched between us.

"I'm not opposed to the idea," Dimitri finally stated.

"Neither am I," Dominic agreed, inclining his head slightly.

"The Queen of Brisa has her own trusted council; I think with so many of us, we could make good progress quickly," I said, hope blooming cautiously in my chest.

"Are you feeling well?" Dimitri asked, his brow furrowing as he studied me.

"I'm feeling better now that the clerics were here," I tried to assure him, though the weakness in my limbs contradicted my words.

"You should step outside of the tent, then," Dimitri suggested, tilting his head towards the flap.

Vero stood from her spot on the ground, her scales bristling. "She is still recovering! What do you want her to hurt herself doing now!"

"I think it's important we establish now that we only want the best for her. She's not just a Goddess; she's our savior," Dominic explained, his tone placating.

Vero narrowed her scaley eyes. Her face was covered in displeasure, smoke curling from her nostrils in agitation.

I stood, feeling the weight of exhaustion but no pain, and moved to the tent. My heart raced at what could be on the other side, pounding against my ribs like a caged bird. I closed my eyes and pulled the cloth back. I opened one eye at a time, bracing myself for whatever awaited.

Outside of my tent stood a crowd of vampires. They were still as messy as I was, but their faces were rosy with color. Blood had returned to their cheeks, vitality to their eyes. Their voices carried as if they hadn't been on the verge of death just a short while before. The evening air was filled with their excited murmurs.

"Savior! Savior! Savior!" They all chanted in unison, the sound washing over me like a wave.

An older woman ran to the tent and wrapped her arms around me. "You saved my granddaughter. I can never repay you," she sobbed, her tears soaking into my already stained clothing.

A younger woman followed her and wrapped her around my other side. "My husband had no chance without you," she cried, her grip almost painful in its intensity.

I still held the tent, not them. I didn't know how to respond. I woke thinking it would be another day, hoping to make progress with them. I would sleep knowing they were all with me and not able to be taken by Helia or Deimos again. Not under my eyes. The realization settled over me like a mantle of responsibility.

When I killed Helia, I'd give them the guarantee of that. The promise crystallized in my heart, as solid and unbreakable as the blood magic that flowed through my veins.

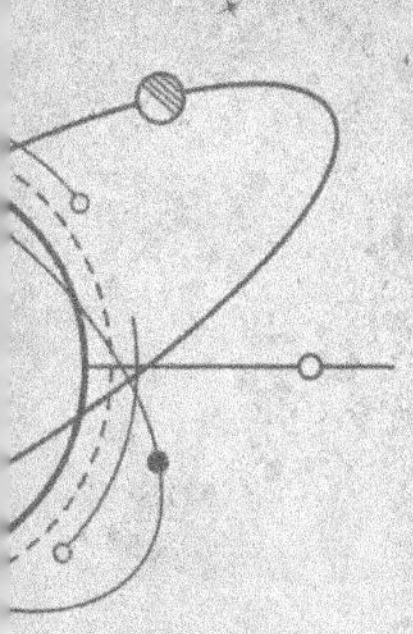

CHAPTER NINE

THE PROGRESS THE REALM NEEDS

SELMOR: THE CURSED FOREST.

Selmor is the remains of the island that the realms collided with. The cursed forest holds the creatures of Nikola, who were still alive when the realms crashed together. Not many people venture to the island. They claim it is haunted by ghosts of souls from another place. There are whispers that a witch lives there, banished from the rest of the realm. She protects the souls in her solitude, content to live around the dying land and cries of spirits.

ASTRA

Aero, the God of Justice, was the most punctual being that I had ever known until he met Fennic. The two of them together had no sense of time management. I did not run Orest and take care of the Sunlight Garden by being left to wait around and lose precious time. The steady ticking of the clock on my wall seemed to mock me as I paced. The two of them did things like rescue cats and give mortals manual labor as punishment. I didn't know why I expected them to consider my invitation to meet seriously. The thought made my jaw clench.

I tried my best to stop my leg, and it was shaking. The vibration traveled through the floorboards beneath me. I was feeling endlessly restless with Ruri's graduation. I spent four years with her under my eyes. Four years of not having to worry about what she was up to or who she was with. Four peaceful years of knowing none of the other Gods could get their hands on her. Now, I had to wonder and worry about who was moving in on her. The uncertainty gnawed at me like a physical ache.

I missed her. She wasn't that much different without her memory, and she still looked the same as she always had, but our shared experiences were missing. The part of her that could understand me in a way that no one else could be missing. The part of her that knew why we had to be the way we were. The absence felt like a phantom limb - something that should be there but wasn't.

I missed the openness that used to sit between the two of us. Ruri gave me the space to say anything I needed to without fear. I wanted to speak to her about Nikola. I knew he wasn't gone. That he had found a way to lurk in our realm. He had the ability to get inside our heads, and he was getting inside of mine. He showed me images of him going into a dragon egg as a soul. He cracked the shell after some time and then appeared as a newly formed man with Sahir by his side. The memory of these visions sent a chill down my spine, raising goosebumps along my arms.

The only comfort that I found was in the notion that he could not simply get a dragon egg from anywhere. They were guarded in Ashbell. I still had a small flutter in my stomach at the thought of the images coming to life. The flutter sent waves of adrenaline over my body. He was a shadow over our life for so long. The taste of dread was bitter on my tongue.

I didn't openly discuss what memories I gained with

anyone, but I had gained a handful. One of the memories had to be a gift. I recalled the day that Dahlia knew Nikola would lock her away. I remembered the plan she laid to ensure she would wake up again. Nikola thought the only way to get Dahlia out of the tree was with all of the girls together, but I knew that was wrong. The secret knowledge felt both precious and dangerous.

The door to my office swung open and in walked the two gods I had been waiting for. The sound of their entrance echoed in the room, breaking my reverie. The backup plan was one that only Dahlia and I held tight.

"The Shadows of Justice have arrived. There's no task we can't handle!" they said in unison, striking matching poses in the doorway.

I felt my lips turn down in disgust. "You two are late." The words came out sharper than I intended.

"We had another needy mortal in line before you," Aero explained, his tone unapologetic.

"It went successful, even though you didn't ask," Fennic added with a smirk.

"I didn't ask because I didn't want to know." The scent of smoke and something herbal clung to them, telling me more than I cared to know about their previous adventure.

I pointed to the two seats in front of my desk, and they sat. The chairs creaked beneath their weight.

"What is it you need? Orest has so many people I didn't expect to receive a request that couldn't be handled by anyone inside the walls of the school," Fennic remarked, leaning back in his chair.

"That's because no one inside of these walls are the two of you," I responded, trying to keep the irritation from my voice.

"I think we've been training our recruits well. They can handle anything that I can think of," Aero said, but he looked at and spoke to Fennic, as if I weren't even in the room.

Aero was fine to deal with when he was alone. I even

admired him at times. His strong sense of right and wrong was unmovable. Yumi or Dahlia themselves could tell him to do something that he thought was wrong, and he'd still decline. Aero with Fennic was another story. The two of them looked like naïve children. I didn't find it as cute as others did. The way they seemed to exist in their own bubble was maddening.

"It's a job only the two of you can do, all right? Enough," I interrupted, drawing their attention back. "Hesperia mentioned to me that she made the two of you touch the tree of life. She said that having both of you touch Dahlia showed the seal that is keeping her locked in. I think the three of us can get Dahlia out." The weight of what I was proposing hung in the air between us.

I was sure that we could do it. They were the only ones to make the seal appear because they were the only key we kept locked away. If we succeeded in unsealing Dahlia, then we would be more than one step or even two closer to putting the realm back to the order it never should have lost. They didn't seem to remember, but I did. Aero was the hand of justice for Dahlia. A trusted companion that helped Dahlia even if it meant his life. The memories were clear in my mind, if not in theirs.

"You want us to enter Semper?" Aero asked, his playful demeanor suddenly serious.

Fennic looked at him and then back to me. "The realm guarded by blood guards." His voice had dropped an octave, the gravity of the situation settling over him.

The way they acted and finished each other's sentences as if they were a married couple was only made worse by the matching outfits they wore. Aero was adamant that they were uniforms. That the mortals used the uniforms to point them out when they were in trouble. Matching clothing made me uncomfortable. The last time we had matching clothing around was when we all decided to be covered in crimson instead of white. When we all wanted to symbolize the blood stains Yumi left behind on all of us. The memory made my skin crawl.

"The realm that we are wanted in. That we face certain death in?" Aero leaned in closer to me with every word he spoke, his breath smelling faintly of mint.

It was this kind of thing that I didn't enjoy about them. They were too much. I wanted to yell at them, of course, that one! The words nearly escaped before I caught them.

"Let's do it!" They spoke in unison again, their expressions brightening.

"We were just talking about needing a challenge," Fennic said, slapping his knee with enthusiasm.

"Mhm," Aero agreed, nodding vigorously. "We are getting too good, too proficient in our work in Cylla. It's all save this kitten and get a prize. Save this man from the tree he thought he could chop down and get a statue erected of us. There's no real danger!"

Fennic nodded in agreement, but I could only roll my eyes. If I had any other option, I would have taken it. The alternatives, however, were non-existent.

"What's the plan, then?" Fennic asked. His voice dropped and was filled with seriousness.

It didn't suit him after listening to him with Aero. The others claimed that Fennic was a hardened soldier in the fractured realm, but I didn't see where that kind of personality could be hidden when I looked at the man in front of me now. The contrast was jarring.

"I have the best advantage of everyone. I've convinced Helia that I am Thann. She doesn't question me," I explained, the words leaving a sour taste. "I can move freely and do as I please as long as I bite back my bile and kiss her. No one will question the two of you entering Semper with me. If they do, we can tell them we are looking into Astra. No one knows I'm Thann but our tight group. It'll be easy to cover my own tracks. It will please Helia to know I've set my sights on myself." I looked between the two of them, who looked to be in deep thought, their brows furrowed in identical patterns.

"It could work," Aero said to Fennic, stroking his chin.

"It could work," Fennic nodded back. "With us there, it's sure to work out."

Why couldn't I have had any other choice of who to work with? The question echoed in my mind as I suppressed a sigh.

"I have to be honest, Astra," Aero frowned, his expression suddenly vulnerable. "I was beginning to feel useless. The girls have no memory to look after them. There are so many important things going on. It felt like we had nowhere to be."

"It felt like we had nothing to offer," Fennic inserted, his shoulders drooping slightly.

"We wanted to do something better for everyone, but any idea we had seemed to be too small compared to the things everyone else was doing," Aero finished his statement, genuine emotion in his voice.

There was a flash of sadness behind his usually happy eyes. As much as the two of them together annoyed me, I had hoped that there would be someone, something that remained happy and untouched by the cruelties that could happen if you moved too deep into the layers of secrets. My back still held phantom pains anytime I tried to find peace. My mind still betrayed me in my sleep and reminded me of everything that I wanted to forget, and my days still brought the pain of knowing my son was gone. The realization that even they carried their own burdens was sobering.

"The two of you understand that if we are caught, we risk death?" It was only fair they understood before agreeing. The weight of responsibility pressed down on me.

They looked at each other, again, in the same way they had since they arrived. Silently speaking through the shifts in their eyes, a language only they understood.

"Of course!" Their voices rang with conviction that belied the seriousness of my warning.

I sighed, "I will send for you when I've found us the best chance to move."

The two wasted no time getting to their feet and talking in unison, again, of all the things they would be doing to get prepared for the mission only they could do. Their excited chatter filled the room as they backed toward the door.

I followed behind them and clicked the lock on my office door when they closed it. The sound was final, definitive. I had other things to attend to that were not at Orest. The thought of my next destination brought both comfort and pain.

Some deities had to walk everywhere if they didn't have a crystal. Some of us had such a deep connection to other things that we made the choice to walk. I picked up two bouquets of assorted flowers, their fragrance filling the air around me, and cut a slice of the air open. The tear in reality shimmered at the edges, pulsing with power. I stepped through, and the other side was a black, endless space filled with stars and moons. The cold vastness engulfed me, yet felt familiar. I stepped across the star-lit path and cut a second slice open to leave space and enter back into the Cylla. The transition was immediate, jarring.

The other side was Brontide. Kyra and I set up a memorial on the top of the stone spire she lived on. The wind whipped at my clothing, carrying the scent of ozone and distant rain. The entire kingdom lived inside of rock spires. Stairways from the ground to the tip swirled the stone. Each one of them was carved out of natural stone. The homes carved out inside of the rock were also built of marble and gold. The craftsmanship was breathtaking even after all this time.

Kyra's castle was the only thing built on top of the spire. Bridges of the same marble were built between spires, and it was common for citizens of Brontide to climb to the top and watch the sky. The barrier that Ruri left could be seen shimmering a deep purple and tinted the star's color at night. The protection that kept us all safe, yet trapped.

I set one bouquet of flowers on the memorial for my son. Together, we named him Merikh. Kyra had her best artist hand carve it into his tomb. The stone was cool beneath my fingertips as I traced the letters of his name. I pulled out a match and slid it across the stone until it glowed. His candles needed to be lit for the evening. The small flames danced in the breeze, casting flickering shadows across the memorial.

"He would love those flowers," Kyra said. She stood beside me and set her own bouquet down. The sweet scent of lilies mingled with the crisp mountain air.

Her dark blue curls bounced with the movements. She turned to look at me. Her bright green eyes smiled even where her lips didn't, and I lost all senses. I placed one arm around her hip and pulled her towards me. The warmth of her body against mine was a comfort I craved. She did the rest and connected her lips to mine. The softness of her lips, the taste of honey and mint, was overwhelmingly familiar.

Peace washed over me in a wave of tingles. She was my home, my happiness. She tucked her head between my neck and chest, and I held her tighter. Her heartbeat against mine was the most grounding sensation I knew.

"I met with Fennic and Aero today. They agreed. So we will be moving forward," I whispered against her hair.

I felt her tense against me, muscles going rigid. "You don't need to do this. There are more than enough of them." The edge in her voice was unmistakable.

"But none of them in my position," I said, drawing back to look into her eyes.

"You can still change your mind. Let someone else play pretend and dress up as Thann," she pleaded, pulling back so that our eyes could speak as well. Her hands gripped my arms with surprising strength. "You can stay here with me. Ruri graduated, and she went off to be with Caym and her temple. We can take this chance to focus on us, our city, our people, our son." Her voice pleaded with me to agree, desperation tingeing each word.

If my heart could crack, that's what I felt happening while she spoke to me. The pain was almost physical.

"I can't abandon Ruri or Dahlia," I said. My voice cracked, betraying my emotion.

"It feels like you can only sleep at night if you abandon me for the memory of Ruri," Kyra tried to pull away, but I stopped her, holding her in place.

"If I don't do what I can to help and the barrier on Brontide is lost and I lose you, I'd never be able to sleep again. If I don't do what I can to ensure our city stays protected and you stay untouched by the deities outside, how will I be able to look at our son and tell him I did my best to protect you?" I moved the hair from her face so that it was in full view, the silken strands sliding between my fingers.

I could see in her eyes that she had more to say but chose not to say it. The unspoken words hung between us, heavy with meaning.

"Talk to me," I urged her, my palm against her cheek.

"If something happened to you, I wouldn't forgive any of them. I wouldn't forgive you. I'd curse you and your afterlife for not listening to me when I told you to stop," Kyra said, her voice breaking on the last word. A single tear tracked down her cheek, catching the fading light.

I pulled her closer to me. Until even air couldn't find its way between us. The scent of her - thunderstorms and wild- flowers - enveloped me completely.

"Even if something happened to me. Even while you were cursing my afterlife. I'd be fighting every Nola there was on my way back to you," I whispered, my lips against her temple.

"You wouldn't have to if you just stayed," Kyra repeated, her fingers digging into my back.

I knew I wasn't going to change her mind. I had to be careful what I discussed with her and when because this was the result. I understood her position. I didn't want to leave her any more than she wanted me to. I wished just as much as she did that we already had our happily ever after. The longing for that simplicity was a constant ache.

Without returning Ruri to her life, I could never find peace in my own. She never picked her own happiness over mine. She never left me to Yumi alone. She gave her own flesh in place of mine more than once. She shared my pain, and I held her tears. She was as close to a sister as I could have ever had. The memories of our bond were etched into my very being.

I'd never find the kind of peace Kyra was looking forward to if I didn't get Ruri and Dahlia first. The certainty of this knowledge was the only thing keeping me on my path.

"I want nothing more than I want our life together. I want to do everything you've dreamt of us doing. I want you to enjoy everything I dream of us doing. For us to do that, I have to set things right. I have to know you support me in it. I have to know that if the worst happened, if by some small chance, something did happen to me, you would step in, in my place, and help. For my sake, for my peace. You can not blame anyone else for my choices. No matter how they end up," I begged her, my voice thick with emotion.

Her grip on me didn't loosen, but I felt the change in her. A subtle shift in the way she held herself. "I can't promise you any such thing." The words were cold despite the warmth of her breath against my neck.

"You can," I said, desperation creeping into my voice.

"I won't." Kyra leaned back and dropped her arms. "I won't." The finality in her tone brooked no argument.

She was open in her discussions on how she felt. She was

always loud in her disdain for my love of Ruri. She was set in her frame of mind. To her, I valued Ruri more than I loved her. In my mind, she held her anger higher than her love for me. The impasse between us seemed insurmountable in moments like these.

From my perspective, the rage she felt over being abandoned by Ruri was stronger than any other feeling she held. And that realization broke my heart anew every time I faced it.

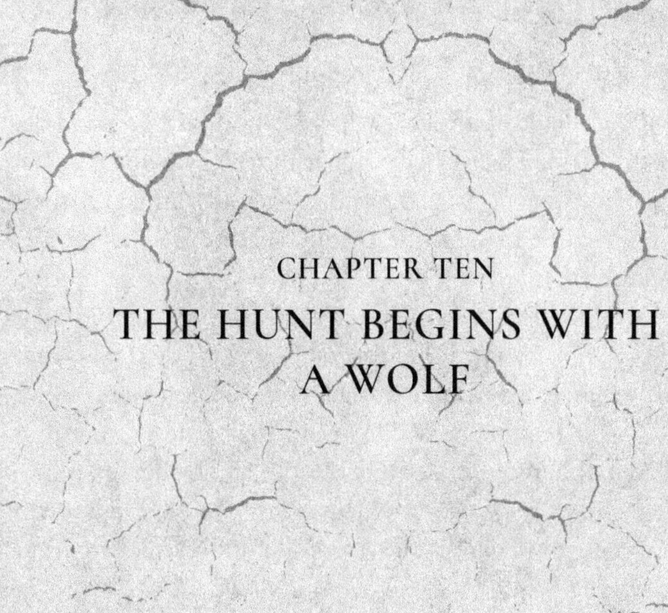

CHAPTER TEN

THE HUNT BEGINS WITH A WOLF

ASHBELL: THE LAND OF FIRE.

The Goddess of Magic built the land of fire around the only volcano in the realm. She hoped the heat of the molten liquid would keep most away. She infused the soil with healing magic not found anywhere else, and burning trees that dropped ash grew from it. The land holds many secrets that have yet to be discovered. It is one of the oldest lands next to Orest and one of the few to still hold the bloodline of the ruler that was hand-picked by the Goddess.

COY

When the realms collided, my memories did, too. I remembered so many things from the Age of Moonlight. I recalled the army that my siblings and I built up. The images flashed through my mind with startling clarity, faces of soldiers long gone, battle plans sketched in blood. I knew who Ryujin was. I remembered in an instant that he was the one we put in charge of our army. I remembered the bloody battle between Gods and mortals that ended our world as we knew it. The screams of the fallen still echoed in my dreams. I remembered the day that I held my brother when I found him far too late. The weight of his lifeless body still haunted my arms. I recall Caym begging me to save the girls. To leave him and send Ryujin to guard Dahlia. His desperate pleas rang in my ears as if he'd spoken them yesterday.

I remembered Sina stopped Ryujin. I remembered that she begged him to stay and protect her. The tears that streaked her face, the tremor in her voice. I remembered her efforts to keep him to herself. I recall that I never saw him again. I remembered without any doubt Deimos helped Sahir. Sahir begged her brother not to leave her behind. Their whispered conversations played through my mind like music from another time.

I seemed to be the only one who could recall Juniper, the Goddess of Wrath and Nikola's daughter, helping mortals get away from the creatures attacking us. I remembered watching her fight by our side like it was her side. The fierce determination in her eyes as she cut down enemies who had once been her father's allies. No one mentioned it, and everyone trusted her with a garden that seemed to be their lifeline to everything they had left to help them in the sister's absence. The contradiction sat heavy in my thoughts.

I also seemed to be the only one who recalled the tool that Olexei gave Shivani to find the traitor without a doubt. I could see them in my mind; I could hear them. The gleam of metal in the half-light, the whispered instructions. It was still too fogged to be certain. The mist that hung over the memory of them was just enough to keep them safe. I was sure that if I could get close to them, that if I could feel them, I'd know who it was. The certainty of this knowledge burned in my chest.

The first thing that I had to do was calm a colony of dragons. They were restless. Some of them were deities who knew what was going on; others were new souls who had never experienced anything before outside of the storytellers that kept them occupied. They all wanted to leave their island and cause chaos until they could roam freely. The energy of their discontent was palpable, like heat rising from stone.

I understood the feeling of being restless. I was restless, too. My skin felt too tight, my thoughts too loud. I was not rash or reckless. I wanted to ensure no stone was left unturned and hidden from me. I would not be careless again. If I had to, I was prepared to kill all of the other guardians to be sure there was no one left against us, and Dahlia came back. I would carry the weight of my actions, and I would answer to Dahlia for them. The resolve hardened in my soul like cooling metal.

The one thing that I had that my siblings didn't have was no bond. Something happened when our realms collided, and although everyone felt strongly for the sisters, I couldn't recall a single detail about them. I couldn't feel them in the same way the others described, either. The emptiness where that connection should be was a hollow ache. At first, I thought it meant I had to be the traitor, but if I was, then my sibling's side of the realm wouldn't be the way it is. If I was the traitor, the sisters would not have been sent to live as mortals and reset again. The logic was inescapable.

Something scrambled inside of me or fixed itself. I wasn't sure which. I was either back together and focused on the protection of all the sisters like I should have been or broken and unable to bond with the one that I was made for. The uncertainty gnawed at me in quiet moments.

I felt for Hesperia as a boy with a crush did. I enjoyed her company. The sound of her laugh sent warmth through me. My mind told me that I knew her in some way. What that was, I didn't know. I decided to look at the situation as an advantage. I could sort through everyone with a level head. Without the need to be hovering, the sisters stopped me from making choices that needed to be made. The freedom of emotional detachment was a weapon I could wield.

Hesperia was hurt; she didn't speak it, but I saw it all over her face. The pain in her eyes when she looked at me was unmistakable. I didn't need to be bonded to her to see her pain. If we were to be anything in the future, and my mind stayed broken, then we would have to hope we could fall in love with each other again. The possibility seemed distant and fragile.

For now, love was the bottom of what needed to be done. I had tougher choices to make. The weight of responsibility pressed down on me like a physical burden.

I stood on a stone stage in Elowen that the dragons had carved with their talons and fire. The rough surface was warm beneath my feet, still holding the heat of their flames. In front of me stood a crowd of them, roaring and flapping their wings. The sound was deafening, the wind from their wings strong enough to make my clothing snap against my body.

I would admit that if I had to be locked on a stone island with hardly anything to look at, I would be displeased as well. The idea I had when I thought of their land was not what I entered. They had burnt, poisoned, and frozen the land until it was stone in every direction. The barren landscape stretched out beyond the horizon, broken only by jutting peaks of rock. I wasn't sure how they had anything left to eat. The desolation was complete and self-inflicted.

The entire realm hung by a thread. The truth was there if anyone wanted to say it out loud or not. I could feel the precariousness of our situation in my bones.

"Dragons, Deities. I've come today to hear your concerns," I called, my voice barely carrying over their clamor.

I was already tired of talking. My patience was wearing thin. I wanted to create a plan and see it through. Discussing everyone's thoughts and feelings only held up time that I could be using in other places. The frustration simmered just beneath my skin.

"Did you bring meat?" One called, the question cutting through the noise.

"Are you any closer to Dahlia? Has she come back to us?" Another demanded, smoke curling from its nostrils.

"Where are the sisters?" A third roared, its voice shaking the very ground.

"When can we leave?" The chorus of questions grew louder, more insistent.

I glanced to Ryujin, who saw my displeasure. He stomped his massive clawed paws in my direction. His grey and black scales shimmered in the sun like polished metal, and the ground shook with every step. The vibration traveled up through my legs.

"If you didn't act recklessly and burn your own home, you'd have endless meat!" Ryujin roared, his voice like thunder.

Silence ran over the crowd like a wave. It was the same kind of wave that washed over me when he took over, and I could tighten my lips shut again. Exactly how I wanted things. The sudden quiet was almost as startling as the previous clamor.

"We are working to get Dahlia and the sisters back, but do you think that will help you? Do you think that they will come back and be pleased to see how reckless you are? How destructive? Do you think they would just look past the things you've done to their island?" Ryujin shifted his snout between the sides of the crowd, his hot breath washing over them in waves.

"We want to know what you plan to do," a dragon called, its voice defiant despite Ryujin's display. "How can we be concerned with a punishment for things that don't exist anymore?"

"I'll be sure to report that back to Dahlia," I pointed, my tone carrying a clear threat.

Ryujin used his snout and pushed me back to my spot beside him. The scales were surprisingly smooth against my back.

"We plan to sort out the traitor and have it done by the month's end," Ryujin called, his voice carrying to the farthest reaches of the gathering.

"It'll take longer than that unless you have some sort of secret!" A voice called from the back of the crowd.

What made him think that we would tell him if we did? I recalled the tool Olexei made. I already had a dragon that Ryujin picked searching for it. Would I tell them that and ruin all of my careful planning? No. The thought was absurd.

"It would be reckless to share if we did," Ryujin growled, a plume of smoke emerging from his nostrils.

"The more time we waste here, the less we can use else-where," I said, impatience edging my words.

"You would be less restless if you focused on rebuilding your island and learning some manners!" Ryujin demanded, his tail lashing behind him in agitation.

Silence was their answer. The only sound was the soft rustling of wings and the hiss of breath. They had to have known, as we knew, how disastrous they looked. The truth was written across the barren landscape they'd created.

I climbed up Ryujin's scales and sat on the bottom of his neck. The texture was smooth but warm beneath my hands, like sun-heated armor.

"Go. We've been here long enough," I said, patting his neck.

Ryujin listened, took flight, and headed as far above the clouds as he could. The wind whipped past us, cold and biting at this altitude. The higher he flew, the less time it took us to arrive. I wanted to travel as fast as some deities did, but I had no special ability to place myself into a vein between realms. I had to stick to normal travel. The limitations chafed at me.

Our first stop was Sephtis. The land of grand architecture and sand. I was told they had grand buildings and homes. They enjoyed bright colored paints. I was told that even though they were still trying to sort themselves out after half of them were cursed to be shifters and the other half were still average human mortals, it was still a sight to see. The descriptions had painted an image in my mind that I was curious to confirm.

I wasn't going for a vacation or sightseeing. It would have been fine with me if the place was burnt to the ground. I was only going to be near Koa. To watch him in his own land and to see what he kept busy with. I wanted him to know he had many eyes on him. To see if the ones around him would hide his secrets. I wanted to sniff him out and cross him off my list or kill him today. The purpose of my visit was clear in my mind.

I was as restless as the dragons were. I wanted life back. I wanted action. I wanted to fight. The hunger for it gnawed at me from the inside.

I dozed off a time or two until Ryujin dived for the ground. He gave no warning, no steady descent. He tilted his snout down, and he dived for the ground as if he were trying to dig us into the center of the realm. I gripped the scales on his neck with both of my hands, my stomach lurching into my throat. The wind screamed past us, tearing at my clothing and hair.

"A warning would have been nice!" I shouted over the roar of the wind.

"Sorry to disturb you, sleepy head," Ryujin growled back. "I didn't realize I was a bed." The sarcasm in his voice was thick enough to cut.

Maybe I would kill him, too. The thought was darkly satisfying.

Ryujin landed, and all four paws with a shake of the ground. All of the men and women that could be seen were running and screaming in all directions. The sounds of panic filled the air. They looked like ants from my view, scattering in terror. Koa hadn't trained hardened citizens if Ryujin had scared them. He was hardly the biggest dragon. If enough of them gathered spears, they could take him down and have food for years. I wanted to ride Divala. The stories of how big the thunder dragon was came from everyone. The size of Ryujin suddenly seemed inadequate.

Ryujin lowered his head closer to the ground and let out a roar that blew a few mortals back onto the ground. The sound was physical, a wall of noise that made the air itself vibrate.

"Hey!" Koa yelled. "Stop scaring them on purpose!" His voice carried over the chaos, authoritative despite the circumstances.

I climbed down the side of Ryujin and jumped to my feet. The sand was soft beneath my boots, shifting with each step.

"Haven't you trained them on how to take down a dragon?" I asked, brushing dust from my clothing.

"Haven't you been trained on entry manners?" Koa snapped back, his eyes flashing with anger.

"Of course I have. I use them, and your people use defensive skills, as well," I nodded, a smile playing at the corners of my mouth.

"If you've come to show off defensive skills, I guess I can make time," Koa shrugged, the tension in his shoulders belying his casual tone.

There was a bite behind seeing him the way he was now. In this life, he was praised as a skilled fighter. The respect he commanded was evident in how quickly his people regained their composure at his arrival. In a past life, Olexei had to spend extra time on him. He was the last of us to become efficient and the weakest of us when he did. The contrast was stark.

"I've come to offer a helping hand," I said. "Hesperia is busy, and so I wanted to see if there was anything I could help you with." The half-truth flowed easily from my lips.

"You don't want to keep an eye on her?" He asked, his gaze searching my face.

"Of all the things she does need, it's not my assistance. Anyone that doesn't fear her deserves to find out on their own why they should," I said, the words holding more truth than I had intended.

"Have you started remembering her?" He focused his prying eyes on me, watching for any reaction.

"I have not," I answered, keeping my expression neutral.

"How is she taking that?" He asked, still prying, his tone deceptively casual.

She's taking it like anyone madly in love with someone unable to return their feelings. She's taking it as anyone would who waited year after year to see the one they considered their person. The weight of her disappointment was a burden I carried but couldn't fully comprehend. No matter how she took it, it was not in my power to change it. I wouldn't admit that I was putting less than zero effort into trying. I truly did enjoy having a clear mind and being in the position to see everyone the way they needed to be seen. The freedom was intoxicating in its way.

It wasn't the time to be worried about any of that. I reached into my pocket and pulled out crystal dust. The fine powder glittered in the sunlight. I made sure my hand was covered in a layer of it so that when I touched him, the truth crystal was thick enough to work. I could not guarantee that it would work without fail, but it was all I had for now. The risk was calculated and necessary.

"If the only help you require is this, I'll go," I patted him on the shoulder with my dusted hand. The crystal powder transferred to his clothing, invisible to all but me.

If there was no glow, then there was no lie. I watched carefully, looking for any telltale shimmer.

"No, no. I was just checking on you. If you want to help, today we're getting displaced kids into homes," Koa explained, his tone softening. "A lot of mortals couldn't handle the shift, and they died. Kids are younger and stronger. They were left alone to help the younger kids. They did a good job, but they lived on the edge of starvation. The hollow look in their eyes was something I never want to see again. A lot of the mortals that didn't shift are afraid of them. Sephtis was already on the brink of perishing because of Deimos. When he kidnapped my sister, he did a good job covering his tracks and hiding things. That, or I was just a really bad brother." Koa's hazel eyes dimmed the longer he spoke, shadowed with old grief.

"Tell me where I'm needed," I said, unwilling to dwell in the emotional miasma he was creating.

I could listen to him speak all day long, but in the end, I was the wrong one to look to for emotional support. Sympathy was not a weapon in my arsenal.

"We've got a few more pieces of wood to hammer in, and their new home will be complete. So you can help me sort through which children may still have relatives to go to and which need to be housed in the orphanage," Koa said, gesturing toward a distant structure.

"What if their relatives don't want them?" I asked, the question blunt but necessary.

Koa looked at me as if I had grown an extra set of eyes, his expression a mixture of shock and disgust.

"You said some of the mortals are scared of them. What do I do with children whose relatives don't want them because they are shifters?" I asked again, unmoved by his reaction.

"Give them a room," he answered firmly, his tone brooking no argument.

I moved aside so that he could lead the way. Sephtis was beautiful, despite my earlier indifference. The golden sand caught the sunlight, making the whole city seem to glow. Their temple was clear to see from where we walked. A large pyramid with the statue of the Goddess of Healing on each side of the entrance. The stone gleamed, polished to a mirror shine. It all looked hand-carved. The mortals ensured every detail of Koa's sister was captured in the statue. If they blamed anyone, it wasn't her. The devotion was evident in every carefully rendered feature.

I stopped at the folded tables Koa had set up in a line. Several other men were already sitting at them with lines of children in front of the tables. The sight gave me pause. Koa underplayed how many of them there were. There had to have been hundreds, maybe more. One home wasn't going to be enough. Two wouldn't cut it even if he put them doubled up. The scale of the problem was staggering.

I took a place at the table beside Koa. He wasted no time picking up a quill and talking to the children. I turned to my own line, and it wasn't the idea of how long it would take that was daunting. The idea of how many children lost their families because of the rage of a Goddess that they still worshiped was crushing. The weight of it settled over me like a shroud.

"Sir? Aren't you going to ask me if I'm alone?" A small girl asked, her voice high and clear.

I nodded, finding my own voice suddenly unreliable.

"I have my bunny and my sister!" She smiled, revealing a gap where her front teeth should be. "Bunny won't need her own bed. She sleeps with me, but my sister kicks too much. Can she have her own bed now?" Her hope was palpable, shining in her eyes.

I nodded and grabbed the paper. "Name?" My voice came out rougher than intended.

"I am Nissa, this is Bunny, and my sister is Elizabeth! We are six and two," she announced proudly, holding up her stuffed rabbit for inspection.

Mortal children were stronger than most of us. The

resilience in her was humbling. I signed their names to a room with two beds and handed her the paper. She skipped off to an older girl, hardly a teenager, who held her sister. The little one's arms were thin, but her grip on her sibling was fierce.

There were so many more to do. The line seemed to stretch endlessly before me.

I could not bring myself to believe that Koa was the traitor while he was also doing this. I believe the traitor would be doing plenty to look innocent. Their goal would be to convince us through their actions, to make us look crazy for thinking it was them. This was too much, even for that. The dedication required went beyond any pretense. I couldn't believe that Koa would be so invested in these lands, in the children, and be betraying us, too. The contradiction was too great.

He had to be clear, but once I found the God of the Sun's tool, I would test him with it all the same. Trust was a luxury none of us could afford anymore.

Until then, I would stay to see if he needed help building another home. The children deserved that much, at least.

CHAPTER ELEVEN

EVEN THE TEMPLE CAN'T STOP LOVE

EDUR: THE LAND OF ICE.

The Goddess of Space started the land of ice, and she didn't get far before she was pulled back to the realm of the gods to stay put in the sunlight garden. Her intention was to fill the land with endless animals, but she hardly got the chance. The Land of Ice struggles to support a large population, and they depend largely on trade, but with low resources to offer in return, every aspect of life in the Land of Ice is limited.

RURI

Belladonna shrunk herself to size and rested on my shoulder in silence. Her diminutive weight was familiar and comforting against my collarbone. She didn't question out loud why we were still standing at the entrance to the temple of magic. Inside was the order. The order that I was to spend the rest of my life protecting. I was excited to start what I had spent my whole life working towards, but a sense of sadness outweighed my excitement. It sat like a stone in my chest, heavy and cold.

I wasn't sure why, but I suddenly did not want to walk inside. My feet felt rooted to the ground.

The temple sat on top of a platform surrounded by magma. It flowed from corners of the temple like waterfalls on each side and into the mote that was only cut off by a golden sheen obsidian bridge. The heat rose in shimmering waves, making the air ripple around the structure. The other side was a stairway that looked as if it would take half the day to climb. Smaller buildings sat inside of the mote and around the temple.

Orchids and cherry blossoms were entwined and carved into the frame of the temple. Their delicate petals rendered in stone seemed to flutter in the heat. Ash trees were carved into the doors, and a different dragon was carved as a pillar that helped hold up the temple. Each scale was meticulously detailed, catching the red-orange glow of the magma below.

"Are you going to go inside, little one?" Belladonna asked, her voice soft in my ear.

"Of course. I have to, right?" The uncertainty in my own voice surprised me.

"We can leave; you have not taken a vow yet," she answered, her tail twitching against my neck.

"It's not that. I want to serve the temple; it's just that I feel like I know this place somehow. That's crazy, right? It is. Of course, it is. It's just nerves," I feigned a laugh that sounded hollow even to my own ears.

"It is normal to feel nervous. I will fly you away if it is what you ask," Belladonna said, her breath warm against my cheek.

Belladonna's burgundy fur blew in the breeze that hit me as well, tickling my skin with each gentle gust. Her eyes were as bright as grass when I tilted my head to look at her. She was looking forward. She was so confident-looking that I felt foolish. Of course, I wanted to go inside. I would go inside. I trained for this day. I dreamt of entering this temple as a dragon guardian. The certainty of this should have steadied me.

It was a feeling I had a hard time with. I climbed the stairs. Belladonna's talons dug into my shoulder just a bit tighter. It matched the increase in my heart rate. With every step I took, it beat quicker, pounding against my ribs like a caged bird. Sometimes, I had dreams of what I thought was another life. Maybe this was something similar. Perhaps I was feeling the memories of a past life. The thought made my skin prickle with goosebumps despite the heat.

"Why do you hesitate?" The man's voice sounded in my head, deep and resonant as if he were standing beside me.

"Can you see me?" I asked, my own voice barely a whisper.

I checked over both of my shoulders, but there wasn't a speck of dust, let alone an entire man. The emptiness behind me was somehow more unsettling than if I'd found someone there.

"No, but I can hear you," he said, his voice carrying a weight that made my stomach tighten.

"How often?" I asked, dread creeping up my spine.

Did he hear when I had nightmares? When I was alone with my lover? Did he hear me when I doubted myself or when I thought how much better I was than the other dragon guardians? The possibilities made heat rush to my face.

Did he have his own opinions of me because of what he could hear? The thought was mortifying.

"Always," he whispered, the word like a caress against my mind.

"Always?" I flinched, my hands clenching involuntarily.

"Every time you think too deeply about something or someone, I hear it," his voice sounded as if he didn't enjoy what he heard. There was a weariness to it, an ancient exhaustion.

"Who are you?" I asked, my voice barely audible over the rushing magma below.

I was afraid to know the answer. The not knowing was somehow safer.

"It doesn't matter. Get inside," he demanded, his tone hardening to steel.

"No," I retorted, surprising myself with my defiance.

"No?" He chuckled, the sound rich with dark amusement.

"Now I'm not going inside at all," I snapped back at him, crossing my arms over my chest.

"Why?" His voice sounded amused, which only irritated me further.

"I don't know who you think you are, but you can't just tell strangers what to do," I hissed, my voice rising with indignation.

The air grew colder, and the sky filled with dark clouds. The sudden change was jarring, like stepping from summer into winter in a single breath. A mist showed beside me, and the Nola from the school appeared. His form solidified from the fog, translucent at first, then gaining substance with each passing second. He picked me up and tossed me over his shoulder. His grip was ice-cold through my clothing. He ran me up the stairs to the doorway that was double our size. He kicked it open with skeletal feet that I didn't believe he had until I saw them, the bones clicking against the stone floor. I was inside the temple before I could have said another word, deposited unceremoniously onto the polished floor.

"I think I am the one that can make you do whatever I want you to do," he said, satisfaction evident in his tone.

I wanted to be offended. I wanted to pull out something witty to say in response, but the only thing that I could think was not appropriate. The words died on my tongue.

Was I amused by him? The realization was almost as startling as being carried into the temple.

The Nola sat me back on my feet and bowed before he

disappeared quicker than he arrived, dissolving into mist that dissipated in the warm air of the temple. Belladonna was the next thing in my line of sight. She sat in the doorway with disgust on her face, her fur standing on end.

"Sorry," I whispered, smoothing down my rumpled clothing.

"Ruri!" A woman in emerald robes lifted her hands in joy, her voice echoing in the vaulted space.

I knew she was the high priestess by the staff with a glowing full moon floating on the top. The orb pulsed with a soft white light that seemed to emanate from within. I knew because of her crescent moon headdress covered in the largest emeralds that I had ever seen. They caught the light, sending prismatic reflections dancing across the walls.

This time, I bowed, the movement formal and practiced.

"Oh, stop it!" I noticed her furry pink ears wiggle on the side of her headdress, the movement so natural it startled me.

Was she a cat? The realization struck me suddenly.

"Do you want to touch them?" She asked as she stood in front of me, leaning forward with a mischievous smile.

Our eyes sat level, and she was taking advantage of it. The deep and prolonged eye contact made me uncomfortable. Her pupils were vertical slits, unmistakably feline.

"I knew a girl once who looked at them the same way, and when I offered her the same thing, she did not hesitate. It became a normality for her to scratch them anytime I saw her," the girl chuckled. The sound did not match the pain in her eyes, a shadow of old grief that darkened their amber depths.

Against my better judgment, I reached up and used two fingers to scratch the back of her ear. It was a quick movement that I regretted immediately. The fur was soft and warm beneath my fingers. She was the high priest of my new position, and I was scratching her cat's ear. The absurdity of it made me want to laugh and cringe simultaneously.

"I'm Inola, the high priestess of the Order Of The Arcane Tome. I wanted to come and meet you myself!" Her voice was less of what I expected from a high priestess and more of what I would have expected when meeting a friend. She practically vibrated with excitement.

I was sure that she would be more uptight and that the entire temple would have a harsher atmosphere. Even the view outside had a harsh visual aura. The land was stunning but so dark and hot. I was caught off guard. The warmth of the welcome did not match the imposing exterior.

"Not much of a talker, all right. So your duty will be to check in visitors. We want to allow people to worship safely. You will also be checking the treasure vault every day and protecting us when we need to travel. We often bless the Ash trees before the healing ash is collected. We also visit the volcano for dragon flower hatchings. The celebration of the Goddess of magic is soon. The coliseum will be alive with virgin men fighting to join the Goddess in the afterlife. We will be skipping that this year. Getting you settled is more important!" Inola grabbed my arm as if we had always known each other and pulled me beside her. Her grip was surprisingly strong for her slight frame. "Do you have any questions?"

"I do have one, but it doesn't have to do with my duties here. I've been training so long for them; I can recite them and the rules of the temple from memory," I said, finding my voice at last.

"Ask away, anything at all," Inola smiled, her eyes crinkling at the corners.

I pulled the silver chain from under my top and held it up until the piece of citrine caught the light. It sparkled with an inner fire, almost as if alive. "Do you know anything about God artifacts? I found this because I heard a voice from it."

Inola leaned her head down closer and then looked up at me, her expression thoughtful. "This is not an artifact. God artifacts are left at death. They're a piece of the deity and its very core magic. This, although precious, is not that. Citrine was what the God of Death gifted the Goddess of Magic. Maybe she wanted to bless you with this before you came. You two do look an awfully lot alike after all."

Bless me? She's long since been dead. If she did have a way to talk to mortals, why would she spend that energy on me? The questions swirled in my mind, unanswerable.

"They haven't finished your room yet, but you are free to roam until they do. Make yourself at home," Inola said, patting my arm.

She gave me one last look up and down before another generous smile. She was off with the same grace she showed up in front of me, her robes swishing around her feet, the sound like rustling leaves.

I walked back outside. I wanted to walk the pathway around the temple and hide myself so that I could try and call to Deimos. I wanted to see him, to let him know that I was okay. The deck was so close to the magma falls that if I had reached up, I could have touched it. The heat was intense, making sweat bead on my forehead. When I made it to the back, it was as I had hoped. A simple balcony overlooking the land. The vista spread out before me, breathtaking in its savage beauty.

I whispered his name in the wind. I knew he would come to see me. He cared about me and helped me keep from having any magical outbursts. He wanted to see me safe, and I loved him for it. The words felt right, yet somehow hollow.

I watched the Seere of Ashbell live their lives. Some were playing with children; others were using machines that I was not familiar with to process the ash they collected. Their laughter carried up to me on the wind, light and carefree. They looked so peaceful. Ashbell had been nearly silent since my arrival. The only sounds that penetrated the air were those of happiness. It was a serenity I hadn't expected.

My cheek felt moist, and when I reached up to touch it, I was crying. The tear was warm against my fingertip.

Why was I crying? The emotion welled up from somewhere deep and unexplained.

"You called?" Deimos asked from behind me. He leaned down until his lips were beside my ear, his breath warm against my skin. "If you'd like me to kill them, I will. They seem to be bothering you."

"No!" I jumped, my heart racing with sudden fear. "I'm just happy to finally be here, I think. It took so long to get here, I thought I may never see the day, that's all."

"All you need to do is ask," he repeated, his voice velvet over steel.

His words sent a fire through me that I did not recognize. The idea of the Seere I was watching being murdered in front of me for simply existing put me in a place I had never been before. The revulsion was visceral, making my stomach turn. Maybe being here was not the best thing for me after all. There were so many emotions pouring out of me that I could hardly process any of them. The conflict left me dizzy.

It had to have been from the relief. From the weight of stress being lifted off of me. That was the logical explanation, wasn't it?

"How are you settling in? I can feel the surge of magic in you getting ready to erupt," Deimos said, his fingers playing with the ends of my hair.

He still cradled me from behind; this time, it felt less loving. I felt as if I were in the wrong place or with the wrong person. His embrace, once comforting, now felt confining.

"I'm settling in nicely. I found this necklace before I left Orest," I said. I twirled it between my fingers, the stone catching the light.

His head peered over my shoulder to look at it. "Who gave it to you?" There was an edge to his question that hadn't been there before.

"No one. I found it inside of a book," I answered, keeping my voice light.

"I can take it for you. I can find out where it came from," he offered, his hand reaching for the pendant.

The feeling of panic washed over me again, and my heart raced. "No!" I tried to settle my voice, hearing the fear in it. "Inola says it's probably a gift. I should keep it. To be safe. The last thing I want is to upset a deity after I just arrived." I turned to face him, and he looked at me as if he knew I was lying. His mismatched eyes narrowed slightly, searching my face.

I reached up and grabbed each side of his face to pull him closer. I let him look into my eyes before I kissed him. His lips were cool against mine, familiar yet somehow wrong.

"How are things going for you?" I asked, desperate to change the subject.

I wanted the subject to change from my new necklace quickly. I felt oddly protective of it, my hand curling around it instinctively.

"They're going well. I've been working hard, and I'm nearly in the position I want. The head of trades and supplies for Ashbell is right in front of me," Deimos said, his eyes gleaming with ambition.

"It's an important role! You'll be in charge of supplying every land in Cylla with healing. I know you'll do a good job in the position. Without you, so many lives would be lost," I smiled, the praise automatic.

I was happy for him. It was a good job for him. He cared about so many. He was a good man. The thought felt rehearsed, like words I'd been taught to say.

"I don't have time to help you practice today. It wouldn't be wise. There's bound to be someone looking for you soon," he leaned down until his lips were over mine again, his breath mingling with mine.

I knew what he was going to do instead. It was something

he did often. I wasn't any more adjusted to it. It hurt. It felt like I was losing a piece of myself. My body tensed in anticipation.

His lips met mine, and I felt him pull from me. When I opened my eyes, it looked as if he were pulling a bit of my soul from me. A purple cloud left my mouth and entered his, carrying with it a piece of my essence. I felt the surge of magic inside of me lower until it disappeared. The sensation was draining, like blood being drawn. He cut ties with me, and I let out a sigh of relief that it was over. I was never sure if I felt better because he helped me or if I felt empty because he hurt me and I didn't understand it. The confusion sat like lead in my stomach.

I trusted him to protect me, and I was sure that he was doing it. The doubt that crept in felt like betrayal.

"I'll visit you again soon," he said, his eyes lingering on my necklace for a moment too long.

He was gone before I could respond, and I felt half of myself and lonely again. The emptiness expanded inside me like a void.

I leaned over the railing with the beautiful etching of the orchids and cherry blossoms and lost the contents of my stomach. The acid burned my throat. All I could do was hope it would miss anyone and end up in the magma. I kept myself leaning over the rail for more breaths than I could count. I knew the feeling of being ill would go away; it just never went fast enough. The nausea lingered, a reminder of what had just happened.

Once I gathered myself well enough to hide any lingering feelings, I followed the path back inside the temple. The cool air was a relief against my clammy skin.

There were a lot more members than I thought there would be. They all chatted and looked happy, their voices creating a pleasant hum throughout the space. There must have been something wrong with me because so many happy people in one place made me feel as if there was something that I was missing. I was sure it was all in my head. It said more about me than I did them. They weren't doing anything wrong; I was just not opening up to the environment. The disconnect was unsettling.

I expected to have to be rigid. Silent. To have to be as hard as a rock and have too many duties to have free time. I had only just arrived a few hours earlier and was already being left to find my own way around after petting my high priestess. The freedom was disorienting.

The Order of the Arcane Tome was not what I expected. Not at all.

I stopped in front of the statue of the Goddess of Magic. It was hand-painted, and the small out-of-line colors that didn't blend as well as others made that clear. It was beautiful all the same. She was beautiful. Her features were delicate yet strong, a paradox in stone. She was covered in fresh flowers at the base of the statue, their fragrance mingling with the incense that burned nearby. She wore a simple emerald gown, but it was the citrine necklace that caught my full attention. The detail was exquisite, each facet of the stone lovingly rendered.

It did look just like mine. She did look just like I did. The resemblance was uncanny, like looking into a mirror made of stone.

A man stood beside me. I tried not to look at him and make things uncomfortable. It was a temple for worship, after all. He should have been free to stand as close to her statue as I was without judgment. I didn't want to be the reason he could not ask for guidance in whatever he came for. My eyes still shifted to try and gaze at him, even against my will, drawn to him like a moth to flame.

He wore a black trench coat over an emerald vest. The fabric looked expensive, draping perfectly over his tall frame. Long black hair was tied in a low ponytail. I could see his hands without having to turn my head to look at him. His arms were crossed, and on the back of his hands were green tattoos. As if lightning had struck him and left its mark on his skin. My thoughts were sent into a spiral. They were like the marks the man from my dreams had. The realization made my breath catch.

Sometimes I got the feeling that even though my dreams showed me one thing, it was a lie. Sometimes I felt as though the man who hurt me and helped me were switched. The thought came unbidden and unsettling.

"Are you all right?" He asked, his voice deep and resonant.

His voice was like the one in my head. Deep and commanding. I knew my jaw was hung too low because my tongue dried with how long I had to have been staring at him. Heat rushed to my face in a wave of embarrassment.

"I'm fine," I stuttered, the words catching in my throat.

I blinked enough times that my lashes could have caused everything in the room to have blown away. The rapid movement made my eyes water.

I was embarrassed enough that I didn't need to reach up to question that I was flushed red. I could feel the heat radiating from my cheeks.

"Do you need to sit down somewhere?" He asked, genuine concern in his voice.

"No, no," I shook my head. I tried to hide my face with my hand, the gesture futile.

When his beyond-deep green eyes were on me, I only wanted to giggle as if I were a young schoolgirl. My first day as temple dragon guardian was going horribly. I was not anything close to a strong stone wall. I was the exact opposite. Flustered and blushing at the first man to speak to me. What would Deimos think of me? He'd be ashamed, that's what. The guilt rose like bile in my throat.

He would be disappointed to know that I hadn't even been in my new life for one day, and I was already tossing him aside as if he were trash and not the love of my life. I was doing it for a pair of emerald eyes in a trench coat! My standards and morals were both clearly low. The self-recrimination was automatic and harsh.

"I need to go. I'm sorry. Enjoy the temple," I tried my best to smile and be polite, but I only wanted to keep my face hidden. The mortification was complete.

The man reached out to shake my hand, but I dreaded the idea. I took his hand in mine. I wanted to give a quick shake and run. What if he were someone important? I couldn't risk a bad reputation on top of bad morals and betrayal. His skin was warm against mine, the contact electric.

When our hands were fully clasped, I felt a spark of pain run up my arm. Lightning seemed to course through my veins, burning from fingertip to shoulder. I opened my mouth to let out a scream, but I was pulled into my own mind instead. The temple dissolved around me, replaced by something entirely different.

I was on my knees in a garden brighter than any I had ever seen before. The colors were vivid, almost painfully so. I could feel the warmth of the sun as if I were against it. My flesh burned and throbbed, and I was sobbing, screaming so loud my throat ached. The pain was all-encompassing, reality reduced to agony.

"I'm sorry. Stop this!"

"You aren't sorry yet, but you will be! Do you think that you can talk to me the way your mother used to and I won't do anything about it? You think that you can tell me how to treat Astra? Thanks to you, she will receive double whatever I give you here. You'll watch it, too!" The woman dressed in silver screamed at me before she cracked a whip against my arm and cheek. The impact was like fire across my skin.

She gave me no time to rest, no time to speak in protest

again before she pulled the whip back and cracked it down on me again. The sound of it cutting through the air was almost as terrible as the pain that followed. She used her foot to shove me backward into a tree. The tree towered over me, covered in pink blossoms. Their sweet scent was a perverse counterpoint to the violence being inflicted.

The silver woman grabbed me by my hair and flipped me onto my stomach. She shoved my mouth into the dirt at the base of the tree and held me there with her bare foot. The taste of earth filled my mouth, gritty and choking. I felt the whip crack along my spine. I didn't count how many times it happened. I didn't want to count how many times. The fire I felt pulsed through me said that it didn't matter. The pain transcended numbers.

I coughed on the dry dirt that filled my mouth and shoved as much of it out as I could before shoving my head back down. I had almost forgotten what air felt like when I opened my eyes and was back in my own body, in the temple where I was supposed to be. The transition was jarring, reality snapping back into place with sickening speed.

I could still feel every lashing I had gotten, stinging the skin on my back. The memory of pain lingered, phantom wounds that shouldn't exist. The green-eyed man held my head on his lap, but I was not yet in control of anything to do with my body beyond my eyes. My limbs felt leaden, disconnected from my will.

What happened to me? The question echoed in my mind, unanswerable and terrifying.

CHAPTER TWELVE

CAUGHT IN BETWEEN TWO NIGHTMARES

MIDORI: THE LAND OF EARTH

The land of Earth was one of the pieces of land claimed and formed by mortals. The land flourishes with plants and animals. The land has had book after book filled with different types, and there are still scholars who make trips to record the discoveries of more. Although the land is beautiful, it is prone to poor luck. Natural disasters happen so often across Midori that it is hard for the land to keep any reputation beyond the land of bad luck. Most do not refer to it as the land of earth but the land of death.

RURI

I was pinned against the wall. Hot breath was against my neck, sending shivers down my spine despite the heat. Arms held me in place as if they were a prison, unyielding and suffocating. Bits of long black hair escaped his ponytail and tickled my cheek, the silken strands a stark contrast to the rough grip on my arms. I knew I wouldn't be able to fight him off of me, but I knew Deimos would not be far behind.

I held back my tears when I felt his lips trail down my neck, leaving a path of revulsion in their wake. He never missed a moment, never allowed me to be alone. He was always able to tell when I was alone, and he always made a move for me. The predictability of it was almost as terrifying as the act itself.

I opened my eyes, and there Deimos was. He marched with a fury, his mismatched eyes blazing with rage. There was something different this time. I was wearing the necklace that I found. It grew hot on its chain, the heat intensifying with each passing second. I thought it might burn me, leave a permanent mark on my skin.

The heat brought with it a shock to my senses, and my eyes grew heavy. I closed them, nearly forgetting that a man still had me pinned to the wall. When I opened them again, things were changed. Where Deimos should have been marching to save me, the man with green markings took his place. The shift was jarring, reality rearranging itself before my eyes.

It was the first time that I could see his entire face since I was a child. The man with green markings matched the man that I met at the temple. That couldn't have been right. They could not have been the same men. Yet there he was, identical in every detail, from the emerald lines on his skin to the depth of his gaze.

The man grabbed Deimos and ripped him off of me. The two of them were on the ground, but it was hardly a fight. The man with green markings won by a landslide, his movements fluid and precise. I thought he was going to take Deimos's hand. I thought I should have intervened. I was watching the love of my life be hurt by a strange man, and yet, I wanted it. The realization hit me like a physical blow.

I wanted the man to hurt Deimos worse than a hand. I wanted him to die. I had a wave of relief over the idea that he would no longer be around. As if so many things may have been a little better, easier if he had died. The darkness of my own thoughts frightened me. I hoped that, with every piece of myself, the man would remove Deimos's head and not just a hand, but I could not say it out loud. The viciousness of my desire was overwhelming.

I refused to let myself speak it into life because some part of me knew that if I said it, it would come true. All of my dreams left me waking in a sweat, panicked and afraid of the man with marks, but this moment, this dream, he was the only thing that gave me hope for peace. The contradiction made my head spin.

There had to be something, some kind of crystal magic influencing me. Deimos was my protector; he was my lover. He cared for me, and we would have a future together soon. I couldn't allow some kind of lie to get between us. The justification felt hollow, rehearsed.

I shot up in my bed, finally awake before the man could do any harm to Deimos. The sheets clung to my sweat-dampened skin. I reached up to touch the necklace, but it was still hot, burning against my fingers. Was it the reason my dream was different? Maybe it was filled with magic. The possibility was both frightening and exciting.

Today was my first official day as a dragon guardian at the temple of magic, and it would not be ruined by a nightmare. I wouldn't allow it. I would go outside for some fresh air. I would refocus myself, and then I would start the day again. The resolve steadied me, gave me purpose.

I grabbed my golden robe and threw it on. The fabric was cool against my heated skin, smooth and comforting. It was the robe I would wear inside of the temple every day for the rest of my life and golden leather when we traveled. Belladonna was still asleep on the other side of my bed. She hardly noticed me getting out of bed. The small slit that she opened her eyes when I stood up had only lasted a few seconds. Her soft snores continued uninterrupted.

I opened my door, and there wasn't a person in sight. The silence was profound, broken only by the distant bubbling of magma. The sun had not yet risen, nor did anyone who lived at the temple. I was given my room, and it was not talked about properly. It wasn't just a bedroom. It was a home. I had a full bathroom and a kitchen.

The space was larger than I had expected, and far more luxurious. I was surrounded by multiple other homes, and we all shared a courtyard. I had already witnessed someone with a two-headed magma hound taking them out for a walk before I went to sleep. The creature had left scorched foot-prints on the stone path.

The courtyard we all shared was lit by the glow of lava and stars. The crimson light bathed everything in a warm, eerie glow. Obsidian benches sat scattered and surrounded by bushes of red and orange petaled flowers. Their scent was heady and sweet, filling the air with a perfume unlike any I'd encountered before. The courtyard was still positioned perfectly to have a clear view of the volcano that sat in the middle of Ashbell. The massive peak dominated the skyline, smoke curling from its summit like a living thing.

I hesitated to move forward when I recognized the man with green markings already standing and watching the volcano from the edge of the courtyard. My heart leapt into my throat. I would have been lying if I said that I wasn't curious who he was. I wanted to know his connection to my dreams. I thought that when I figured out who the man was, I would be scared. Maybe angry. The expected emotions never came.

I was not; I was curious. I wanted to know who he was. Why was he haunting me? If he was connected to me. The only fear I felt was the idea that I didn't know myself. I should have been scared of him. I should have turned around and walked the other way. My feet were already moving toward him instead, as if drawn by some invisible force.

"It's beautiful, isn't it," he remarked, his deep voice carrying in the still air.

I stood beside him and leaned against the smooth obsidian railing. The stone was cool against my palms, grounding. "It is."

"I used to watch the sunrise over the volcano with someone very special to me," he confessed, his voice softening with memory.

I didn't speak. I wasn't sure if it was the right thing to do. It seemed like he just needed someone to listen to what he was saying. Something about him made me want to listen. Something about the stranger felt easy, familiar in a way I couldn't explain.

"She loved Ashbell. She built a home here," he continued, his gaze still fixed on the distant peak. The first hints of dawn were beginning to touch its summit.

"Does she live there now?" I asked. The question slipped out before I could stop it.

I wasn't going to ask but he seemed as if he wanted me to. The longing in his voice was palpable.

"She died," he responded, the two words heavy with grief.

"Is that why you're here?" I questioned, drawn deeper into his story despite myself.

"Yes. I'm helping the Timekeepers in her absence," he admitted, finally turning to look at me. His green eyes caught the light, seeming to glow from within.

I lifted my hand to stop him from talking. Alarm bells rang in my mind. I didn't want to be put deeper in a position to have to turn him over to Inola. The mention of the Timekeepers was forbidden.

"You aren't allowed to speak about them. They're housed at this temple in secret for their own protection," I cautioned, keeping my hand up to silence him. My heart raced with sudden fear.

"Aren't you a guard? Shouldn't I be able to trust you?" He lifted a brow at me, his expression challenging.

"If I were a guard worth trusting, then I should turn you in now. What is your name?" I demanded, trying to sound authoritative despite my inner turmoil.

"Caym," he stated simply.

My heart sank and then corrected itself, only to beat out of control. It happened too fast, so fast that I thought I may have passed out. The name hit me like a physical blow. Turning him over to Inola would mean nothing, but he could have me removed from my position. The realization made my mouth go dry.

"From Solaris?" I asked in a low voice, barely above a whisper.

"So you've heard of me?" He smiled, the expression not quite reaching his eyes.

"You're the general." The words felt inadequate, as if there should be more to say.

He didn't speak this time. He only looked at me. He looked at me with hurt in his eyes. His eyes said he was expecting something else. That he was trying to tell me something that I could not understand. The silence between us was charged with unspoken meaning.

"Can I be honest with you?" I asked. I wanted to stop myself from speaking, but the words tumbled out regardless.

"Sure," he nodded, his full attention on me now.

"I dream of you nearly every night. I know it sounds unbelievable, but I do. Every night, I dream that you hurt me and someone comes to save me from you. I don't know why I'm telling you this or what I think it will accomplish, but I have been scared of you for so long, and somehow, being in front of you feels less like I thought it would and more—" I shook my head and turned away from him, unable to finish the thought. The confession left me feeling exposed, vulnerable.

I turned back to the view of the sun coming over the

volcano. The sky was beginning to lighten, painted in shades of gold and crimson. I wished that I hadn't spoken at all. That I would have stayed inside. I looked like a fool now. I didn't even know how to finish my own words. The embarrassment burned in my cheeks.

"Who is the other man?" he asked, his voice gentle despite the intensity of his gaze.

He didn't speak as if he thought I were a fool. The acceptance in his tone emboldened me, but wariness remained. I didn't want to answer him by saying my lover. Deimos wanted our relationship to remain a secret so that it wouldn't affect our lives or dreams. Caym was the general of Solaris; if he wanted to ruin me, he could simply speak to the God Kyrell, who rules the land there, and I would be ruined. The risk was too great.

"All of our secrets stay here," he assured me. "You can turn me in for telling you that I'm here for the Time Keepers if I say a word." His offer was sincere, a peace offering between us.

"I'm not sure who he is," I lied, the words bitter on my tongue.

All I could think of was the rage he had in my dreams and the fact that I did not try to stop him from hurting Deimos. I couldn't be sure enough of myself to tell him the truth. I didn't know him, and yet I was sure that reaction was the realest thing I did know. The contradiction tore at me.

"I don't think you're crazy. The God of Dreams must have a reason for what he's showing you," I heard a pinch of that same anger in his voice, a subtle shift in his tone that made me tense.

I was far from understanding why the God of Dreams would show me Caym or Deimos. The purpose seemed just beyond my grasp, tantalizingly close yet impossible to reach.

"You should get back inside. Your day starts soon," he suggested, his expression unreadable.

He was right, but I wanted to stay a bit longer. The peace of the moment was seductive. I did not allow myself to do so. I did not allow myself to even say goodbye. The temptation to stay was too strong.

It wasn't just him; it was the entire temple. It was the necklace. Everything around me felt as if it were pulling me in a different direction. Screaming at me to pay attention to it. I felt as if I were living with a pain in my head that I couldn't get to stop throbbing. The pressure was relentless. I felt as if I knew everything about the temple, but I could not recall anything about it. I never second-guessed my path until now. The feeling of being ripped in every direction wasn't something that I thought I could live with forever. The strain was becoming unbearable.

I was so sure that I somehow knew more than I could remember when I stood in front of the statue that held the Goddess of Magic. The marble figure seemed to watch me, her stone eyes somehow alive. I leaned down and pressed the pinky toe. I could not explain why, but I knew it was a button. It popped open and startled me, the click echoing in the empty chamber. It was scarier to be right than to think I knew secrets that The Order of the Arcane Tome held. The confirmation of my suspicion was more terrifying than the suspicion itself.

Two boxes sat side by side in strange little boxes that I did not recognize. The sound from them was clearer than anything I had heard in my lifetime. It was my own voice asking me to put myself back together. To eat what was inside and become whole again. The words were both familiar and alien, my voice yet not my voice.

"Ruri? You shouldn't touch those," Inola cautioned from behind me, her sudden appearance making me jump.

I watched her shove the compartment back into the Goddess's foot, her movements quick and precise.

"What are they?" I asked, curiosity overriding my surprise.

"Are you good at keeping secrets?" Inola looked at me with a blank face, her cat-like eyes unblinking.

"You're the high priestess; I have to keep your secrets no matter what they are," I answered, the oath binding in a way I hadn't fully appreciated until now.

"I'm the Goddess of Spring, and I'm protecting that for the Goddess of Magic and her sister," the more words she spoke, the lower her voice became, until it was barely above a whisper. "It's a shattered piece of their heart."

Was she expecting her to come back? The question formed but remained unspoken, the implications too vast to contemplate.

"Isn't the general of Solaris also the God of Death?" I asked, the connection forming in my mind.

I didn't know why I was asking another question when I had hardly begun to process the other words she spoke. I found myself unable to care about a Goddess when I didn't know who the man I kept running into really was. The hierarchy of my concerns surprised even me.

"Yes," she said simply, watching my reaction carefully.

"The God of Death and the Goddess of Magic are, well, they were together?" I phrased it as a question, but I knew it as a truth. Everyone did. The legends were as old as the realm itself.

"Correct," Inola confirmed, her expression softening.

"So that's why he's really here? The two of you are trying to bring her back?" I pointed a finger at her as if I were catching on to a great mystery. The pieces were beginning to fit together, forming a picture I wasn't sure I wanted to see. "If this necklace is hers, that must be why I feel so strange here! Are you planning to use me as a sacrifice?" A wave of fear ran over me, cold despite the temple's warmth. "Why have I never heard of the Goddess of Spring?"

Was she joking with me? The absurdity of the situation made me question everything I thought I knew.

Inola wrapped her arm around mine and pulled me with her, her grip surprisingly strong for her appearance. The contact was both comforting and constraining.

"I'm going to show you a room that no one is allowed in but a very small circle. Since you are sworn to keep my secrets, it seems it won't hurt to show you," Inola smiled, her expression knowing.

I knew she was happy because her little furry ears wiggled. The movement was endearing despite the gravity of the situation. Did she do it on purpose? The question seemed trivial against the backdrop of revelations.

"You haven't heard of me simply because I want to remain secret for now. There are deities that want to see some very poor things happen, and it would be better if I kept a tightly kept secret," she looked at me with warning in her eyes, the amber depths holding centuries of caution.

I nodded, understanding the gravity of what she was sharing.

"I was there the day the Goddess of Magic was born," she spoke playfully but with pride, her voice carrying the weight of millennia. "There are not many of us older than the sisters of creation, but those of us who have too many memories to keep in our heads."

She unlocked a door with a key that had to have been made of magic. The metal glowed briefly as it turned in the lock. She motioned me inside and locked it behind us. The room was filled with shelves and paintings. Books, scrolls, jewelry, bones. There were so many things inside of the room that I didn't know what to begin to say about it. The collection was vast and eclectic, spanning what must have been ages of history.

"Everything here belongs to a sister of creation or a seasonal deity. It's all yours to explore if you'd like to. I assume you'll take your vow in a few days and be here with us, so it's only right you get to explore a little," Inola explained. "We also keep safe the artifacts for the God of passion, mercy, fear, and the Goddess of the sky."

I wasn't sure if I was going to take my vow. I wasn't sure if I could live feeling the way I had been. The uncertainty gnawed at me. I heard Deimos's voice in my head anytime I considered it too hard. The man who was speaking to me hadn't been back since I entered the temple. It was something that I could add to the pros of staying. The silence was a relief in itself.

I reached up for a tattered brown leather journal. Maybe exploring would help me decide. Maybe I could find something inside that would convince me of the right choice. The binding was worn, the pages yellowed with age.

I opened the journal, and the name written inside caused me to sigh. How many times could something like this happen and be considered a coincidence? Inside was the name Caym. The God of Death's secret thoughts were right in front of me. Only the flip of a thumb away. The temptation was irresistible.

I glanced at Inola, who was busy looking at something else, and I flipped through pages. The handwriting was bold and flowing, unmistakably masculine.

I thought that I wouldn't make it through watching her die the first time. That I would never be able to pick myself up out of the darkness I fell into. That I would slaughter everyone, friend or not if they couldn't give me an answer to undo the things that had been done.

When I saw you again, when I felt hope, and you died the second time by Helia's hands, I knew that I was right. That the word friend or foe meant nothing to me. That the term brother held next to nothing in my eyes. I realized, seeing you die a second time, that I had only a thread holding me together, and I wanted to cut it myself.

I was training the Nola how to kill Gods. I was learning how to forge my own weapons. I was gathering every secret from every deity and realm I could.

Until there, you were a third time. You asked me if I was a God. You asked me if I could stay and tell you stories. How could I ever tell you no?

The things I did to our friends. The things I threatened to do to them if they moved for you—you'd be disappointed in me, but I don't take it back. I was never more blessed than when I watched you have our child. I wanted Kyra to be with us, but she didn't approve of my choices either. When you died holding our third child, I knew it was because of a broken heart, and the only thing I could find peace in was knowing that you wouldn't remember any of it.

I'll get you back again. I'll bring our children back, too. I've already rebuilt our home in Ashbell.

I closed the journal without reading any further. The words burned themselves into my mind. If I thought my head hurt before, I was wrong. It hurt now worse than any pain I had felt before, a splitting agony that threatened to tear me apart. The only thing I could see was two little girls with the blackest hair. One was swaddled tightly and held by the other. The image was vivid, real in a way that defied explanation.

The pain in my head intensified, and with it came a certainty I couldn't explain. Something was being kept from me, something vital. And somehow, I knew that Caym, the God of Death, was at the center of it all.

CHAPTER THIRTEEN
THE LAND OF WATER CALLS

EREBUS: THE LAND OF SHADOW.

The Goddess of Night wanted something tucked away from the bright sun. She raised the ground and carved into the rock until there was enough land to live in. When she was finally finished, there were multiple cave mouths, but they all connected to each other. She hardly put any effort into the land above ground. It was largely barren and dry. Cracked dirt and empty tree branches sat scattered among cactus plants. She placed all of her pride inside the caves. Crystals decorated every inch of the caves, and glow mushrooms gave them light. The Goddess of Night spent most of her time in the caves until, one day, she never returned.

HESPERIA

I wasn't sure that we would find a ship that would allow Sina to travel on it. Not many captains were fond of the idea. The tension in the air was palpable as each one eyed her with suspicion. There were many dragons that could fit on a ship; some of them were the same size as hounds. The captains said it was bad luck to travel with one. The dragons belonged to the sky. I disagreed, but trying to talk a mortal out of their superstitions was next to impossible. I could stand the deity that they claimed taught them to be cautious of such a thing right in front of them, and they'd still argue it. It was a pointless endeavor, like trying to push water uphill.

Sina looked as displeased as the captain, her scales rippling with barely contained irritation, but I was happy to be on the sea and not the sky. I preferred walking the in-between, but the sea was as close as I could get to the same feeling. The gentle rocking of the ship beneath my feet felt almost like the weightless drift through the veil. The smell of salt was the only thing that kept my mind convinced I was at sea and not in the in-between. The briny scent filled my lungs with each breath, sharp and cleansing. I could not have taken Sina with me in the in-between. Not everyone could enter. Sina did not have enough experience with death. The boundaries were clear, even if she couldn't see them.

"Are you enjoying the view?" I asked Sina. She stood firm in the middle of the ship, her claws digging into the wooden deck with each sway of the vessel.

"I am not," she answered, her voice flat.

"Is there anything that I can do to help?" I asked her, searching for some way to ease her obvious discomfort.

"There is not," she answered, not even bothering to look at me.

I nodded. She glanced at me from the side of her eyes. She had changed so much since our original life, and yet she still held the same hard aura around her. Standing beside her, I felt as if there was an unbreakable shell holding me out. The invisible barrier seemed impenetrable. It felt breakable once; I recalled it. The memory of a time when we had been closer brought both warmth and sadness.

"Do you remember when Dahlia was still around?" I asked the question, slipping out before I could stop it.

"I do," she answered. "I never experienced what it was to lose that memory." Her voice softened slightly at the mention of Dahlia, like ice beginning to thaw.

"Me either," I said. "Does it ever feel heavy?"

"To know that others have forgotten and we have not? No. I feel pity for them. If many of them could remember, if we could speak freely, I think much would be different," Sina said, her antlers catching the sunlight as she finally turned toward me.

"So do I. I think things would have ended before they progressed this far," I said, the breeze catching my words and carrying them across the water.

If everyone had their original memories, Yumi would never have been able to get as far as she did. Astra would have pulled all of the souls from the stars. We would have put the realm back together so much sooner. The certainty of this knowledge sat like a weight in my chest.

"Do you really think so?" Sina interrupted my thoughts. "I think maybe not." There was something odd in her tone, a note of challenge I hadn't heard before.

"What?" I asked, startled by her disagreement.

"If Yumi knew anyone would remember, don't you think she would have killed them before bringing them back?" Sina still did not look at me directly, her gaze fixed on the horizon where sky met sea.

"I think Yumi hardly ever had the power to kill them, to begin with. I think she only made it as far as she did because of others. She took advantage of her position and slipped into the cracks she found. Nothing more, maybe a little less. I think she has always been weak, and she has never been a threat," I was beginning to feel my blood boil at the conversation topic, heat rising to my face.

"I think you're right. I think there are many other, much more powerful forces at work in the shadows. I think Yumi was only a distraction," Sina said, her tail lashing against the deck in agitation.

Something about her tone and her stance, while she spoke, sent a shiver down my spine. The sensation was like cold fingers tracing my vertebrae. I couldn't put my finger on what it was. It wasn't her words specifically that made me feel uneasy; it was something about the way she said them that made me fully consider the idea that Yumi was far more useless than even I thought. I never gave her much credit, but maybe even that was too much. The implication hung in the air between us, unspoken but unmistakable.

"At least we can say the realms are back together," I said, my voice softer than intended.

It was more for myself than for her. I was confident that I could kill Yumi. I was confident that even if no one else could, I could help kill the counter gods. Sahir was already dead. I knew Nikola was taking his time and gaining his strength, and he was something that I could not face alone. Right now, I was alone. Caym remembered a lot more than he admitted to anyone else, but like my sisters and I, he was not as strong as he could be with the guardians united. We needed to be them and unite them all. The task seemed to grow more daunting with each passing day.

"Yes, it's just too bad that everything else we wanted to keep out came with it," Sina said, her words sharp as talons.

She spoke in a way that made me think she was blaming me. I felt my brows furrow and my face scrunch with confusion at the idea. The accusation, if that's what it was, caught me off guard.

"Sina, do you have something else to say?" I asked, trying to keep my voice steady.

"I simply meant that some precautions could have been taken to prevent us from being in an even deeper hole with hardly any way out," she answered, frost forming at the edges of her words.

"There was hardly time," I scoffed, the wind carrying my indignation out to sea.

"I'm not trying to say that it was a failure only on your part; it was a group failure," Sina finally looked me in the eye, her gaze piercing.

Her powder blue face was hard, and her white antlers were unmoving. The sun glinted off them like polished bone. Did I truly miss this? Was that the root of what felt stuck between us? She blamed me for the creatures in the cursed forest. She blamed me for Nikola being with us. The realization stung more than I expected.

"I won't apologize," I stated, my voice hardening. "You hardly have the right to speak or toss judgment on a situation you weren't around for. We didn't have a choice or time to plan. No one knew anything until we were crash-landed into Cylla."

I left her where she stood, the sound of my boots against the wooden deck punctuating my departure. I knew that she wouldn't follow. She and I were alike in that. Neither of us was one to chase after someone. I knew it was better to end the conversation where it was then for us to do or say something that we would regret because that was the only way things ever went. The bitter taste of our argument lingered in my mouth.

"Do you still trust her?" Nikola's voice slithered through my mind, smooth as oil on water.

I refused to give him a response, clenching my jaw against the intrusion.

"She seems a little odd, right? She seems like maybe she's not the same friend you left," he chuckled, the sound echoing inside my skull.

"We've arrived!" The captain called from above us, his voice carrying on the wind.

Relief washed over me at the words. I snapped my fingers and moved between the veil that separated the living from the dead. The familiar weightlessness embraced me, the world around me taking on a ghostly translucence. Sina would get off the ship with everyone else. We were close enough to shore. If she wanted to move faster, maybe she should learn to use her wings. I entered back into the realm of the living at the edge of Daxon, the transition jarring as gravity reclaimed me.

The land of water was beautiful. Their castle looked as if its single-pointed tip could touch the sky, the spire gleaming silver in the sunlight. The brightest colored coral sprouted as far as my eyes could see, pinks and purples and blues forming an underwater garden visible through the crystal-clear water. I thought I liked Sina covered in blue, but Daxon's soft blue hues against the crystal-clear water and the golden sand was the most perfect combination I had ever seen. Pastels gave a softness to the land that not many others had. The scene was breathtaking, like something from a dream.

A noise sounded off in the distance. It startled me, breaking the serenity of the moment. A man blew into a shell and moved closer, the haunting note carrying across the water. He blew into the seashell twice more, and I wondered how he was doing it with the face of a puffer fish. His cheeks expanded with each breath, his spines rising slightly. An entire group of water folk followed him. They were all dressed in blue and green fabric that seemed to flow like water itself. Shells adorned their chests and jewelry with hints of pink here and there. I was too deep in examining them and their beauty to consider what they were doing. The procession had a solemn, ceremonial air.

"The Queen has arrived!" The pufferfish with the shell called, his voice surprisingly melodious.

The most interesting thing about the land of water was their advancements. They were able to walk, talk, and breathe on the surface, and anyone who received an invitation to the underwater city could do the same. The magic or science behind this ability remained a mystery to many outside their realm.

The Queen approached where I stood. She wore such a big pearl on her necklace, and it was the first thing that I noticed. The opalescent sphere caught the light, refracting it in rainbows. The sight of the pearl was only pushed to the background by the sight of the tentacles flowing from her dress. They moved independently, like living extensions of her body. Her face looked the same as any mortal siren, with high cheekbones and luminous eyes, and she looked displeased to see me, but I was ecstatic to see her. The familiarity of her features brought a strange comfort.

She stood in front of me with enough anger on her face to tell me that she did not return the sentiment. Her force of octo-guards surrounded her with the same displeasure. Octopus men in all different colors stood on two feet holding spears with shark fangs. Their weapons gleamed wickedly in the sun, clearly not for decoration.

"I received word you were coming, but not from you. I don't appreciate the unannounced visit during penance. Frankly, I don't appreciate the unannounced visit at all," the queen declared. The tentacles on her dress moved as if they had a mind of their own, curling and uncurling in agitation.

"I didn't realize there was something happening?" I felt embarrassed to have shown up in their land and not have considered something like that. I should have. The oversight was uncharacteristic and annoying.

"We are preparing our sacrifices for the upcoming cere-mony. They are being cleansed and prepped to give their lives by jumping into the entrance to the deep sea left by our Goddess," the Queen explained, her voice carrying the weight of ancient tradition.

"The entrance made when the water Goddess was thrown to the bottom of the sea?" I didn't want to sound as if I weren't listening, but I wanted to make sure I knew what was going on before I spoke. The clarification seemed necessary.

"Yes. Every year, the original families give up a member of their line as penance to our Goddess for failing to protect her from the Goddess of Chaos. You've picked a poor time to decide to seek an audience," she was still covered in annoyance, her eyes cold as the depths of the ocean.

"If you would allow it, I'd like to help. I agree that it was a poor choice not to seek information before I made an appearance; if you'd allow me, I'd like the chance to make it right. The last thing that I wanted to do was offend you. I came not just to seek information but to help your entire kingdom stay safe from a threat I am following. It's inappropriate for me to question anyone right now, but I think it would be as inappropriate for me to turn around and leave without offering the same kind of apology to my own family member," I offered, choosing my words carefully.

I wasn't in the realm when any of it happened. I wasn't around to stop Sahir from doing whatever she liked. My sisters hardly stood a chance in the state that they were in, but it didn't change the fact that the goddess they were mourning was someone who was part of my realm. She was part of Semper and a Goddess I was meant to help protect, too. She was part of my family in the same way. If apologies were being given, I should be giving one as well. It was the stolen ability to use my fate chains that held her at the bottom of the sea in a prison; even if I didn't do it myself, I still felt responsible. The weight of this guilt was something I carried everywhere.

Sina was right to give me the attitude; she was just wrong about where it should have been placed. I failed to get back sooner. To protect anyone faster. I was the only one of the four of us to not lose a single memory. Which meant I should be the one to have things fixed by now. The burden of remembering was sometimes heavier than I could bear.

"If I allow it, and you stay, you must start the fast now. We are not allowed to eat or drink until after the ceremony is over," she stipulated, her expression unchanging.

"That's no problem," I said, nodding my agreement.

I didn't need to eat their food anyway. I just enjoyed it. I needed sleep. That was how we recovered and healed. We slept deeper than any mortal did. The subtleties of our existence were often misunderstood.

"I know who you are," she warned, her voice dropping to a menacing whisper. "If you cause one single problem, we will not fail to harm a deity again."

I couldn't stop the smirk that formed from her words. The mortals amused me. I could crush her and her afterlife if I wanted to. The pulse of power in my veins reminded me how easy it would be. Yet some of them still held no fear for us. I admired the strength some of them carried. It was what kept me filled with hope for them and their future. They had such spark inside of them. The audacity was both foolish and admirable.

"Yes, ma'am," I bowed, the gesture both respectful and slightly mocking.

She gave me one last look and turned to leave with her guards, the sand shifting beneath their strange gaits.

I waited on the shore for Sina to arrive. I watched the ship shift back and forth with the waves, the wooden vessel looking small and fragile against the vastness of the ocean. The smaller boats carried other mortals and Sina ashore, the oars slicing through the water in rhythmic movements. When Sina arrived, I would join the water folk in their rituals. The thought brought both anticipation and dread.

"How dare you leave me behind!" Sina yelled. Even in anger, she stomped to me as if running or a light jog was beneath her. Her claws left deep impressions in the wet sand.

"You made it," I remarked, struggling to keep the amusement from my voice.

"No thanks to you! Did you think waiting here for me was some sort of gift?" Sina scoffed, her breath coming out in steamy puffs.

"I only waited because I already talked to the queen," I answered, keeping my tone neutral.

"Why did I come? Hm? If you were going to do all of this without me?" Sina growled, her scales rippling with irritation.

"I assumed it was because you enjoyed my company," I answered, the sarcasm slipping out before I could stop it.

She gave her loudest fake laugh. "Are you going to fill me in or not?"

"They are in the middle of a ceremony. We aren't to question anyone until it's over," I said, watching her reaction carefully.

"That's foolish! Do you think Nikola will agree to that? You can try to be nice to these mortals, but what will they care when they're all dead?" She widened her eyes at me in demand, her tail lashing behind her.

"I'm standing right here. I would protect them," I answered, my patience beginning to fray.

"From Nikola? The one thing that even your mother couldn't truly defeat?" Sina was mocking me now, her voice dripping with derision.

"If you don't want to be here, if you can't follow the terms of an agreement already made, then leave," I pointed back to the ship. "I can't smell any trace of him as it is."

"Of course, you can't. He's not a fool," Sina hissed, a small jet of frost escaping her nostrils.

I knew she wanted to get a rise out of me. She had to have known by now that she would not get one. She didn't rile me up by doing these things. She was upset, but I didn't see anything wrong with the things going on. The pettiness was beneath us both.

"Sina. You aren't to interrupt the mortal's ceremonies. They are important to them; I shouldn't have to tell you that. I should not have to explain that Mother will be back and that she will also consider these things important," I kept my face blank, though my fingers itched to form fists.

She shot air from her snout in anger and turned her back to me without another word. The frost in her breath crystallized in the air before dissipating.

I was going to leave her to pout. I was going to pretend I forgot she was around and wander into the city. A siren found me first. He walked to me with no confidence and smelled of only fear when he stopped in front of me. His scent was sharp with anxiety, almost overshadowing the natural brine of his skin. His skin was covered in shimmering scales. Orange and yellow hues that looked as if they were soaking in glitter and somehow still wet even on land. The patterns shifted with each movement, hypnotic in their beauty.

His arm extended to give me a letter, and I accepted it. The parchment felt damp and cool against my fingers. He did his best to walk away calmly, but the quickness behind his steps gave his true feelings away. The tension in his shoulders was visible even from behind. When his feet reached the water, he jumped in the air, and a tail formed.

The same fiery fall colors as the rest of his body covered where his feet once were. The splash of water should have been impressive, but I was all too disappointed to no longer be able to admire him. The transformation was both beautiful and sad, a return to his true form, but a departure from my presence.

I opened the wax seal in the shape of a siren tail and pulled the page from inside. The paper was surprisingly dry, considering its journey through the water.

Goddess of Fate,

I know why you have arrived. Meet me in the underwater city, and we can discuss ways to help each other. Inside are two pills. Get them wet, and they will turn into mechanical gills. Swim in the coral garden, and I will find you.

I closed the letter and shook the envelope until the two pills dropped into my hand. They were small and blue, innocuous-looking despite their potential importance. If I blindly listened to the letter, I could play right into Nikola's hands. It was a toss-up if the letter were an honest plea or a trap waiting for me. If I were smart, I would ignore it. I would say that there was nothing I needed to discuss with a mortal. Nothing they could offer me to make me walk straight into what could be my death. The rational decision was clear.

Luckily for me, I was smart and strong. So, I was going to answer the letter. The thrill of danger stirred my blood, and besides, sometimes the most dangerous path was the only one worth taking.

CHAPTER FOURTEEN
THE SECRETS THAT LAY UNDERWATER

MOIRA: PIRATE ISLE.

Moira is made up of three islands made by mortals who didn't agree with their own kingdoms. They live together outside of the rules and trades of other lands. They do not attend Orest. They teach each other the skills they know and often spend their time stealing anything else they need. They consider themselves free and honest.

HESPERIA

Sina was upset that I refused to relent on my stance. Her scales had been rippling with barely contained frustration since our arrival. She didn't want a wasted trip. She wanted to question everyone, diplomacy be damned. I considered her wise, intelligent, and logical. I saw her as someone to be trusted. However, her weakness was the same line of traits. Sometimes, she considered herself too wise and too smart, and she didn't allow anyone else's opinion to enter the conversation once her mind was set on something. The rigidity of her thinking was a wall between us.

This was hardly our first argument because of it. She had already left to wait on the ship, her tail lashing angrily behind her as she departed. I told her I would be more than a day, but she pretended to hear nothing, her antlers held high in defiance.

She had been hard to read since our reunion. I tried not to focus too hard on it. The distance between us was a wound I wasn't ready to examine too closely.

I stood on the sparkling shore on the opposite side of the island. The sand looked as if it was littered with glass the way it glinted, catching the sun's rays and throwing them back in brilliant flashes. The sun was rising as it left the sky pink over the water, painting the waves in shades of rose and gold. I could hardly focus on Sina and the situation between us with the Daxon hourglass in front of me. The beauty of this place was a momentary balm to my troubled thoughts.

The hourglass sat on a stand of stone wrapped in seaweed, the green tendrils swaying gently in the breeze. Inside of it was a miniature land. The castle, the homes, and the beach were inside of the top, and liquid filled the bottom, shimmering with an inner light. Daxon was different than any other kingdom because it wasn't just one land; it was two, controlled by the hourglass. The surface held the land, and when the hourglass was flipped, I would be thrown into the ocean and transported into the underwater city. For me, it wouldn't be upside down. My world would flip, but I was the only one who would feel it, and anyone else traveling with me, of course. The magic of it was both beautiful and terrifying.

I pulled out the mechanical gills and attached them to the back of my ears before I flipped the hourglass. The metal was cool against my skin, clinging to my flesh with a subtle tingling sensation. Water filled the city, and the ground shook. I watched the chunk of land shift, and the movement threw me onto the ground with it. The impact knocked the breath from my lungs. In a quick motion, the island flipped entirely, and I was tossed into the water. I held my breath out of habit, forgetting about the gills for a moment. The cold rush of water enveloped me, seeping through my clothes.

Jellyfish swarmed me and guided me forward, their translucent bodies pulsing with otherworldly light. They lit up the sea, but my body still felt lost. I was trying to adjust to breathing while I knew I was underwater. The sensation was disorienting, my lungs working as they normally would, drawing in what should have been water but felt like air. I was trying to process that I should have been upside down, but I was not, and I was in awe of the view in front of me. The disorientation was worth it for the spectacle that unfolded before me.

Some deities think they should have access to everything, but I felt differently. I was happy to see, by invitation, the underwater city. Towers of rock beat in by the water stood one after another, their surfaces smoothed by centuries of currents. Clam shells bigger than I believed they could become were crammed into different places on the rock formation, their iridescent interiors gleaming like pearl-lined rooms.

Starfish hung, luminescent, as lamp posts all around, their five arms casting a gentle glow across the underwater land-scape. Seaweed gardens covered what would be considered their ground, swaying rhythmically with the current, and schools of fish swam in and out, flashes of color against the blue-green backdrop.

The jellyfish guided me the rest of the way to the coral garden, where a gazebo made of seashells was placed. The structure was delicate yet sturdy, crafted from countless shells of every shape and size. A siren swam in after me; his peach skin was covered in red and green scales that matched his tail. The pattern was hypnotic, shifting with each movement. He wore a mask made of pearls that hid most of his face, though his eyes were visible, alert, and wary.

"What should I call you?" I asked, my voice carrying strangely through the water.

"Names are useless yet," he answered, his tone cautious. "If we form an alliance, then we can exchange them."

"I'm willing to listen," I said, keeping my expression neutral.

I wanted to remain hardened. I didn't want him to think that I was too enthusiastic. Even if I was. I wanted to have as many creatures of the realm on my side as I could gain. If I hadn't gotten information on Nikola, it would still not have been a wasted trip. The potential for alliance was too valuable to dismiss.

"I am part of a secret order trained and sent on one mission for my entire lifetime. To find the descendent of the water Goddess. She should be on the throne as our Queen, not the impostor that occupies it now. I know who and what you are. I know you can help me achieve my mission. I know that you can do it without failure. In exchange, I will vow my entire army to you. We will help you in any fight you ask," he proclaimed, his shoulders squared, his posture rigid with conviction.

"Then you are the general?" I inquired. "That's how you can make such a promise?"

"You'll have to trust me," the man answered, his tail swishing slowly in the current.

"I don't hand out blind trust," I stated, crossing my arms.

"Nikola was indeed here. Our current Queen gave a statement to the Fae that helped him become king and enter the high court," the man revealed, his voice dropping even lower.

"I want a name first," I demanded, unwilling to proceed without this small token of trust.

He stared at me with blue eyes through his mask as if to challenge me, but I stared back just as hard. The silence stretched between us, filled only with the soft sounds of the water. It was hard sometimes, with the way life was shaped now, to remember that I was one of the most powerful beings around. I wanted to help the mortals; I always had. I didn't realize that I would have to bow so many times as if I weren't powerful in order to do it. The indignity of it chafed.

He wavered as if he could read my thoughts, his posture softening slightly. "Alec."

"All right, Alec, you have a deal. I have one last question before we part ways. Explain to me how the water Goddess is trapped," I requested, settling on the stool inside the gazebo made of pink coral to make myself comfortable and give a clear picture that I was not ready to leave yet. The structure was cool beneath me, rougher than it appeared.

"She is chained to the sea floor by four fate chains. Each limb is held down, and so is her neck," Alec explained, his voice tight with restrained emotion.

"Have any of you reached her?" I asked, curiosity mingling with concern.

He looked at me as if I had lost my mind, incredulity evident even behind his mask. I hadn't. I wasn't fully informed of all the things that had gone on in the realm while I was not a part of it, and there weren't a lot of opportunities to become informed about everything else there was to do. The gaps in my knowledge were frustrating but unavoidable.

"There is a barrier around her that we cannot get through," Alex clarified, his fingers flexing with obvious frustration.

I nodded. "There's nothing else?"

"That's more than enough to keep us out and away from our Goddess," he frowned, a bitter edge to his words.

I didn't want to get their hopes up in case I failed, but if it was only fate chains, my fate chains, I should be able to release her. The realization sent a surge of hope through me.

Shouldn't I? The question lingered, unanswered.

"I have one more question," he ventured. "What are

counter gods? In helping save scrolls from the great library some of us have read things we do not understand."

I decided to skip the lecture and consider it mortal curiosity. His thirst for knowledge seemed genuine.

"Long ago the god of insanity and the goddess of starlight wanted to harness the power of the fate sisters. The goddess of starlight did succeed in the creation of four vessels. Four divine bodies capable of holding the power of the fate sisters, of taking their places. The goal was for starlight's creations to eat the hearts of the originals before the fate sisters killed them. When a false counter is too close to the real sister they grow weak and powerless. The goddess of moonlight however, put a sort of seal on the real fate sisters so that even if their heart was eaten they wouldn't be absorbed. It is a complicated history," I admitted, condensing millennia of conflict into a few sentences.

He watched me and took in my words, his gills fluttering with each breath. He nodded with satisfaction at them, his eyes wide with new understanding.

"I've been here long enough. I need to go, and you shouldn't linger, either," Alec advised, glancing nervously over his shoulder.

He swam away, kicking up bubbles with his tail, his form quickly disappearing into the blue distance. I didn't need to ask any other questions. If their queen was on Nikola's side, it was no wonder she was not pleased to see me. She would not take lightly my presence in the underwater city, either. I understood well enough that I had to stay playing by mortal rules while our lives were in such a fragile place. The precarious balance could tip at any moment.

Daxon had been through its fair share of trials. Sahir's daughter was the original creator and in a fit of jealousy, Sahir sent her daughter to the bottom of the sea. Ruri was successful in hiding the child born from the goddess of water and a mortal but the sirens spent years searching for the like to reunite their kingdom. The weight of their history pressed around me, as tangible as the water.

I was disappointed that my journey didn't come with my own tail. I had to swim with my own two feet, which felt clumsy and inefficient in this environment. My limbs moved sluggishly against the water's resistance.

I didn't have time to keep wallowing before the space around me started to glitch. The water, the city, it all shifted into blocks of black and white. The sudden change was jarring, reality fragmenting before my eyes. My body felt heavy, as if I were no longer floating in the water. A pressure built around me, squeezing the breath from my lungs. The glitching kept happening in front of me, and it sent shivers through my mind until everything was black and white, like an old photograph come to life.

"I have missed you," Nikola said. His voice came to me in waves, distorted yet unmistakable. "I'd be lying if I said I didn't expect this. I knew after so long together that you'd miss me, too." His echoed laugh came next, wrapping around me like cold fingers.

"I don't miss you; I want to kill you," I declared. My voice sounded the same as his. As if it were traveling through something that distorted it, stretched and warped.

"You and I aren't that different. When you can see that, we can work together," Nikola suggested, his form flickering in and out of existence.

"We are nothing alike," I scoffed, disgust rising like bile in my throat.

"Aren't we? We're both willing to do things others would consider too far in order to get what we want," Nikola challenged, his voice insidiously reasonable.

"The difference is you did it for yourself, and I do it for my family," I insisted, my hands clenching into fists.

The shift in my tone was the only rise he would pull from me. I wouldn't give him the satisfaction of seeing me truly angry. He was right about one thing: we had been together for so long that I knew him well. He left me in a locket, but he didn't leave me completely alone. The memories of our time together were etched into my very being, impossible to erase.

"Wrong. You've convinced yourself that doing things for others is not the same as doing it for yourself, but it is. You spin your mind in webs to convince yourself that you're right-eous. I'm only what you would look like if you stopped doing that. I've seen you murder without hesitation. I've heard your thoughts, and I've not forgotten the things you did in our first lifetime. You've so easily forgotten that. Why? Because you and I aren't that different. We want what we want. You could have so much if you opened your eyes in a mirror," Nikola taunted before disappearing into shifted black and white blocks, his parting words lingering in the now-empty space.

The mechanical gills placed behind my ears shifted and dropped into the water, still grey, to a place that I could not see. I scratched at my throat as I tried to pull in air, panic rising as my lungs began to burn. A black abyss opened under me, and I felt myself fall. The speed sent a wave over me, wind rushing past my ears, and I was encompassed in dark-ness. The sensation of falling seemed endless, a descent into oblivion.

I sat up, gasping and pulling in air. Everything around me was so bright that I could hardly see, my eyes struggling to adjust after the darkness. Sweat slicked my skin, my heart pounding in my chest.

"Hesperia? Are you all right?"

I kept blinking, but my sight was slow to come back. The world was a blur of color and light.

"Can you hear me?"

I sniffed the air. My nose was more reliable than my sight anyway. The familiar scent triggered something deep within me.

"She's awake."

I stopped when my face was against the one beside me. My sight was coming back, and sky-blue eyes were the first thing that I saw. Moon white hair was next, and I took the deepest breath through my nose that I could. He still smelled of milk and honey, the scent as familiar to me as my own.

"You smell amazing," I whispered, the words escaping before I could stop them.

"Thank you," Coy responded, his expression a mixture of confusion and something else I couldn't quite name.

"Where am I?" I asked, reluctantly pulling back slightly.

"The Shadows of Justice headquarters," he explained, his voice carefully neutral.

"How?" I questioned. I had yet to remove my face from his, drawn to his presence like a moth to flame.

"You were dropped through a rift in the roof," Coy clarified, his eyes meeting mine.

That explained the darkness. The memory of falling returned, a phantom sensation that made my stomach lurch.

"You've been asleep for three days. How are you feeling?" he inquired, concern evident in his voice.

"Three days?" I exclaimed, my voice rising with alarm. "I was just in Daxon!"

"Sina should be here soon. I can assure you that you were not, just in Daxon," Coy stated, gently putting distance between us.

I could feel that he still didn't remember me the way I remembered him. The hollow where our connection should be ached like a physical wound. The Coy I remembered would have moved in closer. He would have had his lips on mine the instant that I was close enough. My Coy would have had his hands all over me, his touch both comforting and electric.

Even the Coy I knew before the realms shifted together was closer than we were. That Coy didn't know exactly who I was but he at least knew that he liked me. That he wanted to be close to me. This Coy was burdened by the same things that weighed on me. The distance between us felt insurmountable.

He hated that he failed. He hated that he couldn't have already fixed it. I knew because it's how I felt, too. The parallel was both comforting and painful. My hope sat with how many times he glanced down at my lips. There had to be a part of him that was not as indifferent as he tried to make me believe he was. There had to be a part of him that remembered me in some capacity. I was willing to wait. The patience cost me, but I would pay it gladly.

"Milk baths used to be your favorite," he whispered. He was still looking at my lips while he spoke, a flash of something like recognition in his eyes.

I resisted the urge to move myself forward until we were fully touching. The temptation was almost overwhelming.

"I cleared Koa. He's not a traitor," Coy announced before he met my eyes. He pushed his chair back and walked out of the room, the door closing softly behind him.

I could wait. I would have patience. I wouldn't pressure him or his memory. I'd wait an endless amount of lifetimes if I needed to. It didn't change the hurt I felt every time I thought we might get close again, and we didn't. A little piece of my heart chipped away every single time I was caught in a moment like that. The ache was becoming familiar, a constant companion.

Koa was not the one that I was cautious of. I was happy that Coy was keeping busy, but I was still hopeful that it would somehow trigger him. The possibility, however slim, kept me going.

Coy turned himself to the noise that was coming from the other side of the door that held us in together. He didn't look back at me when he stood and left. I followed him out. Things were a lot more crowded. Astra talked to Sina, their voices low but intense. Vespera sat in a corner, alone. She looked beyond annoyed, her fingers drumming impatiently against her thigh. Aero and Fennic were, in their own word, hardly aware of any other presence, absorbed in their own conversation.

"Hesperia! You're awake!" Astra called out, her voice cutting through the background noise.

Only Sina acknowledged her and looked in my direction, her antlers tilting in recognition.

"What happened?" Astra questioned, concern evident in her pink eyes.

"Nikola did something; I'm not sure what it was. He stood in front of me, spoke to me, and then I woke up here," I admitted, the memory still fragmented and confused.

"He spoke to you!" Sina exclaimed, her scales rippling with alarm.

"Did he try to hurt you?" Astra asked, moving closer to examine me.

I shook my head. "If he wanted to, he could have tried, but here I am," I said, spreading my arms to demonstrate my unharmed state.

"Did he give you anything important?" Sina pressed, her tone urgent.

"He just taunted me," I replied, unwilling to share the details of his words. They had struck too close to home.

She looked disappointed. Her scales dulled slightly with her reaction. She wasn't nearly as dissatisfied as I was. He was in front of me and slipped away. As upset as she was, it was nothing in comparison to what I felt. I hardly put in any effort to truly stop him. The missed opportunity gnawed at me. He was right about one thing: we had spent enough time together over the years to get to know each other well. I would do more than I'd admit if it meant success was guaranteed. The thought was unsettling in its truth.

"Is there anything else we should know?" Sina questioned, her eyes searching my face.

"I have nothing to offer," I admitted, the confession tasting bitter.

"I do," Astra interjected. "I somehow envisioned that we would all have more time together than we have. I think I sit with Coy when I think about it. I'm sick of sitting so idle. Ruri and Sage are sensitive, Shivani, too. The rest of us? What's stopping us from making real moves? I took things into my own hands. I'm taking Aero and Fennic to wake Dahlia up. We're going to get her out of the tree."

"Can you do that?" Sina asked, her voice sharp with disbelief.

"I can't guarantee that we can, but we haven't really tried, have we? In fact I don't think we truly tried much. We've done a lot of talking, waiting, and watching others make big moves. We did a lot of telling others they have to be calm and wait," Astra explained, looking between the two of us, her gaze challenging.

"They agreed? Did you tell them it could kill them? Unlocking a seal with that kind of power?" I asked, unable to keep the concern from my voice.

The way she looked at me told me what I needed to know. Her eyes slid away from mine, guilt briefly flashing across her features. If Fennic and Aero were aware of a consequence, she didn't make it as clear as it should have been.

Something inside of me twitched with the need to speak up. To allow them the chance to make the most informed choice they could, but a louder part of me said that she was right. Some kind of sacrifices needed to start happening in order for us to make any sort of changes. Nikola wasn't asking any what they wanted. The pragmatism of this approach both repelled and attracted me.

Would it be so bad if he was right? Would it keep me up at night? Would I lose time thinking of all the ways I should have proved him wrong instead? The questions echoed through my mind, unanswerable.

I looked back to the two men chatting and laughing before glancing back at Astra. The two of them were bonding well, their faces animated with genuine joy. If they did die, they would have lived well. The rationalization felt hollow, but necessary.

They were the closest brothers I had ever seen, their bond palpable even from across the room.

"This is outrageous!" Sina roared, her voice vibrating through the room. "You're willing to let others die because you think you're above the rules? All of the sisters must be awake before touching Dahlia. That's how it works. They must know who they are so that they can safely break the seal. You're seeking casualties that don't need to be! Rushing won't put you in a better position. Bad men make poor, quick choices, and it's why they lose. Do you want to join them in that?"

Sina stormed off, and her stomping paws shook the building, dust falling from the ceiling in small clouds. Her righteous anger was a tangible force, leaving us in stunned silence.

Astra watched me, but I wanted to speak first. I didn't need persuasion. My mind was already made up.

"Do it. Tell no one else," I whispered, the words barely audible yet heavy with consequence.

Astra nodded and grabbed my hand, her grip tight with shared purpose. If the two of them died, it would be Astra and I that carried the guilt. I was willing to do it. Astra clearly was, too. I would do what I needed to if they died, but I agreed with Astra. I couldn't take another lifetime of remaining passive and pretending we tried to make a difference. I wanted my sisters. I wanted my mother. I needed my lover. The hunger for resolution was consuming me from within.

I was willing to kill to do it. The admission should have frightened me more than it did.

"Hesperia?" Vespera interrupted, her approach tentative,

as if she were interrupting something. Her eyes darted between Astra and me, curiosity evident in her gaze.

"Yes?" I cleared my throat, releasing Astra's hand.

"I wanted to ask you a favor. I was told you can bring things back from the dead if you have a bone? Can you bring Sage's sprites back? I know there are bones in the cursed forest. I think it could trigger her memory without any of us pushing it on her," Vespera suggested, hope lighting her eyes.

I clapped my hands together, and she jumped at the sudden sound. Excitement rushed through me at the possibility.

"That's a great idea!" I exclaimed. "I'm ready to go when you are!"

The chance to act, to do something concrete rather than wait, was irresistible. Perhaps Nikola was right, perhaps we weren't so different after all. The thought should have troubled me more than it did.

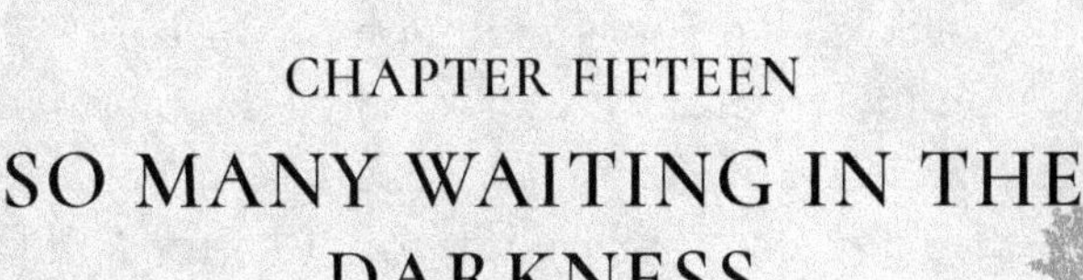

CHAPTER FIFTEEN

SO MANY WAITING IN THE DARKNESS

SOLARIS: THE LAND OF LIGHT.

The land of light has been ruled by the false God of Life since its creation. The land has undergone multiple changes and terraforms in its lifetime with the help of other deities. The God of life largely lacked the ability to do it all on his own. His single success was helping bring the God of death into existence when the Goddess of Starlight slipped on her hold over the Goddess of the Moon, and she was able to aid in his creation. The Goddess of Chaos was the most notable help in the boom, and that is Solaris. She offered her abilities and assistance in exchange for the God of life's unquestioned loyalty. He still wears the mark of their bond to the current day.

SAGE

I could not stop my fingers from tapping the tabletop, the rhythmic sound amplifying my anxiety. There were crates of stolen crystals in the alleyway just a few feet from where I sat. The wooden boxes contained enough power to level half the

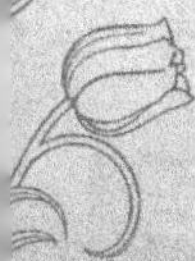

city, hidden behind a pile of refuse. One wrong person saw it, and there would be a lot more bodies than there already had been since this venture started. The thought made my mouth go dry.

A mug of blended apple and mushroom wine steamed in front of me, the aroma sweet yet earthy. The mushrooms of the area had known effects, and this tavern enjoyed using them to their benefit. I enjoyed it, too. I ensured the wine I ordered would ease my anxiety. I wanted the memories of the temple gone and as far away from me as possible. The screams still echoed in my head when I closed my eyes.

I wanted the meeting with the King over, too. The anticipation was almost worse than the meeting itself.

I sipped from the mug, looking at the door every few minutes. The warm liquid slid down my throat, bringing temporary relief. One of my mercenaries occupied the ally with directions to where the crystals were being stored. Maybe I'd get lucky, and that would be enough. He would have one of his men take them, and I'd go on about my business. The hope was thin but persistent.

I sighed and threw my head back straight into the arm of the King. The impact made me jolt forward.

"Shit," I muttered, the word slipping out before I could catch it.

He sat down across from me, his cloak rustling as he settled. "Watch your mouth."

Who did he think he was? The indignation rose hot in my chest.

"Did your men meet the puppies out back?" I asked. I tried my best to watch my words in case anyone was listening, my voice barely above a whisper.

He nodded under his cloak, the fabric shifting slightly. "Indeed. Beautiful purebred samples. As expected from your work."

"Good. I'll be on my way then," I said, already shifting to stand.

Before I could get to my feet, he held out his leg and stopped me. The pressure against my shin was light but unmistakable.

"I wasn't done yet," he said. "The temple of magic is next." His voice was lower than before, edged with something that made my skin crawl.

I shook my head. "No, it is not. Not for me. Find someone else." The words came out firmer than I felt.

"You'll do it, or I'll put your head on my throne," the King said simply, no emotion in his voice.

My eyes narrowed against my control. "Do you know what I dealt with just to get you there?" I tried my best to lower my voice, but the pounding in my chest made it difficult. "You underestimate the flame you're playing with."

"I am the only flame to fear," the king grabbed my mug and took a drink for himself, his lips curling in distaste at the flavor. "I will pay you double to clear that temple. Orest will be sending new guardians. It'll be a quick in and out for you." He leaned in closer, his breath hot against my face. "Are you going to let all the girls under your care that are still alive starve?"

I wanted to flip the entire table. To make him eat his words. I wanted to shove the mug he kept picking up down his throat until he choked on it. I didn't. I wasn't a fighter, and I knew it. The restraint made my muscles ache with tension.

"It better be double," I pointed, my finger trembling slightly.

I saw his smirk from under his cloak, a flash of white against shadow. He stood and left with the same smug demeanor he entered with, his boots making no sound on the worn wooden floor.

I hardly had the chance to take a breath before his place was quickly filled with Onyx, who also stole my mug. Where the king took a sip or two, he chugged, his throat working as he drained half the contents. I watched droplets hit his well-kept beard, catching in the red-brown hair. I crossed my arms. They needed to stay close and tight, protecting me from the world. From him.

"You owe me a drink and an explanation of why you're following me!" I demanded, my voice sharper than intended.

"Can't you just accept I'm a wonderful protector and you're terrible at making deals?" He asked, setting the mug down with a thud.

"Onyx." My tone was warning enough.

"What would you like, Darlin? Help with another temple? My life story?" He said, leaning back in his chair. "I only wanted to check on you and see how things went."

"They went like any royal being told no would go," I answered, avoiding his gaze.

Onyx reached across the table and touched my hand. The contact was electric, but not in a pleasant way. I knew he was trying to comfort me, but I didn't find it comforting. I found pain in his touch. Flashes ran through my mind of my head being held underwater. Of pain and panic, and death. I couldn't breathe, and I knew it was the end. I felt betrayed and surprised. So much sadness. The images were vivid, terrifying in their clarity.

I moved my hand away from him and held it close to my chest. "I need to go," I said, my voice shaking.

I looked down at my hand, and small blue markings started to appear, like tree branches spreading across my skin. The sight sent a jolt of fear through me.

By the time my mind felt settled, I found myself in front of Vespera's bookstore. I didn't know how I had gotten in front of it from the tavern or how I lost so much time. I only knew I felt as if I needed to be there. The lapse in memory was disturbing, but the need to see her was stronger.

I pushed the crimson-painted door open, and when I

stepped inside, three cats cornered me, their tails high and curious. The smell of mushroom coffee filled the air, rich and earthy, and plants hung from every corner. Vines climbed the walls and cascaded from shelves. They were strung along the ceiling as well, creating a living canopy.

I couldn't be sure how big the building was on the inside because the shelves covered in books went for what felt like miles, disappearing into shadow and green. A kitten clawed its way up my pants and stopped once it was perched on my shoulder, its tiny claws digging into my cloak. If ever there was a place that fit Vespera, it was indeed her bookstore. The organized chaos mirrored her mind.

"I'll be with you in a minute. Coffee or tea is on the side table, free," Vespera called from somewhere in the maze of books.

I slid myself into a row of bookcases. I unclipped my cloak and hung it on a corner. I pulled the mask that covered my face down onto my neck and let it hang. My black hair tumbled out with nothing left to hold it back, the weight of it familiar against my shoulders. I grabbed a book and sat down in a chair, one leg on the other. I wanted to look cool and casual. I didn't want her to know that my heart was beating so fast it would soon bust out of its home. The thudding was so loud I was sure she could hear it.

I definitely did not want her to think that I was blushing or maybe even a bit nervous to be visiting her at her store. The thought made my cheeks burn hotter.

"Something tells me it might be your first time holding a book," Vespera whispered from behind. She removed the book from my hand, flipped it around, and handed it back. "Now it's correct."

Her voice in my ear made me jump, heat rushing to my face.

"I wasn't paying attention. I know how to hold a book," I

stuttered, taking the volume back and staring blindly at the now-right-side-up text.

Even the way she peered over the book at me made my stomach flip. Her eyes sparkled with amusement, crinkling at the corners. I always thought she was beautiful, but she was the smartest person I knew, too, and it's what made me so nervous around her. The way her baby blue bob was shaped perfectly around her face made my eyes fill with joy, and the way her eyes matched was a beautiful picture to watch. It was her mind, though, that was the biggest delight. Her intelligence shone brighter than any crystal I'd ever stolen.

I watched her sit beside me and lean back, her movements graceful. "I didn't expect to see you here today."

"I thought I'd do something nice for you," I answered, trying to sound casual. "I was in town, so."

I was truly doing something nice for myself. I could have slipped and landed on her lips and given us both a bigger gift if I could be sure she would want it, too. The thought was both thrilling and terrifying.

If I told her that I was having visions, would she think I was insane? The markings on my hand had faded, but the memory remained.

Her eyebrow lifted with a twitch as if she heard my thoughts, and we both looked at the ground. "What is it you need from me?" she asked, her tone softer than before.

I sighed and sat up. "Please don't take it like that." The disappointment in her voice stung more than it should have.

"Stop." She held her hand up, palm out. "You haven't spoken a word to me since the temple. I know you aren't here to just spend time with me. What do you need?"

"I wanted you to back me up at today's meeting," I confessed, swallowing harder than normal.

"Another job so fast?" She asked, concern replacing disappointment.

I nodded. "The king wants the crystals from the temple of

magic next. I don't want to take it. The pay isn't high enough. He says Orest is rotating new guardians, but-"

"But it wasn't guardians that scared you before," she finished, her eyes searching mine.

I looked at her but didn't speak. What could I say? That I'd seen things no mortal should see? That I was still haunted by the screams?

"I do not know why you felt the need to ask. I'd follow you in any direction you took me. Luckily for you, I agree stealing from the temples isn't a wise choice," Vespera said, her hand briefly touching mine.

"Good," I agreed, relief washing over me.

Vespera stood up and rolled her shoulders. I heard her neck crack before she put speed behind her steps. She stopped at bookcase after bookcase, grabbing random books—too many for me to keep track of, too fast to count. Her fingers danced along spines with practiced familiarity. She filled her arms and sat them on a table before making a new pile. A wave of fear rushed over me when I realized they were all for me, and I sunk back into my seat, tossing my head back. The thought of so much reading was somehow more daunting than facing the king.

"When the meeting is over, you can take a look at these. It's everything you need to get started on your reading jour-ney," Vespira announced, hands on her hips, pride evident in her voice.

"Started? This pile is more than a start," I scoffed, eyeing the mountain of books with trepidation.

She brushed me off and grabbed my cloak. She tossed it to me with a look I understood. It told me not to hang my junk on her precious items. I couldn't help but smirk. I threw my cloak back on, the familiar weight settling on my shoul-ders. She and I put our hoods up in sync, and I followed her out. The coordination made my chest warm with something I didn't want to name.

"I'll organize the books for you by fun. Some of them have inns with one bed. Some are lost princesses. Some just make you wonder for days about what you read," Vespera talked so quickly that I could hardly take her seriously. Her enthusiasm was infectious, though.

Was she nervous as well? The thought was oddly comforting. It would be better to keep the idea that I was hallucinating to myself for now. Some things were better left unsaid.

She kept talking, but I could hardly listen. The blue branching pattern on my hand flashed in my memory. I knew it wouldn't be a struggle to get her to speak up at the meeting, but I would be lying if I said I still didn't feel a small ounce of guilt. I had never backed us out of anything before. I made this group; I made the rules. I was strict with the rules. I was punished for breaking the rules. I told everyone it was always black and white, yes or no. Now, I was the one bringing to the table the idea that we break them. I asked questions and got involved, and now I had to deal with it. The hypocrisy sat bitter on my tongue.

I let her stay in front of me and enter first. It wasn't that I was scared of them. I was disappointed in myself, and it was a new feeling. This group was my first priority in everything I did and every rule I made and choice I took was what I considered to be their best interest. To help move them forward. To help move us together into riches fatter than the King's. Now, I had to give up enough coin to let us live in luxury for more than the year's end. The loss felt like a physical ache.

"Hurry up," Vespera said as she leaned out of the door, her impatience clear.

I sucked in my cheeks and took one last sigh for the coin about to be lost and entered Wraths Tea and Taco's Tavern. I paid a high price to the stingy gnomes that ran the place to make sure it was only us for the evening. The girls had already pushed tables together and crowded around a packed table-top. The smell of their food filled every corner of the space— spiced meat, fresh vegetables, the yeasty scent of ale—and fires roared in hearths along the walls, casting dancing shadows across the room. It would have been the most perfect entrance I could have come into. If I wasn't feeling my heart break over what it would cost me on top of what I already paid. In coin and life. I could already hear those starlight-forsaken gnomes complaining and adding fees for every tune they had to listen to. Their greed was legendary even by my standards.

I pulled out a chair at the head of the table. Feeling like the only responsible one sitting among a crowd of feral toddlers. I shrugged to myself, looking at all the food. I may as well have just one taco before we get into it all. One small little treat for emptying my pockets on all of this. The meat steamed invit-ingly, chunks of juicy beef mixed with peppers and spices.

"Ah, ah. I think not," Lia slapped my hand, and all the contents, down to every last vegetable, dropped out of the back of my taco. "Not before discussions are finished." She glared, her green eyes sharp.

I tossed the shell that was once filled to the brim with the warmest, juiciest meat and stood back up. I slammed my fist on the table once, twice. "Shut it already!"

"Rude," Lilac grumbled, tossing her feet on the table, her boots leaving marks on the polished wood.

"I called the meeting so we can talk about the next job that was offered and the last one we did," I cleared my throat, trying to project authority. "The last one was a close call. Closer than any of us there want to admit. It paid well, but some of us won't be able to hold any of the coins." The memory of the bodies made my voice catch.

"Less to split," Lia joked, her laugh grating on my nerves.

My eyes lowered in her direction. "The next job will be even worse."

Cheers came from all around, glasses raised in anticipation.

"Finally, some fun!" Arles shouted, her face flushed with excitement.

"I'm getting nowhere with you all," I crossed my arms, frustration building. "I want to deny the job. Before you all start with me, I know it's against the rules-"

"Rules you made up," Lia interrupted, pointing her fork at me accusingly.

"I know!" I pointed with my eyes. "But I don't want to die! All right! I want to eat tacos and drink mushroom wine. I don't want angry gods cutting me up for their dinner after I steal their prized possessions!" I whined, the words bursting out more desperately than I intended.

"Gods?" Arles scoffed. "I bet they'd fetch a good price!"

"I know," I threw my head back. "I had the same thought!"

"Even if we all went together, do you really think we could kill a God with no magic of our own? I know you all used the few crystals we had for scams!" Vespera said, standing up, her voice cutting through the chatter.

I wiped a hand across my forehead and sighed, sitting myself back down. I was glad she stepped in. I was starting to convince myself that it might be worth it for the coin, too. The voice of reason in a sea of greed.

"If we did have any crystals left, it would only be illusion stones, and that would only get us so far. What if it was the God of knowledge? Those wouldn't work. It's the goddess of magic's temple that we are talking about robbing. What if the rumors are true?" Vespera said, looking around, her gaze intense.

"They aren't!" Lilac yelled, slamming her mug down.

"They could be," I said, remembering the strange visions, the blue markings on my skin.

"They aren't," she repeated, stubbornness in every line of her body.

"What if we go in thinking that and then find out too late that they actually are true? What if we go in there and the ghost of the goddess really does haunt her statue? What if the gods that loved her come through the temple and eat you? Who will take your shares of the coins?" Vespera glanced at me when she finished speaking, a small nod meant only for me.

"Let's take it to a vote!" Lia yelled, standing on the table, her boots among the food. "All in favor of coin and maybe catching a god?"

All hands went into the air, including Vespera's, which slowly lifted in the hopes that I wouldn't see it. The betrayal hit like a physical blow. I couldn't stop myself from slamming the plate that held my once-together taco across the table into the disaster the group had already created. The crash was satisfying, if only for a moment. I couldn't believe it. I'm trying my best to keep them all alive. Doing what I can to take responsibility for the loss in coin. Paying for their whole evening, even Vespera stabs me in the back. I hope she doesn't think I'm still going to do all that reading after this. She can pick five of those books now. That's all I'll accept. The petty thought was small comfort.

"We took vows. We know what we signed up for. Now, let's honor them with a drink!" Lilac yelled, raising her mug high.

"Exactly! Now it's time for the real fun the boss paid for for the night!" Arles said, lifting her cup, ale sloshing over the rim.

Coin, coin, coin, it's all they think about. Who cares if we all die or if I go broke before I can die? I crossed my arms, hardly holding myself from kicking my foot into the table just to feel better. I didn't think my night could get any worse, but I was wrong. There was a familiar breath breathing into my hair. I sat up and turned around to see Onyx smirking, his orange eyes gleaming with amusement.

"Who invited you here?" I demanded, heat rising to my face.

"You did," he said, his smile widening.

"I did not. I would not," I insisted, the lie obvious even to me.

He pointed me to the rest of the room, and when I turned around, there was a whole group of men carrying axes and swords, shirtless with tight leather cut-offs, hardly holding in their bottoms. The sight was as ridiculous as it was unexpected.

No, she did not. Did she spend my coin on men? I turned back around, fury building.

"You came with them?" I demanded, my voice rising.

He nodded, entirely too pleased with himself.

"You haven't dressed the part then. I won't pay you," I said, looking him up and down pointedly.

"I've already been paid," he said, patting his pocket, the jingle of coins unmistakable.

"I'm going home," I announced, pushing my chair back. No matter how good he would have looked dressed like the others, I wasn't staying. The thought itself was treacherous.

Before I could stand up, he put his hands on my shoulders and sat me back down. The pressure was gentle but firm. I watched him make a plate of tacos and slide them in front of me. He didn't speak, only nodded his head in command. If he thought I'd listen to that, he was wrong. I paid him, without knowledge, and through Arles, to be here. He was mine to demand around, not the other way around, I thought, taking a bite of taco. It was so good, the flavors exploding on my tongue. He wasn't even dressed right. Who did he think he was? Taking a job and not even listening to the guidelines.

Where was the wine? I looked around, suddenly desperate for a drink to wash everything away, the fear, the frustration, the blue markings that had appeared on my skin. Just for tonight, I wanted to forget it all.

CHAPTER SIXTEEN

SOME AREN'T MEANT TO HOLD SECRETS

THE ORDER OF THE ARCANE TOME

The Order of the Arcane Tome runs the temple for the Goddess of Magic. Located in Ashbell, Inola, the Goddess of Spring, is the high priestess and is in charge of all that goes on inside the temple walls. The royal family works in close relationships with the temple for all matters related to Ashbell. They stay true to the teachings left by the Goddess of Magic: heal and make allies. As a result, the temple holds many relics and secrets for other lands.

SAGE

I slept at Vespera's bookstore. She gave me her guest room, the invitation extended with casual grace that belied its significance. I loved receiving the offer, but I hadn't realized her home was above her shop. The outside did not allow me to believe that she had an entire home inside. If I hadn't laid my own eyes on it, I'd never believe it. The entire place was, somehow, exactly what I pictured for her.

Velvet and forest green covered every surface with hints

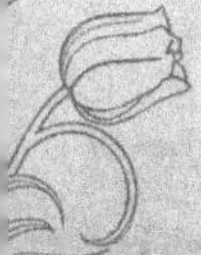

and highlights of brown. The fabrics were rich and inviting, begging to be touched. Perfectly potted plants decorated every nook with hand-molded candles accenting them, their scents mingling in the air, earthy and sweet.

Her home was like walking through the dimly lit woods. I could have made a hot cup of tea and watched the view from her upstairs window for the entire day and never become tired of it. The way the light filtered through the leaves outside cast dappled patterns across the floor, ever-changing and mesmerizing.

Vespera was an even split of mysterious and predictable. If one day she and I could somehow feel the same about each other openly, I hoped she would make our home feel like the one she kept. The thought was both terrifying and exhilarating.

Warm, like home. Like I had always belonged inside of it, with her. The certainty of this feeling scared me more than any job I'd ever taken.

Even though I was more comfortable than I had been in a long time, I hadn't slept as well as I had hoped I would. I tossed and turned because every time I closed my eyes, I saw myself being held underwater, and I only woke up seconds before I died.

The sensation of drowning was so vivid, the burning in my lungs, the panic, the realization that this was the end. Every time I woke up, the blue markings on my skin glowed for a few brief minutes, pulsing with an inner light that illuminated the dark room, but they never grew larger. I was happy for that small blessing because I needed them to stay hidden. I could wear gloves for now to keep them secret. The leather ones I'd picked up in Erebus would do.

I was using the dreams as a crutch in the end. I doubted I would have slept without the newly added nightmares. I had too much to think about, my mind racing with questions and observations. It was easy to keep secrets I didn't know that I was holding. That's why I made the rule for the guild not to ask questions. It wasn't that way anymore. The ignorance I'd once cultivated was crumbling around me.

I couldn't pretend I was a secret keeper. I was not. I was dying to talk about the fact that I knew the masked king's name was Nikola. The knowledge burned in my chest, demanding to be shared. I needed to tell someone that I was now being haunted by visions that felt more like memories than dreams.

I was cracking under the guilt of the temple deaths and didn't want to do another temple job ever again. The screams still echoed in my ears in quiet moments. Something told me that I needed to keep the marks on my hand a secret, but it was painful to listen. On top of that, I still seemed to be the only one who knew Onyx held dragon eggs. The web of secrets was suffocating.

A knock sounded at the door as if it were fated timing. The soft rap against wood was like divine intervention. A sign that I should open up and spill the things I needed so that I didn't overflow. A nudge from the universe that maybe sharing could bring Vespera and I closer. Letting her in and opening up to her could give me the help I needed in deciding which person I should pursue more seriously. The temptation was almost overwhelming.

"Are you awake?" Vespera called through the door, her voice muffled.

"Yes!" I answered, sitting up in bed, the sheets pooling around my waist.

She slowly creaked the door open and stepped inside. The morning light caught in her baby blue hair, making it glow like a halo around her face. She was already dressed, her clothing neat and pressed, while I was still in my rumpled sleeping clothes.

"Are you all right?" she asked, concern evident in her eyes as she took in my disheveled appearance.

I hesitated. I knew I should have kept at least one mystery, at least one thing, so that I could preserve my own sense of reserved mystery, but I didn't. The dam broke. I opened my mouth, and words poured out as if they were a waterfall, unstoppable and reckless.

"Did you know Onyx has dragon eggs? He says that he's protecting them. That it's important. I've just never heard of dragon eggs being allowed outside of Ashbell. It's strange, right? He has to be doing something shadier. Do you think he's helping poachers? Maybe he's running a side business stealing and selling dragons? I'm also having the craziest nightmares, and then these lines started showing up." I lifted my hand so that the blue markings were visible and instantly regretted it. The branching patterns glowed faintly even in daylight, a luminescent blue against my skin.

I didn't keep a single crumb to myself. The confession left me feeling exposed, vulnerable in a way I rarely allowed myself to be.

Vespera watched me as if she were waiting to see if I had anything else to say before she opened her mouth. She was patient and kind. She was smart, too. I looked like a fool right now, and she looked like a statue that would be sat in the middle of a town square to be admired for centuries. Her composure only highlighted my chaos.

"I'm sure that all came out sounding messy," I chuckled, trying to regain some dignity.

I was suddenly feeling less like a fool and more like a nervous teenager talking to a crush for the first time. I felt the heat from my cheeks rising, betraying me further.

Was I blushing? Do not reach up and check. Do not do it. I mentally commanded myself, knowing that would only make it worse.

"Do the nightmares scare you?" she asked, her voice gentle as she moved to sit at the edge of the bed, the mattress dipping slightly under her weight.

"While I'm inside of them, yes. As soon as I opened my eyes, no. I'm not scared anymore," I answered, hoping that made me sound brave to her.

"If you were seeking my opinion, I would keep the markings and the dragon eggs to yourself," she advised, her expression serious.

"Do you know what it is? Or why he has the eggs?" I felt my heart on the edge of bursting, the questions tumbling out before I could stop them.

"Do you really think I should answer those questions? Knowing that you'll need to talk to someone about it?" Vespera crossed her arms and titled her posture, one eyebrow raised in challenge.

She made a point, but I didn't have to like it. The truth of her words stung.

"Can you tell me anything? I'm not trying to say he stole them, but honestly, he probably stole them. How else would he have gotten them?" Every word I said had my hands flinging back and forth, gesturing wildly as if movement could make my point clearer.

"Maybe you should go tell him that you feel like telling everyone about what you saw. It could motivate him to give you some answers," she suggested, a slight smile playing at her lips.

She was right. Of course, she was right. Maybe if I made him think that I was going to start talking, fear would scare him into telling me what he was actually up to. The strategy was underhanded but effective.

"Do you have a specific reason this is bothering you now? Do you think this has anything to do with the guild taking the control of decisions out of your hand?" She looked at me, already knowing the answer, with a smirk on her face.

The observation hit too close to home. I stood abruptly, nearly tangling myself in the sheets.

"I don't have time for this. It's a long walk to the black-smiths," I said, trying to sound busy and important.

I grabbed my cloak from where it hung by the door, the familiar weight settling on my shoulders.

"It's a block away," Vespera pointed out, amusement dancing in her eyes.

"Gotta go!" I called back to her, not daring to look back as I fled.

I threw my hood up and jogged to the city center. It was as bustling and busy as usual, merchants calling their wares, children darting between stalls, the scent of fresh bread and roasting meat wafting from nearby taverns. The guard outside of the door to Onyx let me in unchecked. I wasn't surprised by that, but I hadn't expected to see the shop empty. Onyx seemed to always be inside guarding the fires. The silence was eerie, broken only by the soft crackling of flames in the forge.

I should have used that moment as a learning experience. I should have turned and left, returning when he was present. I did not.

I lowered myself into the fireplace that had black steel bars around it, the heat from the dying embers warming my face. I clipped the bar holding it closed. When I pulled the bars open, there the eggs sat. Two dragon eggs that I knew shouldn't have been with him.

One was a deep crimson that seemed to pulse with inner fire, the other midnight blue with specks that glittered like stars. No matter what he would say, I just knew there was no good reason for them to be outside of Ashbell. It wasn't even time for the pollination ceremony to grow the dragon flowers. The wrongness of it settled in my stomach like a stone.

"Sage?"

I jumped and slammed the bars closed before I stood up, my heart leaping into my throat.

"What are you doing?" Onyx asked, his voice deceptively calm.

"I was just looking for you," I said, the lie transparent even to my own ears.

"I'm honored that you missed me enough to finally come to seek me out," he said, moving into the room from a back entrance I hadn't noticed before.

His golden eyes never left mine. I expected him to be mildly upset, but if he was, he hadn't shown it. He moved closer to me, one step at a time as if he were expecting me to stop him. The chains that hung from his under armor clicked together with every step he took, a metallic rhythm that matched my quickening pulse. I didn't stop him any better than I tried to stop my heart from thumping at the sight. The heat from the forge suddenly felt insignificant compared to the warmth rising within me.

I didn't know how many more days I could take being on the edge of a heart attack from the two of them. If I were smart, I would decide on neither and stay alone. If one choice was causing me so much distress, maybe I wasn't ready for any choice. The realization was unwelcome but necessary.

"Why do you really have these?" I asked, gesturing toward the fireplace.

My words were hardly above a whisper. Any louder would have felt like yelling, with how close he was to me when he stopped walking. I could smell the forge on him, hot metal and coal mixed with something spicier, uniquely his.

"Have they been bothering you that much?" He watched my mouth while he spoke, not my eyes. The intensity of his gaze made my skin prickle.

"You'd look less dodgy if you just answered the questions you were asked," I said, trying to regain some control of the situation.

Why did I suddenly not care about the eggs? His presence in front of me nearly made me forget why I had come to begin with. The question that had seemed so urgent moments ago now felt distant and unimportant.

"You wouldn't believe me even if I told you, and I don't want to scare you away," he said, his voice dropping lower.

"Scare me away?" I shook my head in confusion, genuinely puzzled.

"Isn't it obvious that I'm in love with you? It's important to me that you see me as who I am before you start learning of the things I do in the dark," he confessed, lifting his hand and placing it on my cheek. The contact was electric, his calloused palm warm against my skin.

A shiver ran through me with the flick of his thumb over my skin. It brought with it another chip in the wall I tried to keep up until I could sort out my own feelings. He said he was in love with me, and on the surface, it made sense. He was always guarding me. He protected me as if I were precious to him. If I thought deeper about it, it was only possessive. He made me feel as if I could fall in love with him, but it wasn't that I was actually in love with him. He only tried to convince me that we could be something when he wanted a distraction. The manipulation was subtle but undeniable.

It was hard to listen to the logical side of my thoughts when he hovered over my face. I wanted to move forward and make contact, but I closed my eyes and fought myself. He had some sort of pull about him, but I knew that the difference that mattered was knowing I was in love with Vespera, not the idea of her. The clarity of this thought was startling.

Her presence made me feel safe to be lovesick. His presence made me feel sick in love. I was hardly making sense to myself, but the distinction felt important.

"Why do you have the eggs?" I asked again, forcing myself to focus on the question that had brought me here.

He sighed and backed his face up if only a few inches, his exhale warm against my skin. "I'm protecting them because they are what's going to bring back the moon Goddess and the sun God."

"What?" I laughed, the sound sharp and disbelieving. "You're drunk then?"

"I told you that you wouldn't believe me," he said, a flash of disappointment crossing his features.

"How am I supposed to believe that?" I challenged, frustration rising.

"It doesn't matter if you believe me as long as you forgive me for making you think I was ever trying to hide something from you," he said. He still brushed my cheek with his thumb, the repetitive motion almost hypnotic. "I don't want you upset with me. I don't want you to think that I ever want anything other than to protect you."

He wanted to treat me like I was a fool. That's what it was. I backed up until there was an arm's length between us. I needed the space to breathe again, to clear my head from whatever spell he seemed to cast over me.

"Not believing what I tell you is not the same as me telling a lie," he insisted. "The eggs are to bring Gods back. That is the truth. Don't you want a better world? Sure, this one could be worse, but it could also be better if it were blessed by the originals. If you had the chance to do it, wouldn't you? If you didn't need to take jobs stealing and murdering, wouldn't you pick that life?"

He was serious. He was really trying to convince me that he was going to use those eggs for reviving Gods. The audacity of it would have been amusing if it weren't so concerning.

"Who else knows? Ashbell? The temple? Even if I said that I believed you, I still don't understand how you got them in the first place," I pressed, unwilling to let him off so easily.

"They were given to me to protect until we could gather the rest of what we needed. I can't tell you any more than that," he stated, moving closer to me again, invading the space I'd tried to create. "Can you forgive me for keeping secrets?"

Metal armor clacked and banged at the doorway, breaking

the tension. "Sir. There's a royal guard here with a message for Sage. The King requests her presence before he leaves." The interruption was both unwelcome and a relief.

"I'm on my way," I called out, seizing the opportunity.

I pushed myself past Onyx and left with the royal guard. I wanted to escape. Being away from him was how I could collect my thoughts and sort them out. He was overwhelming. The feelings he gave me were overwhelming. If meeting the king was how I had to do it, how I had to be pulled out to make an exit, then so be it. I didn't want to work with him again, but it wasn't only my choice, and my choice was made by a majority vote. No questions; Only coin is what the girls said. The mantra had once been comforting; now it felt like a trap.

The guard stopped at an alleyway and nodded me in. I hesitated; my mind was still too foggy to truly consider that meeting someone in a dark alley, even a king, was a poor choice. The shadows seemed to lengthen, reaching for me.

The guard pushed me into the alley before he turned his back on the entrance to keep anyone else out. The sight and the smells were evenly matched: damp stone, rotting food, and something sharper, more metallic. My escape, although it came with a lower heart rate, felt like a downgrade. I traded one dangerous situation for another

"I wanted to give you one last chance to accept the job I'm offering you before I go back to my own land," the masked king said, his voice echoing slightly in the narrow space.

"If I don't accept?" I asked, feigning a confidence I didn't feel.

"Then I make your insides outsides, and we start again," he threatened, his tone chillingly matter-of-fact.

I was taken aback by his entire sentence. Did he want a dark, lonely meeting place so that he could kill me? I was a guild leader, not a king killer. The realization of how precarious my position was hit me with full force.

"I guess it's good for both of us that I've decided to accept," I managed, unsure of what tone to use because I couldn't read how serious he was.

I wanted to think he was joking, but I didn't think he was. There was something in the stillness of his posture that suggested complete sincerity.

"I wouldn't have minded either way," he answered with a shrug, the gesture somehow more menacing for its casualness. "I want you to kill everyone you see in the temple of magic. Take the crystals and find a very special box for me before you leave."

"How will I know it's the right box?" I asked, the question practical despite the horror of what he was asking.

I wanted to keep my questions to a minimum. He was intimidating in a way I hadn't seen from him before. I didn't think he would enjoy me telling him that he was asking for a lot to happen at one time in one of the highest-guarded temples in the entire realm. I'd have to get past a lot more than just a dragon guardian. The gods that still roamed with mortals all had interests in keeping that temple guarded. The task seemed impossible, which made me wonder if that was the point.

"You'll know that it's the right box because when you touch it, it will glow. Bring it back to me, and your pay will be triple," he promised, the words falling like stones in the silence.

What good was triple the coin if he decided to kill me? The way he was talking had me convinced that he was going to kill me. Even if he didn't kill me himself, the fact that I couldn't refuse him and his jobs were increasing in difficulty would kill me. I was going to die. That's all there was to it. I was as good as dead. The certainty of this sat cold in my stomach.

The masked king, Nikola, left me in the alley. He felt like he was coming into his role well. He started as approachable and quickly became comfortable with having unending power. The transition was as impressive as it was terrifying.

He now treated me the way he should have, as a lowly member of the realm who listened or paid the price. Looks like I needed to get ready to go to the temple of magic. The thought brought no excitement, only dread. Either way, I was walking toward my death; it was just a question of whose hand would deliver it.

CHAPTER SEVENTEEN

OUT WITH THE OLD, IN WITH THE NEW

SHIVANI

The area was unusually quiet, considering how many men had ropes tied to the statue of the God of Rebirth. The scent of determination hung in the air, mingling with the earthy smell of stone dust. They proclaimed that it was the wrong statue to have on top of their temple. They discussed wanting it gone, and although I tried to change the subject and move it to things I thought were more pressing, they denied me and declared that it was a symbol of change. That tearing the statue down would symbolize their new way forward. It was the last reminder of all the things they had been through.

I had yet to truly understand what they had gone through, but I didn't need to understand the full story to hear their words. It wasn't a place for my opinion, only my cheering. So I did. I stood in front of the crowd, the cool morning breeze ruffling my hair, ready to help if they couldn't tear it down themselves. Even if the shift in our lives was happening at a pace that made me uncomfortable, I would still cheer them on. It had taken so long to get to the point that we were finally at, and it was a bit like a nervous dream, both thrilling and unsettling at once.

The first sign of the solid stone tipping happened, and every other vampire behind me roared with joy. The sound vibrated through my chest, sending a thrill down my spine. They yelled and cheered like their vocal cords paid no price. It gave the men pulling the ropes a renewed sense of energy, and they got the statue further into its lean.

Dominic used the crystal inside his staff to shoot electricity into the statue. Blue-white sparks crackled and hissed against the ancient stone. I worried that the magical interference would bring the vampires down and prevent them from seeing it through on their own, but it didn't. The stone tumbled off of the temple roof and shattered into so many pieces the ground looked like we had been through an avalanche. The crash echoed through the valley, punctuating our moment of victory. It was me who felt nervous about magic. I considered it a hindrance and not a help these days, not them. I pressed my lips together tighter, careful not to ruin their joy.

The vampires on the roof roared as loudly as the ones that surrounded me.

"It looks like you made a lot of progress while I was away," Koa remarked.

I had to blink multiple times before I could fully take in that it was him standing in front of me. His familiar scent of pine and leather washed over me like a comforting blanket. I jumped into his arms and wrapped around him. It was easy to love him when I didn't think too hard. It was easy to allow myself to be happy if my mind didn't have time to run over anything that had happened or was bound to happen.

"Koa, you won't believe how much has happened since you left!" I exclaimed.

"I know enough about you nearly killing yourself. You'll have to fill me in on the rest," Koa muttered.

I was instantly disappointed in myself for considering that

he would simply be happy for me. It was hard for me to bond with him as deeply as I thought we would have when he was so sure that I would fail. The excitement from the vampires surrounding me had yet to dwindle down, but my excitement simmered into the usual shame for myself I carried. The joyful atmosphere suddenly felt distant, as though I was hearing it from underwater.

I loosened my grip on him, but he didn't loosen his.

"I only meant well," he whispered.

I pushed against him to force him to let me go. "I know."

He put me back on my feet but kept himself close, his breath warm against my cheek.

"You aren't taking care of yourself," he pressed.

"If this was all you came for, you need to leave. Vero does this enough." I turned to leave him where he stood, but he grabbed my arm, his fingers pressing into my skin.

"I came to see you," he insisted. "I wanted to warn you that temples are bracing for more break-ins. I wanted to help you better secure your camp. I wanted to see you."

I held my hand to his mouth to stop him from talking, feeling his lips move against my palm. "Of all the places in the realm, I promise this one is the safest. If you placed any more guards or spies here, then your land would be barren."

"Shivani—"

"Stop," I demanded.

"I do want to hear of all the things that you've accomplished. I do," he emphasized.

"Then start with that. Don't treat me like a child. You forget that I'm much stronger than you are," I reminded him.

"If you knew how to wield yourself correctly, sure. But there are forces at play that know how to manipulate you better than you know how to control yourself," Koa pleaded, his eyes searching mine for understanding.

"I received word from the Queen of Brisa. She is going to let the vampires stay. We can start building a city now." I ignored his words and shifted the conversation in my own direction, letting the sweetness of this victory wash away the bitter taste his concern left in my mouth.

His voice only matched the one inside of myself.

"Are you going to check on Sage?" he questioned.

"I know that I'm supposed to, but it seems like she has enough of a following that my presence won't change much," I responded.

He looked at me with judgment. Like a parent reprimanding a child. I felt heat and rage bubble up inside me, my fingers tingling with the urge to lash out.

"Instead, I plan to kill Helia," I announced.

Koa laughed. "What?"

"I mean it. Now that the vampires have decided we can work together, she's next on my list. I need her heart, and if she's around, they'll never be safe. None of us will," I clarified, my voice steady despite the hammering of my heart.

"I don't think you should do it," he cautioned.

"You can't treat me like I'm incapable forever!" I yelled, my voice cracking.

"That's not what I mean to do. I came to check on you because I was having nightmares of you. That you died by Helia's hand. To hear you talk about it as soon as I arrive, I don't think you should make any rash moves." His eyes were filled with pain, the amber flecks in his irises catching the light.

Was he telling me that I was supposed to stop all plans because of a few dreams? Was he a fortune teller after his time away? The way his eyes pleaded with me made me doubt myself and my choices for a moment. I couldn't allow it to be longer than a moment. I wouldn't let him convince me to change my mind. The weight of my decision settled like a stone in my stomach, heavy but necessary.

"If I'm not sure of what I'm doing, I won't risk it," I stated.

"I don't want to lose you," he whispered, his voice barely audible. "We hardly have time to create a life together, but we will. I know we will. I want you around for it. I've seen what it does to someone to lose the only thing they care about."

"If I'm not confident, I won't act. I'm not looking to die," I repeated, a chill running down my spine despite the warmth of the day.

When we had distance between us, it was easier to think that things would be a happily ever after tale. I thought he was cute because of the way that he was so overprotective in his tone. I didn't find it as cute of a quality in him when there was no space between us. I kept hearing that it was the guardian bond and all of the things going on around us that made him act out.

It wasn't his fault; they were just wired that way. I didn't hear Hesperia talk about Coy acting like she couldn't handle herself. I hardly had time with any of the others yet, but I hadn't heard a word of them being so possessive, either. It was hard to give him the benefit of the doubt when it felt like he never allowed me space for error, either. The thought sat heavily on my chest, making it difficult to breathe.

"I understand what you're saying. I wouldn't want you to take risks with your life either. It doesn't change that some things need to happen. I have to kill Helia. Today, or in a year. I have to do it. Not you, not your army. If you can not handle that, you need to leave. If you don't believe in me, you need to leave." I stopped to take a breath in. I said too much, and I felt the words I had been holding back ready to pour out, bitter and sharp on my tongue.

"That's not what I wanted you to take away from my words at all," he protested.

He didn't offer me a chance to keep going even though I was ready to. He grabbed my arm and pulled me into him until I was pressed so flat I felt my cheek squish.

"I know that you're strong. You're smart and beautiful. You have the power to do much more than I do. I only admire you. It doesn't stop my mind from wandering and worrying.

I've watched your sisters die as if they were nothing. Some of the most powerful deities are murdered as nothing more than flies simply because they've been switched off. I'm afraid every day that if I had to watch you go through what your sisters did, I may be worse than Caym." He stopped talking and squeezed me harder, his heartbeat drumming against my ear.

"If you keep getting tighter, you'll be the one to kill me," I gasped, the scent of his sweat and fear filling my nostrils.

I felt a tinge of guilt when he spoke, but my own need to prove that I was capable overpowered the guilt. Maybe I was selfish. Maybe I was wrong for not considering the effect things have had on him. I hadn't done a single thing in my own realm. I only made it worse. If I hadn't gone to the castle at all, I never would have set in motion the death of everyone in my realm. I not only failed to help my realm, but I got them all killed and helped Nikola get back to the rest of my family.

I took Fennic's only friend down with the realm, and he hasn't spoken to me since. He said he had too much guilt for killing me, but I know it's because of Mori. I can't live an eternity in this realm and fail at everything, too. If I only made choices based on what Koa might be feeling, I'd be a sprite in a cage over a king's throne. The thought made my skin crawl with claustrophobia.

I let out a breath of relief when the ground shook so hard that it tore us apart. The tremor rumbled through the earth, rattling my teeth and sending small stones skittering across the ground. The idea that a disaster was on a doorstep ran through my thoughts, but I welcomed it in a small way. I hardly knew how to approach Koa in a way that made both of us happy in the end. I needed to accomplish something that proved he should be my equal, not just my guardian.

"Shivani!" Dimitri yelled. "There's a dragon!"

Dimitri lost his harsh tone for the first time since I met him. He sounded worried, his usually composed face now pale with concern. I left Koa to see what was going on. Dragons leaving their island wasn't something seen often. I knew that much. A crowd stood around black and white scales that gleamed like polished obsidian and pearl in the sunlight. He was large enough that I could see him perfectly through the crowd, his massive form casting shadows over the gathered vampires.

Dimitri followed me through the crowd. "That's not a dragon," I corrected.

"What?" He looked at me with rage, his nostrils flaring.

"It's a Wyvern. It walks on its wings. Dragons don't walk on their wings," I explained.

"Does that matter right now?" Dimitri spat, droplets of saliva catching the light.

"It always matters," I snapped back.

The wyvern picked me out of a crowd as if he could smell me. His eyes, amber and intelligent, locked onto mine with unsettling focus.

"Why are you here?" I asked it.

He shot a gust of air from his nostrils at me. The hot, sulfurous breath made my eyes water as he made sure that it was straight in my face. "My name is Akiva. I was sent here to offer my protection to Shivani and the vampires," he announced, his voice deep and resonant, like stones grinding together.

"Who sent you, Akiva?" I inquired.

"Belladonna," he answered.

"Ruri's dragon?" Koa interjected.

"Does Ruri have her memory back?" I asked, hope flickering within me like a fragile flame.

"Not yet. Will you accept me or not?" Akiva demanded, his scales shifting with impatience, creating a sound like metal sliding against metal.

I looked to Koa, but I instantly regretted doing so. It didn't help me prove that I was strong enough to make my own choices if I looked to him first. The moment of hesitation felt like an eternity, stretching between us like an unspoken accusation.

"I accept," I nodded.

"Good. The pouch on my side has the things you requested from Ashbell," Akiva informed me.

Koa was the one to grab the satchel from the wyvern's side, but I was as quick to snag it from him. The leather was warm to the touch, and I could feel the weight of my future plans nestled inside.

"What was that for?" Koa questioned.

"I need it," I replied.

"You won't tell me what's inside?" Koa's tone grew increasingly frustrated, a vein pulsing at his temple.

"Not yet," I said as I tucked the bag inside of my coat, feeling the contents press against my ribs. "I need to go. Can you help Akiva?"

I didn't allow Koa the time to accept or deny before I pushed him and Dimitri into the crowd. I ordered the guard outside of my tent to keep everyone out. I didn't want any interruptions. I did have a plan. When Koa left, Dominic, the high priest, was going to start evacuations. He was going to move the vampires to Sephtis in secret. We already sent men ahead to set up camps on the edge of their border. Helia's next visit was on the horizon, and I would kill her.

I wanted the area clear of any possible casualties. With the statue being knocked down, she may even show up sooner. We didn't know what to expect, so we were all moving fast. I asked for a special kind of poison from Ashbell. I expected more resistance and more questions. Instead, I learned that Ruri, being my sister, allowed me access to anything I wanted without question, and as hard as I would try not to abuse the perk, I was happy to have experienced receiving it.

I was confident in our planning. In our abilities, and with the addition of a dragon on our side, we would be that much better off. I just needed to mix the poison with blood and not mess up the portions. The vials clinked together in the pouch, a deadly symphony of glass and liquid.

Helia would arrive at the temple confident in herself. I would poison her and kill her. The metallic taste of anticipation filled my mouth as I pictured her fall. I would not fail like I did in my own realm. I would carve out a place in Cylla and be a sister to be proud of when I stood next to the others. This time, the blood on my hands would be justified.

CHAPTER EIGHTEEN

THE DAY A DEITY DIED

SHIVANI

I sat at my desk and tapped my quill against the wood, the rhythmic sound echoing in the silence of my tent. I'd be a liar if I said I wasn't nervous. I was confident that I could kill her. Why wouldn't I kill her? She was only a false version of me. A weaker version. She was like me, but she wasn't as good as me. She was a poor creation from a Goddess that hardly had a grip on her own being. Yumi failed more than I had, and she'd learn that again today when I killed Helia. If Helia, trying to use my abilities, could curse an entire land of people, then she was nothing in comparison to me.

I groaned and tapped the quill harder, leaving tiny indentations in the wooden surface. The thought of failure still crept into my mind. I was trying so hard to convince myself. I thought if I said it enough times, I would have to remove any space I held for doubt in myself. I was wrong. I tried to repeat how much of a waste Helia was, but instead, I only drifted deeper into doubt.

What if I failed again? What if I was doing it again? What

if I was letting myself believe that I was better than I truly was, and I did die? The bitter taste of fear coated my tongue.

If the universe or my mother were looking out for me, they would have Helia bring the traitor with her, and I could be the hero of both. I could hold her heart in one hand and the traitors in the other. If I were a blessed daughter of creation, like I kept hearing, then my mother would open the sky and use her might to help me solve the problem of Helia. Wouldn't she? The silence in response to my thoughts was deafening.

My tent opened with a soft rustle of fabric, and Dimitri and Dominic entered. They took their seats in front of my desk and looked at me without a word. It's what I asked for. The position of being in charge and calling the shots. I still shifted in my seat when the two of them looked at me, clearly awaiting orders, directions, or demands. The leather of my chair creaked beneath my weight.

"These two jars and this blood bag have my blood and a special poison inside. They are mixed perfectly, so do not ingest it yourself. The poison is concentrated enough to knock out even a god for a short period of time. The combination of my blood will give her just enough of a high that she won't question why it's not renewing her or making her stronger until it's too late. When she is having a hard time staying focused and awake, I'll take my chance to kill her. I want the two of you to leave as soon as she starts feeling the first symptoms." I tried my best to command, forcing my voice not to waver.

Dominic nodded. He looked proud of me. His eyes gleamed with an approval I'd never seen before. It was a strange feeling to think that the vampire I hardly knew meant something to me. I had spent so long trying to see him, to find a way that we could work together, and now, in what felt like a dream, he was not just in front of me, but he approved of me. The realization warmed me in ways I hadn't expected.

"The evacuations are complete. They went without a hitch, and Koa has not said anything about the relocation yet, which means he hasn't found out either," Dimitri reported.

Dimitri stood, bowed, and left the tent. He was already wearing the tattered crimson robes that he had been when he left the temple. It pained me to see him in them again. He had recovered so well that he looked like a new vampire. He didn't just put the robes back on; he smeared himself with old blood and dirt to complete the look, and I hated it. The metallic scent of dried blood clung to him like a shroud.

"You are doing well," Dominic affirmed. "I can see the doubt on your face. I can sense that you're nervous. Anyone would be. I can imagine that sometimes it is hard for you to remember that you're a goddess since you've always lived as a mortal. You are still a goddess, though; you can do so much more than any of us. We all believe in you." He stood and left the tent, too, his footsteps fading into the morning bustle outside.

I didn't follow him out. I wanted an extra moment to sit with myself before I put action into motion. Dominic said words that should have comforted me, but the haste that Dimitri left with made me nervous. Did he expect me to fail? Vero wouldn't talk to me before she left with the group. She knew as well as I did that even if it killed me, I had to kill Helia. Only one of us could be alive, and things can't move forward until we learn which one it would be. The weight of that knowledge sat heavy on my shoulders, pressing me into my seat.

I left from the back of my tent instead of the front doorway. It was early enough that the sky was still filled with pinks and yellows. The cool morning air kissed my skin, carrying the scent of dew and earth. I could see hundreds of stars and moons around the sun. They looked as if they were embracing the sun, and I took it as a sign. I knew it meant nothing, but I wanted it to mean that my parents, at least, approved of my choices.

I kept to trees and bushes as I moved to the temple, the leaves rustling softly against my clothing. I did not take the stairway so that I could avoid being seen. I entered through the back of the temple. The temple was lighter than it had been the last time I was inside. The walls and floor were cleaner, too. There was a feeling of warmth that hadn't been there before. Helia would no doubt have something to say about the change. Dimitri hoped by looking a mess in front of Helia that he could play down the way the temple looked, but if she were as smart as she was made out to be, it wouldn't work.

The best advantage I had was not knowing her. I could be told hundreds of stories, but I would never carry the same fear of her as anyone else because my own eyes had never seen her through their lens. I only saw her as someone weak enough to need mortals and their services to get anything she wanted done. I would never be like her, and I would not allow her to leave and continue spreading her diseased thoughts around to infect anything else. My determination flowed through me like liquid fire.

I followed their voices once I heard them. Dominic guided me to them without knowing it. I tucked myself as tightly into the decorations outside of the room they occupied. The grandfather clock made it simpler, its shadow concealing my presence, the rhythmic ticking masking the sound of my breathing.

"This is it?" Helia asked, her voice sharp and impatient.

"No, the others will be back for more. Shivani has made it hard for us to do our duties," Dominic explained.

"She made it near impossible for me to feel good either," Helia hissed.

I heard her toss the cork from one of the jars onto the ground, the small object clinking against the stone floor. One in, the clock started. I'd have her heart soon enough. I'd be one step closer to being myself soon.

"When they come back, I presume you'll separate the ones I'm taking back?" Helia's words were asking a question, but her tone was making a demand.

"I will. Will you be bringing the others back to visit?" Dominic inquired.

My palms started to sweat, dampness spreading between my fingers. It hadn't been enough time for him to get cocky. She popped the cork on the second jar and tossed it. The sound of her gulping the poisoned blood down was nauseating. She sounded like a starved calf that finally found its mother after days of being alone. The wet, desperate sounds made my stomach churn.

"You should remain grateful that I put you in charge as it is. Don't forget your place, Dominic. I'm not in the mood to play games with you," she growled. "The temple already looks as if it's in the middle of a remodel. If you've switched sides, you should say so before I find out on my own. What I've done to others will look like a joke compared to what I'll put you through."

My curiosity won, and I leaned my head into the doorway. I wanted to see her. I needed to know if she had truly drunk both jars already. I was taken aback by how similar we looked, yet how different. Her skin was so pale that I knew my presence in the realm was taking a heavier toll on her than it was on me. Her eyes and hair were as red as mine, but lacked the vibrant life I knew shone in my own.

Her hair was long, as long as mine used to be before it was cut off at Rivens castle. Those days felt so far away when I stood steps away from a Goddess that I was supposed to kill when I hadn't even killed Nikola as I thought. I was still haunted by nightmares of both events, the images flashing behind my eyes in moments of doubt.

"I'll need more blood than this," Helia demanded. She bit

the bag open and started downing it, too, crimson droplets escaping from the corners of her mouth and trailing down her chin.

"I can see that," Dominic agreed. "It seems the stolen Goddess blood is no longer helping you as it once did."

"Maybe I should try yours." Her teeth ground together with her words, the sound like stone against stone.

She did look ill. I was sure at one point she was beautiful, but in front of me, she looked tired. She was sunken in as if she hardly had meat on her. The paleness of her skin hardly even held any pink. It was the arrogance inside of me that felt a boost of confidence from the sight. She looked so weak I wondered if I even needed the poison.

"I have a feeling it wouldn't make much difference now," he laughed.

I watched her sit straighter with the wave of realization. She was smart and quick, yet still not perfect. I lunged into the room. I was afraid to miss my chance. I was running out of hope. I was not an expert in gods, and I was no god killer. I could only say that I was good at convincing others that I knew what I was doing. My heart thundered in my ears as I made my move.

Helia looked up at me while I dived for her with rage. She carried no glimmer of surprise or shock. She did her best to stand but dropped to her knees. She still had the strength to slide the table away from her and slam it into the wall, the wood splintering on impact. The poison wasn't perfect, but It was enough. It only ever needed to be enough.

I threw myself at her like she was my next meal. I lunged and threw her backward onto the cold stone floor. I hardly recognized myself. The anger I felt made me nauseous and scared. My hands were around her throat, but they shook. I was positioned correctly. I had her where she needed to be, but I was already scared of the way I felt, and I had only just touched her for the first time.

Our skin being connected made my eyes haze over in red. I felt real for the first time. I felt full of energy. I hadn't realized until touching Helia that what I had felt was hollow. I was a shell of who I could have been. I hardly noticed anything but the surges going through my body until I saw red. I was bashing her head into the stone, and she was bleeding from it. It flowed from her, and it felt as if it were flowing into me. The scent of her blood—my blood—filled my nostrils, metallic and intoxicating.

The sensation was unlike anything I had ever experienced before. My skin was covered in chill bumps despite the sweat that dripped from my forehead onto Helia's skin. She let out a scream from underneath me and landed her fist into my side. The air left my lungs faster than I could have taken it in, pain exploding through my ribs.

She shouldn't have been strong enough to hurt me as badly as she had. She acted as if she had never been poisoned. She flipped me over as if I weighed nothing and locked her legs around me. Fist after fist hit me. My face, my shoulders. She hadn't aimed for any specific spot. She was satisfied with landing wherever she landed. Each impact sent shockwaves of pain through my body.

"Did you think it would be that simple? I outsmarted Yumi, and you thought that you could just kill me with two hands around my throat?" Helia screamed.

She made no effort to keep her voice from echoing through the temple walls. She gave the same care to the level of her voice as she gave to my body when she pulled me to my feet by two hands full of my hair. My scalp screamed for relief. Hair snapped at the root and left spikes of pain through the top of my head. It seemed like nothing compared to the impact of my body against the stone wall.

Helia threw me into the wall hard enough that stone crumbled around me and caused me to inhale dust while I coughed for air. The cracks and pops I felt in my bones made me sure that I had broken something. I didn't have the strength or courage to move and test the thought yet. Every part of my body pulsed with pain. My vision blurred, darkness creeping at the edges.

"I'm glad you were this stupid. I'm sick of feeling weak. Tired of playing games with you because I'm ordered to. I think you are useless. Pathetic. A waste of time. If I had it my way, I would have killed you the moment you landed in my realm. I would have if it hadn't been for someone informing me that Nikola was back. There's nothing to be done now. You attacked me first. He will just have to accept your death and move on," she continued screaming, her voice vibrating through the temple walls.

She formed a fist of blood the same as mine and slammed it in my direction. The only thing that I could do was wrap my wings around my body and roll. I was still trying to catch my breath. I had no strength to defend myself yet. The taste of blood filled my mouth, coppery and warm.

"You won't be the only one. When one brick is pulled, they all become weak and tumble," she spat. "I should thank you a second time for allowing me to be in a perfect position. Nikola thinks that when the four of you awake, he can absorb your powers. I think it would be better if I did that and kept my throne." She laughed, the sound hollow and cruel. "After you, your sisters next. They came to avenge you, is the story I will tell."

She used her foot and slammed it into my stomach. I coughed blood hardly seconds after contact, the force of the blow sending another wave of agony through my already battered body.

"If they're as easy as you, It only proves how weak Nikola truly is," she spoke without yelling for the first time.

I tasted iron and sweat. They ran together on my face. I had to have been bleeding from more than one place. Did Dimitri and Dominic make it out? Were they safe at the camp with everyone else? I was less worried for myself, although I ached in every bone, and more concerned with what she would do to them if I failed.

It was too late to go back now. It was too late to decide that maybe Koa was right when he thought I was too weak to defeat her. If I failed, Helia would no doubt kill the boys. She would consider this a betrayal on their end, and I was sure she wouldn't ask them a single question before their death. I didn't doubt that she would kill my sisters, either.

I knew that I had two choices: use my magic or call for Koa to help me. Koa already played the savior once. He found a way to travel the universe to do what he needed to do. That was no small accomplishment. I didn't want to wield magic that hurt people. I didn't want to be like her. I wanted to be like Koa. Brave without question. I wanted to be so strong and so confident that I never considered what could happen; I only saw the straight line ahead of me and followed it.

I wanted to be like my sisters and have people tell stories of me when they ate dinner. I wanted to be like they were. The thought filled me with a determination that burned through the pain.

I closed my eyes and felt them shake. I focused, and I paused time. I only had a few moments. The quickness behind my heart rate reminded me how fast those few moments would go. I pulled from what I knew.

Two arms grew from my sides, the flesh stretching and forming with a strange tingling sensation. With my mind, I controlled the two additional fists. I hit her with everything I had, and as time sped back up, she didn't hit the wall; she went through it. A haze stood between us from where the wall crumbled. What would my sisters do? It was hard to know when I hardly knew them, but I knew if this were one of their stories, they'd keep going.

I moved through the haze. I tried to breathe in, but the dust dried my mouth, coating my tongue and throat. I pushed it down and hit a second time, then a third. I hit until I felt my blood fist make contact with her again. I knew I had done it because when Helia went through the next wall, sunlight filled every corner of the once-together temple, streaming through the fresh opening and illuminating the destruction we'd caused.

Helia faced the ground. She was on her hands and knees. She coughed blood the same as I had, dark red spatters staining the stone beneath her.

"If you thought that a few hits would give you a win, you were wrong," Helia coughed between her words.

"I didn't. I'm not that foolish," I spit my own blood, the acidic tang making me grimace.

I reached into my chest and pulled at the blood pumping through my heart. I pulled until I held a hand full of my own blood, and I formed it into a claymore. It pulsed at the same rate as my own heartbeat, glowing with a deep crimson light that cast eerie shadows across the temple floor.

I imagined that I had to look as poor off as she did. Both of us had to have broken more than one thing. She stood up well enough that I knew it also had to be true that we were both running off of adrenaline, our bodies pushing beyond what should have been possible.

She ran at me with her own blood fist, ready to strike. I sliced through it with my blade and tried to allow no time between the strikes. I twirled my wrists to lift the blade back and meet her flesh. I wanted to take her head, but I only sliced her arm. I had to have done a better job than I thought I had because she held her arm close and nearly forgot I was present, her face contorted in pain.

I watched her try to open a vine portal back to Semper, but she failed every time, her attempts growing more desperate with each failure. Instead, she was running in Orest's direction, leaving a trail of blood behind her.

I wanted to follow her, but my feet did not listen. My legs

trembled, and I realized I was swallowing blood. My vision swam, the temple tilting and swaying around me.

"I tried my best not to intervene. I tried to stay back and give you the space you so desperately wanted. I can't do it any longer. You're going to die. She's retreating. Please, let me help you. I won't touch Helia. I won't lay a finger on anything you tell me to stay away from, but I'm begging you, let me help you," Koa pleaded, his voice cracking with emotion. "If I force my hand, you'll hate me. If I stay idle and let you get hurt, I'll hate myself. Give me something, please."

My responses didn't matter. My thoughts didn't have time to flow. I felt his touch, cool against my burning skin, and I saw darkness, falling into it like sinking into a deep, bottomless lake.

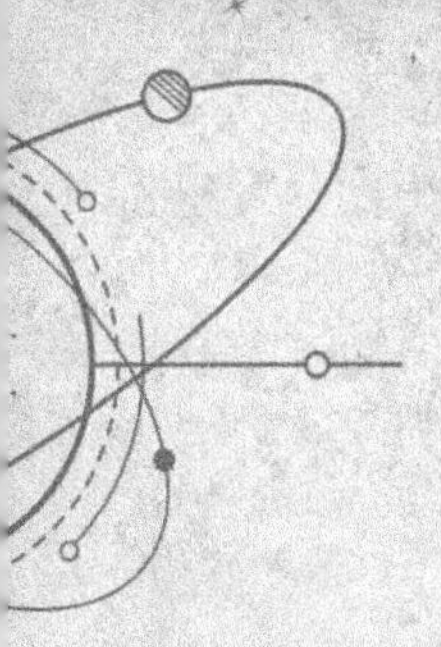

CHAPTER NINETEEN

ONE STEP FORWARD, FIVE BACK

ASTRA

Fennic and Aero stood behind me. They watched the vine portal that I opened, but none of us moved our feet. The shimmering green edges of the portal pulsed with energy, casting ethereal shadows across our faces.

"I'm going to warn you one more time that if things go downhill, they're really going to go downhill. It will happen fast, and we aren't likely to come home. It'll be the three of us against a lot of problems," I cautioned. "Entering Semper disguised as Thann has been easy because I don't stir any pots. When I enter as myself, I am guarded and only allowed to do my job."

I turned to look at both of them and although Aero looked confident and ready to move, his jaw set with determination, Fennic's eyes didn't agree. He looked as if he wanted to change his mind and leave on the spot. The fear in his gaze was palpable, his fingers fidgeting at his sides. I wouldn't blame him if he had. Semper was always cold, but it was much different with not just Helia in charge but Deimos as

well. Helia made blood guards, and Deimos cut down any he deemed weak.

The good side of that was none of them were very smart; the downside was that if you weren't used to fighting, you weren't fighting your way past them. They were stronger than they looked. I felt closer to Fennic than Aero for the first time. I was scared to get caught and needed to fend off a realm full of blood-hungry guards. I worried the most about the lingering darkness that seemed to grow over the realm of the gods. The weight of it pressed down on my shoulders, making each breath feel heavy.

Since the realms crashed together, there was something I couldn't put my finger on that took away from the joy of having everyone back on the same plain. It was the constant lingering feeling of doom. The sensation that someone was always watching, eyes burning into the back of my neck when I least expected it. I didn't understand what Nikola was, but my gut told me that he wasn't just a deity made by Dahlia. I hadn't laid a single eye on him yet, but I felt his effect every-where, like a cold shadow that never quite left.

Aero walked through the vines first, so I followed a step behind. The portal hummed as we passed through, sending tingles across my skin. I tried to silence my racing heart, but it pounded in my ears, drowning out all other sounds. I didn't look back to see if Fennic followed me in because I knew that I wouldn't blame him if he changed his mind and decided to stay. I reached into my pocket and ran my fingers over the illu-sion crystal so that I was fully disguised as Thann, the God of Rebirth. The crystal was cool to the touch, its power seeping into my being.

I disguised myself as him so often, for so long, that when I knew I looked like him, It was easy to become him. I tucked myself and anything that I may be feeling away and became the image of him that I remembered. Spoiled and selfish. Aero looked back at me with a frown, his nose wrinkled in disgust. If he thought it was unpleasant to look at me this way, he had no idea what it felt like to go from a woman to a man. I didn't even want to date men, let alone become one. The sensation of my altered form made my skin crawl, every movement feeling foreign and wrong.

I moved in front of Aero and guided us behind the throne in the Chamber of Starlight. The massive golden chair loomed above us, its ornate decorations glinting in the ethereal light. I wanted to stay out of sight so we could take the back door. The same door that Yumi used to take when she was free and roamed Semper. The doorway, she would walk to check on me and go to her room. To punish me in front of the tree.

I hadn't stopped thinking about the tree and the way everything was done to us; we had to be in front of it. Knowing Dahlia was in the tree, and she had to watch, helpless to intervene, for years. It added a new layer of vile to Yumi. She was so hard on us, not because she cared for us. It was all to taunt Dahlia. To rub in Dahlia's face that she was powerless and there was nothing to be done about it. The thought made bile rise in my throat. It wasn't just the physical punishments that Dahlia had to watch; she had to spend day after day seeing all of the souls trapped inside of the stars, too.

We made it to the edge of the garden. We stood so close to the golden and green room that I felt the warmth from inside before an axe was lowered in front of me and halted our movement. The polished metal gleamed dangerously, reflecting our startled faces.

"Halt. No one enters without a guard," the blood guard growled, his voice like gravel.

I reached into my pocket and pulled out the coin Helia gave me when I convinced her that we needed to keep our relationship low. When I wore Thann's looks and held her at Orest. It was a symbol of my free access to anything I wanted as her lover. The gold coin felt heavy in my palm, its edges digging into my skin. It had been years, and the idea didn't disgust me any less than it had on the first day I had to hold her, the memory of her touch making my stomach turn.

"This coin gives me permission to be wherever I want. Do you want to explain to Helia why you denied me access? There won't be a second chance if she's brought into this," I threatened as I held the coin to the guard's face, keeping my voice steady despite my churning stomach.

He looked from the coin to me and then behind me. I saw the thoughts run through his mind, as well as the blood guards could have, at least. His crimson eyes narrowed in suspicion, but uncertainty flickered across his features. He lowered his axe and moved for us to pass, but he kept himself stationed at the doorway, his massive form blocking the exit. It wasn't the most ideal, but the outcome could have been worse.

Fennic and Aero followed me inside. The two of them remained so silent that I could have forgotten they were with me. I guided them to the center of the garden, where the tree of life sat. The massive tree towered above us, its branches stretching toward the ceiling, leaves shimmering with an inner light. I didn't want to call it Dahlia. It was where she remained locked away, but I was able to keep my distance between myself and the too-hard facts if I didn't fully acknowledge the tree out loud.

"I feel like she's already yelling at me," Fennic shivered, his voice barely above a whisper.

"I'm confident that you deserved it if she did," I remarked dryly.

"Do you remember her?" Fennic questioned, his eyes fixed on the tree.

There hadn't been a lot of time to talk about the subject, and if we didn't talk about it as a group, I tried not to think about it. The memories were like shards of glass, painful to touch.

"Not as well as I would like to. I don't remember as much

about our entire lives as I want to," I admitted, the words leaving a bitter taste in my mouth.

"I don't remember how we died," Aero interjected, his voice uncharacteristically solemn. "I think about it all the time."

"Can I make a confession in case we die?" Fennic asked, his voice trembling slightly.

I wanted to deny him. I wanted us to stop wasting time in a place that I shouldn't have brought them. I wanted to focus on the task at hand and not on our fears. I didn't. Even if he frustrated me nearly always, he deserved to have some peace if he died. The scent of fear and uncertainty hung heavy in the air between us.

"Sure," I nodded him on, bracing myself for whatever was to come.

"I can't stop thinking of how I killed Shivani. I always think of how much everyone must hate me deep down. I agree to do this because it has to be done, but I don't think that I want to be here when Dahlia does come back. I don't think that I have the courage to face her," Fennic watched the ground while he spoke, his voice breaking with emotion.

I wasn't prepared for that to be his confession. Part of my natural annoyance with him was that he killed Shivani. We hardly brought her back. He acted like the side we fought against but still stood with us. He was right in his fears. The revelation hung in the air between us, heavy as stone.

"Have you talked to Shivani about this?" I inquired, studying his face carefully.

His eyes widened in horror, "Of course not! You aren't going to tell her, are you?" The panic in his voice was palpable.

"That's not my place. It just seems like this conversation would be more productive with her and not us," I pointed out.

"Do you tell every thought of yours? You don't hold any

guilt that you keep to yourself?" Fennic challenged, his words hitting closer to home than I'd like to admit.

Of course, I did. I failed Ruri. I let her die. Just like I failed Dahlia, my son, and Kyra. I failed everyone I loved, and all I had to hold onto was the bits of ego I could gather and hold together. The weight of that guilt pressed down on me constantly, threatening to crush me. I didn't deserve those bits, either. Not discussing the depths of my shame was what kept me on my feet. I hardly allowed myself time to think about it, pushing the thoughts away whenever they surfaced.

It was none of his concern. The thought of sharing my own failures made my throat close up.

"Hey, the God of Justice can't be wrong on these subjects. Which means whatever I say has to be accepted. I judge that, at the time, you were only half yourself. You didn't understand that the things you were feeling were your need to do your duty as the God of Protection. You did what you thought best," Aero narrowed his eyes on Fennic and left no room for argument, his voice ringing with authority. "We can move forward now."

"Can we move forward now?" I asked, impatience coloring my tone.

I didn't want to be insensitive, but the silence around us, the knowledge that a blood guard was outside and aware of us all, made my palms sweat. The scent of soil and ancient magic filled my nostrils. The addition of the two of them trying to be sickly sweet added nausea to my sweaty skin.

Fennic and Aero nodded to each other for encouragement as if they knew what to do. I knew that they didn't. We were all only guessing. They nearly had me convinced when they both laid their hands on the bark, and it immediately started to glow under them. The light pulsed beneath their fingertips, warm and golden. None of us had magic beyond what we had for our duties since Ruri was sent into the mortal realm to be reborn, but they began to glow as if they were filled with magic again, their bodies outlined in shimmering light.

Despite how convincing and beautiful the sight was, nothing happened. The air around us remained still, the anticipation building until it was almost suffocating.

"What now?" I asked, frustration creeping into my voice.

"You listen now," Dahlia commanded, her voice resonating from the tree, powerful and ancient.

The three of us jumped in unison at the sound, the unexpected voice sending shivers down my spine.

"My efforts to unite what once was shattered was well received, I see. All pieces placed back together but one. Until you bring the artifact left by my dear one, we shan't move forward," Dahlia coo'd, her voice like honey and steel.

"We just had it in the other realm, so it should be easy to get, right?" Fennic asked, hope edging into his voice.

"I can get it," I declared with more confidence than I felt.

"Find it and release me," Dahlia demanded, her words echoing around us.

I could see that there was no reason to say anything else. The bark hardened on the tree of life with an audible crack, and I knew that she wouldn't be answering us again. The moment had passed, leaving us once again adrift.

"Let's go," Aero urged. He had his hands on Fennic, moving him toward the exit, his fingers digging into Fennic's arm.

I had one more thing that I wanted to do before we left. If today was going to be the day that we tested how much we could accomplish, I wanted to test what I could do with the stars, too. I moved to the back of the tree and waved my hand across the sky until it shifted from daylight to darkness. Hundreds of stars shined down on me, glittering like diamonds against the velvet sky. I reached up and grabbed one with my bare hands. If Ruri could do it, I should be able to, too. I could collect them and deliver them to Ashbell. The star was cold against my palm, vibrating with energy.

The first star didn't budge, so I reached for a second. The second star gripped my fingers as if it were a hand as well. It pulled me with a force I almost couldn't resist. Silver shimmering hands reached up my arms and gripped me tight enough that I thought I might lose my arms. The touch burned like ice and fire simultaneously. Hissing and growling filled the air around me, the sounds crawling into my ears like living things.

There was no face, but there were teeth in my view next. So sharp they looked hand-carved and long enough to be in an animal's jaw, gleaming with malice in the starlight.

Aero's hands gripped my arm and ripped me back. I heard him hit the ground with the force it took to pull me back, his breath leaving him in a painful grunt. I felt the hottest shock in my body that I had ever felt before I hit the ground beside him. A sharp pain ran through my side and into my stomach, like a knife being twisted inside me, before Fennic pulled me to my feet.

We took the same path through the Chamber of Starlight and behind the throne to leave as we had taken to enter. On the other side of the vines, we were back in my office, the familiar surroundings providing little comfort to my rattled nerves.

I moved quickly and wrote a note to Hesperia. I needed her to get the artifact of the sun god for Dahlia. The quill scratched against the parchment, my hands still trembling from our encounter. I handed the letter to a Fiia before I tossed myself into my chair, the cushions offering little comfort to my aching body.

It wasn't just my body that ached; it was my mind. It was a deeper part of me that I had never felt before. As if something attached itself to my soul. To the essence, that made me who I am at my core. I felt those rough, starlight-covered fingers digging into parts of me that I didn't know existed, leaving marks that no one could see but I could feel with every breath.

The office door flung open before any of us could compose ourselves, the wood crashing against the wall with a bang that made us all jump.

"We need you! There are two Goddesses fighting. They've already knocked down an entire wall of the castle! They're killing each other!" The guard bellowed, his face contorted with panic.

I got to my feet as quickly as I could, ignoring the protest of my muscles and the lingering pain from the star's touch, but the men were still faster than I was, their footsteps already echoing down the corridor as I hurried to follow.

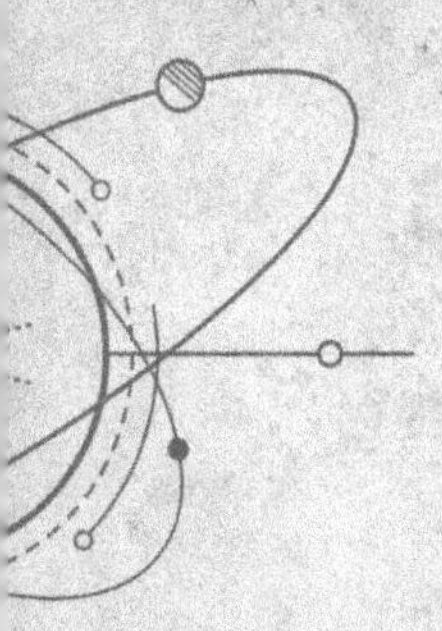

CHAPTER TWENTY

ONE CURSE TO RULE
THEM ALL

ASTRA

I didn't make it outside before I saw parts of the castle in ruins. Dust filled my lungs with each panicked breath, the scent of scorched stone hanging heavy in the air. Students screamed and scattered in all directions, their footsteps echoing across the shattered courtyard. The staff had no answers for me. It didn't matter who I asked; no one knew more than the last. They only knew that there was fighting on our grounds, their voices tight with fear as they pointed toward the commotion.

I reached the entrance of Orest and saw Koa. The color washed from his face, and his eyes searched for something as hard as my own. The wind carried the metallic scent of blood, making my stomach clench in anticipation. We weren't searching for long when the blood splattered the ground in front of us, and Shivani's body came sputtering across the stone courtyard. Helia trudged her way up the staircase. She was bloodied and dragged her leg behind her, leaving a crimson trail that glistened in the harsh sunlight.

I saw flesh torn from Shivani with the force behind her

toss on the stone, her skin raw and exposed where it had scraped away.

Koa grabbed my arm, and what I expected to be a firm grasp was only shaking. "Tell me what to do," he pleaded, his voice barely audible over the chaos.

"Tell me what's going on?" I heard my own voice tremble as my heart hammered against my ribs.

Helia was problematic because none of us could be sure what she was actually capable of. None of us had any solid proof that Shivani being near her would make Helia weak enough to be an easy kill. None of us knew enough of anything. We had guesses and ideas from the way that Yumi acted. We had ideas based on the way Kyrell lashed out or became weak around Ruri.

We had a strong belief that the stronger Shivani was, the weaker Helia would be. We didn't have any proof that it would or wouldn't be the same the other way around. If Shivani refused to use her abilities and grew weak because of them, would it make Helia stronger? The thought made my blood run cold.

"Shivani is going to die. She's determined to kill Helia today, but she doesn't want my help. She doesn't want any help," he muttered. He used his free hand to push back his blonde hair, but he streaked it with blood. "She already passed out in my arms once. I can't lose her, but I can't live if she hates me." His voice cracked on the final word, his fingers digging into my arm.

Seeing the God of War crumbling in front of me wasn't something I ever expected to see. I understood that he wanted me to step in and help so that the blame would fall on me. I didn't care if I held all of Shivani's hate. I did care to lose my position in Semper before I could save Dahlia. The position Koa was putting me in was complicated. I needed to save Dahlia, and I couldn't do that if Helia locked me away.

Many things were worse than death. If Helia killed me,

then I would peacefully forget all of the problems that surrounded us. Everyone would be down another helping hand, and I would never be bothered by the idea. That was worse than dying. If I was locked away, then I could no longer pose as Thann. I would no longer have free roam of the realm of the Gods. Kyra and Ruri would lose their hand up in the game we were forced into. The thought weighed on me like a stone in my chest.

I was holding our most solid piece. My choices kept us in the game or handed us a loss.

If I let Shivani die, Dahlia would not forgive me. I didn't need full memory to know that much. Ruri would not forgive me. I had enough knowledge to know that was true. My mouth went dry at the impossible choice before me.

Helia grabbed Shivani by the hair and dragged her across the courtyard to the water fountain that decorated the entrance of Orest. I could hear the rasp of Shivani's body against the stone, see the strands of hair pulling free from her scalp. I had a choice to make. Shivani or my position. Koa still looked at me with pleading eyes.

I couldn't help him this time. If Shivani needed to be reborn like her sisters, then that's how it would have to be. I couldn't guarantee the same thing for myself. The realization sat bitter and heavy on my tongue.

The two of them shoved and hit until they were at the fountain of the courtyard. Water splashed around them, darkening with blood where it touched their wounds.

Helia shoved Shivani's head under the water. I heard my own breath from how rapidly my heart was beating at the sight. I had to make the choices that he didn't want to make. He didn't consider the position that he put me in when he let them come here. It made sense for Helia to come and seek out Thann, but it didn't make sense for Koa to allow Shivani to keep following Helia.

"I have an idea," I announced to Koa. "I'll be back."

I turned and ran back inside. Aero and Fennic passed by, but they ignored me. They were focused on the sight of Shivani turning the water in the fountain to blood and using it to form limbs and strangle Helia. The air grew thick with the coppery scent of blood, coating my tongue with each breath.

Aero pulled out a small white handle and transformed it into a large white glowing scythe. The weapon hummed with power, sending vibrations through the air around it. Fennic was close beside him, already wielding a black claymore with the brightest red flame burning from the blade. Heat rolled off it in waves that I could feel even from a distance. They hit in unison, taking both of Helia's arms off.

Shivani used the sight of Helia and the men in front of her as a way to renew herself. It was clear in the way she stood and formed her own claymore of blood that she felt energized despite the blood pouring from her or her swollen face. She didn't have both eyes fully open, but she stood above Helia all the same, her stance firm despite her injuries.

My chest started to hurt. Not from their fight. If Helia died, I would not be upset. The pain was radiating from my side where the stars struck me. I moved my top, and when I looked at my chest, I saw the image of a burnt black star. It pulsed with each beat of my heart, sending shock waves of pain through my body.

Shivani took Helia's head from her shoulders, and Koa stopped it with his foot. The wet thud of flesh against stone made bile rise in my throat. I took the break in pain and walked back outside. I wanted to be back in sight before their fight was over. Koa got what he wanted; someone else helped Shivani, and I kept my hands clean in case she lost.

Maybe it made me a bad person. I think I was okay with that if it meant that I was alive to keep the secrets I held safe and the lives that depended on me safe, too. Shivani's sisters died. They died more than once. If they could be strong through it, so could she in the end. If Caym lived through

Ruri's death, Koa could live through Shivani. I needed to believe that to justify my inaction.

She mattered to me as Ru's sister. As Dahlia's daughter. She didn't sit on the list of people that I'd give my life for.

Shivani yelled and grumbled over Helia's headless body. She dug her arm into the hole in Helia's throat until her arm was as far in as she could get it. I saw no elbow on her arm. The wet, sucking sound of flesh against flesh made my stomach turn.

Shivani pulled her arm out and held Helia's heart up for all of us to see. It still pulsed weakly in her grip, blood dripping between her fingers and pattering on the stone below. I wanted to pretend to celebrate Shivani's victory, but the pain that started as a throb in my chest grew into a stabbing every breath I took.

I dropped to my knees and gripped my chest. Was I being punished for not helping Shivani? The thought flickered through my mind like lightning before darkness overtook me.

"Astra?" Aero yelled.

His voice sounded muffled, fuzzy, as though I were underwater. The world tilted sideways as consciousness slipped away from me.

I woke up in a daze. Everything around me was warm but so bright that I couldn't focus. I held my hands over my eyes to block the light, the harsh glare piercing through my eyelids.

"You're awake!" Kyra cried, relief washing through her voice.

"I didn't realize I was sleeping," I murmured, my tongue feeling thick and clumsy in my mouth.

"What were you doing to end up so hurt? Divala had to fly healers straight from Ashbell here because the medicine we had wasn't enough," Kyra demanded, her words tight with worry.

I lowered my hand and opened an eye. Kyra was kneeling at the side of the bed. Her green eyes were bloodshot, dark circles shadowing the skin beneath them. The scent of healing herbs hung in the air, mingling with the warmth of candles burned low.

"I'm all right," I said as I tried to sit up, wincing as pain shot through every nerve.

"All right? What were you doing?" She pressed me harder like I was in trouble, her fingers digging into the bedsheets.

"I was just trying to pull souls from stars in Semper, but something strange happened. It should have been easy to do with Yumi locked up and the stars being my duty while she is. It's not a big deal," I explained, trying to keep my voice steady despite the pain.

"Yes, it is! You're going to die for someone who doesn't care about you!" Kyra yelled, her voice breaking with emotion.

I sighed, the movement sending fresh waves of pain through my chest. "Please don't do this right now. This has nothing to do with anyone but me. I made a choice, and it had a poor outcome. It's that simple." The words fell flat even to my own ears.

"I just don't understand how you can always be so willing to put yourself at risk like this." Kyra let go of my hand and stood up, her chair scraping harshly against the floor.

I wasn't as willing as she thought, but it would sound worse if I told her that I was just willing to let one of Dahlia's daughters die so that I could make it home to her. The truth would only put more distance between us.

"I understand that you're upset Ruri never said goodbye to you, but that doesn't mean you can keep holding me account-able like this. You can't keep blaming every choice I make on her. Ruri is only one small part of the entire picture. Even if I never spoke to her again, we would still have to do the same things and make the same choices to save our realm from not just Yumi but Nikola." Kyra stopped me with a sharp gesture, her eyes flashing with anger.

"I'd watch it all die and help you create a new one if it meant your safety," Kyra whispered fiercely.

She left me and slammed the door to her bedroom on the way out. The sound reverberated through my aching head, making me flinch.

I moved my clothing off of my chest again, and the star was still burnt into me. Black streaks came from it and extended in every direction across my entire chest, like dark veins pulsing beneath my skin. The pain was still near unbearable, each breath feeling like fire in my lungs. I needed something stronger than the medicine that was given to me already.

I tried to stand. I needed to find a cleric. I didn't make it far from the bed before I was on my knees again. The same glistening hand gripped my heart and squeezed. I felt a mixture of Yumi and Helia's presence at my fingertips. I didn't know how I knew it was them, but I did. Their malice was unmistakable, cold and familiar as an old enemy.

I felt them draining me, pulling my essence away like water slipping through cupped hands. The room grew dim around me as my strength ebbed, and I wondered if this was how it would end, not with a heroic sacrifice, but with a silent curse that no one saw coming.

CHAPTER TWENTY-ONE

SECRETS NEVER STAY BURIED

COY

Being a guardian meant that I didn't need to hunt for my brothers. I knew where they were, like I knew where my limbs were. My brothers were as much a part of me as any other part I had. I stood a distance away from the crowd surrounding the Ash trees, but I was far from hidden. The warm breeze carried the scent of burning leaves and mineral-rich soil to where I watched. Caym helped the Seere that inhabited Ashbell gather ash from the burning leaves, his movements precise and methodical.

The Seere were a strange group to me. Other mortals pumped blood through their bodies, Seere pumped molten lava through theirs, and it was visible around their black scales. The orange glow pulsed beneath their obsidian skin like a heartbeat. They were built to live near the volcano and its heat. I wiped the sweat off my own forehead, the moisture making my fingertips glisten. The thought made me aware of the heat's effect on me, my clothes clinging uncomfortably to my damp skin.

I spent a lot of time traveling Cylla, and I felt as if I had lived in three different worlds. Our original world was so much different. Golden and green. It had a vibrancy and an order that no other place had. The air there tasted sweet, like honey and sunlight. There was one kingdom run by the gods. The shattered realm was dark and cold. Run by one puppet moving to the strings of an even older enemy. The very air there had felt sharp, like breathing in tiny shards of glass.

Cylla sat somewhere in the middle. Run by mortals and a few gods who cared to stay around. Some places were vibrant, but it was all cold. Something was missing from our current realm. Maybe it was peace; maybe it was simply memory. It seemed the more others remembered, the more comfort they had. The thought left a hollow ache in my chest that I tried to ignore.

I wasn't going to dwell. I didn't want my memory yet, and I'd stay firm on it. With their comfort came the inability to make choices that weren't based on specific individuals. That was the biggest weakness I had seen since we collided. The words felt rehearsed even in my own mind.

Someone told me that if I repeated things enough times, I would eventually believe them.

It hadn't worked as well as I had hoped yet.

"What are you doing here?" Caym questioned, his voice cutting through my thoughts.

He walked towards me in the presence of someone much older than he was. The way he talked, and the way he stood. I hadn't seen so much as a wrinkle on his undershirt or a string on his corset vest out of place. His boots didn't even carry a speck of the ash that covered everything else in sight.

"I'm here to check on you," I answered, forcing my voice to remain steady.

Caym chuckled, the sound warm and familiar. "I heard that you were coming to check on each of us. Koa said you did a pretty good job building homes in Sephtis. I can't let him be the only one that gets an extra set of hands, so if you're going to be here, you're going to have to help here, too."

I nodded. I didn't need to speak to be given instructions. He pointed me ahead, and I listened. I had never gathered the healing ash, but it was clear enough from watching the Seere that I scooped it into a special sack, tied it closed, and put it into the pile of bags. The ash was surprisingly warm against my palms, almost alive with energy. Caym took his own bag and scooped.

"Have you made any progress?" Caym inquired, his voice low enough that only I could hear.

"I've cleared Koa. I've sent dragons to find a special tool that will confirm my findings or prove me wrong. I've nothing else to report," I responded as I gathered another scoop of ash, the fine particles clinging to my fingers.

I drove my hand into the pocket of my pants that still carried crushed truth stone and brushed a hand against his arm. I moved in a way that could be considered an accidental consequence of our closeness. The stone tingled against my skin, detecting no falsehood in his presence.

"I won't ask about the tool. I think it's good you're taking charge of this. You're the only one we can clear. You weren't here for anything," Caym remarked, his eyes focused on his task.

I wanted to save Caym for last because of all the deities I've seen or spoken to; he was the one I admired. I worried that being around him would crack the wall that I worked so hard to build for myself. His steady presence was already making hairline fractures in my carefully constructed defenses.

"Have you seen Ruri?" I asked, the question slipping out before I could stop it.

He filled his bag with another scoop of ash. He didn't look at me. "She is convinced that she is in love with some mortal man. Having me around confuses her this time." His voice remained even, but I could hear the pain beneath the carefully controlled words.

The sadness in his eyes was exactly why I didn't want to remember Hesperia. I was too afraid to be consumed by the feeling. I wanted to be far from her and the emotions that tapped at my door, persistent as raindrops on a window.

"I considered it unjust to check Koa and Onyx without also seeking you out, but I never truly suspected you. I thought maybe you were making the perfect play. Putting your hands in everything so that you have control of all information. You felt like the perfectly placed traitor until I met you. I realized you were just doing the best you could." I bit my tongue after the words came out, tasting blood.

I spent years eating every feeling that wasn't related to a plan. It was around Caym that I cracked, my carefully constructed walls beginning to crumble.

"I won't hold that against you. I can see how I would look suspicious to someone who didn't know me. I know that if you were in my place, though, you would make the same choices," Caym observed. He still had not looked upset or startled by my presence, his movements remaining smooth and controlled. "Can I ask you a question? Did you seek me out because you wanted to clear me of being a traitor or because you were growing tired of fighting yourself?"

"Both," I admitted, the word feeling raw in my throat.

"If there's one thing that I'm confident about, it's your ability to make the right choices and admit that you might miss Hesperia, too. You're right that there isn't much information that gets away from me. You and Hesperia are alike in that you both want to look unbothered on the outside. It doesn't make you weak to say it out loud to her," Caym pointed out. He tied off his bag and set it to the side, the fabric pulling taut around the ash inside. "If I were the traitor, I'd have taken my own life for Ruri's sake. Why don't you take this time to go see Hesperia?"

"Before I decide to take your offer, can I ask you another question?" I requested, my heart pounding at the thought of seeing her.

Caym nodded, his eyes meeting mine with understanding.

"Do you think it's Onyx or Koa?" I asked. "Truthfully."

Caym's gaze drifted off into the distance for a moment before he answered, his shoulders tensing slightly. "I think in the end, neither answer will hurt less." He shifted his head to face me, "I've spent a lot of time with both of them. Defending both of them. I've trusted them both. I've called them both brothers and believed that if they were put in a position to betray us, that it had to be for a good reason. That it had to be against their will. I've come to the conclusion that there has to be a puzzle piece that I'm missing to make them pick the side they are. I hold hope that they are actually helping in their own way." He sighed, the sound heavy with the weight of centuries.

The both of us let a few moments of silence pass. The crackling of burning ash leaves filled the void between us. I was so sure that Caym had found some sort of secret to cope with our circumstances. I was confident that he would have a secret cure that would somehow flip a switch to harden me. Instead, I found him carrying the same burdens, just with more grace.

Caym opened a rift beside us and nodded his head in its direction. The portal shimmered with energy, casting prismatic reflections across our faces. He was right. Talking to her was worth at least one try. I stepped through the rift and was surprised to see that I was still in Ashbell. Only now, I was closer to the temple, the massive stone structure looming before me.

Hesperia turned and looked at me with disbelief, her golden eyes widening. "Coy?"

I swallowed harder than usual, the sound audible in the

sudden silence. I didn't speak because I wasn't sure yet what to say, my practiced words evaporating like morning dew.

"What are you doing here?" she asked, her voice a mixture of confusion and guarded hope.

"I could ask you the same thing," I raised an eyebrow, instantly regretting my defensive tone.

I was off to a poor start, the tension between us thick enough to cut.

She crossed her arms and leaned to the side, the fabric of her dress rustling with the movement. "I'm here on business. I received a letter from Astra. She needs the Sun God relic we hid in the temple. I have also started making allies, unlike you. I've been pouring over lineage trackers from the Timekeepers to find the lost descendant of the water Goddess. If I deliver them safely, they'll swear an army to me. The lineage tracker says the last known location was Ashbell. Where do all the important things in Ashbell go? The temple."

"That does seem to be where all lost or important things go," I agreed, my voice softening.

"Now you listen to me!" She pointed, her finger inches from my chest.

Both of my brows shot up. They were preparing my defense before my mouth was, my body tensing automatically.

"Wait, did you just agree with me?" she asked, her hand faltering mid-gesture.

I nodded, the movement stiff. "If you'd allow me, I'd like to stay and help you complete your mission," I offered, the words clumsy on my tongue.

"No. Absolutely not," she frowned, her expression hardening like a shield being raised.

I wasn't sure what I expected, but it wasn't what I received. Caym made me feel so confident that I had convinced myself she would fall into my arms and I'd have a relationship like his immediately. The rejection stung more than I was prepared for.

"I don't understand," I confessed, my voice barely audible.

"I think that I should sooner take you to a cell and lock you away until we have time for a healer to examine you," her frown turned to disgust, her nostrils flaring slightly.

"Have you decided that you no longer want me around?" I questioned, a hollow feeling spreading in my chest.

"I hardly understand where this is coming from?" She shook her head, her dark hair catching the light. "You've made it clear that you want distance, and I gave it to you. Suddenly, you wake up and change your mind. Did you have a fall?"

"Can I request that the distance be shortened?" I asked, the words feeling foreign in my mouth.

The way she looked at me hadn't changed, suspicion mingling with hurt in her golden eyes.

"I apologize. I shouldn't have assumed that you would be okay with my sudden shift. I didn't consider that you may be too hurt to make such an adjustment."

I turned to leave, my boots scraping against the stone floor, but she grabbed my arm and pulled me back. The warmth of her touch sent a jolt through me. She wrapped her arms around me and buried her face in my chest, her body trembling slightly against mine. I felt myself crack a smile. I ran a hand through her hair, and although the movement felt stiff, I could have gotten used to it. Her scent surrounded me, jasmine and starlight achingly familiar yet new all at once.

"I think it's cruel of you to dangle this kind of idea in front of my face only to half-heartedly try and love me," Hesperia whispered, her breath warm against my chest.

"It's not my intent to be half-hearted," I responded, my hand still awkwardly frozen in her hair.

"You're hardly holding me," she pointed out, disappointment coloring her words.

It was heartbreaking to hear the quiver in her voice in the same way it was to hear Caym admit that he feared learning the truth of the betrayal lurking behind us. I didn't need to look at her to know tears flowed from her. The sound of her breath told me it was true, each inhale catching slightly in her throat.

I should have stayed away from her. Maintaining distance between us at least kept her from the kind of pain that made her cry. Yet as I stood there, my arms gradually tightening around her shaking frame, I wondered if the greater pain was in the distance itself. The walls I'd built to protect myself were crumbling, and I found myself uncertain whether to rebuild them or let them fall completely.

CHAPTER TWENTY-TWO
IN THE ARMS OF A HERO

RURI

Inola sent me to be locked away in the secret room of the temple with Lui for the day. She said that she hadn't gathered proof but that she knew that I was sneaking around with someone. Inola said if I couldn't be responsible on my own, she would make sure that I was on her own. I didn't understand why it was such a transgression for me to have a relationship. My arguments meant nothing because, at the end of the day, I signed up to be Inola's property. The thought left a bitter taste in my mouth.

If she said that I was to spend my day with the old man still hanging onto his days as a Timekeeper, then that's what I had to do. The musty scent of ancient scrolls filled my nostrils as I sat beside him.

"Once, before the Goddesses were lost, these scrolls used to line walls tall enough we needed magic to reach them all," Lui reminisced, his voice crackling like parchment.

"Mhm." I nodded, tracing patterns in the dust on the table with my fingertip.

The old man enjoyed talking, but I wasn't as interested in

what he had to say as he was in saying it. His stories rolled over me like waves, one after another, never quite making landfall in my mind.

"When we rebuild, you're welcome to come," Lui offered, his rheumy eyes brightening.

"Do you really think that you'll rebuild the great library?" I asked, unable to keep the skepticism from my voice.

I didn't think that they would. The ambition seemed too grand for the broken world we inhabited.

"I do. The king of Ashbell offered us a place here. The Queen of Brontide did as well. Daxon lent us sirens to help recover what scrolls we can." He leaned into me to whisper, his breath smelling of mint leaves and age. "Between you and I, I think they've been stealing scrolls."

"What would they need it for?" I asked, wrinkling my nose at his closeness.

He truly was something else, this old guardian of forgotten knowledge.

"There are things in here older than even I am." He pointed to a scroll above me as if I were to retrieve it, his gnarled finger trembling slightly.

Lui was the kind of person who may be pointing me to the greatest joke he had ever heard or the biggest secret he had ever kept. I wasn't sure which one was inside of the scroll he pointed to, but I didn't care, either. It was most likely to get me in trouble, too.

"Ruri."

I jumped to my feet at the sound of the deep voice, my heart leaping into my throat.

"I was sent to retrieve you. Inola requested that you come with us for the day," Caym announced, his tall frame filling the doorway.

I scoffed, trying to ignore the way my pulse quickened at the sight of him. "I thought I was to stay here and keep an eye on Lui? Now, I can't be left at the temple without her around?"

"It'll be worth going to see the dragon's hatch," Caym suggested, his voice like warm honey.

I would have said yes because if Inola had said I was to go with it, it wouldn't just be my job but my duty to do so. If I wanted to resist or deny it, the smile that formed above his soft, round chin would have caused me to agree. My resistance melted like snow in summer heat.

The small smile met his eyes and showed the points on his canine teeth. They also showed a new weakness in my knees. I must have developed it suddenly because it had never been a problem before. I hardly walked straight following him out of the temple, my feet feeling as though they were floating rather than touching the ground.

I felt my eyes dry out from staring. Had he always been so beautiful? Seeing him in the darkness, with only the stars and the volcano to light him up, had been a sight, but seeing him in the full light made him look like he had been chiseled by a god. There was something about him that I couldn't put my finger on. He felt so familiar, like a favorite melody played after years of silence.

I couldn't recall seeing him growing up. I just knew that I knew him from somewhere. The sensation tugged at the edges of my memory, just out of reach.

I knew that his hands would be soft, even though they looked as if they would be rough. I somehow knew that he smelled of burnt food in the evenings and lavender in the morning. I knew if I asked, he would agree that he liked stews. Why would I know that? The certainty was as disorienting as it was inexplicable.

I recalled the gloves he wore, too. I recognized the special string they were made of. Where was it from? The pattern etched into the leather seemed to tell a story I once knew by heart.

"Are you all right?" he asked, his brow furrowing with concern.

"I'm sorry," I stuttered, heat flooding my cheeks. "I just think I know you from somewhere. I feel like I need to touch you."

I felt the heat in my cheeks intensify after the realization that I spoke out loud and no longer in my head. He didn't seem as embarrassed as I was. He moved closer to me and lowered his face to mine, his scent enveloping me rosemary and starlight and something uniquely him.

I thought I may have died under the closeness of his gaze, my heart pounding so hard I was sure he could hear it.

"Touch anything that you'd like to," his words were strung together like poetry, each syllable caressing my ears.

They made my heart slow to a point where I thought it might stop entirely. I reached up and brushed my hand across his bare cheek. The contact felt like lightning, electric and overwhelming. Suddenly, a movie was playing in front of me. A vivid memory of his body on top of mine while he whispered in my ear. The vision was so real I could feel the weight of him, the warmth of his breath against my skin.

"Are you sure that you're all right?" he asked. His words were the same familiar whisper I had just heard in my memories, sending shivers down my spine.

There my legs went. They let me down and gave out, but he didn't. His arm was around my waist quick enough that it felt as fast as the flash of memory I had. The strength in his grip was reassuring, anchoring me when everything else seemed to be spinning.

"You can touch me again if you need to," he smirked, his eyes darkening.

Caym's arms were around me, and the closeness of his lips already had me sitting on the edge of what I was sure was an explosion that would make the volcano look like a small pool. I felt myself leaning into his lips, which were so close to me that we could have been one being. The world around us faded, leaving only the magnetic pull between us.

I would have kissed him if it wasn't for the quick and small sound he made when he felt me leaning in closer. It was a sound of wanting. As if he needed me as much as I thought I needed him. The raw vulnerability in that tiny noise broke through my haze.

I didn't know him, but I could have been convinced that I did. Every fiber of my being recognized him, even if my mind couldn't place how or why.

I backed up and inhaled a silent breath until my lungs were too full to take in anymore. I couldn't be near him. The air between us felt charged, dangerous.

It wasn't fair to Deimos. What I was doing was bordering a person that I didn't want to be. I didn't want to have to look at Deimos and tell him that I kissed another man. The thought of betraying him sat like a stone in my stomach.

"Are you sure that you're all right?" Caym asked, concern evident in his voice.

I cleared my throat, fighting to regain my composure. "Yes. I'm fine. I-I," I couldn't stop myself from stuttering, my tongue and thoughts hopelessly tangled. "We need to go. Inola will be waiting."

I walked ahead of him, my steps quick and uneven. I needed to create space between us. I didn't know what I saw when I touched him, but it was too intimate of a moment for me to see. If I wasn't with Deimos, I may not have denied the sight. But I was with him; I didn't need to consider such thoughts. The guilt and confusion swirled within me like opposing currents.

I looked beside me to where Caym stood, and he watched me out of the corner of his eyes with a smile larger than he had since I met him. The fondness in his gaze made my heart skip a beat despite my best intentions.

I looked back down immediately. I didn't want him to

know that I saw him looking at me. The only thing that took my attention from him was the sight of emerald lightning strikes growing up the back of my hand. I lifted my hand into the air, the skin glowing with an otherworldly light, but he looked at it, too. I pulled my sleeve down and tucked my hand into the pocket of my cloak, panic rising in my throat.

His eyes were as wide as mine felt, but he stayed silent, the unspoken understanding between us more terrifying than any accusation.

When we arrived at the volcano, the king of Ashbell was already waiting to greet Inola. The heat from the molten rock below washed over us in waves, making the air shimmer. Inola moved to the side, and although it had to be my imagination, it was as if she had done it on purpose. The king nearly dropped to his knees, his face draining of color as his eyes fixed on me, and I didn't think; I just moved to grab him.

"When you said that it was striking, I didn't think you meant identical," he spoke to Inola but hadn't blinked while looking at me, his voice trembling with something that might have been awe or fear.

"The resemblance is striking to see," Inola agreed, her tone carefully neutral.

My training hadn't told me how to respond to a king standing in front of me looking as though he'd seen a ghost. I helped him stand back up and give me another full look, his eyes drinking in every detail of my face as if committing it to memory.

"Let's go," Inola commanded. She motioned us forward, breaking the strange tension.

My mind felt fuzzy again, and I was somewhere else. I still looked like myself, but I was somehow not. I stood in front of the king of Ashbell, and he knelt in front of me. I held the crown he still wore on his head while he stood in front of me earlier. I placed it on his head, and he looked up at me with so much pride that it was contagious. The memory, if that's what it was, felt as real as the ground beneath my feet.

I blinked again, and I was on the rim of the volcano between everyone, the heat stinging my eyes and making my skin flush. My mind kept moving between my present and someone else's past, like a stone skipping across water, never settling in either time.

A group of women wearing simple and plain white gowns walked in a single-file line down a carved set of stairs into the volcano. Their movements were measured and reverent, steam rising around them in ghostly tendrils. They each carried an egg different from the last, shells gleaming with jewel-like colors. One by one, they lowered the eggs into the lava, and sparks came from the magma, shooting upward like golden fireworks. It only took moments for the smallest-scaled babies to come flying out of the liquid, their newborn cries piercing the air.

I was so transfixed in the sight that I didn't notice I was leaning too far forward. The idea of falling into the volcano scared me enough; the small grip I still had on the rim was lost, and I stumbled. My heart skipped a beat when I watched myself tumble forward, the heat of the lava rushing up to meet me.

"You're already hatched. You don't belong in there," Caym declared.

He pulled me up by my waist, and this time, he held me with both of his arms. He held me as if he knew me as well, his touch sure and familiar. He touched my face to move my hair, his fingers cool against my flushed skin, but it sent my mind spiraling again.

I saw him, through what had to be someone else's eyes, in another lifetime again. He fed me strawberries in a hot spring. One that looked similar to what Deimos took me to. The juice stained his fingers and my lips, sweet and tart on my tongue.

When I blinked and saw him through my eyes again, lightning bolts were coming from the sky above us, splitting the air with deafening cracks.

"I can explain!" I shouted, panic clawing at my throat.

I had done so well at quieting my magic. I should have met with Deimos more. Now I'd be in a cage, or worse, dead. The thought sent ice through my veins despite the volcano's heat.

"It's not on purpose!" I cried, tears stinging my eyes. "It must be some kind of curse, or—or," I stumbled over myself, words failing me in my terror.

Caym placed a hand over my lips, his touch gentle but firm. "Take a breath, Ru."

It was hard when he kept taking all of the air from me. Even harder when I saw the dragons as they sat and watched me, their ancient eyes reflecting the lightning in eerie flashes. The king and Inola held their eyes on me, as well, their expressions unreadable.

I was the center of everyone's attention, just like Deimos said I would be if I slipped. The realization settled over me like a shroud, heavy with the weight of inevitable consequences.

CHAPTER TWENTY-THREE

IS IT TOO GOOD TO BE TRUE

RURI

I didn't know how long I had been pacing my room, but it felt like years had passed since they sent me to be alone. The wooden floorboards creaked beneath my restless feet, marking each anxious step. Inola tried to assure me that they would keep my secret, that it wasn't a big enough problem for me to panic over, her voice calm in a way that only made me more suspicious.

Of course, she would say something like that. She wanted me calm and locked away until she figured out what to do with me. I called and called to Deimos, my whispers growing increasingly desperate. I needed him to come and rescue me. He was busy, and I tried my best to understand that under most circumstances. This was one where it was hard for me to feel so understanding, my patience wearing thin like frayed silk.

I slowly turned the knob on my door and pushed it open, wincing at the soft creak. I couldn't pace in silence any longer, the quiet room amplifying my racing thoughts. There were no guards placed anywhere. Not a single person was out of place.

Everything was so normal that I questioned if I had rained lightning down at all. The familiar scent of incense and candle wax filled the corridor, oddly comforting in its normalcy.

I snuck to the back of my quarters and called to Deimos again, my voice barely a whisper. This time, he stood in front of me, materializing like a shadow given form.

"Why didn't you answer sooner?" I asked as I shoved him, my hands connecting with his cold chest.

"I was doing my best, but you didn't leave your room. You wanted me to go inside of it? After you called to me, telling me you were under watch?" He looked at me with furrowed brows and a frown, his golden eyes flashing with annoyance.

"I wanted you to help me," I scoffed, the taste of fear bitter on my tongue.

"I am," he said simply, his voice lacking the warmth I craved.

"It doesn't feel like it," I snapped, crossing my arms to hide my trembling hands.

He grabbed me and pulled me into an embrace, his movements quick and possessive. "Does it now?" His scent of ash and night surrounded me, yet failed to comfort.

It didn't. His arms felt cold and empty compared to the fire I had felt from someone else. Was his ever loving? Did it only feel that way because it was all I had felt? The realization sent a chill down my spine.

"You will be okay," he stated. "If I had entered your room, and I was seen by someone like Caym, how could I have helped you then?"

"Do you know him? Are you that afraid of him?" I couldn't believe what I was seeing from him, this crack in his usual confidence.

He shoved me and nearly knocked me down, the force sending me stumbling backward. "I am not afraid of him." The tip of his false finger that sat on his lost hand was in my face, cold metal gleaming inches from my nose. "But you should be. He can be cruel to you if you're not careful. Haven't those dreams taught you enough about him? Aren't you afraid of him enough to keep a distance?" His voice roared and echoed around us, his breath hot against my face.

His words felt more like venom than a cure. He had never yelled at me before, and the shock of it left me breathless.

The shift in reality happened again. Something about him triggered my mind to pull me back into it, the world around me blurring and refocusing.

This time, I was pressed against a wall. I was disgusted and angry under a hot breath. Deimos leaned over me, and I felt as if I'd vomit, his fingers digging into my arms. Caym grabbed him and threw him to the ground, the impact reverberating through the floor. Deimos' hand was the next thing to hit the floor, severed and bloody. Caym's eyes were locked on me. Commanding me to take in the seriousness behind his actions, their intensity burning through me.

Who was that man? What was this memory that felt so vivid yet foreign?

I came to and puked at Deimos's feet, acid burning my throat. He backed up in disgust, the hem of his robes splattered, and before I could look up at him, I noticed more markings on my other hand. Emerald patterns crawled up my wrist like living vines. What was happening to me?

"What is wrong with you?" Deimos yelled, his disgust palpable.

I didn't have time to respond before I was walking beside Inola in a golden city, the sunlight blinding in its brilliance.

I vomited again, the sour taste overwhelming, and when I looked up to see Deimos in front of me, I was filled with so much heat that my fists shook. I shot a lightning bolt out of my hand at him, the crackling energy singing the air.

He dodged it, his movements unnaturally quick, and I shot a purple ball of flame at him. I wanted him to die. I hated him. I hated Deimos more than I understood the word hate. The emotion consumed me like wildfire.

Why did I hate him? The question floated distantly in my mind, but the rage overpowered it.

"Ruri!" Hands grabbed me and turned me around to face them. "If you don't stop, you're going to crumble the entire temple." The grip was firm but gentle, grounding me.

"I know you," I said, staring into eyes that sparked recognition deep within me.

"Of course you do. I'm Hesperia. You know me from Orest," she said, her white hair glowing in the light.

"No." I shook my head. I felt the shaking in my hands start again, energy crackling between my fingers. "I know you!"

My head throbbed. My chest felt like it was going to explode, heart hammering against my ribs. What was wrong with me?

"I know you. I know you. I know you."

I shook my head, trying to search my mind for the answer. Was I screaming? The sound tearing from my throat barely sounded human.

"Who are you?"

The corner of my eye caught sight of my nails scratching away my own skin on my arm, leaving angry red welts. I looked back up at the girl in front of me, her face blurring through my tears.

I needed to kill her, too. The thought came unbidden, shocking in its intensity.

She held me too tightly. Her grip left a burning sensation on my body, her touch both comforting and searing.

"I'm sorry," the girl said, regret flashing in her eyes.

I felt a pain in the back of my neck before darkness claimed me, pulling me under like a wave.

I took a deep breath before I stretched and groaned. My pillows were warm, the sheets tangled around my legs. I opened my eyes, and Hesperia sat in front of me, her posture tense with anticipation.

"How are you feeling?" she asked, her voice careful.

I narrowed my eyes on her and sat up. She hit me. I reached behind my head and touched my neck, feeling the tender spot where pain bloomed under my fingers.

"You hit me!" I yelled, indignation rising within me.

"It was for a good reason!" She yelled back, her hands clenched in her lap.

I took in the sight of her white hair down to its flyaways before looking back into her eyes. "You still hit as if you've never fought a day in your life."

Hesperia clicked her tongue and looked at me with a curled lip. "It was clearly hard enough to knock you out, so if anyone is weak, it's you." She leaned back in her chair, mumbling under her breath before she shot back up, eyes widening. "Wait, what?"

"You better mark this day in history. When the rest of them wake up, no one will ever believe you knocked me out," I said, a smirk playing on my lips.

The air was pulled out of me when she ripped me up and wrapped her arms around my neck, nearly lifting me from the bed.

"I thought I'd never see you again," Hesperia sobbed, her tears dampening my shoulder. "I see your face, but it wasn't you inside of it."

"You won't see me again if you keep this up," I choked out, the embrace threatening to crush my windpipe.

Hesperia only loosened her grip enough to allow me the smallest oxygen flow, her fingers digging into my back.

"What's going on?" I squeaked, struggling to breathe.

"It's a long story," she said through tears, her voice thick with emotion.

"I have time," I answered, patting her back awkwardly.

"What do you remember?" she asked, finally pulling back to look at my face, her eyes searching.

"I remember Nikola slaughtering deities and Yumi stealing souls," I said, the memories flooding back with sickening clarity.

"He locked me in a necklace and kept me with him," Hesperia said. "He talked to me as if I were his personal diary." Her words sent a chill through me.

A sadness washed over her face. One I never would have believed she could wear, her usual confidence replaced by something fragile and wounded.

The door opened and jolted both of us. She released me from her hold, and the two of us looked like children caught in a cookie jar, freezing in place.

"Inola sent me to check on the situation," Caym said, his deep voice filling the room. "Onyx also sent a messenger with a new set of weapons Ruri apparently commissioned him to make for her. He said she was quite scared of him, so he didn't want to bring them in person." Caym laughed and shook his head, his eyes crinkling at the corners.

He stopped and stood stiff in the doorway, recognition dawning on his face. Hesperia didn't look at him; she only gave me the biggest smile she could make, her eyes glistening with hope.

I felt like it had been hundreds of years since I had seen him. Touched him. I shoved Hesperia with a pillow out of my way and jumped over her chair. I would test how he had been keeping up with his strength over however long it had been. I jumped from the chair into his arms and wrapped my legs around him, my heart soaring.

I smirked when he still caught me as if it were second nature, his arms strong and sure around me.

"I see you've not neglected your training," I said, my voice light with joy.

He didn't answer me at first. He held me, but I felt the

distance between us. It was an uncomfortable feeling, like a note out of tune in a familiar melody.

"Did he forget me as well?" I asked, doubt creeping in.

"Forget you?" He spoke with disbelief, his eyes wide. "You're the only thought I have."

"You said the same thing while we sat on the roof of the golden castle. We had snacks then, though," I sighed, the memory warming me from within.

"You, remember?" His voice was slow and full of hesitation, barely daring to hope.

I leaned back and placed both of my hands on each of his cheeks, his skin warm beneath my palms. "I don't believe I ever truly forgot you."

He was still hesitant, but I wouldn't let it stop me. I grabbed his face, and I kissed every inch of his bare cheeks and chin, tasting salt from tears he wouldn't admit were there.

"Where is Belladonna? Jeb?" I kissed too many more times to count, punctuating each name with affection. "Astra? Sage?"

"I can't believe you're back," he nearly sobbed, finally tightening his embrace, holding me as if he feared I might vanish if he let go.

CHAPTER TWENTY-FOUR
A LOST FRIEND HOLDS THE ANSWERS

HESPERIA

"Are you sure you don't want to stay on the shore?" I asked Vespera, the damp air clinging to my skin like a second layer.

She didn't answer me, but she didn't need to. When I looked back at her, the grimace across her face was clear, her lips pressed into a thin line. The cursed forest was a place I didn't enjoy going, either. It was filled with the creatures from Nikola's realm, their unearthly growls echoing through the mist. They hadn't discovered a way to get across the water that surrounded them. It was a relief for me, but not for what was already an angry creature. Killing them never seemed to have a lasting effect either, like trying to extinguish a fire that constantly reignited.

I wasn't happy to leave my newly awakened sister so soon, but I also didn't want her to see the state of the forest, the corruption that had seeped into every tree and patch of soil.

I was fine with doing what I needed to do. Killing the creatures meant nothing to me. Vespera wasn't weak, but it was hard to make someone understand what they were dealing with unless they laid eyes on it themselves. The creatures were taller than most things in Cylla. Large enough to compete with the golems of Orest, their twisted forms defying natural laws.

"So, are you any closer to helping Sage get her memory back?" I asked, stepping carefully over a gnarled root.

"If I was, do you think that I'd be here doing this?" Vespera answered, her voice sharp enough to cut.

"I would think that you'd still want to do something nice for her," I said, glancing over my shoulder.

Vespera let out a small scoff, the sound bitter in the heavy silence of the forest.

"All right," I said. I turned to face her, my boots sinking slightly in the soft earth. "What is it? You've been passive and avoided me the entire trip."

Vespera's cheeks flushed, and she looked as if she were going to pounce at me, her hands curling into fists at her sides. It washed away in an instant and was replaced by something else entirely. Something closer to sadness, a vulnerability that seemed foreign on her always-confident face.

"We're far away from anything that could hear you. Talk to me," I pressed, the scent of decay and rot filling my nostrils with each breath.

"It's complicated," she murmured, her eyes fixed on the ground.

"No, it isn't," I forced my tone to be rougher, hoping to break through her walls.

"I just didn't expect things to take so long. I thought that, even if she didn't remember me, maybe she would remember the feeling of me, like Ruri and Caym. I didn't expect to be in competition with Onyx for so long. I pictured myself killing Onyx by now. Now I'm watching Ru come back. Friends, sisters, and lovers are all happy again. Why isn't it me, too?" Vespera stomped forward through more bare tree branches, the dead wood cracking beneath her feet.

My feet slid through the sludge of mud and moss that

covered the ground, each step releasing the pungent scent of decay. "Ruri and Caym are not the rule; they are the exception."

If they were, I wouldn't be spending all of my free time convincing myself that somewhere inside Coy, he still knows who I am. The thought sent a familiar ache through my chest.

"Shivani and Koa aren't perfect, either. Coy and I are complicated. It's more common for us all to struggle. It's hard for me, too, but it would be harder if we were all sent back to the start. I think you're on the right path. Trying to rescue her sprites is something that she will be grateful for when she gets her memory back," I said. I grabbed her by the arm and made her stop walking so quickly, her skin cold beneath my fingers. "She will get her memory back."

I saw a glimmer of pain in Vespera's eyes, like light catching on fractured glass. Even while she spoke and admitted so loosely that she was struggling, she did it with a harshness. She acted as if she were stone that I couldn't see through. The glimmer of suffering that ran over her was easy for me to recognize because it felt the way that it looked, a familiar weight I carried myself.

I suffered in silence, too. I preferred to shove down the pain of the way we lived now the same as she was doing. I think she was suffering worse than I was. I only had to half swallow down the bitterness of Coy's memory loss, while her love barely recognized her existence.

Nikola did a good job of hardening me over the years, saying that it was only him and I. The part of me that truly felt pain was all but broken. I had been where she was, and I had to find something to hold onto. What I grasped at was positivity, fragile as it sometimes seemed.

I pulled at the strings of hope and did my best to ignore the tunnels of darkness. I never wanted to be swallowed by them again, the void that had nearly consumed me during my captivity.

"You need to believe that we will get there. That she will get there. Holding onto hope is the only way you can keep moving forward," I urged her, squeezing her arm gently.

"Then let's keep moving," she answered, her voice flat.

The way she pulled my arm said she only spoke to please me, not because we were friends. I could lead her anywhere she wanted me to, but I could not force her to accept any answer she wasn't ready for yet. I could try my best to tell her that I had already learned these lessons, but the sad thing was, no matter how many times I wanted to show her that she could skip the journey and see the result, she'd never see the same thing as I did without digging through the same dirt that I had. The realization weighed on me, another burden to carry.

Our walk through the rest of the forest was without any further words. Vespera walked ahead of me, and I didn't try to catch up to her. There was always a tenseness to her, but she was unusual this time, her shoulders rigid with unspoken emotion.

I nearly forgot that Sina was also behind us, her footsteps so light they barely disturbed the fallen leaves. Maybe that was why Vespera hadn't wanted to open up to me. Vespera might not have wanted to seem vulnerable in front of multiple people. We began to enter trees that were clearly charred from a fire that burned too hot, too quickly. The blackened trunks reached toward the sky like skeletal fingers. It meant we were closer to the bones.

I knelt in front of them and reached into the middle, the pile shifting beneath my hands. I used my nose to sniff out what I was looking for, the scents of death and magic mingling together. I knew there were bones of fire sprites and earth sprites, but I hadn't seen or heard of others. I smelt the wet grass of the earth's sprites. Many deities had a problem with theft in the Golden City. If an earth sprite's back was licked, it was said to have hallucinating properties. I hadn't tried it myself to know.

I pulled a bone out of the pile and pulled the soul from the in-between. It was only a man, not a sprite. I pulled another, then another, each one sending a jolt of energy through my fingertips. My nose was having a hard time adjusting to the realm, I suppose. I leaned myself down and took a bigger whiff, the scent of ancient magic tickling my senses.

"I found it!" I yelled as I dug deeper, excitement momentarily breaking through my caution.

I pulled out the sprite bone, but I also grabbed a second. A bone bigger than the sprites would have been, but I was pulled to it. I heard it calling me, and I felt as if I needed to pull it up, too, the compulsion overwhelming my better judgment. I handed the smaller sprite bone to Vespera, who stood behind me. I kept the bigger bone. I held it up and took a deep pull of its scent. It smelt of—

I tossed myself to the side of the bone pile and vomited into the mud, the acidic burn of bile scorching my throat. The feeling that washed over me was the same as when I was with Nikola, a sickening drain that left me hollow. I didn't enjoy thinking of my time with him; I didn't want to openly talk about it with anyone. The idea that they may feel bad made me feel worse. When he felt weak, he would pull from my roots to bring himself back from death. Touching the bone was the same feeling, like having my essence ripped away.

"Are you all right?" Vespera asked, concern breaking through her indifference.

I lifted my hand and shook it at her so that she would stay back, my stomach still heaving. "I'm fine," I managed to gasp, the taste of sick bitter on my tongue.

I didn't want her to sense that I had a slip. When I fully lifted my head, the trees made a tunnel that called to me, an unnatural pathway through the tangled forest.

"Do you see that?" I asked, pointing with a trembling hand.

Vespera leaned down and tried to see from my view. "The tunnel?"

I stumbled to my feet and rubbed my thumbs against the sides of my lip. I wanted to be sure that there was nothing on my face from emptying my stomach, the shame of weakness burning in my chest. I did not look back to direct Vespera to follow me. I would have been happier if she hadn't. I was feeling too embarrassed. I followed the small, tunneled path to the end, drawn forward by curiosity stronger than caution.

A small round hut sat in the middle of the trees. The entire thing was made of logs and moss, a wisp of smoke rising from a crude chimney. I didn't consider any consequences; I only followed my curiosity. I pushed open the log door, and I was in shock when inside, there was a familiar scent, herbs and incense that triggered memories long buried.

"Minna," I whispered, disbelief coloring my voice.

"Of all the faces I thought I would see, yours was not it," Minna said, her voice unchanged despite everything.

I scrunched my brows, "Were you expecting someone?" My heart raced at the implication.

"I've been haunted by the ghost of Nikola often," she answered, her eyes darting to the corners of the small space.

"You've seen him?" I closed the door behind me before Vespera could enter, the wood rough beneath my palms.

I didn't want to chance anyone clamming up, the information too valuable to risk.

"I've seen an apparition of him," she said, her hands trembling slightly as she busied them with herbs hanging from the ceiling.

"What does he want?" I asked, moving closer, the floorboards creaking beneath my feet.

"You, your sisters. For me to join him in continuing the

plan he always had," she said, her voice dropping to a whisper. "He offered me divinity back."

"What is the plan?" I moved further in, the warmth of the small fire in the center barely touching the chill that had settled in my bones.

"I don't know the entire plan. If I did, I would give it to you as a thank you for the second chance you gave me. I am using it. I don't want anything to do with him. I've rammed some of the creatures left behind. I have a peaceful life," Minna sounded sincere, her eyes meeting mine without wavering.

I nodded but didn't speak. I believed her. There wasn't anything about her that looked like a liar, no telltale signs I'd learned to recognize during my captivity.

"Yumi placed a curse on the stars in Semper. She left it as a sort of backup plan," Minna continued, her voice dropping even lower. "She told us that if she weren't around to reset the trigger on them, anyone who tried to pull the souls from the stars would be cursed. They would slowly have their soul corrupted until it shattered. That they would be broken in a way that ensured they could never come back. The only other one that knew how to handle the curse was Helia. You'll need to get those answers from her before you kill her, too."

"How would I know if the curse was present?" I asked, dread pooling in my stomach.

"It creates a star shape on the chest," she answered, her finger tracing the pattern over her own heart.

The ground under her hut shook, and cries of pain rang out, the walls trembling around us. She had not been honest enough about the number of times she was visited by creatures of Nikola. Vespera charged out as if she were ready to die for anything. She did not have a plan of action or any grasp on what she was running into, her recklessness evident in every line of her body.

I followed Vespera out of the hut only to see her held up

by the tentacle of a pile of sludge. The thing rolled and shifted itself into more tentacles to toss Vespera between them, her body flailing helplessly in its grip. The stench of rot and decay rolled off it in waves, making my eyes water.

"This is what you get for never listening to me!" I shouted, frustration bubbling over.

"Are you kidding me?" Vespera screamed, her voice strained as she struggled. "Do you think now is the time for an I told you so?"

"Yes, I do! If I'm going to have to rescue you, then you can at least promise not to rush without a single thought in the future!" I pointed, anger fueling my magic.

"Fine! Now save me!" Vespera growled, panic edging into her voice.

The pile of sludge and moss tossed her from one tentacle to another as it rolled to me, its movements unnaturally fluid for something so massive. I knew Vespera was just telling me what I wanted to hear, but I'd still be able to remind her of it later, if we survived this encounter.

I drew a moon into the air, my fingers leaving trails of silver light, and opened a passage to the veil. I turned myself into a white skeleton and used my voice to sing to the spirits that lingered around us, the melody ancient and haunting.

It only took a few hushed hums of the tune before soul after soul took form from the veil and the bones around us. They listened without command, a ghostly army answering my call. The sludge pile of Nikola's design was bombarded with attack after attack until it tossed Vespera to the ground with a hiss that seemed to pierce the very air.

Vespera hit the ground with a yelp and glared at me before she did anything else, mud splattering across her face and clothes.

"I saved you, didn't I!" I yelled, power still crackling around my transformed form.

Deimos seemed to be neglecting his duties in Cosima.

There were far more spirits roaming than was reasonable, their ethereal forms mingling with the mist. Some didn't want to move on and be sorted, but the amount around me was far too much for even that to be the reason, a clear sign of neglect.

He took claim of my realm without a second thought. He claimed that the God of Dreams would be the best fit to sort my soul, but then he neglected my land and the job, leaving chaos in his wake.

He was pitiful, and as I stood surrounded by the souls he'd abandoned, I felt my resolve strengthen. I would reclaim what was mine, no matter the cost.

CHAPTER TWENTY-FIVE
A MOIST RESCUE

I talked to Inola, and she gave me the Sun God's artifact. The golden relic hummed with ancient power against my palm, warm to the touch as if it contained the essence of sunlight itself. I sent it to Astra with a note about the curse. I didn't know if I believed it, but if it happened to be true, then the most important thing was for her to know. I didn't want to risk carrying the information that could save someone's life and not share it. The weight of that responsibility pressed on my shoulders.

Communication was key.

I sent a second Fiia with the bone of Nikola's that I found in the pile. The bone felt unnaturally cold, as if it absorbed warmth rather than emitted it. I couldn't guarantee that they could use it to find him, but I didn't want to miss that chance, either. I was willing to use any lead, no matter how small or disturbing.

I walked through the path in between and searched for signs or traces of a deity. The air here was neither hot nor cold, existing in a state beyond physical sensation. Souls left different traces. Deities were different from mortals, and mortals with unfinished business left a different trace. Each signature pulsed with its own rhythm, like heartbeats in the void.

The in-between was my favorite place to be. It was an endless sea of colors and ripples to walk through, shifting and flowing like liquid silk around my form.

Just as I felt as if there was no space left in the temple of magic to walk, blue deity sparks appeared on the ground, glittering like shattered sapphires. I moved through the veil back to the realm of the living, and in front of me stood a girl with tight aqua-blue curls that seemed to shimmer with each movement of her head.

"Who are you!" I demanded, my voice echoing against the stone walls.

She looked at me in fear, her eyes wide as pools reflecting a summer sky.

"What land do you come from?" I pointed, taking a step closer.

"I've always been in Ashbell. So was my mother," she said, her voice quivering like a plucked string.

"What's your name?" I asked, softening my tone slightly.

"Nira," she stuttered, fingers twisting nervously at the hem of her tunic.

"I'm sorry to do this to you," I said, truly meaning it despite my determination.

She looked at me with a tilted head, confusion replacing fear for just a moment. I used my pointer finger and moved her flesh away until I saw her roots. The sensation was like parting water, her physical form yielding to my power. They were part deity, and they were turned off. I flicked my finger and brought her root back to life, feeling the spark jump between us.

She immediately sprayed water from her fingertips and screamed, the liquid crystalline in the temple's dim light. I did already apologize. I hit her in the back of the head, and her body fell into me, limp and heavy. I tossed her over my shoulder with joy, her damp hair soaking through my sleeve. I hadn't found Nikola yet, but I found the demigod to earn a watery army. The triumph tasted sweet.

I drew the moon and opened the veil passageway, the air splitting with a silvery tear. She was part deity, which meant having her pass through, as long as it was quickly, should have been all right. I was gambling with her life, but how would I know if I didn't try? If she did die, I suppose I could take the army by force. The thought sent a chill through me despite my resolve.

It would be frowned upon by Mother, but she would have to understand that we aren't strong enough on our own to kill Nikola if even she wasn't. Some risks were necessary in war.

I stepped forward and into the veil. It took only a single breath before she screamed out in agony, the sound piercing through dimensions. I immediately stepped back out; her skin burned in a white light. The smell was awful, like flesh and hair burning at once, acrid and sickening.

It seemed we would be traveling by boat or dragon after all, the mundane path our only option.

"Is everything okay over there?" a familiar voice called, laced with amusement.

"Don't do it," I grumbled, my shoulders tensing.

"I was simply watching from afar and couldn't help but notice you making some poor choices that you already knew were against the rules," the voice continued, drawing closer.

"Ru!" I demanded, turning to face my sister.

She held her hands up, a mischievous smile playing on her lips. "I just thought from the sight of things that you needed a reminder of how mortal lives worked. They can't go in the veil unless they're dead."

"I know! It could have been different now! It was worth a try," I said, frustration coloring my words.

"I'm not sure that she would agree," Ruri crossed her arms, eyebrow raised as she glanced at the unconscious girl.

"She's already back asleep. She won't ever know," I said, adjusting the weight on my shoulder.

Ruri nodded with both brows raised, skepticism written across her face.

"Ya know, Maybe I should put you back asleep, too," I said, a challenge in my voice.

"You want to see if you can do it a second time?" Ru wiggled her brows, electricity already dancing between her fingertips.

I sighed. I missed her. The familiar banter felt like coming home after years away.

"Of course I do!" I tossed the girl's body on the ground and ran after her outside of the temple, the thrill of competition coursing through my veins.

Ruri didn't give me any space or countdown before she tossed purple balls of electricity at me. The air crackled with power, the scent of ozone sharp in my nostrils. I used my own magic to create a shield of bones around me. They shattered under her magic with a sound like breaking glass, but only after they took all of the heat, protecting me from the worst of it.

I shifted myself in and out of the veil to dodge her blasts and move closer. The transitions felt like plunging in and out of water, disorienting but exhilarating. She expected it every time, anticipating my movements with uncanny precision. I didn't fight the smile on my face. She wasn't a little awake. She was not hardly alive. She was herself again. She anticipated me as if she recalled every single brawl that she and I ever had, our battle dance familiar despite the years apart.

When I moved out of the veil to what should have been directly in front of her, she moved from behind me and wrapped me in purple wires. They tightened around my body, humming with energy that made my skin tingle.

"That's cheating!" I groaned, struggling against the bindings.

"That's a win, I think," she said, satisfaction evident in her voice.

"Does anyone know who the girl passed out in the hallway is?" Lui asked from the doorway of the temple, his ancient voice carrying despite its softness.

"She's mine," I answered, still trying to wriggle free.

"You're abducting mortals now?" he asked, leaning on his staff with disapproval etched in the lines of his face.

"Not, exactly. She's not completely mortal," I said, the wires digging into my skin with each movement.

"So, not mortals, but kidnapping is a yes?" he asked, his tone dry as dust.

"It's complicated," I said. "Let me out of these ropes!" I wiggled, the bindings growing tighter with each attempt.

"I kind of think they suit you. The color looks good against you, and it keeps you less mobile," Ruri said, circling me with a predatory grace.

"Let me go," I demanded, failing to keep the petulance from my voice.

"All right, all right," she unwound the bindings from my body with a flick of her wrist.

I looked down to appreciate the view of freedom, relief flooding through me, and when I looked back up, I saw that I was gone from Ashbell and with Nikola. The transition was so sudden, it left me disoriented, the world tilting on its axis.

"Did you enjoy that?" he asked as he stood in front of me, his voice silky and cold.

"Not as much as I will enjoy the fight against you," I said, forcing bravado into my voice despite the fear clawing at my throat.

"Do you believe that there will be one?" he asked as he moved closer, his scent of winter and rot washing over me. "If it's this easy for me to take you from the world you're living in and into the one I decide you can have, do you think that you stand a chance against me? Do you ever consider everything going on to be exactly how I've allowed it to be?"

"I've considered that you want me to think so. I've considered that you need to believe what you're saying is true to keep from weeping," I said, refusing to back away despite every instinct screaming to run.

"Have you come up with a plan yet?" Nikola asked as he ran his fingers through my hair, the touch sending revulsion through every fiber of my being.

"Yes, kill you," I answered, my words sharp as blades.

He laughed and showed every tooth he had, the sound echoing in the void around us. "Having confidence, although attractive, hasn't seen you successful yet. Do you remember our time together while we waited for your sisters? Or did the merge erase them?"

"I wish that they had been erased," I snarked, memories I'd tried to bury surging back like a tide.

"Do you remember when you begged me to kill you? When you cried until your sobs were silent because you longed for peace and could find none. When I offered you the ability to relive the deaths of your mother and sisters so that you could remember their faces? Do you recall when I put their heads as lanterns in my throne room and used their bones to create our silverware? You couldn't kill me then. Why would you think that you could now?" He ran his hands over my shoulders and arms as if we were close or loving, each touch leaving a trail of ice beneath my skin.

"Do you recall when I took the fork you carved from Olexei's hand and shoved it down your throat until it was embedded inside of you?" I mocked, clinging to defiance like a lifeline.

"And I still didn't die because it was an awful plan. If you had thought it out further and had a second round waiting for me, then you may have gotten further," he waved his finger at me, talking like a disappointed teacher. "I also remember your punishment after that. I still think about the sounds you made when those hooks entered your eyelids."

"Enough!" I screamed, the word tearing from my throat.

My world spun, colors blurring around me, and I was back in front of Ruri. She hovered over my body and shook me like I was a doll, her face tight with worry.

"I'm fine, I'm fine," I waved her off and sat up, my head pounding with each heartbeat. "Too much excitement, too quickly. I must be adjusting to the realm still."

"Haven't you been here a while?" Ruri asked, suspicion darkening her eyes.

"I have a mortal to get to Daxon," I said, desperate to escape her scrutiny.

I kissed Ruri on the cheek and went to retrieve the girl, my steps quickening with each moment. If I stayed, she would sense the lie that I was telling. For now, she was just confused, but that confusion wouldn't last. Some secrets were too heavy to share, even with those I loved most.

CHAPTER TWENTY-SIX

A NEW SET OF ORDERS
FROM THE ENEMY

SAGE

Vespera and I stood on the cusp of the Ashbell temple. The warm breeze carried the scent of frankincense and myrrh from the open doorway, mingling with the earthy aroma of the lush gardens surrounding us. I didn't want to be involved with the temples from the start. Standing in front of the most heavily protected temple was the absolute last thing I wanted to do. The massive crystal columns gleamed in the sunlight, intimidating in their perfection. I thought that Vespera had to be feeling the same way because since she came back from a trip she needed to take, she had been a bit different and distracted, her usual confidence replaced by a distant gaze.

"I think that you should go back," I said, the words feeling heavy on my tongue.

"What?" She nearly yelled, her eyes snapping to focus on me.

"I can sense something off about you, and it would be better if I went alone. So, you should go back to the others," I said, trying to keep my voice steady despite the tension building between us.

"I'm not going anywhere. I'll be here to protect you in case anything happens, just like any other time, in any other place," Vespera insisted, her hand instinctively moving to the hilt of her sword. "There's nothing off about me; it's you."

When she said things like that, it made my stomach flutter, and I swore there had to be hearts in my eyes while I looked at her. The intensity of her gaze made my cheeks warm. When she started to lean in closer to me, as if she were going to kiss me, I knew I had to be right. My eyes must have been bulging with surprise. I leaned a bit to the side and moved forward to the temple like I had not noticed what she was doing, my heart pounding against my ribs.

There was a large part of me that wanted to admit how much I wanted to be with her. I also didn't want to hurt her. I didn't want to commit to her while I was unsure of how I felt about Onyx. It wasn't fair to her, but I did want her. The contradiction twisted inside me like a knife.

I entered the temple through the front entrance. The marble floor was cool beneath my feet, each step echoing in the vast space. I was hopeful that we would blend in and look like anyone else visiting. We didn't because it was empty. My body radiated dread, goosebumps rising on my arms despite the warmth. Temples weren't quiet or empty. They were always filled with people in and out, the buzz of whispered prayers and shuffling feet.

"Don't overthink it," Vespera whispered, her breath warm against my ear. "If it's going to be an easy in and out, let it."

It only made my palms sweat to hear such loud silence, the absence of sound more threatening than any noise.

The temple was exactly what it promised to be. Beautifully decorated down to hand-carved crown molding, each detail telling a story of devotion. Golden frames held portraits of leadership, the painted eyes seeming to follow us as we moved. There wasn't a speck of dust in sight around the candle holders either, the flames casting dancing shadows on the walls.

The air in the temple was as light as the color scheme, perfumed with incense and magic. If I believed that worshipping the gods would get me anywhere, the temple of magic might have been what convinced me to participate in the rituals. The sense of peace was almost palpable.

I stopped in front of the statue of the Goddess of Magic. It seemed familiar. She seemed familiar. Her marble features stirred something deep within my memory, like a half-remembered dream.

"This is the goddess?" I asked, my voice barely above a whisper.

"Yes," Vespera said, shifting uncomfortably beside me.

"She feels like someone I know," I said, reaching out before catching myself.

"How would you?" Vespera forced a laugh, the sound brittle and false.

She sounded strange again. As if she were hiding something, a secret trembling on the edge of revelation.

"Do you know her?" I asked, turning to study her face.

"That would be just as foolish," she shook her head, but her eyes avoided mine.

I wanted to believe her, but her demeanor made me even more confident that I knew the goddess from somewhere. I felt a burn on my arm, like fire spreading beneath my skin, and when I lifted my sleeve, the markings that showed up on my skin earlier grew further, emerald patterns crawling toward my wrist. I pulled my sleeve down quickly, my heart racing.

"What's that?" Vespera reached for my arm, concern momentarily replacing her evasiveness.

"I'm going to check this way," I pointed and jogged behind the statue, desperate to escape her scrutiny.

The first thing I noticed was a door left open. Every other door was sealed tightly, but this one stood ajar, as if inviting me in. Inside of the room sat a crate of crystals, glowing softly with inner light. The sight was too much for me. I felt set up, like walking into a trap I knew was there. The shelf behind the crate was filled with scrolls and items, ancient knowledge waiting to be discovered.

A small full moon necklace sat beside a scroll, the silver pendant gleaming in the dim light, and I knew it was the secret item I was sent to bring back. I grabbed it and stuffed it into my pocket, the metal warm against my thigh. I didn't want Vespera to know that I took it. I didn't want her to be guilty if we were caught. What I was doing was worse than crystals, the weight of the theft heavy on my conscience.

I hated myself further when my curiosity for the other scrolls became too large to ignore. I grabbed the first scroll that I saw, the parchment dry and fragile beneath my fingertips.

Age of Moonlight, 13

The darkness spoke to me. His voice was like a serpent song. He offered me anything that I desired. He wanted nothing in return.

Age of Moonlight, 24

I made the wrong choice. It was the wrong choice, and I can't put it back. I can't fix it. I can't set things back to the way that they were. I've ruined us. I've ruined the world. I made the wrong choice.

I shoved the scroll back; it was like a bad dream scribbled down by a lunatic. It left my mouth watering for more, the taste of forbidden knowledge bitter and sweet at once. I grabbed another and opened it, the scroll crackling as it unfurled.

Age of Moonlight, 465

Nikola gave a public speech. He told the mortals that he had the same power as Dahlia, but he was willing to share all of his with them. He preached that anyone against the mortals having a share in power and magic should be cut down. He told them that suffering did not need blood. He taught that there were many other ways to reprogram someone's thought process than death. He convinced enough mortals that if they grew more creative, they could condition those against them to move to their side.

The terror lay in watching the mortals bow down to him and his teachings with hardly any second thought. They turned on their neighbors. They drug children into the streets and slit their throats to punish their parents. They hooked eyelids open, so lovers had to watch their other half be mutilated so that unclean minds could not further their lines. The mortals justified their actions by looking to their leader.

The shadow against the sunlight.

I put the scroll back where it was. I was gentler this time because I didn't think that I wanted anyone to know I read it, my fingers trembling as I placed it carefully on the shelf. I opened a book instead. I had hoped that it would have a less traumatic theme, the leather binding cool against my palms.

Age of Moonlight, 476

It was a cruel joke that we were called gods and looked at as the ulti-mate power, but we had half of what the mortals convinced themselves of. Most of the power of a god lay in our ability to form things like ground and skies. We could raise a mountain but wipe out a plague that infected the minds of the weak and turned them into monsters. We were useless against it. Our choices were to wipe them all out and start again or hope that after being patient, enough generations would go by so that they learned something useful.

That choice was a destruction of ourselves. Some of us wanted complete eradication. Others held hope that the mortals, who were truly good, could make a difference. They couldn't bear to see their mortal friends die.

We were stronger than mortals, but nothing compared to the originals and their power. Most of us were only present to keep order in our dedicated subject and nothing more. Slaves to a single idea of life. Helpless and useless to the destruction that the shadow caused on every piece of the life he touched.

I closed the book and got back to my feet, the sound of the binding snapping shut echoing in the small room. That was enough story time for me. I wasn't much for fairy tales as it was. I didn't understand why the temple would have things like those, but it was none of my business. The words lingered in my mind nonetheless, raising more questions than answers.

I turned to leave the room with the crystals but was stopped by the loudest squeals and a rush of bodies. They came from every room. Guards, temple attendants, and even ordinary people. It's as if they were hiding, the sudden flood of humanity overwhelming. The scent of fear hung heavy in the air, sharp and acrid.

Did they see us coming? Were they trying to stay alive? The idea that they thought I'd come to slaughter them all made my heart sink to my stomach, and for a brief moment, I thought about returning the artifact to them. Guilt clawed at my throat.

It was a thought I hardly had time to mull over when half-dead creatures with shredded wings showed themselves inside the temple. Their rotting flesh reeked of decay, the stench making my eyes water. I knew they weren't part of the temple when Vespera and I were no longer a problem, and all attention was on them. Vespera stood, sword ready, as if she were part of the temple, too, her stance protective and familiar.

I dodged temple guards that hacked through creatures, blood spraying across the pristine marble. I wasn't a fighter; I gave orders. A creature flew for my face and pushed me into a wall, its leathery wings beating against my skin, and even though I fought against it, I let out a scream. I was torn between being ashamed of the way my scream sounded and letting out another, terror overwhelming my pride.

Long emerald hair and shimmering green eyes stood tall above the grotesque creature. Her sickle blade tore into the flesh of the creature, and its head rolled into my arms, still warm and twitching.

Who was she? The question blazed through my mind even as I recoiled in disgust.

I tossed it back at her in an against-my-will motion, and when my hands were free, she dived for me as if I were another one of the creatures. I lifted my own sword to stop hers from entering my eye, the metals clashing with a shower of sparks. She put the entire weight of her body into her sickle, and it was clear that she was well-trained, her movements fluid and deadly.

"I surrender!" I yelled, desperation making my voice crack. "I surrender! I surrender!"

"Sage!" Vespera reprimanded, her voice cutting through the chaos.

"I'll apologize! Just don't kill me!" I ignored Vespera and tried to force myself to cry instead, willing tears to my eyes.

She lowered herself from me, her sickle still hovering inches from my face, and Onyx came through the sea of monsters. I sighed a breath of relief, my knees weak with gratitude. I would never do another temple job, not if I lived a thousand years.

"Onyx, save me from this brute!" I sobbed, reaching for him dramatically.

"This is the leader of the Daughters of Steel? This?" The girl looked me over with a frown, her lip curling in disgust. "This is the girl we were warned was going to steal our crystals and cause us problems for the afternoon?"

"How do you know this isn't part of my plan!" I retorted, trying to summon some dignity.

"Looking pathetic is part of your plan?" The girl sheathed her sickle blade, the contempt in her voice stinging worse than any wound.

"Are either of you going to help me?" I said as I looked between Onyx and Vespera, betrayal bitter on my tongue.

"I need to help clear out the flying things," Onyx said and turned away, the dismissal clear in his stride.

Vespera pretended not to hear me, suddenly fascinated by a dead creature on the floor, and the girl pulled out chains to use on me, the metal links clinking ominously. The king better still pay me for getting his secret mission out in one piece. I had the scroll tucked away in my top, still secret and still safe. At least something had gone according to plan, even if my dignity hadn't survived the encounter.

CHAPTER TWENTY-SEVEN

IN SERVICE OF THE TEMPLE

SAGE

Was I an adult or just a child? I hadn't been placed in time-out in so long that I nearly forgot it was a possibility for anyone. I tapped my foot against the ground over and over while I waited for everyone to collect me, the rhythmic sound echoing off the stone walls of my makeshift prison. The smell of incense and candle wax hung heavy in the air, a constant reminder of where I was.

Vespera looked at me nervously, her usual confidence replaced by something fragile and uncertain. It wasn't like her to look so flustered. The best part of her was trusting that she always told the truth. She was always an open book, her emotions written clearly on her face.

The girl who saved my life was apparently the dragon guardian of the temple. She was in charge of my punishment, too. I was unsure if I should have been grateful or not, the weight of the pendant still heavy in my pocket.

"Sage," Vespera spoke, her voice barely above a whisper.

I didn't move, but my eyes shot to her, narrowing slightly.

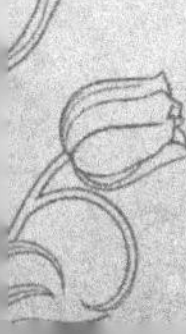

"I didn't want to do this here. I was going to wait until we got back, but it seems like you need a pick me up." Vespera reached into her bag and held her hand up to me, her fingers trembling slightly.

Inside sat a small, chubby thing made of fire. Its translucent wings fluttered with golden embers, casting dancing shadows across her palm, and its skeletal figure was noticeable underneath glowing amber flesh. Obsidian eyes sat so big that I could have gotten lost in them, reflecting tiny flames like stars in the night sky.

"It's a fire sprite," she said, her voice filled with a tenderness I rarely heard.

I reached up to touch it, my fingertips tingling with anticipation, but I was pulled into a memory, the present fading around me like smoke.

I was deep in a lush, green forest surrounded by so many of the little creatures. The air was thick with the scent of moss and earth, the warmth of the sprites creating a gentle heat around us. I taught them how to use magic from the ground. Together, we pulled the magic from the trees, the energy flowing through us like liquid gold. They were doing it perfectly as if they had been born with the natural ability, their tiny hands glowing with power.

Vespera stood over me, a hand on each shoulder. She shook me hard, the vision shattering like glass. I gasped for air as if my head had been stuck underwater, my lungs burning with the sudden intake of breath.

"Is she okay?" The dragon guardian called, concern lacing her voice.

"I'm fine," I huffed, my head spinning as reality reasserted itself.

The girl looked at Vespera as if they were silently exchanging words, an unspoken conversation passing between them. I became further convinced that I was the outsider.

That they had to know each other, the realization bitter on my tongue.

"Do you want to fill in the rest of us? Or do you two want to keep looking at each other in silence!" I yelled, my voice bouncing off the walls.

"Sage, are you jealous?" Vespera mocked, a small smirk playing on her lips.

Jealous? Of course, I wasn't jealous! Why would I be? Jealous of what? The way they kept staring into each other's eyes. The way they looked like long-lost friends. Lovers? The way they forgot that I was able to see them slowly become lovers? Me? Jealous of this loser trying to steal my girl! Heat crept up my neck and into my cheeks, betraying my thoughts.

I stood, ready to fight, my hands balled into fists at my sides, and they both looked at me, waiting for me to say a single word. The tension hung in the air like a storm about to break. I decided against repeating my inside words, outside, swallowing the accusations that threatened to spill out.

"All right, I was only joking," Vespera laughed, the sound forced and awkward.

"My name is Ruri," the dragon guardian said, extending her hand in a gesture of peace.

I nodded but stayed silent, arms crossed tightly over my chest. If she was moving in to take my girl, I'd not be nice. She'd not get my name, or any other courtesy I could withhold.

"This is Sage," Vespera said, ignoring my obvious displeasure.

I shot a fiery glare at her, the betrayal stinging like a slap. How dare Vespera give up the last secret that I had in my control?

"We've talked about it and have decided to let you go. The teachings of our temple call for forgiveness, and so we shall forgive. If you come back and try to steal from us again, your punishment will be service to the temple until your life is over," Ruri said, her tone firm but not unkind.

"My life!" I yelled, indignation burning through me.

"I thought you weren't speaking to her?" Vespera crossed her arms, one eyebrow raised in challenge.

"That's ridiculous!" I said, stomping my foot like the child I was apparently being. "My life is important!"

The girl only stared at me, her expression unreadable. She moved a bit closer and reached into her pocket, the movement slow and deliberate. I lifted my fists in response, my body tensing for a fight. She looked up at me and blinked too many times, clearly taken aback by my stance.

"You'll break your own hands before any part of me," she said, her voice calm as she pulled out a necklace and opened my fists to lay it in. The metal was warm against my palm, as if it had absorbed her body heat. "This will protect you in your line of work."

"Why are you being so nice?" I asked, suspicion coloring my words.

"It won't happen again. I suggest you walk carefully and consider your company. Those creatures that keep attacking the temples are sent by the God of Dreams. Seems he's interested in hurting you," Ruri said, her eyes flickering with something that might have been concern.

I nodded, turning the necklace over in my hand. "Am I free to go?"

"Do you have somewhere important to be?" Ruri asked, her head tilted slightly.

"It's none of your business if I do," I widened my eyes as far as they would open, trying to look intimidating and probably achieving the opposite.

"Are you having some sort of episode?" she asked, exchanging a glance with Vespera.

"An episode is one way to put it," Vespera sighed, running a hand through her hair.

"Do the two of you require help in traveling?" Ruri asked, her tone softening. "I can offer you a dragon?"

"That would be great," Vespera drew her words out in disappointment, avoiding my eyes.

"Yes, you're so generous," I mumbled, the words dripping with sarcasm.

We followed her outside of the temple to not just a dragon but seven of them. Their massive forms blocked the sunlight, scales glinting in what rays broke through. The scent of smoke and leather filled the air around them. Was she trying to show me that she could turn me into a barbecue if she wanted to? I clicked my tongue. If she thought these kinds of gestures would impress my woman, she was wrong.

"I'll fly on this one!" Vespera called as she climbed up the side of a brown and orange dragon, its scales shimmering like autumn leaves.

I couldn't believe Vespera was into this brute. I followed her onto the dragon all the same, the creature's hide warm and surprisingly soft beneath my hands.

The dragon could have flown faster, but it was better than a carriage or ship. Wind whipped my hair as we soared above the landscape, the world below shrinking to a patchwork of colors. The note I received told me that I needed to meet the king at the blacksmith shop. I didn't understand why Onyx would hold a meeting there or why he was involved, but I tried to consider that it was to protect me.

When I entered the blacksmith shop, the heat hit me like a wall, sweat immediately beading on my forehead. Inside, the king stood with no mask beside Onyx. Nikola's gaze felt harsher than a blade, cutting through any pretense of courage I might have had.

"I heard you're empty-handed," Nikola said, his voice as smooth and dangerous as a sharpened dagger.

"There was an attack and a dragon guardian. I didn't get the crystals," I admitted, trying to keep my voice steady.

"I thought of something else that you can help with to make up for it. You do this, and I'll let you be free of consequences over the crystals," Nikola said, gesturing toward a dark object nestled in the glowing coals of the forge.

I wanted to hand him the artifact and demand that it make us even, but a part of me was curious about his offer, drawn to it like a moth to flame despite my better judgment.

"What is it?" I asked, stepping closer to the heat.

"I need blood for this egg. Offer yours, and we're even," he said, his eyes reflecting the orange glow of the fire.

Onyx stood silent, but his eyes shifted between Nikola and I, tension evident in every line of his body.

"Why can't Onyx do it? Or you? What's inside of the egg?" I asked, suspicion prickling at the back of my neck.

"We don't have the right kind of blood. I'll leave it at that. I understand what you've been told about the egg. We want to bring back old Gods. Gods lost to horrible events. We want to make the realm a better place for everyone. You can help us do that. You can help get all of those girls you saved a better home," Nikola said, his voice hypnotic in its sincerity.

My heart pounded so hard I thought it might beat out of my chest, the sound drowning out the crackle of the forge. Part of me said that I shouldn't be involved in things I couldn't see solid proof of. Anything could be inside of that egg, waiting to be unleashed on an unsuspecting world.

"You can be the change we need," Onyx urged, his voice unusually soft.

I didn't want to think about it any longer. I'd say no if I could. I knew it wasn't an option. I pulled out my knife and sliced the palm of my hand, the blade biting into my flesh with surprising sharpness. My arm resisted when I moved it closer to the egg as if it had a mind of its own, every instinct screaming at me to stop. The last line of defense against the action I was about to make. I did it anyway. I placed my bloody palm onto the dragon egg, the shell hot against my skin, and without lapse, it began to shake and shudder.

The egg rolled from the fire and shook harder, making a sound like dry leaves rustling. Crack after crack showed until the egg split in half and out rolled a girl gasping for air. Long, wet lavender hair surrounded her naked body, steam rising from her skin in the cooler air.

My stomach sank, and I regretted my choice instantly. Her limbs folded like a spider's and it made me want to turn and run, bile rising in my throat. There was something profoundly wrong about the way she moved, too fluid, too many joints.

Onyx was on his knees in front of her. He checked her over like a newborn baby, his movements reverent and careful.

"You did well," Nikola said, his hand heavy on my shoulder.

"Who is she?" I asked, unable to look away despite my revulsion.

The girl looked up at me. She still pulled in the air harder than a normal being would until she began laughing, the sound sharp and discordant in the small space.

"Oh, this is golden," the girl laughed harder, her eyes fixing on mine with disturbing intensity.

"Her name is Sahir," Nikola said, something like pride in his voice.

I wished that I knew more about the Gods now. All of this was meaningless to me, but somehow, I still knew I made the wrong choice, the knowledge settling like a stone in my gut.

"I could not have found a better way to come back than by her hands," Sahir still laughed, the sound making the hairs on my arms stand on end.

She got to her feet and stabilized herself quickly, movements too graceful for someone just born. She moved forward and had her hands on me as if we were old friends, the touch sending chills down my spine. She picked at my clothing and hair until she deemed that I was properly tucked away, her fingers cool and dry against my skin.

"You really don't know who I am?" She asked me, her head tilted at an unnatural angle.

I shook my head, a sense of dread growing within me. "Should I?"

"It'll come back to you eventually," she smiled, her teeth too sharp, too white in the dim light of the forge.

CHAPTER TWENTY-EIGHT
A CHEWY BREAK THROUGH

SHIVANI

The table I sat at was less than full. Shards of broken wood scattered the room, splintered evidence of the battle that had brought me here. A second time, I had to eat a whole heart. I never imagined being in such a position. It was somewhere between infuriating and comical that I was in the situation not once but twice. The irony wasn't lost on me, though the copper scent filling my nostrils made it hard to appreciate. Koa offered to cook it this time around, but the thought of knowing body parts were frying away over a fire made my stomach turn. If I was going to do it, I wanted to hurry it along, get the ordeal over with before my resolve crumbled.

Koa came into the remnants of the temple with Vero by his side. Her back was lined with plates, the porcelain clinking softly with each heavy step she took. Her face wore the same familiar frown, scales glinting in the dim light. I never thought a dragon could look so miserable. The ability to crush anything you wanted and still be miserable. If my feet could bring fear to the hearts of most, I'd like to think that I'd have a reason to smile more often.

"Desserts!" Koa exclaimed as he took plates from Vero and sat them in front of me, the sweet aroma of sugar and fruit momentarily masking the metallic smell of heart. "You can take a bite of heart and wash it down with any of these."

Vero grunted as her response, a puff of warm smoke escaping her nostrils. It was better than listening to a lecture, I suppose.

Koa stood by my side and used his silverware to cut a piece off Helia's heart; he joined it with a chunk of strawberry cake before he held it in front of my face. I never envisioned seeing the god of war looking at me with puppy eyes. Big, round, and full of the need to please me. I hated when he looked at me with them. I didn't feel as though I treated him as well as he treated me, the realization sending a pang of guilt through my chest.

I opened my mouth, and he fed me the bite. It was as chewy as I remembered it being. It was as iron-flavored and hard to choke down as my own heart was. The texture was like overcooked meat, fibrous and resistant to every attempt to break it down. My leg began to shake. The motion shook the rest of my body, chair creaking beneath me.

How long had I been chewing the first bite? Seconds stretched into eternity as I worked my jaw.

I rubbed my forehead with the back of my hand, feeling beads of sweat forming at my hairline, and both of my legs shook up and down at a faster speed than my jaw moved. Vero sulked in the side of the dining hall, her massive form casting long shadows across the floor, and Koa's eyes sat fixed on me. He was unblinking, his attention unwavering and somehow making this more difficult. I felt the sweat form on the side of my face underneath his gaze. My jaw still chewed away, muscles growing tired with the effort.

Koa used the fork to pick up another piece of cake, the frosting glistening in the light. His intentions were pure; I knew it, but the sight was the last hammer that cracked me.

"I can't do it this way," I tried, but failed, not to yell, my voice echoing off the stone walls. "It's going to take too long if we do it this way. Please, just let me eat it."

Koa's eyes shimmered in pain, but he stepped back, the fork lowering slowly to the plate. I didn't deserve him. I didn't know how to apologize for the way I treated him, either. The words always seemed to stick in my throat.

I picked up Helia's heart and took a bite out of the middle, the organ still oddly warm in my hands. I only half chewed before I swallowed, then took another bite, the flesh resisting my teeth. I ignored Koa's face, which beat down on me. I didn't want to see his eyes and whatever they screamed at me. I held back the bile I felt rising with every chewing motion I had to make. My eyes watered with how badly my body wanted to get rid of what I was putting inside of it, the saltiness of tears mixing with the metallic taste on my tongue.

I was doing it for the right reasons. The thought became my mantra.

I took another bite, ignoring the way my throat tried to close against it.

Things had become torn apart in the past, but I was making strides to put it right again. I was nearly done. I was one of the sisters running to the finish line. I stood on the cusp of being an all-powerful being with more lives than the vampires in my hands.

My heart sank at the thought, but I took another bite, the taste growing more potent with each mouthful.

I needed to think lighter if I was going to distract myself from the grisly feeling inside of my mouth. I tried to focus on what would come after this was over.

"You've done it! That's the last bite!" Koa cheered, his voice carrying a relief I wished I could share.

I didn't feel as joyous as he did. I felt hot, and my jaw felt stiff. As if it were a new muscle, I had overworked. I forced my cheeks to rise again and meet him with a forced smile, my lips stretching uncomfortably over my teeth.

My hands started to shake like my legs had. Slowly at first, and then so noticeable, I wondered if I was losing my mind at the speed they were beginning to tremble. The room began to spin around me, colors blurring together. Breathing became harder to pull in, and gurgles came from my abdomen, something shifting inside me.

"Are you all right?" Koa asked, his voice suddenly distant despite him being right beside me.

I told my mouth to open and speak, but it did not listen. My body hit the floor instead, the impact sending shockwaves through my already aching form.

"She's having a seizure!" Vero's voice, suddenly human-like in its panic.

"Grab her head! Make sure she doesn't bite her tongue!" Koa commanded, his strong hands cradling my skull.

A dim light pulled my focus. The world around me spun like a jar. Images of trees and grass, flowers and golden homes spun around me like I had been placed into a snow globe. When the images slowed, I was placed back inside of myself. I stood in front of a black door. It was cracked open just enough for me to peek through, the darkness beyond beckoning me closer. A man stood in front of someone else. A woman sat at a desk with her feet thrown on top. She looked carefree, but my heart shuddered with how fast it beat, pounding against my ribs as if trying to escape.

"This is the last time we will have this conversation. If you are too foolish to follow the guidelines that I laid out for you, then I will take you out of the equation," his voice sounded melodic, sending chills down my spine despite its beauty.

The girl watched with amusement, her lips curled in a smirk, but I could not see the other person. The shadows hid them too well.

"If you listen to me, they will do all of the work for you.

They consider themselves too smart to be fooled," he pressed on, each word carefully measured.

"Why should we listen to you? I've heard of how you have been doing things. You stole hairs from Dahlia to create Sahir. You don't seem to have an upstanding idea of progress," the hidden man spoke with venom, his voice hauntingly familiar.

"Like me or not, boy, I'm still the only thing standing that Dahlia hasn't been able to kill," he answered, confidence dripping from every syllable.

The girl casually placed at the desk threw her feet down so quickly it startled me, the chair legs scraping against the floor. "If you don't listen, I'll kill you myself," she said, her voice sweet as honey but laced with poison.

"Sahir, that's enough," the man shifted his body to the side, and I nearly got a glimpse of the hidden figure, my heart racing with anticipation.

"Daddy is the oldest thing next to Dahlia and Yumi. He fought them for centuries already. I think he's far beyond qualified to lead us to their deaths," Sahir smirked, her teeth gleaming unnaturally white.

"You can be on the right side of the history we will create, or you can fall with them. It's your choice," the man hummed, the threat clear despite his gentle tone.

His head snapped back in my direction. The motion was so quick it startled me, and I slapped my hand over my mouth to try to hide my gasp, the sound escaping between my fingers. It hadn't worked.

"Nikola, who's there?" The voice from the shadows grew urgent.

The door flung open in front of me, and his hand gripped my throat. The touch was ice-cold, stealing my breath. He pulled me into him until my lips were against his. He pulled himself back and took with it a piece of me that I didn't understand. Blue streaks of fire came from my mouth and into his, or maybe they were from his and into mine? I couldn't be sure. The only thing I felt was the tear that drizzled down the side of my face, hot against my cold skin.

"Can you hear me? Shivani?" Koa's voice pulled me back, anchoring me to reality.

I pulled a deep and hard breath in until my lungs felt as though they'd burst if I kept going, the air sweet and precious after the suffocation of my vision.

"I saw him. I saw the traitor and Nikola," I cried out, my voice raw and desperate.

"You had a vision?" Koa asked, his eyes wide with concern.

We were surrounded by so many faces, and my world was still spinning, the temple walls shifting and blurring around me.

"I was spying on them while they discussed plans to kill Dahlia. He found me and put something inside of, or took something from me, I don't know for sure," I stuttered, the words tumbling over each other in their rush to escape.

"You did become delirious and ill for a few weeks before the incident that separated us all," Vero said, her dragon's voice thoughtful.

"Did you see the traitor's face?" Koa asked, his grip on my shoulders tightening.

"No, but I heard him. He was reluctant to keep helping," I said, clinging to the fragments of the vision as they tried to slip away.

Koa helped me to sit up, but the action made my stomach unhappy, and I nearly tossed up the contents on him, bile rising in my throat.

"It felt like a conversation that Caym would have," I admitted, the words like ash in my mouth.

A part of me didn't want to believe that it could be him. I knew it wasn't Coy. Caym was the only other one to be so upright in himself. He had a strict code, and he stuck to it. Maybe he was forced against his will to betray his friends. The thought offered little comfort. If anyone else knew something, they hadn't told me.

"There's something else," I said, my voice steadying. "Come closer, Vero."

She looked at me with dissatisfaction, her scaled brow furrowing, but she listened and moved close enough that I could reach her, her warm breath washing over me.

"I don't know how I know that doing this will work, but I do," I said, a newfound certainty flowing through my veins.

Vero opened her dragon lips to speak, but I grabbed each side of her face before she could. I locked her eyes into mine until they both shook, power surging between us like lightning.

Vero's eyes rolled back into her skull, and then they were closed along with mine. When we both opened them, everyone in the room covered their faces. The light that came from her was blinding, pure and white as the heart of a star.

The glow wore off, and she stood on two feet in front of us. Her gown flowed in a hue of oranges and red, the fabric rippling like flame. A crown of golden leaves formed on her golden hair, and she looked up at me with tears in her eyes, the droplets catching the light like diamonds.

"I'm back? Is it not an illusion? I'm really back?" Vero sobbed. She wrapped her arms around herself, her whole body trembling. "This proves that you're whole again. You being whole is the only way I can be whole again, too."

The act sent a surge through me that felt like fire. I felt the blood inside of my veins heat, and a new kind of strength brew inside of me, filling every corner of my being.

"You're back," Koa whispered, awe in his voice. "You did it. You're really back."

I felt complete again, the pieces of myself finally settling into place like they had always belonged there.

CHAPTER TWENTY-NINE

A TIME FOR THE OTHER NEGLECTED PIECES

SHIVANI

The cloth of my tent was pulled open, and inside walked a glowing beauty. Sunlight outlined her silhouette, turning her white hair into a halo of light. She was one I hadn't seen in what somehow felt like centuries, even though I knew it hadn't been long. I was confined to my tent for the last three days to recover from eating Helia's heart. The air still held the faint metallic scent that refused to leave me. Koa and Vero were adamant that I rest, their concerns echoing in my ears whenever I tried to move. Vero was convinced that Nikola would be able to feel what we had done, and he wouldn't sit silently.

Of course, Koa took her words seriously. I didn't blame him this time because I somehow knew she was right, too. The certainty settled in my bones like an old truth.

I had nothing to do but take in every stitch mark along my tent and think of all of the things that I hadn't done since I had been in Cylla. The rough fabric above me had become a map I'd memorized, each thread telling a story I hadn't lived. I had never laid eyes on the moose that held the hide my camp was made out of. I had never stepped foot in one of the taverns that I heard so many stories of, never tasted their ales or heard their songs firsthand.

I wasted so much of my time. Once things were settled, I would stick to setting magic aside and finding other ways to help without using it. Holding power hadn't helped me sort out my head or sort out the vampires. It only held me back, like chains I'd forged myself.

My mind felt foggier than it had before. I knew so many things on the tip of my tongue now, but I couldn't grasp them. They sat on the edge of my vision, tantalizingly close yet untouchable. Edging my lips for release. I could not push them past the border and allow them to flow, the frustration building with each failed attempt.

Hesperia looked at me with a cautious smile, and it brought me comfort like a close sister, but anger that I felt like I knew everything about her but could voice nothing of it. Her familiar scent of jasmine and starlight washed over me, triggering memories I couldn't quite reach.

"How are you feeling?" Hesperia asked, her voice soft like wind through leaves.

"Frustrated," I admitted, shifting against the pillows. "I know you. I know Koa." I shook my head, the motion sending a dull ache through my temples. "Of course, I know you. I mean, I remember you. I remember our mother and you and I fighting constantly. I remember Sage. I know who the traitor is. I just can't spit it out." I sighed between my stuttering, my hands clenching the blankets. "If this is what Coy feels like, I'd become distant, too."

Her brows furrowed for such a brief second that I nearly missed it, a shadow passing over her features.

"Take it a breath at a time. Koa mentioned what you saw in your vision. Nikola may have done something to you, maybe even Coy. We can't be sure of anything yet. Let us help now." Hesperia's eyes were wide with demand, the gold in them catching the light.

I held both of my hands up, feeling the weight of surrender. "I will. The fog on my mind has given me that, at least. Even my mind is screaming to trust what you have to say. Why are you here?" I asked, studying her face for clues.

"Even I felt you wake up. It was like being struck by lightning. I wanted to see how you were before I left for Daxon." Hesperia said, her fingers playing with the hem of her sleeve.

"You won't stay?" My voice trembled, betraying a vulnerability I hadn't meant to show.

Hesperia's soft voice broke, and she wrinkled slightly at the corners of her downturned lips. She moved to the side of my bed and pulled me into her chest. I closed my eyes and gave in to her embrace, the warmth of her body chasing away the lingering chill in mine. Her hands brushed through my hair like they had done it hundreds of times before, each stroke unlocking something deep within me.

"If I thought that you weren't in good hands, I'd stay. I made a deal with the water court that I would return their true heir to them in exchange for their loyalty. They offered me their army. I'll make the trip quick," she said, her heartbeat steady against my ear.

"Is it worth it? What good will mortals do?" I asked, tightening my grip on her, afraid to let go.

I had hoped that I could talk her out of leaving. Even if I couldn't put my finger on all of our memories, I knew in my core that they were there. That I loved her. We were much more than we had been in the split realm or even in Cylla. The connection ran deeper than blood, older than time itself.

We spent the last several years as a fraction of what we were. I wanted it back. The memories, the life, and the feelings belonged to me. I wanted them, and I wanted to punish everyone who took them from me, the anger flaring hot in my chest.

"It is worth it. Mother is strong, but we have something now that she didn't have when she tried to deal with Nikola and Yumi before, and that's ourselves, awake and aware. The four of us can do a lot, but it would be better if we didn't have to start at the bottom. I can raise the dead, but I need a part of them. You can clearly give the mortals a blessing with your blood magic. The vampires aren't a curse; they're something much stronger than they've gotten credit for. Something Nikola hasn't prepared for. Ruri created dragons. Sage created Sprites before our realms ever cracked. Imagine the kind of blessings we can give the mortals on our side when we all work together." Hesperia still held me, her voice vibrating through me. "After all, our purpose is to work with mortals."

She was right, but my mind didn't change. I wanted us together. All of us. It felt safer, the way a child clings to family during a storm.

"Have you found him?" I asked, the question hanging between us like a ghost.

"I'm not sure yet," she answered, tension creeping into her shoulders. "Let me worry about that. For now, let Koa in. Let him hold you, too. Speak with Vero. I know she's been a thorn in your side, but she's been suffering. Coming to terms with everything that happened and not having her body was too much for her." She moved me back and held my face to look at hers, her eyes searching mine. "Let us in. Check on things outside of this tent. Relax. The time to forget what that feels like is coming quicker than we want to admit."

I nodded, and she kissed my forehead, her lips cool against my skin. Being in front of her was a strange feeling. She felt like our mother, the resemblance striking in ways that went beyond appearance.

I stood with her, my legs protesting after days of disuse. Even if I listened to her and let them take charge of things, I still wanted to see her out, to watch her until the last possible moment.

"How is Sina?" I asked as we walked toward the tent opening, sunlight streaming through the gap. "We've talked about my circle, but I don't know anything about yours."

Hesperia looked at me knowingly, a smile playing at her lips. "You won't keep me longer by asking endless questions. Still, Sina is all right. She is under a lot of stress, too. I think she just wants to make sure that there are no mistakes this time. I think she feels like Vero did. In a strange form, in a new world and unready to admit that she feels lost."

"You sound as though you are trying to convince me instead of informing me," I said, crossing my arms.

She sighed, the sound weary with the weight of responsibilities I couldn't yet comprehend. "I need to go now. Rest, I will be back." She turned around, the fabric of her cloak sweeping across the floor. "Oh, Ruri also has her memory back."

"That feels like something you should have led with!" I yelled at her out of the tent, the shock momentarily overriding everything else.

Koa and Vero turned to look at me from where they stood nearby. Their faces matched in reprimand, brows furrowed and lips pressed into tight lines.

"You can't keep me locked away forever," I said, squinting in the bright sunlight after days in the dim tent.

"Shi-Shi," a voice called, high and excited.

It was the girl I watched in the medical tents. She looked like she had never been sick, her cheeks rosy with health. She grabbed my hand and pulled me forward, her small fingers surprisingly strong. We both stopped in front of the temple, which had been mostly rubble days ago.

"Look what we did!" She jumped, her excitement vibrating through her entire body.

The temple stood taller than before, with a statue of my likeness where the false God of Rebirth used to be. The stone caught the sunlight, giving my carved face a lifelike glow. The details were so precise I felt a shiver run down my spine.

"We've been working day and night to have it done before you were well enough to get up," Vero said from beside me, pride evident in her voice.

"I want to go see Ruri," I spat out, the words escaping before I could stop them.

"What?" Vero turned to me, her eyes widening. "I present you this, and that's what you say?"

I wasn't trying to be ungrateful. It was beautiful. A gesture that spoke louder than my gratitude could. It made me realize that I had only been looking at my own nose. I said that I was too preoccupied to help my own sisters. I hadn't even bothered to ask what had been going on with any of them, not truly. The realization settled in my stomach like a stone.

"I think the gift is beyond what I could return. You all did so much in such a short time. It's all of you that deserve the rest. I deserve to pass out apologies and do what I always should have been," I said, my throat tight with emotion. "I don't even know what's going on with anyone else."

"Ruri only just remembered herself. Sage has made no progress. Hesperia hasn't admitted to us if she made progress with Nikola or not. Coy has not gotten closer to the traitor," Koa said from my other side, his voice carefully neutral.

"It feels like things are not on our side again this time," Vero said, a shadow passing over her features.

"That's my point. If I hadn't been so selfish, maybe they could feel that way. If I had moved fast, I would have checked in more. If I had done anything, maybe we could have more progress behind us. Look what you've all done so quickly. I want to go see Ruri." This time, I demanded, planting my feet firmly on the ground.

Koa and Vero looked at each other, a silent conversation passing between them, but I refused to take anything less than yes. I would check in with Dominic, and then I would leave. It was time I helped more than myself. The determination burned like fire in my veins.

I marched forward, determined in my mission, but Koa grabbed my arm and pulled me in the opposite direction I wanted to move. His grip was gentle but firm, allowing no space for resistance. He stopped us at the stream that flowed beside the camp and forced me to the ground, the grass cool and damp beneath us.

He sat beside me with an exaggerated sigh. He didn't speak, and that turned out to be fine. The sound of the water brought its own peace, the gentle gurgling washing away some of the tension in my shoulders. I hadn't noticed the baby birds being raised in the trees around the camp, their tiny chirps creating a melody that seemed to speak directly to something ancient within me.

"We'll figure it out together," Koa whispered, his voice blending with the stream's song. "You don't have to keep me at arm's length. You don't have to treat me like I'm your enemy. If you want me to jump into the river in front of us and refuse to swim, I'll do it."

He didn't look at me, and I didn't look at him. His voice spoke with enough pain, and I felt ashamed for a moment. I wanted so badly to be a hardened deity with no need for anyone. I knew that I made the two of us suffer because of it. He was always open and honest, but I held us back; no, I held him back, like an anchor dragging us both down.

"I need to leave. I need to be helping. I can't focus here; I can't clear my head. I feel like I'm being watched. I feel like something bad is coming. I can't sort any of it out," I admitted, the confession lifting a weight I hadn't realized I was carrying.

"Then we will go," he assured me, finally turning to meet my eyes, his own filled with understanding. "Let it be together."

The last word hung between us, an invitation and a promise all at once.

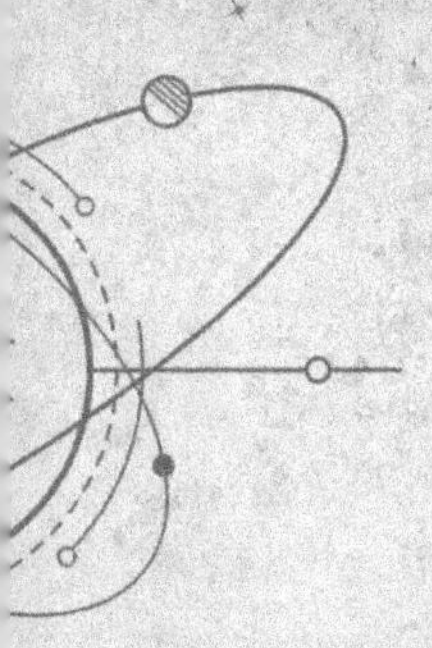

CHAPTER THIRTY

CUTTING UP MOTHER
WON'T HURT

ASTRA

The window inside of my office overlooked the perfect spot of Orest. I had a full view of dragons and students, the scene stretching out before me like a living tapestry. I hadn't done much else the last two days but take in that view. The glass was cool against my fingertips whenever I reached out to touch it, as if trying to grasp the world beyond. I watched lovers run off when they thought no one watched, their laughter carried away by the wind.

I watched friends argue, even though they knew everyone watched, their voices rising and falling like waves. I saw dragons bond and mortals make profound choices that I knew would alter their course. Things they would look back on and wonder if that was the moment, the choice that set in stone their ending. Their faces filled with the weight of decisions they couldn't yet understand.

I wondered the same thing. I only thought of where I would be if I hadn't touched the stars. If I listened and left. Saved the task for another day. I didn't. My path was only suffering because of it. It was a choice, a moment that I was sure set my path in stone, like a signature on a death warrant.

I should have listened and left. Instead, I had to wear long sleeves to hide the marks that were rapidly spreading across my body, black tendrils creeping like poison through my veins.

The mixtures from Ashbell hardly worked, their bitter taste lingering on my tongue hours after I drank them. I dreamt of dying every time I closed my eyes. My heart was pulled apart, like the petals of a flower, until it turned to dust. I woke up in a cold sweat, sheets tangled around my trembling limbs. I lived with a fever that nothing helped lower, my skin constantly burning as if I were standing too close to a forge.

Teas, salves, nothing took the edge off of the aching in my bones. Each movement was agony, though I refused to show it. I wanted to be a hero, and it looked like I was going to die before I would have a chance. The irony wasn't lost on me.

I wanted so many things. I was sure that I would come out the other side with Kyra on my arm, my son in a bassinet, and an entire kingdom to watch my wife rule over. The dream that once felt so attainable now seemed as distant as the stars that had cursed me.

The sun rose, painting my office in hues of gold and pink, and I decided that she would never be my wife. I would leave it that way. I didn't want Kyra attached to the idea of a dead wife she owed something to. I would fade from everyone's memory, and even if hers was the last I faded from, I would still fade. She would move on and be happy, and that gave me a bit of peace, a small comfort in the growing darkness.

Maybe death could bring me an endless dream of the three of us, frozen in perfect happiness.

A knock sounded at my office door, the sound jarring me from my thoughts.

"Astra, we're here," Aero said as he stepped inside, his armor catching the morning light.

Fennic opened his mouth to speak, but my heart pounded

out of its cavity, each beat sending fresh waves of pain through my chest. I didn't want to waste a single second of the time I had left.

"Let's go," I said, pushing myself up from my chair with more effort than I wanted to admit.

"But Kyra wants you to take it easy. She ordered us to make you stay," Aero pleaded, concern etched into his features.

I knew she wanted what was best for me. Kyra always wanted what was best for me. I wanted the best for her, too. I hated that she was always second in my thoughts. I loved her more than I could have expressed, the feeling so vast it seemed impossible to contain in words. She deserved better than what I could hand to her. More peace than I could have given her. Even still, in the face of my death, I only felt I owed Ruri.

Ruri understood the parts of me that I couldn't explain. She understood the dark tunnel I nearly stayed wedged in. Ruri was the only one to trudge through the same agony that I had in Semper. If I was going to give my last breath to someone who would use it to enact revenge in my name, it would be Ruri, not Kyra. Kyra had my breaths in the living world, and she would have my soul in death. Ruri would have my dying breath, a final gift from one survivor to another.

I opened the vines to Semper, the portal shimmering like water in the air. "You move willingly or unwillingly," I pointed, my voice betraying none of the weakness I felt.

A Fiia fluttered in with the artifact, its tiny wings creating a gentle breeze against my cheek. There was no doubt it belonged to the sun god. The Fiia dropped a shard of bright yellow flame into my hand. The heat of it pulsed against my palm, surprisingly gentle for something so powerful. It chittered little words to Aero before leaving through the keyhole in the door, leaving behind a trail of golden sparkles.

"Ruri has her memories back!" Aero yelled, his eyes wide with excitement.

I met him with a forced raise of the lips as my response but still pointed them inside of the vines. I didn't need to believe in fate or destiny. I was a Goddess. The idea was foolish. I shaped destinies. If there was such a thing for us, this would have been the closest thing I had seen. Ruri was back in time for me to go. I was to be a tether for her. An additional lashing to get her moving again. A disruption of peace before it could be felt. Good.

Yumi deserved what would come, the thought bitter and satisfying at once.

I grabbed Fennic by his collar and moved him to the vines. Every nerve in my body winced at the action, fire shooting through my muscles. I was forcing strength I hardly had. Aero moved with him, and they were inside the water image before I stepped through, the sensation of passing through the portal like diving into ice.

Fennic gripped his skull and lowered himself to the ground, his face contorted in pain. The tree was in our sight, its massive trunk reaching toward the golden sky, but nothing else was around us. The emptiness was eerie, as if the world held its breath.

"I can hear her," he groaned, his voice strained. "She says that we need to slice into her bark and insert the artifact."

"I'm not doing that!" I scoffed, the words echoing in the strange silence.

Cut her up? All we could see was bark. What if we cut the wrong part of her? What if she came back without an eye because of it? No. I wasn't doing it. The thought alone made my stomach twist.

"No one should worry. I cut wood all of the time to save cats. I'm an expert in tree chopping," Aero said, his confidence almost comical.

He didn't hesitate. He took out a pocket knife and stabbed it into the tree. The sound of metal piercing wood made me flinch. I lost count of how many times he dug the knife into

Dahlia. Stab after merciless stab created a divot big enough for the sun shard to fit inside comfortably. I was disgusted by how careless he was, every hack making me wince as if it were my own flesh.

The bark grew around the artifact until it disappeared, the wood seeming to breathe it in. The tree took on a yellow glow once it fully ingested the artifact, light pulsing from within like a heartbeat. Fennic and Aero placed both of their hands on each side of the clear scarring in the bark, their faces solemn with concentration.

An invisible fire erupted. I could not see flames, but I felt them, scorching through me from the inside out. The only sight was golden light, so intense it burned my eyes even when I closed them. Everything became so bright, so hot that my body felt as if I were under thousands of pounds of pressure. My bones seemed ready to crumble beneath the weight. It disbanded with a silent scream.

I felt it inside of my mind, but my ears did not hear it. The release was sudden enough that even I dropped to my knees in front of a lifeless-looking body, the figure small and still on the ground before us.

"We did it," Fennic said, awe in his voice. "She's haunted my mind and dreams enough; I know it's her."

Aero picked her up as I struggled to get to my feet, my limbs heavy and uncooperative. I considered Dahlia's presence a blessing in another way when they two were too distracted to notice my struggle, their eyes fixed on the woman in Aero's arms.

We went through the vines, but I did not take us back to Orest. I took us to Kyra. I needed assurance and protection. We needed the secrecy that Brontide could afford us, its walls thick with ancient magic.

Kyra cut the corner of the white and gold-covered hallway. She turned past stone pillars and stopped in her tracks when she saw me, her face draining of color.

"What have you done?" Kyra called out, her voice bouncing off the marble walls.

I hushed her with a finger to my lips, the motion taking more effort than it should have. "We need a room, healing, and privacy," I whispered, my voice hoarse.

She looked at me, her eyes glazed over as if she were trying to process the sight in front of her. Dahlia shouldn't have been that shocking to see. Kyra wouldn't know who she was if I hadn't told her. Kyra motioned and gave out demands, but it all felt blurred around the ringing in my ears, the world tilting dangerously around me.

"Are you all right?" She asked me, stepping closer, her perfume enveloping me in a familiar comfort. "You look worse off than the girl you brought. What's going on?"

There was pleading in her voice. It was followed by fear when her words cracked, the sound breaking through my haze.

"I've just felt stressed lately. Don't worry about me. I'll start to feel better now that I know such an important part of our future is safe here with you," I smiled at her, hoping it reached my eyes.

"Do you think that you can be extra nice to me, and I'll forget that you asked to die?" Kyra growled, her fingers digging into my arms.

I shook my head, the motion sending fresh waves of pain through my skull. "No, but I was hoping that maybe this would help win you over?" I leaned into her and kissed her soft lips before I left a second kiss on her chin, tasting salt and sweetness. "If that doesn't work, maybe you could come with me on a date to walk through the stars?"

"You can't just kiss me and not hear anything else about the way your actions have affected me," Kyra said. It wasn't working, but the way she kissed me back, her lips lingering on mine, said her words were lies.

"How about you give me a list of each thing I did? I will give you a kiss as an apology," I offered, trying to lighten the mood.

"No," she said firmly, though her hand reached up to cup my cheek. "You're going to rest and have a cleric check you over as, not just an apology to me, but so that my mind can rest, too. If a cleric clears you, if they say that you're all right, then I'll stop yelling at you."

Her eyes begged me in a way that even her voice didn't, green depths swimming with fear and love in equal measure, so I gave in and went to find my room and fake an examination. For now, I could pretend, for her sake, that everything would be alright. It was the last gift I could give her.

CHAPTER THIRTY-ONE

THE DAY ALL OF THE REALMS CRIED TOGETHER

COY

I left Ryujin at the entrance to Erebus. The dragon's massive form cast long shadows across the stone pathway, his scales gleaming in the dim light. I didn't want him to be an overly intimidating presence in front of Onyx. Caym urged me to bring him with me, his concern evident in the tight lines around his eyes, but I was confident in my choices. I wanted Onyx to feel comfortable. I wanted him to think he had the upper hand. The only person left to visit after him was Vespera.

I saved the two of them for last because I knew in some part of me that it was one of them. The truth stone in my pocket grew heavier with each step. I did not visit Erebus often, but it felt busy even to me. There seemed to be crowd after crowd around the blacksmith shop, the air thick with the scent of hot metal and sweat. The clamor of voices and hammers created a chaotic symphony. There wasn't much security around the entrance to the main room because of it. Onyx hardly gave me the time for a full glance when I entered behind him, his attention fixed on the blade he was shaping.

"Are you here for a repair, as well?" he asked, not looking up from his work. "Everyone seems to have broken something or other today."

"No," I answered. I let my thoughts run freely, but I didn't enjoy the same idea behind the words that I let flow freely. "I'm here to clear you of suspicions or kill you."

Onyx sighed, the sound weary as he set down his hammer. "I'm growing tired of how many times I need to be under a critical eye compared to others."

"You're the most suspicious," I said, studying his movements carefully. "If you've been under too many eyes, it's not because of me. I visited everyone else first."

"I disagree with you. If you were thinking clearly, you'd say Caym. He's sitting perfectly for a traitor. All important things pass through him." Onyx lowered the blade he was working on and turned to face me, his eyes hard as the metal he worked. "What is it you need me to do? I have no markings, no tie to anyone. My spotlight is already unjust."

"We know you're close to Sage, and that's a good enough reason to look at you. She has been a center target," I said, my hand drifting closer to my weapon.

"You think that I would hurt her?" He laughed, the sound sharp and humorless. "That I am incapable of having a friend that I care about?"

"I do," Vespera said. She glided into the room with a purpose about her, her footsteps silent despite her haste. "I think it's you, too. You push Sage in every direction but the right one. You pressure her and ride the line of resetting her mind every chance you get. You hardly cover up the fact that you want to screw things up again."

"I could say the same about you. Your unhealthy obsession with Sage keeps you right beside her. If anyone had the chance to get away with anything they wanted, it would be you." Onyx pointed at her, sparks seemingly flying from his fingertips with the intensity of his accusation.

"You think that you can dodge these accusations forever, but you can't. I have proof that I'm her guardian!" Vespera yelled, her voice echoing off the stone walls.

She dropped the illusion on her body, and navy-colored vine markings appeared on her chest and arms, glowing with a soft inner light against her skin.

"This proves you're the traitor," Onyx called out, his face contorting with rage. "You only proved you're her guardian, and I'm innocent."

"All I proved is that you can't decide this time who you want to have markings for," Vespera shot back, her hands balling into fists.

"I don't have markings, so why have you placed me in the middle of things?" Onyx asked, his voice suddenly too controlled.

"Should we really be pretending that you are innocent? Do we have to treat each other as if we are not smart enough to fit a few pieces together?" I sighed, growing impatient with the dance. "It's over, Onyx."

"We have to pretend like she didn't take the girl I cared for. We have to pretend like Vespera is somehow a good being when she failed to keep Sage safe and alive more than once. As if she is worthy of a title when she couldn't bring Sage back because Caym said no. I thought that pretending had become a main focus of our lives." Onyx scoffed, his words dripping with venom.

They spoke as if they had forgotten that I was present at all, the tension between them palpable like a living thing. Vespera lunged at Onyx, her movement a blur, and I had half a thought about letting them fight it out. That would be a clear-cut way to sniff out some sort of hint in either direction. I did not want to report back to the rest of the group that waited for us that I watched them kill each other, which meant that I could not allow them to keep going.

Onyx grabbed an axe, the metal gleaming wickedly in the

forge light, and swung it at Vespera, who already had a sword from a table in her hands. They clashed with metals and searched for a final blow, the sound of steel on steel ringing in my ears.

"Enough!" I yelled, my voice nearly lost in the cacophony.

They didn't give a drop of acknowledgment. I moved closer and yelled again, but they ignored me, lost in their dance of death. I ducked out of the way of a swing from Vespera's sword before I moved closer, feeling the wind of the blade as it passed.

"Hey!" I yelled louder, my throat straining. "Enough! This isn't how we're determining anything. We need the traitor alive, so if you care for your innocence or the group, you'd stop."

Vespera dropped herself onto her knees to dodge another attempted blow from Onyx and his axe. She was successful in her dodge, like she had been every time he took a swing at her. His was too slow against her, his movements telegraphed by rage.

I, however, was not as fast as she was.

My first thought was of Hesperia and what I had forgotten when the light reflected off his axe while it moved past Vespera. How many sunsets had I forgotten? Did we prepare meals together? Did we talk of pets or a home? Did we have one? I never asked her because I was confident in the future that waited for us. The regret hit harder than the blade.

The axe was embedded in my abdomen, and crimson flowed freely from the wound when he pulled it back and out of me. The pain was shocking, both hot and cold at once. He showed no mercy even after he saw that it was me he landed in, his eyes briefly widening before narrowing with purpose.

I was so sure that my future was long and would include so much of Hesperia that I could ask her endless details of what I couldn't remember. The taste of copper filled my mouth as I struggled to stay upright.

I was sure that I had time to reconnect with Fennic, too. I may not have been his true brother, but we were brothers still. I pushed him as far away from me and never looked back as I did Hesperia. Every slight and dismissal now weighed on me like mountains.

I was going to die without being able to say as much as sorry. I didn't help him bury or mourn his lost friends when we arrived, and I never reached out after. The realization burned worse than the wound.

I wasted my present betting on my future.

Onyx whistled. It was a tune I had heard from the Age of Moonlight, haunting and familiar. Vespera looked at me with a colorless face. Her eyes were wide, and for the first time, I felt afraid. The genuine horror in her expression confirmed what I already knew.

"Coy?" She got to her feet, and her hands were on my midsection, warm against my rapidly cooling skin. "Coy! Why would you get so close!"

"You're blaming me?" I coughed out, feeling liquid spill from the corners of my mouth.

I felt the initial shock of the axe, but I only felt cold after. I heard my heart pound in my head, each beat growing more distant, like thunder moving away.

"We need to go now. If we leave, Ruri can help, and Ashbell will have something. Someone will know what to do!" Her words were erratic. Her words were a shoved-together mess coming faster than the beating I heard in my ears.

The increased despair in her voice sent me into a spiral. Was I truly going to die? The room seemed to be darkening at the edges.

A black mist appeared, swirling like ink in water, and from it walked a man in a cloak. The temperature in the room dropped noticeably.

"Nikola?" I questioned, my voice barely a whisper.

My voice was low, and my words hurt, each syllable sending fresh waves of agony through me.

"You move too slowly," Onyx grunted, moving to stand beside the cloaked figure.

Vespera looked at me, still wide-eyed and uneasy. "I don't care who you are. I need to get him to help. Move out of my way," she demanded, her voice cracking with desperation.

"I won't be doing that," Nikola said, his voice smooth as silk. "I'll never understand why none of you moved real pieces. You all have played this game as though there aren't any real actions being taken against you, as though you have all the free time in the world. Look at you two now." Nikola laughed, the sound chilling in its emptiness. "Blessed by Dahlia, and yet you smell of fear and shame. You look like cornered rats on the verge of pissing yourself without shame if it meant you'd be granted mercy." Nikola crossed his arms, and the fabric of his robe tightened with it. "You remembered the artifact that could have made things so quick and easy for you, but you sent out others for it? It's truly been boring compared to Dahlia."

I felt nauseous for a moment, the world tilting sickeningly. My body was heavy against Vespera, growing heavier by the second. I dropped to the floor when Nikola grabbed her by the throat, and I had nothing left to lean on.

The stone was cold against my cheek. Nikola held one hand over Vespera's mouth and slit her throat with the other so deeply that I was sure she had lost her head entirely. The spray of crimson painted the walls. I couldn't have looked to make sure when he tossed her body behind him to move for me, the thud of her fall impossibly final.

I didn't have the strength to resist. I hardly had any to speak. My root, my life, it was hardly hanging by a thread, unraveling before my eyes.

I felt myself fade, the world growing dim around me.

Onyx leaned down so that I could see him clearly, his face

the last thing I would ever see. "I could have matched to any of them," he whispered as his body changed to be covered in emerald markings for Ruri, then white for Hesperia. "Maybe I'll give Hesperia the treatment you never could." He smirked, his words twisting like a knife.

"Two at once. If you can finish the other two Guardians, I might actually consider you useful, Onyx." Nikola said, his tone casual as if discussing the weather.

"Caym will be easy. Koa will fall once Caym does," Onyx said, confidence dripping from every word.

"You should hope that you are right," Nikola said. "I'll take the bodies with me."

Nikola reached down and grabbed a handful of my hair to lift my head, the pain distant now, almost belonging to someone else. I watched him take the same axe that Onyx drove into my stomach and aim it at my neck. As the blade fell, my last thought was of Hesperia's smile, bright as the stars we once counted together.

He took my head, as well.

CHAPTER THIRTY-TWO

THE NIGHTMARE BEGINS

RURI

Inola looked at me as if I had two heads, her eyes narrowed with disbelief. "I simply meant that it took less time than I expected to bring me back. I anticipated things to have been harder. I expected to see a whole new world. It feels somehow the same," I said, running my fingers along the smooth edge of the table between us.

"It's easy for you to feel that way when you miss everything in the middle. It's easy to feel complacent when you haven't witnessed the deaths or heartbreaks that came with the years that have passed since you were banished from Semper. You simply took a long nap. I'll only speak for myself, but it's felt like hundreds of years," Inola's cheeks flushed pink while she spoke, her hands gripping her cup so tightly I feared it might shatter.

Was she upset? The tension in her shoulders told me more than her words.

"I'm sure you are right in some way, but it doesn't change that for me. It feels like only minutes have passed," I rubbed my hands against the fabric of my leather pants, and they glided from the moisture on my palms. "I remember bits of the golden city but nothing else of being with our mother. I remember Semper and my death. I don't remember the life I lived in Cylla, though."

Inola's shoulders tensed, and she sat up straight, the chair creaking beneath her. "That's none of my business to tell you," she said, her voice suddenly cold as winter frost.

I had a sinking feeling I was missing something important with the way Inola locked up when I mentioned it, but I didn't want to pry too much yet. I would let her win for now. I had something important that needed to be at the top of the list, and that was Deimos. The mere thought of his name made my skin crawl.

He took advantage of me. That I remembered clearly. I had no blur on his voice telling me Caym was my enemy. I had no muffle on his voice in my dreams trying to convince me that Caym would be my end. I remembered all of the nightmares he gave me of Caym hurting me, the images vivid and sickening. The feeling of remembering scared me. Recalling how far Deimos went, how deep he took things between us, the fire that I felt inside of me burned hotter than any I had felt before, scorching my veins from within.

I didn't want to kill him. I wanted him to suffer for an eternity. I wanted to find a way to keep him alive so that he would hurt longer than I had. The things I may be capable of doing were worrisome because I knew that I had the power to do them. The darkness of my thoughts almost frightened me.

Yumi would be next on my list. I spent day after day confused over her obsession with the Tree of Life. I didn't understand why my punishments were in front of it. Why it was so important that I keep it coated in my blood. I did now. She forced me to be complicit in keeping my mother locked away and then made her suffer by watching me hurt. Each memory made the rage inside me grow, threatening to consume me.

I'd make her pay, too. I'd find something to do to her that would make the way she acted look like child's play. The thought sent a chill down my spine, but I welcomed it.

"I have a few things to do today. I'll meet you back here after?" I asked, already rising from my seat.

Inola nodded, her eyes following me warily, and I stood up and excused myself. I couldn't stop my smile when I heard the sound of my boots against the marble floor, each step a reminder that I was truly here, truly alive. I reached out and ran my fingers across the cold walls. I could have kissed them. I wouldn't take anything for granted again. I wanted to feel everything, to see everything, to imprint every sensation onto my newly awakened soul.

I wanted to live.

I took a deep breath of the hot air of Ashbell the moment I was outside. The scent of sulfur and spice filled my lungs, deliciously familiar. The back of the temple grounds were just as beautiful as the front, gardens of fire-resistant plants blooming impossibly in the heat.

"Ru?"

I turned to face him, my heart freezing mid-beat.

"Deimos! There you are," I cooed, the sweetness in my voice tasting like poison.

He smiled at me, and my body rejected the sight in every way it could. My hands shook, and my teeth ground against each other. His footsteps sounded like drums in my ears. The beat told me to attack, to tear, to destroy. He reached up and grabbed me by the neck to pull me into him. His lips hit mine, and I pushed down bile. I tried my best not to pull away from him too quickly, but even a second felt like it was too much, his touch like acid on my skin.

"Inola will be looking for me; I can't stay long. How are you? Did you get the position in Ashbell you were looking to get?" I asked, forcing brightness into my voice.

"There's something different about you," he said, his eyes narrowing suspiciously.

He lifted my hand and twirled me around, his grip too tight to be affectionate.

"It must be how much I'm learning at the temple," I laughed, the sound hollow even to my own ears.

He shook his head, his gaze never leaving mine. "I don't think that's it." He took my hair between his fingers and twirled it, the gesture possessive rather than loving. "You have a sweeter scent. Like old times."

"Shouldn't that make you happy?" I asked, fighting the urge to step away.

"Are you concerned that I'm not happy?" he asked, his voice dropping to a whisper.

He danced around my words, and I simply could not imagine a lifetime where I had willingly decided that I was in love with him. That I wanted to be touched by him. That I wanted to touch him. It was stomach-turning, the revulsion so strong I could taste it.

I formed an ice dagger in my palm and shoved it into the side of his rib cage. The weapon materialized in an instant, cold and deadly. Deimos grabbed his side and stumbled backward, his expression more surprised than pained.

"That could have been painful, Ru. Did what we have over these years mean nothing to you? I knew what your plans for today would have been once I smelled you. I just wanted to taste you on my lips one more time. It's a shame that I couldn't have tasted other parts of you again before you went back to him," Deimos laughed.

It was deep and set the fire inside me ablaze, rage burning white-hot behind my eyes. He disappeared into a mist, his form dissolving before my eyes. He hadn't gathered the courage to come and see me in person.

"Coward!" I screamed into the wind, my voice echoing across the temple grounds.

I stormed back into the temple, my footsteps thundering against the stone, and there he was, like the most beautiful addition to any room; he waited patiently. Caym's presence immediately calmed the storm raging within me, his familiar aura washing over me like a soothing balm.

"It didn't work. He came only in apparition," I sighed, frustration evident in every line of my body.

"You still looked gorgeous while trying," he said, a small smile playing at his lips.

He seemed less than shocked by the idea that Deimos would have done it. Had I missed so many things that now I was the one behind? Locked out of everyone's secret plans? The thought stung more than I wanted to admit.

"I need to find Kyrell. If killing Deimos isn't the first thing that happens, killing Kyrell instead should be," I said, pacing the marble floor.

"It's less possible to kill Kyrell. He went back to Semper when he heard you may really wake up this time. He sought out the protection of a realm beyond your grasp. You'd have to find a way into Semper to get to him," Caym said, his voice steady and practical.

I clicked my tongue and shook my head, the sound sharp in the quiet room. "I could ask Astra to get us in. She still has access to Semper. I wanted to avoid her for fear that she may be upset with me. I hadn't sought her out yet, nor had I even sent a message since I woke up. If I apologize, maybe she will still be on our side?"

"Astra has been looking forward to you waking up as much as the rest of us. She would not be upset that you didn't send word yet. We all have a part to play, and we've understood that," Caym said, his confidence reassuring.

"We all need to be together, then. We need to be in one room so that we can all openly share what we know. I don't want something as simple as the idea that none of you can communicate correctly to be what stops us and causes us to fail. We need to gather and make a plan on how to proceed before any other footsteps are taken," I said, conviction strengthening my voice.

Caym smirked at me. Its shape grew wider the more I spoke. If I were any weaker of a girl, I'd have caved in, and we would be hours behind sending messages to gather. The knowledge of his faith in me warmed something deep inside.

"I need to go find my heart box," I said, already planning the next steps.

I kissed him and lingered a bit longer before I reluctantly left him behind, the taste of him infinitely sweeter than the memory of Deimos. If we didn't get things moving, there would be no future for us to have. We would be lost to each other again, waiting for the hope one of us would be back.

I couldn't do it again. Not when I had just found him once more.

ONE MISSING LINK

RURI

Shivani was the first to arrive at the temple. The golden light filtering through the stained-glass windows cast colorful patterns across her face as she entered. It had to have been something she decided to do before we sent word. She had been talking for a while about Helia and vampires, her voice animated with passion.

She seemed to have endless tales of her time in Cylla. The idea that Helia set off some sort of curse by using things that didn't belong to her was not a shock to me. It made sense. It explained how she became so strong and what she was doing while the rest of us were being handed task after task. It lead me to wonder what else Helia or the other gods had been up to while Yumi kept our noses pointed. The scent of incense hung heavy in the air as I listened.

What I wanted to know more about was her time in the shattered realm. I wanted to know more about Nikola. She was a stranger to me in the sense that we hadn't been beside each other in nearly one hundred and fifty years. She felt familiar all the same. My mind knew her as a sister still, our connection transcending time and distance.

I tried to let her keep going until she was done and felt as if she had nothing more to say, but my face must have spoken for my mouth, betraying my distraction.

"What's wrong?" Shivani asked, her red eyes searched mine.

"I'm listening," I said, running my fingers along the stone table between us.

"Sure, but you aren't engaged. What is it?" She pressed, leaning forward.

"Deimos knows that I'm awake. He knows that we will be moving, so he will be moving faster. I'm just worried that if we don't move quickly, things will fall apart again. It'll be worse this time. More of us are together and pieced together. If Nikola wants us, he has us now. Kyrell went back to Semper, so I cannot merge with him. I'll remain only half as strong as I could be," I sighed, the weight of it all settling in my chest like a stone.

"It's all right," she said with a hand on my shoulder, her touch warm and reassuring. "Sage is the only one left to wake up. He can't kill us all until then."

"You should be reminded that against my will, I was feeding him power. Theres no way to tell how stronger he has become." I said gently.

"We've got it."

I knew she meant her words as encouraging, but they were not. I didn't hold any information that assured me he needed all of us alive. I only knew that he needed us whole. If her stories were all true, then Hesperia and Shivani were on the list to go first. The thought sent a cold shiver down my spine.

"I feel a bit behind," I admitted, my voice smaller than I intended. "I was the one that carried all the information before I died. Now there's Nikola; I have two more sisters. Helia mastered your magic, which makes me wonder if Kyrell has been secretly using mine. Hesperia and you already killed two people that I feel as though I just saw yesterday. It sounds like everyone knows so much, and I'm just here."

Shivani smiled, the gesture softening her usually fierce features. "Don't be fooled. I wouldn't have killed Helia if it wasn't for a lot of help. Hesperia is kind of scary, so it's fitting that she killed her counter, and we hardly know much more than I think you do. We know Nikola is as old as our mother and father, but I haven't found concrete information about where he came from. There is still a massive block standing between the people who know things and are able to speak. I think you woke up at the best time that you could have."

"I don't mean to interrupt the bonding happening here, but the Fiia sent word. Astra got Dahlia free of the tree and Semper. She is in Brontide with Kyra," Caym said as he entered, his footsteps echoing against the marble floor.

I jumped to my feet, the chair scraping loudly behind me. "What?"

"Dahlia isn't responsive yet, but they do have her," he repeated, his face showing guarded optimism.

"We need to do something, too!" I called, my heart racing with excitement. "I'll go wake Sage up. I'll make sure she gets her memory back!"

"That's a poor idea," Shivani said, her expression suddenly serious.

"I can drop off scrolls. She will follow them, and it will lead her to the truth," I said, my hands moving animatedly.

"If it were that easy, don't you think we would have done it by now?" Caym asked, his voice gentle but firm.

I threw myself back into the seat beneath me, the cushion letting out a small puff of air. "What about her guardian!"

"We haven't figured out if it's Vespera or Onyx yet," Shivani said, exchanging a glance with Caym.

"Oh. I guess I have missed a few things," I mumbled, tracing patterns on the table with my fingertip.

"Only a few," they said in unison, the shared moment almost making me smile despite my frustration.

"Maybe we should go to Astra then? I can't just sit here. I'm restless. I feel useless. If there's nothing we can do here and we can't help Sage, can we at least take healing supplies to Dahlia?" I asked, the need to act burning through me.

Caym nodded, his eyes softening at my plea. "We can do that. I'll send a message for everyone to meet us there instead of here."

The relief of having a purpose, even a small one, washed over me like a cool wave. At least we would be moving forward, taking one more step toward whatever awaited us all.

CHAPTER THIRTY-FOUR

YOUR GUT IS ALWAYS RIGHT

HESPERIA

The trip back to Daxon was filled with chatter and Sina's frown. The girl I learned was named Nira never seemed to run out of words, her voice rising and falling like waves against our ship. She held a keepsake from her past generations, and I was able to confirm that it was a tooth from the Goddess of Water, the ancient enamel gleaming with an inner light when she held it in the sunlight. She told me all about how much she loved swimming. That her first pet was a fish, I could have written a book filled with her words, each story tumbling after the last like water over stones.

The sight of land was almost welcome, so she could find distraction in the scenery, the coastal city of Daxon rising from the mist like a jeweled crown. I hadn't gotten time to explain what would happen once we arrived. To inform her that I would be handing her over to other strangers and leaving her behind. She was so innocent and naïve that I almost felt bad for what I was doing, guilt settling in my stomach like a stone.

The idea of giving her over when she knew nothing and

was easily influenced felt as if I were making a poor move in favor of Nikola. The thought left a bitter taste in my mouth.

Still, taking her to Daxon was the best place for her. She would be met with a shock and an adjustment but then she would help unite the kingdom under the rightful heir and we gain allies in a world where our abilities as deities are cut down. The politics of necessity rarely left room for kindness.

The ship docked on land, and the captain shouted the go-ahead to disembark, his voice carrying over the creaking of wood and splash of waves. That was the final straw for her. She finally stopped talking and nearly dived off of the boat, her aqua curls bouncing with each step.

A familiar man in a hooded cloak waited for me on the edge of the docks. His eyes locked with mine, dark and knowing, and I knew that he was there for business. I nodded at him, and he reciprocated, the subtle movement heavy with meaning.

"Are you positive? Did you confirm?" he asked, his voice barely above a whisper.

"Yes. She's the right one," I said, watching Nira as she spun in circles, fascinated by the harbor.

"It looks like we have a deal then," he said. "Where should we be starting?"

"Our plan is to destroy the realm of the gods so that they have to come to Cylla and fight where the Goddess of Starlight made us weaker. Once that happens, we will bless you with abilities beyond your own. My sisters and I will ensure you and your army are strong enough to be God killers," I said, each word carefully measured.

"How do you intend to do that?" he asked, suspicion edging into his tone. "I'd just like to know what's going to happen to my body."

"We will give you all four types of our magic to use freely," I said, keeping my voice steady despite the enormity of the promise.

The man raised his head so that I could see underneath it. His eyes were widened, and his brows were furrowed, the skin beneath his hood paler than it should have been. He understood enough to know that even gods didn't hold all four types of magic. It was one per person. The revelation seemed to shake him.

"I'll send word to our allies in Solaris. I'll tell them that they should also ready themselves," he said, fingers tapping nervously against his thigh.

I shook my head, the salt-laden breeze catching my hair. "That's a problem we haven't dealt with yet. Their leader must die. I doubt they will want to help us after."

"I disagree. The army there has been loyal to Caym since he started training them. They'd deliver their ruler's head if he asked it," the man whispered his words, breath warm against my ear.

I pulled Nira forward so that she stood in between us, her slight body a buffer between two plotting immortals.

"Will you tell me more about you now?" I asked, curiosity finally getting the better of me.

I hadn't expected much, but I couldn't leave without the attempt. The question had been gnawing at me since our first meeting.

He leaned into me and whispered, his voice changing timbre slightly. "I am a sea titan, created by the Goddess of Water before her death. In my true form, I look nothing like a man. I told you I run a hidden group ready to play our part in return for your assistance."

I nodded with a forced smile, hiding my skepticism behind courtesy.

"Nira, this man you can trust. Do what he tells you," I said, giving her shoulder a gentle squeeze.

I turned and made my way back down the dock to my ship, wooden planks creaking beneath my steps. I wanted to leave as quickly as possible. I may have handed her over to her death disguised as her happily ever after. I didn't need to see it. I did my part. The thought sat heavy in my chest.

I didn't expect much, and yet I was still unhappy with the answer I got. A titan? A sea titan? Did he think that he was funny? I'd be asking about this. Someone should have to have a list of all the things living in the realm. The claim felt too convenient, too perfect.

A Fiia hovered over me, its tiny wings creating a gentle breeze against my face, and I stopped walking. Why was it in front of me? Its glow seemed dimmer than usual, tinged with urgency.

"Coy missed his meeting with the dragons. Astra has Dahlia. She shows no signs of life. Ruri travels to Brontide," it chittered and flew off without asking me if I had a message to send back, leaving a trail of golden dust in its wake.

Sina looked at me expectantly, her feline eyes narrowed. She could not understand them. I wasn't sure why, but she couldn't. The limitation had always seemed strange to me.

"The Fiia said Coy missed his meeting," I said, my voice betraying more concern than I intended.

"What?" Sina looked shocked, her ears perking up.

"Have you heard from Ryujin?" I asked, studying her reaction carefully.

"Of course! They're investigating Onyx. I'm sure Onyx would be able to confirm they're there," she said, her tail swishing with what looked like nervousness.

Her reaction made me suspicious and uncomfortable. My stomach did flips, and my gut told me something was wrong. The feeling was too strong to ignore, a warning bell I'd learned to heed.

"Can you go take a separate ship to Onyx and see if they are there? I'll go to the dragon lands and see what they know," I said, already formulating a different plan.

Sina nodded all too willingly. Was she just happy to see

Ryujin? Or did she know something that she wasn't sharing? Her eagerness felt off, another warning sign.

I watched her stomp off on all four paws. Her talons hit the wood in a prance. She had a bubbly pep about her that was unusual, almost inappropriate given the circumstances.

I pulled my own Fiia from my small coin purse, its light casting my face in a gentle glow.

"Go find Coy. Do not come back until you find him," I whispered to it, my voice barely audible above the lapping waves.

I didn't have a solid reason, but I didn't trust anyone or anything to bring back the truth to me but the Fiia. I was going to see the masked king, not the dragon lands. I wanted to keep that close to my chest, too. If my senses were right, it would be where Nikola sat. Then I'd go see Mother. The path ahead felt dangerous, but necessary.

I wanted to hear word from Coy, but he didn't need me to protect him; he made it clear. Still, as I gazed out over the restless sea, I couldn't shake the feeling that something terrible had happened—something that would change everything.

CHAPTER THIRTY-FIVE

A DREAM STATE

HESPERIA

I stood outside of the gates to the kingdom of the masked king and only waited a moment before the chains pulled the gate open, the rusted metal groaning in protest. A fae came out, his steps measured and precise. He was covered in silver armor with hardly any skin to be taken in, the metal glinting coldly in the afternoon light.

"Name and business," he asked, his voice hollow inside his helmet.

"Hesperia, I—"

"It's the girl! Send her into the king!" He called back, urgency cutting through his formal tone.

A herd of guards jogged out to escort me inside, their synchronized footsteps creating a rhythm that matched my racing heart. If they were waiting for me by name, it painted a worse picture of where Coy had to be. The sense of foreboding grew with each step toward the throne room, the air growing colder despite the warmth of the day.

I followed them inside and to the throne where the masked king sat, one leg over the other in casual dominance. The room smelled of incense and something darker, metallic. He removed his mask and smirked at me in a way I was familiar with, his features rearranging themselves into a face I knew all too well.

"Nikola," I sighed, my worst fears confirmed.

"I'm honestly hurt it took you so long to find me. I expected you here sooner. Then again, so did poor Coy," he pointed to the side of the room, his finger directing my gaze like a weapon.

I didn't want to turn my head because a part of me already knew what would be waiting for me as soon as I heard Coy's name. I expected to see him caged and hurt, clinging to life. My body didn't listen to my mind's pleas, and when my eyes were locked on the sight Nikola wanted me to see, it was beyond what I could have imagined. The horror of it stole my breath.

A scream that echoed in the room left my lips, bouncing off the stone walls and returning to my ears as if from a stranger's throat.

Coy's head sat on a stick beside his body. His chest had been torn open, and his heart was missing, the cavity a dark void where his essence should have been. Without a complete heart, none of us could come back. I could make exceptions for mortals, but not us. The rules that governed our existence were clear and cruel.

I couldn't change the rules for us. No heart, no life. The finality of it crashed over me like a physical blow.

My vision tunneled, the edges of the room fading to black, and I lost control of myself. I had no thought to roll over or a little voice telling me to stop. I lunged for Nikola with a fury I could hardly comprehend, my body moving on pure instinct. Deimos, the God of Dreams, came from behind Nikola's throne and hit me in the side of the head before I reached Nikola. The impact sent stars shooting across my vision. It was a shock that stunned me enough that I hit the ground on my knees, the stone cold and unyielding beneath me.

"If only you still had time to run off and gather your sisters," Nikola laughed, the sound like broken glass. "You and I discussed at lengths your tendency to act without thinking over the years, didn't we? Nothing I tried to teach you stayed in place, it seems. It's a shame because all I wanted was to prepare you for a less one-sided battle against me. I wanted to give you at least a fighting chance, Hesperia. It hurts me to hurt you. I've grown to consider you a daughter after all of the time we've had together."

"I've seen what you do to those you consider a daughter. I don't feel the same about you. You better hope that you kill me this time!" I screamed, my voice raw with hatred.

"I could change the sentiment to wife if you'd like that more. You are alone now, after all," Nikola mused, his casual cruelty twisting the knife deeper.

Deimos held his fingers over my eyes, his touch cold and invasive. I felt a force shove me through a blur of light before I was placed back on my feet, reality shifting around me like quicksand.

It was the same as before. The same as when I was locked away in a separate realm from my sisters.

Coy stood in front of me. He looked me in the eyes while Onyx held him and took his head. The sound of blade meeting flesh was sickening, wet and final. A tear ran down the side of his face, but he did not waver. His body hit the ground first before Onyx tossed his head, and it rolled to my feet, leaving a crimson trail across the stone.

I wanted to scream, but my mouth did not open, my voice trapped inside my throat.

Time rewound itself until Coy was whole again, the horror playing out like a performance for my benefit alone. But this time, Nikola took the axe from the ground and used it to remove Coy's head, the blade catching the light as it arced through the air.

I was stuck in a loop. A dream where I had nothing to do but watch Coy die by their hands, over and over. I knew there was nothing that I could do to stop it. All I could do was turn away, but even that didn't stop the sound of his flesh being torn apart, the wet thud of his body hitting the ground echoing in my ears.

I lived so long trapped in a false reality just like it that I knew already there was nothing I could do to stop it from happening. Nikola had already placed me in a similar dream, the familiarity of the torture almost worse than the torture itself.

I sat on the edge of losing my mind last time. I didn't know if I had the strength to hold myself together again. The darkness at the edges of my consciousness threatened to consume me entirely.

The sound of Coy's head being rolled to me played out again, the nightmare eternal in its repetition.

CHAPTER THIRTY-SIX

SOMETIMES TIME MOVES
TOO SLOWLY

SAGE

I stood outside of Nikola's throne room, and his guards informed me that I was denied access. The cold metal of their armor gleamed in the torchlight as they blocked my path. They told me he had no need for me today. That they could easily inform him that I was empty-handed and would remain that way, their voices laced with thinly veiled contempt.

I was suspicious and didn't stop my wondering eyes. There was a dragon inside with him. She had antlers and powder blue scales that shimmered like frost in the morning light. She was the picture of a winter morning, elegant and dangerous all at once. I couldn't hear them, but the fact that they were whispering only furthered my curiosity, the secretive atmosphere sending prickles of unease down my spine.

Onyx grabbed my arm and pulled me away with him, his fingers digging into my flesh. He tugged my arm until we were in a hallway and pinned me against the wall, the cold stone pressing against my back. He didn't look at my eyes but my lips, his gaze heavy with intention. It was almost a sentence in itself, his desire written in the tension of his body.

"Can you guess what I'm thinking?" he whispered, his breath warm against my skin.

I could take a guess or two. What I wanted to know was why he was coming onto me so strongly all of a sudden. Did he know something about the king's meeting? If I ignored those things, I could allow myself to think what I knew he was for a brief moment, curiosity mingling with something deeper.

One kiss couldn't hurt, could it? It may even help. One kiss may let me see if there was a spark between us or not, answer the question that had been lingering between us.

He leaned into me closer as if he could read my mind, and I finished closing the distance until our lips were together. Sealed with the wish of love. Love wasn't the word he was hinting at when he allowed his hands to wander down my back to squeeze more than he was offered. The scent of metal and leather clung to him, overwhelming my senses. He took liberties with his tongue in my mouth and added aggression and force that I didn't consider passionate, his hunger more predatory than romantic.

Vespera's face flashed in my mind, her eyes filled with something I couldn't quite name, and I pulled away from him and his panting breath. One kiss didn't help me decide that I was in love with him; it made me question if I even held a liking for him or if I was just confused. The taste of him lingered, neither pleasant nor unpleasant, just... wrong.

"What's wrong?" Onyx asked, frustration evident in the tightness of his jaw.

"Nothing," I cleared my throat and moved under his arm and off the wall, straightening my clothes with trembling fingers.

A man with a mask and cloth wrapped around his face approached me with my own card. The familiar symbol of the Daughters of Steel gleamed in the dim light. He held the card out for me to accept, his gloved fingers careful not to touch mine. He came to seek me out and offer me a job. I glanced back at Onyx and grabbed the strange man's arm. I dragged him with me until we were out of sight, his footsteps reluctant but compliant.

"What? Get to it," I demanded, my patience worn thin by the day's events.

"There is a man in the dungeons of Orest. He must die," the man whispered, his voice so low I had to strain to hear it.

"Sounds simple enough. What are you paying?" I asked, crossing my arms.

"A king's treasury," the man answered, the promise of wealth heavy in his tone. "There are strict rules that must be followed. First, you have to go alone. You and only you must be the one to kill him, and you will need to remove his heart and bring it back. It must be intact. You understand?"

"You're serious? You lost me at heart. Do you take me for one of the vampires? Why would I do that? Kill him, sure. Mutilate? No. No way," I shook my head, disgust rising in my throat.

"I'll pay you triple," he countered, the words hanging between us like a physical temptation.

Triple? I audibly groaned, the sound echoing in the empty corridor. I did like coins, and Vespera would, too. If she found out how much I turned down, she'd have my head. The mental calculation was quick and decisive.

"Fine! But you tell no one I mutilated a corpse the way you've demanded," I pointed, my finger jabbing the air between us.

The dead were sacred. They needed their heart for the afterlife. I didn't want that kind of reputation following me, the superstitious dread making my skin crawl despite my pragmatism.

"There's one more thing," he said, shifting his weight from foot to foot.

I lifted my hand and pointed my finger at his nose, close enough that I could see his eyes widen behind his mask.

"When you're done and back, you must have dinner with me. I'll pay separately for that," he said, an unexpected request that caught me off guard.

Dinner? That was easy enough. I held out my hand to shake his. It was an important part of things. If he didn't hold up his end, it would be the hand I cut off. I chuckled to myself, the sound dark even to my own ears. It would be the hand Vespera cut off. The dungeon man would be one of a tiny list of things I killed myself. It was mostly tacos that died by my hands.

The thought of Vespera returned unbidden. What would she think of all this? Of Onyx? Of this mysterious contract? The questions swirled in my mind, unanswered but persistent. I pushed them aside. First the job, then the complications. One step at a time.

CHAPTER THIRTY-SEVEN
A BLOODY DUNGEON

SAGE

I stood on the mountainside of Orest, a stone's throw away from being inside of the walls, when the entire mountainside started to shake. The rocks beneath my feet trembled, sending loose pebbles cascading down the slope. In the distance, where Ashbell was, I could see some sort of giant creature, some kind of titan, standing tall from around the volcano. I shouldn't have been able to see it, but it was so large in size that I could. It stood with armor embedded into its stone-like skin and horns atop its head, gleaming wickedly in the sunlight. It looked big enough to slice the world in half, its massive shadow falling across the land like an omen.

It was the first time I had felt as if the realm was changing that it started to carry a strange sense of doom around its corners. The air felt heavy, charged with something ancient and threatening.

I needed to do my job and leave. I needed to get back to Vespera. If the world was going to go to the dogs, I needed to be by her side. I needed to keep her safe. Maybe I needed her to keep me safe. The thought sent a flutter through my chest that I wasn't ready to examine.

I moved inside of Orest and to its dungeon. There wasn't a single soul in sight, not from the courtyard to the hallways. The eerie silence pressed against my ears like a physical thing. I didn't need to sneak if I decided against it. I could have walked carelessly through the entire school and never had a single sighting, my footsteps echoing against the stone floors.

A small green creature with wings appeared in front of me. It was chubby, and its eyes were bigger than cups when it looked up at me, glittering with an intelligence that made me uneasy. The thing was covered in leaves instead of clothing and fluttered with wings that looked like they were made from stringing together blades of grass. It buzzed around my head and motioned me to follow it, but it never spoke, the soft hum of its wings the only sound it made.

I had never seen anything like it before. Against my better judgment, I followed, drawn by curiosity and necessity. It guided me down the stairwell to the dungeon, the air growing colder and damper with each step. Seemed that we were both going to the same place, though I couldn't fathom why such a creature would be here.

When I rounded the corner at the bottom of the stairs, a man stood in blackened armor, but the red streaks across his skin stood out the most. They were like veins on the outside of his body, pulsing with an unnatural glow. He looked at me as if it were a casual run-in. As if he had expected to see people walking around in the dungeon, his posture relaxed despite his menacing appearance.

"I wondered when they were sending the next guard for the prisoners," he said, his voice carrying an odd metallic quality. "Carry on."

He moved around me and did not look back, his armor scraping softly against the stone walls. It felt wrong, like a setup. Suspicious and regretful. I was already on the cusp of completion. I just had to hurry up and finish the task so that I could leave. There was no way that I had come the whole way and was going to leave empty-handed. I needed money to build some sort of underground home that would protect us from whatever now lurked outside, the image of the titan still fresh in my mind.

The dungeon was empty except for one man. He was chained to the wall with something that glowed, casting strange shadows across his face. It wasn't normal steel, the metal humming with power I could feel in my teeth. I was happy to only have to take his heart and not his body, though the thought still turned my stomach.

I picked the lock to the cell and walked inside, the door creaking open on reluctant hinges.

"I'm happy you're the one to show up," he said, his voice surprisingly strong for someone in his position.

"Do you know who I am?" I asked, tightening my grip on my dagger.

"I shouldn't be surprised that you don't know who I am. You can call me Thann. I know you've come to kill me. I've been ready for a while."

He mumbled on as if we were close, or I had come to take a record of his last words, his voice strangely familiar despite my certainty we'd never met.

"I've made a lot of mistakes. I've done a lot of things that I'm not proud of. When you have a clearer understanding of what you're doing here. When you look back, look in peace. I'm happy it was by your hands, Sage." Thann closed his eyes and opened his chest to me, acceptance written in every line of his body.

I took a deep breath, the musty air filling my lungs, and plunged my dagger into his chest, and pulled it down until I heard it hit bone. The sound of blade meeting flesh was sickening, the warm spray of blood coating my hands. Breaking his ribs wasn't as easy as I expected it to be, the crack of bone echoing in the small cell, but I made it to his heart and removed it. It pulsed once in my hand, impossibly warm and alive.

I shoved it into a bag, then into a box. The weight of it felt wrong, unnatural. I didn't want to know it was there, but I could confirm the man was dead, we were alone, and it was by my hands only. The deed was done, the evidence secured.

Thinking on his words made my mind hurt, a strange pressure building behind my eyes.

I had flashes of his face on my mind. A long grey beard and he sat in a garden, sunlight dappling through leaves onto his serene face.

A second flash and I saw him holding a baby under water, tiny limbs thrashing as bubbles rose to the surface.

How did I know him? The question echoed through my mind, unanswered but persistent as I made my way back through the empty halls, the titan's shadow still visible through every window I passed.

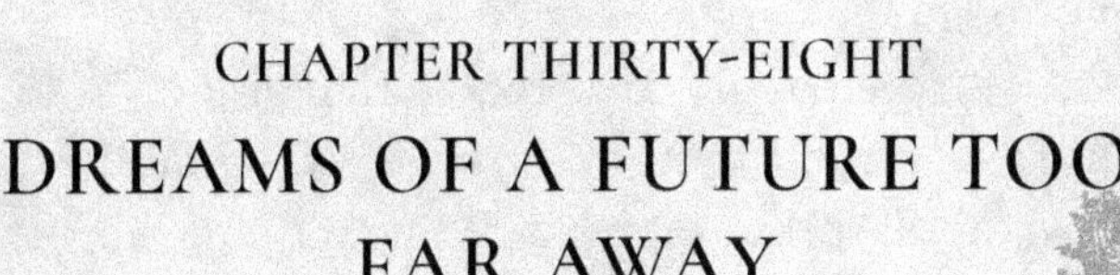

CHAPTER THIRTY-EIGHT

DREAMS OF A FUTURE TOO FAR AWAY

ASTRA

My dreams have always been the same since the stars appeared. I held my son in my arms again, his weight perfectly balanced against my chest, his tiny heartbeat fluttering against mine. I nurtured him into childhood, watching his first steps across sun-dappled floors, hearing his laughter echo through halls I'd never walked in waking life. Kyra and I had three more children, their faces blending features from both of us in ways that made my heart ache upon waking. Life was everything we fought so hard for, golden and perfect in those fleeting dream hours.

Somewhere, my son had resentment, and he hid it well beneath smiles that never quite reached his eyes. He grew up, and it bubbled over until he became a force much more devastating than Nikola had ever been, his power casting shadows longer than mountains across the lands we'd tried to save.

Most of the originals had gone to sleep or died. There wasn't the same force to push against him, and he knew it, his confidence terrifying in its completeness. I always woke up before I saw the outcome, drenched in sweat and gasping. I couldn't bring myself to believe that it was anything more than a curse pulling up my deepest fears, though the images lingered like smoke long after waking.

"Are you awake?" My door opened, a sliver of light cutting through the darkness.

"Yes," I answered, my voice rough from disuse.

Ruri came in and shut the door gently behind her before she ran, in a full sprint, to my bed. She hit me with the force of a wall before she wrapped her arms around me, the scent of pine and lightning surrounding me. The happiness from having her back was as high as the pain she inflicted on me, her embrace pressing against wounds both seen and unseen.

She pulled back and grabbed each side of my face, her hands cool against my fevered skin. "What are you hiding?"

"I just haven't been sleeping well lately," I answered, avoiding her piercing gaze.

"I meant this sickness, but we can discuss this, too," she said, her thumbs brushing across my cheekbones.

I sighed; of course, Kyra told her. The betrayal stung less than it should have.

"I've had dreams of my son destroying the world. It started the same time this did," I said as I pulled my shirt from the star on my chest, revealing the blackened mark that pulsed with each heartbeat.

"Astra!" Ruri yelled, her face paling. "Why would you hide this? This looks bad. Your skin is rotting around it. I haven't forgotten about your son, but if you die from this, who will raise him?"

I couldn't hide my smile. Having what should have been my sister back to reprimand me was good to hear, the familiarity of it warming something deep inside.

My smile led to a laugh, which led to a cough, and before I could tell my body to stop, I was vomiting blood. The metallic taste filled my mouth as crimson spattered across the white sheets. Ruri called for help, her voice cracking with fear, and a crowd ran in, their footsteps thundering against the floor.

"Stop, stop," I begged, wiping my mouth with a trembling hand. "It's fine. I'll let you do what you need to try and fix whatever this is, but you have to allow me to check on Dahlia."

"Fine. I agree. It's better than chaining you down like I was going to do," Ruri said, her attempt at humor belied by the worry in her eyes.

She stood and held out her hand for me, and I took it, my fingers cold against her warmth. I didn't want her to know how much I was hurting either, but it wasn't as easy to hide from her. When I grasped her hand, she looked at me as if the sparks of pain were felt inside of her, too, her face flinching in momentary shared agony.

"I never could hide things from you," I chuckled, the sound hollow in my chest.

"I'll help you," she whispered, her voice for me alone. "You don't need to say anything. I'll heal you anyway."

I wanted to believe her, but I knew it was too late. I felt my body failing, each breath more difficult than the last. The largest part of the pain I felt was in my heart. It physically felt as if it were shattering, like glass breaking beneath a hammer.

I followed her into a separate building where Dahlia was laid and covered in blankets. The air inside was heavy with the scent of herbs and healing magic. Healers stood around her, injecting things into her arms that I didn't understand, the glowing liquids pulsing as they entered her veins. The advancements they made in Ashbell always shocked me, a reminder of how much I'd missed.

They had brought color back to Dahlia's cheeks, the pallor of death replaced by the faintest pink. Ruri nodded me ahead. A silent message that I was free to approach her first. I sat on the edge of Dahlia's bed and watched her, drinking in the face I'd thought I might never see again.

I reached up to move her hair and tuck it neatly atop her head. Her braids flowed over the pillow like rivers of gold. I took a damp cloth and dabbed her forehead, the coolness soothing against her skin. I dropped the rag on the ground and nearly dropped myself off the side of the bed when she shot up and tossed herself over my lap. I looked over her to the naked body lying in bile on the ground, my mind struggling to comprehend what I was seeing.

"Did you just throw up, Olexei?" I shuddered, the stench making my eyes water.

"Astra," Dahlia was breathing too hard to speak for long, her chest heaving with effort. "I've missed you, but you smell of sickness."

I had nothing to say in return. What could I have said? The truth seemed too cruel to voice aloud.

"A dark curse on your heart. It smells of rage and sorrow," Dahlia huffed, her hands moving over me as if reading my ailment through touch.

"Attack! We're under attack!" Guards screamed as they ran past the doorway, their armor clanking with each frantic step.

"Stay here," Ruri yelled before she took off in a run, purple lightning crackling at her fingertips.

Dahlia grabbed my hands and tried to use magic. She placed her hand over my heart, but nothing happened again, no warmth, no healing light.

"Dahlia, are you powerless?" I asked, the realization sending a chill through me.

She didn't look at me; she only kept trying to touch me, her fingers trembling with effort against my chest.

"What a perfect sight," Deimos laughed from the doorway, his voice like ice water down my spine.

He walked to me and touched my chest himself. I let out a scream that tore from the depths of my being. Dahlia's touch hadn't done anything, but his touches sent a wave of ice over me. I didn't need to ask him what he was doing because when I looked down, I could see his fingers wrapped around my heart. He was freezing it to shatter, and I felt every small chip fall off, the pain beyond description.

"You can't be here!" I gasped, black spots dancing at the edges of my vision.

"Yes, Brontide is protected. The thing is, your mind isn't. I can be with you, no matter where you are, if we're inside your mind. You can also die here, too. I thought that you would be my biggest obstacle, but you let Ruri run off with any guy she felt like seeing, and it was so easy to convince her with fear that she should feed me her power. It was a regular routine for her and I. She'd fill me with her own magic until she was near death. The amount of things that I can do now? You wouldn't believe it," he boasted, his fingers tightening around my heart.

I gripped my chest. His grip was so tight I could hardly have a thought, each beat of my heart sending fresh agony through me.

"Do you want a fun last thought? Even after your failures, you get to leave one last scar. Anyone around you will be able to see you dying, but they won't be able to stop it. Goodbye, Goddess," Deimos laughed, his voice the last thing I heard as darkness began to claim me.

CHAPTER THIRTY-NINE
THE SPIDERS RETURN

RURI

Grotesque creatures stomped through Ashbell, their massive legs cracking the stone beneath them. Winged skeletal monsters filled the sky, blotting out the sun and casting the world in shadow. The scent of decay and scorched earth filled my nostrils as I recognized the nightmare unfolding before me - I knew it was Deimos. I had seen them before. I had seen the spiders, too, their chitinous bodies gleaming with an unnatural sheen. I was stunned by the thought that Sahir was around. One of the first things that I was told was how Sage killed her, yet her presence lingered in the air like a foul memory.

Kyra did not allow me to stay in Brontide. It was as shocking to me that she hated me so much, her eyes hard as ice when she ordered me away. I hadn't considered that it would be a possible outcome of leaving her with another Goddess, the betrayal still fresh for her, while ancient history to me. We had only been back home long enough to start treatment on Astra when everything exploded in chaos, the world turning upside down in the span of heartbeats.

Onyx held an axe and moved through the monsters, the blade glinting crimson in the strange half-light. His movements were too purposeful, too synchronized with the creatures around him.

"Onyx!" I yelled as I ran to him, my boots slipping on the blood-slicked ground. "Where is everyone else? Are they safe? I raised my Titan already. I know it's just another secret I kept, but he will help."

"Titan?" he asked, his voice oddly calm amid the chaos.

"Yes," I pointed him towards the volcano where my creation stood enormous against the horizon.

My Titan stood tall; he slapped creatures from the sky on the horizon, each swipe of his massive hand sending dozens of them plummeting to the earth. I turned back to Onyx, and he had his axe in the side of one of my Seere's necks, the guard's eyes wide with shock and betrayal as life drained from them.

"Onyx?" The question hung in the air, unanswered.

He raised his axe and took down another guard before he walked past me as if I were invisible, blood spraying across my face, warm and sticky. He was the traitor. It was him all along. The realization hit me like a physical blow. I charged after him, but was met with Sahir moving in front of me, her lavender hair flowing around her like liquid silk. I connected my fist to her cheek instead of his, the impact sending shockwaves up my arm. She was just as guilty for where we were now. We could have all lived in separate corners of what we must have, and be peaceful. Was this the better option for them? This destruction, this chaos?

"I heard you were back, and I just had to come see you myself," Sahir smiled while she held her jaw, a trickle of blood running between her fingers.

She pointed behind me, and I turned, dread pooling in my stomach. Onyx held down Caym on his knees, the God of Death's face contorted with pain and rage. I had to be in a dream. This couldn't be real, couldn't be happening.

"Part of me always knew it was you," Caym said, his voice steady despite everything. "I want you to know that I still consider you a brother, and I'd still defend you if I knew that this was the outcome. I'd still keep it to myself and hope that you would make the right choice."

Deimos held his hand to Caym's forehead, his fingers glowing with malevolent power, and Caym stopped struggling, his body going rigid. Onyx stood, and time stood still with him. His axe was through Caym's neck in slow motion, the blade reflecting my horrified face as it arced through the air.

"I never needed your protection," Onyx ground his teeth together while he spoke, spittle flying from his lips.

My Caym. My husband. He was dead. The world shattered around me, reality fragmenting into pieces I couldn't hold together.

"This is the last thing we do together," Deimos said, wiping blood from his hands onto his robe. "Our deal is done. Now you're on your own."

Sahir had her hands on my arms and pulled me to my feet, her grip bruising. I hadn't realized I wasn't on them. I never felt the ground hit my knees, the numbness spreading through me like poison.

"Do you know how he got Caym to stop struggling? He stuck him in a nightmare where you were the one to die if he didn't. He died thinking you were going to die again," Sahir laughed, the sound like broken glass. "Coy is dead. Vespera is dead. Hesperia is trapped in a nightmare. We're going for Sage next. If anything, I should thank you. Your death gave us the time we needed to gain the upper hand."

I gave them the time they needed. Was I to blame? The thought drove into me like a knife, twisting deeper with each breath.

I dropped back to my knees without her grip on me. I couldn't hold the weight of myself and process her words. The world around me continued to burn and scream, but all I could see was Caym's face in those final moments, all I could hear was the horrible sound of metal meeting flesh. Everything we'd fought for, everyone we'd loved - slipping away like sand through desperate fingers.

CHAPTER FORTY
THE NEW KINGDOM

SAHIR

I knew when I watched my dreams come true, it would have been fulfilling, but I didn't realize it would be so filled with joy. The satisfaction spread through me like warm honey, intoxicating and sweet. Ruri saved Dahlia and Olexei, but they were useless, broken shells of what they once were. I wanted to kill Sage, but she still had no memory, her mind a blank canvas waiting for our influence. Nikola wanted her on our side because of it. He said there was no need to make things harder, and who was I to deny him when he was clearly right? His wisdom never failed to impress me.

I had to admit that there was a bit of joy in having her by my side, after everything, willing to look at me as a friend and influential Goddess worth her time. The irony was delicious enough to savor.

Sage sliced her hand open and let the blood drip over the second egg that Onyx kept. The crimson liquid flowed down the shell's surface, glowing faintly where it touched. Not a single movement came from the egg, but I knew it would work

all the same. If it worked for me, it would work again. The certainty hummed inside me like a physical thing.

Sage began to look around the room as if she had done something wrong, her eyes wide with uncertainty, and before I could take a chance to play along and punish her, a fist pushed through the egg. The shell cracked with a sound like thunder. I grabbed the edges of the shell and pulled them off, fragments falling to the floor with soft clicks.

He stepped through and cracked his neck, the sound echoing in the chamber, and I bit my lip at the sight. His perfect form emerged like a dark god from primordial waters. Nikola grabbed me by the waist and pulled me into him, his touch both familiar and electric. Our kiss was filled with more passion than I remembered it, his lips tasting of power and promise. I allowed my hands to wander over his body, feeling the strength beneath his skin, but he stopped me, his fingers encircling my wrists.

"How do you feel?" I asked, breathless with anticipation.

"Complete," he growled, his voice resonating with newfound strength. "Walking around as a spirit had its benefits, but now it's time we finish our plans. We have an audience to greet," Nikola declared, his eyes flashing with purpose.

He grabbed pants and a white button-up shirt before he turned and walked out to the castle balcony, the fabric hardly containing his power. I followed Sage as she walked on his other side, the three of us united in dark purpose. I didn't mind sharing Nikola with her because I knew that I was better at everything, my superiority as obvious as the sun above us.

"A war between gods and mortals is on the horizon," Nikola yelled to the crowd, his voice carrying to every corner of the gathering. "It will shape our new world. I will grant my followers power like they've never seen before and promise the most devoted a seat beside me in the new kingdom."

I let my smirk turn to a smile that showed all of my teeth when I noticed Ruri and Shivani in the crowd. Their hoods hardly hid their identity, their features too distinctive to truly conceal. Bringing Nikola back in full form was more important than they were. Their time would be soon, their deaths a delicious dessert after this main course of triumph.

When Nikola's speech was finished, I urged Sage to move forward and kiss him so that it was the last thing her sisters had to think of, a final twist of the knife in their grieving hearts.

"Is what you offer true?" Sage asked, her voice carrying an innocence that was almost painful.

"It is," Nikola answered while the crowd still cheered in the background, their adoration a physical force. "I'll extend a seat to you, too."

"What is our next move?" I asked, stepping between them, the scent of jealousy rising from me like heat.

I wanted to interrupt them. I allowed Sage to kiss him for one reason, and it wasn't for them to grow closer. The possessiveness surprised even me.

"Be calm, Sahir. The mortals are used to us, but they still fear us because they know without us, they are weak," Nikola soothed, his fingers tracing my jawline. "Our part should be small for now; let them cling to the idea that they have a chance to be equal to us. They are nothing that we can count on, and if we want them to do half of the work for us, we only need to convince them that some are stronger than others. Turn them on each other. They will fight over the chance to be the ones on top and touch the power we are born with."

I ran my hand through his beard before I kissed him again, feeling the coarse hairs against my palm. It was good to have him back, solid and real beneath my touch.

"Daddy's home!" I danced, twirling with childlike glee that belied the darkness of our triumph.

If Yumi was starlight and Dahlia was moonlight. If Olexei

was sunlight, then Nikola was the darkness that they all rested in the void that gave meaning to their light, and would ultimately consume it all.

DRAGONS

Ryujin—Second in Command of the Armies from the Age of
Moonlight, in dragon form.
Sina—Winter Goddess in dragon form
Vero—Fall Goddess in dragon form
Cyrus—Summer God in dragon form
Belladonna—Ruri Dragon

Usha—Erebus Guardian
Divala—Brontide Guardian
Kaida—Onyx Dragon

TEMPLE LEADERS

Dominic—High Priest of vampires
Dimitri—Lower Priest of vampires
Inola—High Priestess of the Order of the Arcane Tome

Temples

Temple of Rebirth
Temple of Magic
Temple of Vampires
Temple of Healing
Temple of Water

REALMS

Semper—Realm of the Gods
Cylla—Realm of the Mortals
Cosima—Realm of Dreaming Souls
Merripen—Realm of the Dead

Original Deities

Dahlia—Goddess of the Moon
Yumi—Goddess of Starlight
Olexei—God of the Sun
Nikola—God of Insanity

SEASONAL DEITIES

Sina—Goddess of Winter
Vero—Goddess of Fall
Cyrus—God of Summer
Inola—Goddess of Spring

Sisters of Fate

Ruri—Goddess of Magic
Sage—Goddess of Nature
Shivani—Goddess of Time
Hesperia—Goddess of Fate

DEITY-LED KINGDOMS

Ruri—Ashbell
Kyrell—Solaris
Thann—Orest
Astra—Edur
Kyra—Brontide
Orla/Sage—Erebus
Izaria—Daxon

Other notable inhabitants

- **Fiia**—A small fluttering creature made of starlight that helps send messages back and forth.
- **Lui**—Leader of the Timekeepers.
- **Jeb**—Commander of the Nola.
- **Nola**—Keepers of the underworld, helpers to the God of Death.
- **Vina**—Cave protectors
- **Seere**—Clerics of Ashbell, created by Ruri. They are covered in black scales with magma-colored

veins, orange eyes, and black hair. They commonly wear masks to avoid breathing in the excess ash on their land.

- **Mita**—Nearly transparent skin. Golden eyes and tinted skin. Black hair. Their golden veins pulse with the thunder magic they wield.
- **Angels**—Guardians created to protect Yumi and the realm of the Gods.
- **Timekeepers**—Collectors and protectors of knowledge from the Age of Moonlight.
- **Blood Guards**—The Second created guardians of Semper. Made by blood from Helia, the Goddess of Time.
- **False deities**—Deities created in the likeness of powerful originals in order to take their place. Helia, Minna, Thann, Kyrell.

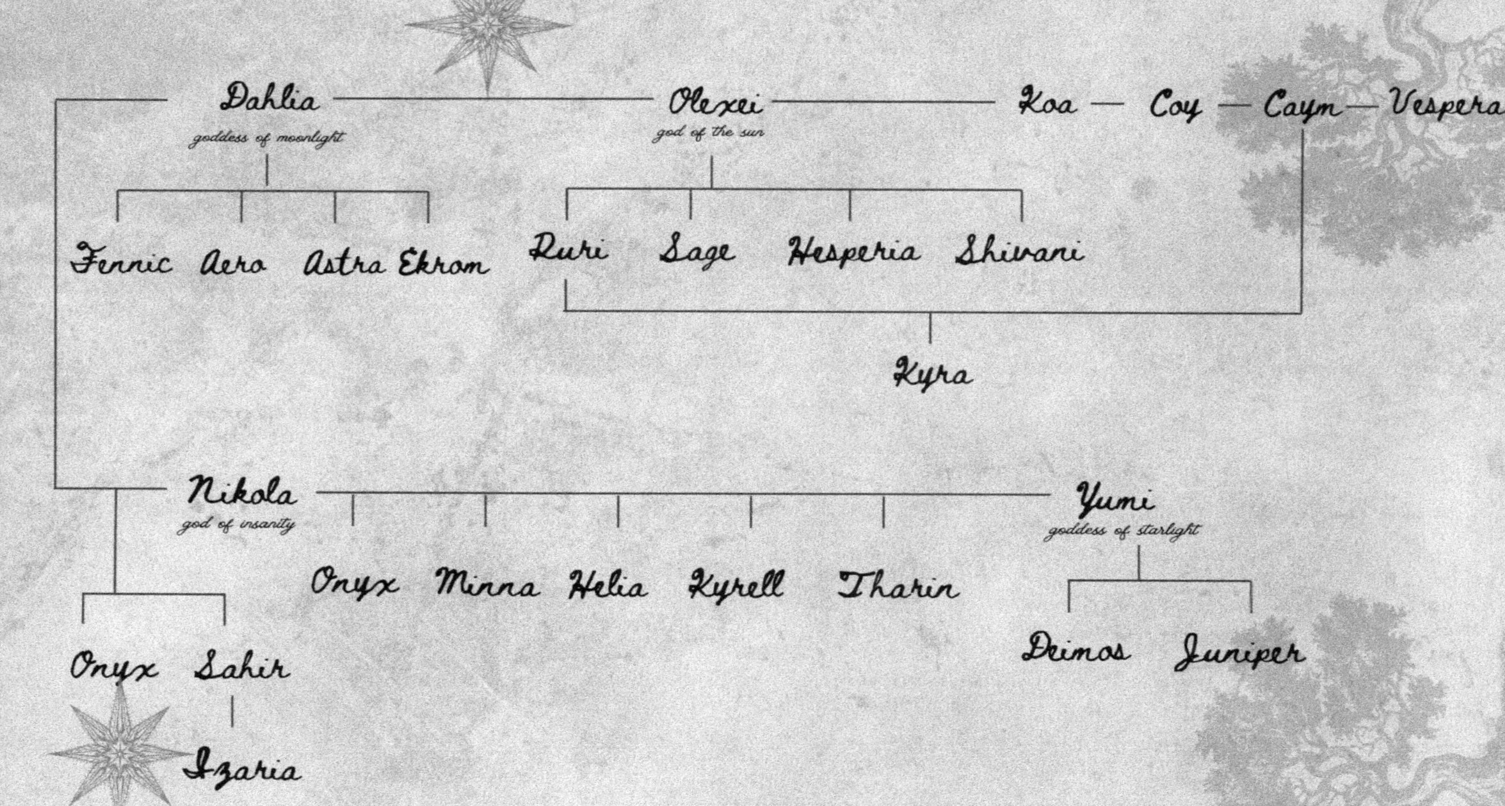

Dahlia
goddess of moonlight
Olexei
god of the sun
Koa — Coy — Caym — Vespera
Fennic   Aero   Astra   Ekron
Ruri   Sage   Hesperia   Shivani
Kyra
Nikola
god of insanity
Yumi
goddess of starlight
Onyx   Minna   Helia   Kyrell   Tharin
Onyx   Sahir
Izaria
Deimos   Juniper

ALSO BY HARLEIGH KNIGHT

Coming Soon…

Origins of Cylla

Rage of Gods and Dragons, Book Four

The Bloodborn Inheritance

A Prophecy of Ruin, Book One

Hourglass of Blood, Book Two

Shadow of the Last Born, Book Three

The Bonebound Court

The Hollow Crown, Book One

Bound By Bone, Book Two

Midnight Oath, Book Three

Keep up to date with the latest news and release dates by following on social media.

Find Harleigh Rose Knight on all platforms.